KIND of BLUE

Also by Miles Corwin

The Killing Season
And Still We Rise
Homicide Special

KIND of BLUE

A Novel

MILES CORWIN

Oceanview Publishing
LONGBOAT KEY, FLORIDA

ISBN: 978-1-60809-007-5

Published in the United States of America by Oceanview Publishing,
Longboat Key, Florida
www.oceanviewpub.com

2 4 6 8 10 9 7 5 3 1

PRINTED IN THE UNITED STATES OF AMERICA

For Leni

KIND of BLUE

PROLOGUE

Lieutenant Frank Duffy trudged up the five flights of stairs from the Felony Special squad room to the tenth floor, where the LAPD command staff was based. By the time he had walked down the long hallway to Assistant Chief Vincent Grazzo's office, he was already wheezing from exertion and beads of sweat speckled his brow. He knew he should have taken the elevator, but his doctor had ordered him to get some exercise and these days walking the stairs at the Police Administration Building—Los Angeles Police Department headquarters—was his only opportunity.

"I got something for you," Grazzo told Duffy, who dabbed at his brow with his knuckles.

Grazzo sat upright in his chair, tightly gripping a pencil in one hand. Short and pudgy, his midnight blue LAPD uniform fit him like a wet suit, and rolls of flesh spilled out over his collar. Duffy always thought that overweight police officials in their fifties and sixties looked as absurd in their uniforms as tubby baseball managers waddling to the mound.

"Last night, an ex-cop by the name of Pete Relovich got clipped at his house," Grazzo said. "Looks like a B and E."

"The name is vaguely familiar," Duffy said with a faint Irish inflection.

"When he was a young cop, he saved his partner's life in Watts."

"That was a long time ago, but I remember hearing something about it."

"They were on a robbery stakeout in the projects. Just about to take down a gangster pistol-whipping an illegal with a pocketful of cash, when a few homies fired on them. The partner took one in the gut. Pete was hit in the nose by a fragment. It traveled through his fucking nasal cavity and ended up in his mouth. He spit the hot metal out, shielded his partner with his body, then carried him to the squad car. And Pete still had the balls to return fire and drop one of the cocksuckers." Grazzo shook his head with admiration. "He was one macho cop."

"Wasn't his father a captain in Newton years ago?"

"Yeah, that was his old man," Grazzo said. "He retired a while back. Pete had thirteen in and pulled the pin last year."

"Why not wait for the pension at twenty?"

"Who knows."

"Anything interesting in his package?"

"He's got a handful of excessive force complaints. But as far as I could tell he was just a hard-nosed street cop who was doing his job and ran into some whiners.

"Anyway, the chief's got a hard on for this case. He and Relovich's old man go way back. They were young boots together at the old Venice station. This one's personal for the chief."

"The father still alive?"

"Naw. Heart attack five years ago. But the chief wants this case cleared. He owes the old man that at least."

"Where did Relovich live?"

"San Pedro."

"Why isn't Harbor Homicide handling the case?"

"Why did the chief bring back Felony Special after the unit was shitcanned in the nineties?"

Duffy wondered if a prerequisite for being named assistant chief was learning how to answer a question with a question—and then answering your own question.

"Power," Grazzo said. "He now has the power to take any case from the divisional dicks—from a jaywalking to a homicide—and give it to the Felony Special guys. They're *supposedly*," Grazzo said, pausing for a moment, "the best detectives in the city. And the chief wants the best detectives handling this case."

"Major Crimes," Duffy said.

"What?" Grazzo asked.

"Back in the nineties, they called the unit Major Crimes."

"Who gives a shit what they used to call it."

"Okay," Duffy said. "I'll give it to the on-call team right now."

"The chief doesn't want it going to the on-call team."

"You know that's how we do it," Duffy said.

"The chief doesn't want this case going to the luck of the draw. He wants your best detective on the case. The best of the best, so to speak. So who do you wanna put on it?"

Duffy stroked his neck. "Let's see. Saito is my best scene man. McKay's my best interviewer. Griego used to work at Harbor Division and knows all the gangbangers and pipeheads down there, so he might be a good choice. Raymond's a bulldog and he'll—"

"Chief wants your best guy—overall."

"My best guy overall quit eleven months ago."

"Who was that?"

"Ash Levine."

Grazzo tapped his index finger on his chin. "Asher Levine? The guy involved in that Latisha Patton fiasco?"

Duffy nodded. "That's right. I hated to lose him."

"You suspended him, didn't you."

"I did. But I never thought he'd quit over it."

"Quitting the department just because he loses a wit and gets suspended? The guy sounds fucking unbalanced."

"I don't think so. He just was in very deep on that case."

"What's he doing now?"

"Sitting on his ass. Doing a little gofer work for his brother's law firm."

"Jew?" Grazzo asked.

Duffy nodded.

"What was a smart Jew doing working as a street cop?"

"Levine's an odd duck. He's a combat vet, too."

Grazzo lifted his *Semper Fidelis* coffee mug in a mock toast and took a sip. "Don't tell me he's a fellow Marine."

"No. IDF—Israeli Defense Forces. Dropped out of college, moved to Israel, and joined up. I've known him since he was in patrol and I'll tell you, he's a hell of a detective. He doesn't think like a normal person. He sees things other guys miss. I remember a time when we were both at Pacific Division and he was just a young patrolman at the time. We were working the crime scene when—"

"You're a chatty fucking Irishman," Grazzo said.

Duffy shrugged.

"You want to bring him back?" Grazzo asked.

Duffy grabbed a Kleenex off Grazzo's desk and mopped his brow. "He's a pain in the ass. But yeah, I'd love to have him back."

"The chief wasn't happy when the Latisha Patton hit stirred up all that bad press for us, but he didn't want to lose Levine over it. He thought Levine's work on the Spring Street Slasher case was outstanding." Grazzo tugged at his collar. "What was it—four, five vics before he scooped up that psycho?"

"An even half dozen," Duffy said.

"I say go get Levine."

"How about the background checks, shrink visits, and all that other LAPD bullshit?"

"I'll fast track the paperwork and put him on temporary. You get him an appointment with the shrink. He can finish the rest of it next week. Can you run him down now?"

"Today?"

"Yeah, today."

"I don't know if I can find him this afternoon."

Grazzo checked his watch and frowned.

"But I know where he'll be tonight."

"Where's that?"

"Where else would a divorced Jewish cop—with no life and no kids—be on a Friday night?"

Grazzo frowned. He didn't like it when someone else—especially someone lower on the LAPD chain of command—answered a question with a question and then prepared to answer it.

Duffy chuckled and said, "At his mother's."

Duffy could not find a spot in front of Mrs. Levine's duplex, the duplex where he knew Levine was raised, so he parked two blocks away and strolled down the sidewalk, crunching across dried palm fronds that carpeted the street after the breezy afternoon. He recalled cruising down this street when he was a young patrolman in the Wilshire Division. The other cops called the area—east of Fairfax and south of Pico—the Borscht Belt because of all the elderly Eastern European Jews who clustered there. The neighborhood was modest, filled with duplexes and small apartment buildings, but the places were tidy then and the landscaping was well tended. Now, Duffy saw how it had deteriorated. Slabs of stucco had crumbled from a number of the apartment facades, tufts of crabgrass peeked through the cracks in the asphalt driveways, and the narrow lawns in front of most of the duplexes were dusty patches of weeds. Rusty air conditioners teetered from a few windows and metal shopping carts were abandoned in the gutters.

There were still some elderly Jews left—like Levine's mother—but Duffy noticed a number of Hispanic kids in diapers playing in front of the apartments and several surly black teenagers wearing blue nylon do-rags leaning against cars. On a few garage doors, he saw the spray-painted tags of the Mansfield Family Crips. Duffy walked up the brick path to the duplex Mrs. Levine rented, which was squeezed between two small apartment buildings, beige boxes with water stains beneath the rooflines. The duplex, with its red-tiled roof, wrought iron light sconces, and small courtyard, once must have had a stately elegance. But Duffy noticed that many of the tiles on the roof were split, the sconces were bent and nicked, and the wooden steps leading to the upper unit sagged in the middle.

Duffy glanced at the side of the duplex and noticed that all the windows were shielded with thick black security bars. He wiped his feet on the mat and, before ringing the doorbell, paused for a moment, rehearsing a few possible approaches, trying to decide which would be the most effective.

CHAPTER 1

I just finished mumbling my way through the *Bir Mat Hamazon*—grace after the meal—when I heard the doorbell ring and Lieutenant Duffy call out, "Open up, Ash, I know you're in there."

My mother padded across the room and peered through the peephole. Then she quickly glanced at me with a pained expression, her eyes filling with an amalgam of anger and dread, and opened the door.

"Shabat Shalom, Mrs. Levine," Duffy said, smiling. He reached for her hand and then patted it gently.

She glared at him.

"I learned a little Hebrew in the seminary when I had a class in comparative religion."

"Very little, I assume."

While he prattled on, trying to charm my mother, I sat slumped in a dining room chair. My temples felt like they were being squeezed in a vise. In an instant, I was transported right back to that street corner at 54th and Figueroa, where I saw Latisha Patton splayed on the sidewalk, her head encircled by a pool of blood, brain tissue and skull shards blown into the gutter. Why? Because of my stupidity. Or incompetence. Or carelessness. Or all of it. I felt as if I had killed her myself. For the past year I had been trying to bury the agonizing memory of that afternoon. And now, seeing Duffy brought it all back again. When I set my hands on my lap, I saw that I had left sweaty handprints on the wooden arms of the chair.

My mother glanced over at me for a moment. She could always read me better than any suspect. Turning to Duffy, she said in a loud whisper, "I wish you'd just let him get on with his life."

She looked particularly small and frail at that moment. Pale and freckled, her bright red hair was so lacquered and spherical it looked like a football helmet. She had an energy that made her seem physically imposing, but when people stood next to her and realized she was only about five feet tall, they were always surprised. Of course, standing next to Duffy would make anyone look small and frail. He was six foot five and somewhere between burly and fat, like an offensive lineman a few years past his playing days.

"I just need a few minutes with your son," Duffy said. "Then I'll be on my way."

I could see that my mother looked painfully confounded, torn between the desire to berate Duffy and the compulsion to offer him food. "You eaten?" she muttered through clenched teeth, as if the words escaped from her mouth against her will.

"Just had a delightful supper with my own dear mother."

Duffy eased into a chair—encased in a protective plastic coating—across from me. When I smelled his breath—beer laced with Tic Tacs—I knew he had spent the past hour—not with his mother—but downing beers at El Compadre in Echo Park, a Felony Special hangout.

"But," Duffy added, "I wouldn't say no to a cup of coffee and perhaps a slice of your challah." A loaf of braided egg bread was centered on the dining room table between a pair of dripping candles. "Sometimes Ash used to bring in sandwiches made from your delicious challah and he'd occasionally be kind enough to share them with me."

She rolled her eyes and trudged off to the kitchen. I crossed the room and slumped on the sofa.

Duffy looked around the monochromatic living room, everything a pale celery green, including the walls, carpeting, porcelain lamps, faded silk lampshades, and chintz sofa. "Your mother must like green."

"You must be a detective," I said sarcastically.

"I guess she's the obsessive type—like you," Duffy said, smiling.

This was just like Duffy, I thought, to ignore my mother's discomfort and my glare, and just make himself at home. I had always admired Duffy's ability to strut into a South Central living room, filled with cop-hating gangbangers and, with complete confidence, toss off a quip, ease a tense situation, and begin asking questions. Maybe it was his size. He was a presence that demanded attention. Maybe it was because Duffy, with his ruddy complexion, empathetic sky blue eyes, wispy silver hair, booming voice, and hale, voluble manner reminded people of the friendly parish priest. The Irish lilt enhanced the impression. I had always thought that Duffy's two years at a Catholic seminary when he was a teenager gave him a great advantage. One Salvadoran murderer who confessed later told me that talking to Duffy in an interview room was like whispering in a confessional to *un padre con placa*. A priest with a badge.

I first met Duffy at a homicide when I was a young patrolman in the Pacific Division and he was a detective. While the other cops were drinking coffee beside their squad cars, I wandered around outside the yellow tape and found a flattened .40-caliber slug imbedded in a wooden porch column next door to the crime scene. Duffy was the primary detective on the case and the slug led him to the murder weapon, which led him to the murderer. After that, at homicide scenes, Duffy always asked me to help him conduct the searches and, on a few occasions, he let me interview peripheral witnesses. When he took over South Bureau Homicide—a division based in South Central—he brought me in as a detective trainee. When I got my shield, he threw me a party at the academy. Years later, when he made lieutenant, was promoted to Robbery-Homicide Division, and put in charge of Felony Special, I was one of his first hires.

It was pretty predictable that I would have a weakness for father figures, and Duffy was an obvious choice. My father, after surviving Treblinka, was so consumed with his own demons, so remote and tormented, that there was not much emotional capital left for his sons. But after the Latisha Patton debacle, when I really needed some paternal guidance and support, where was Duffy? All I got from him was a two-week suspension and a bureaucratic rebuke stuffed in my personnel file. Seeing Duffy now didn't make me angry, just very sad, the betrayal so strong that I could feel it in the pit of my stomach. Many times during the past year I had envisioned how I was going to curse him out when I saw him again, how I was going to denounce him for caring more about covering his ass than taking care of his people, how loyalty meant nothing to him, how he was so consumed with ambition that he'd sell out every detective in the squad room for a promotion. But now, when I had the chance, I was too enervated to utter a word.

"I like your mother," Duffy said. "I like her honesty. In the past, whenever we talked, she always said what was on her mind. Very different from the women in my family. Everything was always fine. No matter what. My older brother would show up for dinner, night after night, dead drunk, and almost pass out on the kitchen table. My mother and aunt would always manage to avoid seeing what was right in front of their faces." Duffy, in a high-pitched brogue, impersonated them: "'Our poor Brendan must be a bit sleepy again this evening. The poor lad is working too hard.'"

Duffy rose and walked over to the mantel and studied my parents' wedding picture. "You don't resemble your mom much." He pointed to my father, who had wavy black hair, an olive complexion, and stared into the camera with an unnerving gaze. "You look a lot like your father. You've even got his Charlie Manson stare. How long's he been gone?"

"Seven years."

"He looks a lot older than your mother."

"More than twenty years."

"You ought to take a page out of your dad's book and find yourself a young babe."

"She wasn't that young when she got married."

"Aren't you the baby of the family?"

"Yeah. My brother's eleven years older than me. When I was kid, and my parents would take me to the park, people thought they were my grandparents."

Duffy edged his chair across the room until it was only a few feet from me.

"I learned that in detective school, too," I said.

"What are you talking about?"

"Cut the distance between you and the suspect. Get in his space. Make him feel uncomfortable. Get leverage over him. Persuade him to do what you want."

Duffy laughed—a deep, hearty belly laugh. "I've been shuffling paper too long. I need to get back on the streets. I'm losing my edge."

"So you want me back."

Duffy looked genuinely startled. "How'd you know?"

"No other reason for you to be here."

"Yeah, I want you back. I never wanted you to leave."

"Then why'd you suspend me? Why'd you stick that chickenshit letter in my package."

Duffy crossed a leg and carefully straightened a sock. He fixed me with a solemn look and said, "Had no choice. And if I hadn't—"

"Maybe someone would have questioned *you*, questioned *your* judgment, questioned how *you* run your unit?"

"Look, Ash, you may not understand now, but one of these days you might be running your own unit, and you'll have to make difficult decisions that will—"

"I doubt that," I interrupted. "And I don't want to listen to any more of your bullshit. I worked my ass off for you. I cleared a hell of a lot of cases for you. Made you look damn good. Whenever you caught some loser case that no one else wanted, you'd never hesitate to call me at three in the morning. And I'd always come running. But when I got into some trouble and really needed you, you left me swinging in the fucking wind."

"You done?" Duffy asked.

"No. I'm not done. I want to ask you a question: After the way you turned your back on me, why should I come back?"

"Because you want this job. Because you need this job. Because you've missed being a detective every single day since you quit."

I took a deep breath and expelled the air with a loud spurt. Typical Duffy, I thought. When it came time to manipulate you into doing what he wanted, he always knew how to cut right through your resistance and arrive at some essential truth that left you sputtering without a comeback. That's how he was able to lead a unit of cocky, know-it-all, prima donnas, each one of whom thought he was the best detective in the city.

I had been lost this past year. Duffy was right about that. But I had been too angry and too proud to come slithering back. I thought I was punishing Duffy and punishing the LAPD when I quit. But I soon realized that the only one who was being punished was me. There are more than nine thousand cops in the department. One less or one more cop, I quickly discovered, didn't seem to matter much to anyone. Except me. I discovered that I had lost everything. Without the job, I felt as if I didn't exist.

But I also wanted to return to the department because of the Patton case. As long as the murder book was moldering in the bottom of some dusty file cabinet, and her killer was roaming the city, I knew I'd always feel that I'd failed. Failed Latisha Patton. Failed myself. I simply didn't do my job and a woman was dead because of it. If I returned to investigate Duffy's case, I could—on the side—pursue Patton's killer. I knew I could never properly track the case on my own, as a civilian. I had to get my badge back.

Now, watching Duffy cross his arms over his sizable gut and stare across the room, eyes half closed, looking like a giant Buddha, I was immensely relieved that he'd offered me a way to come back. But I wasn't going to let him know that. I wasn't going to make it easy for him.

"Why should I come back and work for someone who doesn't back his detectives?"

"I don't have time to play this game now. You going to take this case or not?"

"Tell me about the homicide and I'll think about it."

Duffy scratched his eyebrow with a thumbnail. "A retired cop by the name of Pete Relovich was piped last night in his house in San Pedro. His dad was a captain in Newton years ago. Looks like a B and E. Did you know Pete?"

"No. But, but I crossed paths with the old man at a crime scene years ago."

"I want you to come back and take over the investigation."

"Why's Felony Special handling a B and E hit on a retired cop? Sounds pretty routine."

"The chief was friends with his old man."

"So why me?"

"Chief wants my best detective. So I'm asking my best detective to come back. Grazzo's given me the okay. He's fast-tracking you. You can start right away and finish up the bureaucratic crap over the next few days."

My mother returned carrying a tray with two mugs of coffee, a bowl of sugar, and nondairy creamer. She grabbed two pieces of challah from the table and set them on a plate in front of Duffy.

"Many thanks, Mrs. Levine," he said. "Can I trouble you for some butter on that challah?"

"Didn't they teach you anything in your seminary class about our prohibition of mixing dairy and meat?" she said in an accusatory tone. "We had brisket for dinner."

Duffy laughed and said, "Maybe that's why I ended up at a police station instead of a parish."

"Thank God for small favors, they must be saying in the parishes," she grumbled as she padded off to the kitchen.

I sipped my coffee and said, "So you worked Grazzo and got him to take me back. It's a twofer: you've expiated some of your Catholic guilt and you get another body at Felony Special. You're always complaining about not having enough detectives. Now you get a freebie without the fight with personnel. You probably told Grazzo I was the only detective who could solve this crime."

"You *are* too smart to be a humble civil servant." Duffy slowly stirred a spoonful of sugar into his coffee and said, without looking up, "I *did* tell Grazzo all that—in essence." He held his hand over his heart. "But listen to me, Ash, my boy, everything I told you was still the God's honest truth," he said, his brogue thickening with each word. I do think you're the best detective that I've—"

"When did your family leave Cork?" I asked.

"When I was ten, why?"

"When you're trying to appear sincere, you really lay on that fucking accent."

"I resent—"

"You know that when your countryman, Brian Callaghan, was promoted to assistant chief—and he came over when he was nineteen, not a kid like you—your accent suddenly got a lot thicker."

"That's not true."

"And when he retired, your accent quickly faded."

"That's a load of horseshit. And it's got nothing to do with why I'm here. Let's stop wasting each other's time. I'm asking you to come back. So make your decision. What's it going to be?"

When my mother reappeared, I realized she'd been eavesdropping. "Why can't you leave him alone?" she asked Duffy.

"Because the LAPD needs him. Because *I* need him."

"Hasn't the LAPD hurt him enough already?" she said. "That Latisha Patton business was devastating to my son. He's risked his life so many times for your department. He's solved so many cases for you. He's given up *everything* for the LAPD. And how do they—how do you—treat him? Like dirt! Anyway, he's considering going to law school. He's been studying for the LSAT test."

"Does the world really need another lawyer?" Duffy asked. "You've already got one lawyer son. Why do you need another one? I admit, Ash probably would be a fine lawyer—for someone starting out so late. But he's already a magnificent detective. A brilliant boy. Truly gifted. Why not let him do what he does best?"

She pursed her lips for a moment and said to me, "You know how upset your father was when he first saw you in uniform? He saw the uniform and thought of one thing, those SS officers who—"

"Enough!" I shouted. "Why does everything in our family have to lead back to this? Why does every discussion in this house end in hysteria?"

"You're *meshuga* if you go back," she said. "You don't need the *tsoris*. I don't need the *tsoris*. Remember, your brother said as soon as you finished law school he'd hire you."

"Marty's got to get out of rehab first," I said, disgusted. "Why is it more honorable to have a son who's a drug addict lawyer than a son who's a sober cop?"

"A *goyishe parnosseh*," she muttered. A gentile trade. "It was the dream of your father that you and Marty open the law offices of Levine & Levine."

"You're really bringing out the heavy artillery tonight."

"Me, I'm just worried about you getting hurt," she said. "I don't want to go back to spending my nights worrying that some *shvartzeh* in Watts is going to shoot you."

"Mom, I haven't worked South Central for years."

Duffy clasped her hand in both of his and said, "We've got an ex-cop murdered. *He's* got a mother grieving for him. The killer may kill again if he's not stopped. This is honorable work, Mrs. Levine. You know that. That's why Ash cares so much, why he puts so much of himself into each case—"

I held up my hand. "Save the speeches for El Compadre. I want a few things."

"I'm listening," Duffy said.

"I pick up my pension benefits from the date I left."

"I think that can be arranged."

"I don't care what you think. I want a guarantee."

"Okay. I'll make sure it gets done."

"On this case, I don't want to wait months for fingerprint and trace results and a year for DNA—the typical LAPD bullshit. I want you to call in your chits, lean on Grazzo, and promise to get everything back to me within a few weeks."

"You know I can't promise that."

"Then find someone else."

Duffy stuck a hand in his pocket and fiddled with his keys. "Okay. Cutting through the bureaucracy of the LAPD is like moving mountains. But I'll get it done."

"After that Latisha Patton crap, I don't trust many people in that room. If you're going to give me a partner, give me Oscar Ortiz."

"He just partnered up. Can't split them up now."

"Then I'll work alone."

"I don't like that idea and it won't—"

"If you want me back, that's the way it's got to be."

"Just on this first case," Duffy said.

I walked across the room and grabbed a brown leather jacket out of the closet. "I want to go to Relovich's tonight."

My mother wagged a forefinger at me. "Chasing a murder on Shabbes. That's a *shanda*. You should be ashamed of—"

"What about *Pikuah Nefesh*," I interrupted.

"What's that mean?" Duffy asked.

"To save a life," I explained. "Jewish law allows you to break the Sabbath to save a life. Like if I was a doctor." I turned toward my mother. "And I *could* be saving a life. If I don't catch this guy soon, he could kill again."

She swatted the air. "I don't approve of—"

"I don't want to hear it," I interrupted.

She sighed heavily. "I just want you to be happy. I know you haven't been happy this past year. So if going back will make you happy, then go back. You've got my blessing."

"Thanks, Mom."

She kissed me on the cheek and said, "*Gay Gezunt.*"

CHAPTER 2

As we strolled down the brick path toward the sidewalk Duffy complained, "I had to park two blocks away. Not a single spot on this street. I guess there's still enough Jews left in this 'hood who can't drive again until sundown tomorrow."

I wasn't in the mood to chitchat with Duffy; I would have preferred to hit the crime scene alone. But I knew that since I was returning to Felony Special, I would have to keep it civil with him and maintain a rapport. If I wasn't able to do that, there was no point in returning. He was my boss and there was nothing I could do about it. There would be a time to confront Duffy. It just wasn't now.

Duffy kicked an empty Old English 800 malt liquor can into the gutter. "This street has hit the fucking skids. You ought to get your mom out of here."

"I've tried. But she can walk to the synagogue. Her Hadassah chapter's only a few blocks away. And one of her yenta friends still lives down the street. So she won't budge."

Duffy slapped the back of my head. "She's stubborn as hell—just like her son."

We walked the rest of the way in silence, past dozens of families on their way to shul, the men in dark suits and yarmulkes, the women wearing imposing hats and pushing strollers, the boys with their long side curls. We passed a duplex on the corner—Mrs. Pearl's place, my mother's last remaining friend in the neighborhood—with the only other garden that was still lush. The hibiscus in the front yard sprouted blood red blossoms and the flowers on the thick stands of oleander were so milky white they appeared to glow. The breeze carried the scent of gardenias.

We climbed into Duffy's unmarked Crown Victoria, raced down Fairfax, pulled onto the Santa Monica freeway, and then headed south on the Harbor Freeway, toward San Pedro.

"So what's happening with the Patton murder?" I asked. "I assume if someone had cleared it, I'd have read about it in the paper."

"Still unsolved."

"Who at Felony Special is working it?"

"After all the hubbub surrounding the case," Duffy said with a sour expression, "I had to ship it out. It's being handled by South Bureau Homicide."

After Duffy and I left the unit, they changed the name to Criminal Gang Homicide Division, but everyone still called it South Bureau Homicide. "Christ, I mumbled. "They making any progress."

"I have no idea. I'm out of the loop on that one." Duffy flashed me a sly look. "I know you're probably figuring that while you're working Relovich, you'll have time to track the Patton homicide, too. Squeeze in some interviews, check out some suspects. Well, get that out of your mind. I want a full-court press on Relovich. I don't want you distracted. That Patton case has caused you enough grief. Let South Bureau handle it. Leave it alone."

"I was thinking—"

"I want you thinking about the case at hand. Forget Patton. Concentrate on Relovich. I called the Harbor Division lieutenant before I came over and he gave me a quick rundown. Homicide was last night. Coroner investigator gives time of death at around twenty-three hundred. The knucklehead busted out a back window. Probably a junkie hot prowl. Relovich's wallet was open with cash missing. Ex-wife said Relovich always wore his father's lapis ring and old Hamilton watch. Both were ripped off. Neighbors already been canvassed. No one heard the shot. No one saw anybody suspicious on the street. The next morning a neighbor looking for a lost dog knocked on the door, didn't hear an answer, looked through a window and saw the body. Detectives recovered a .40-caliber slug. No casings at the scene."

I nodded, but didn't ask any follow-up questions. I don't like entering a crime scene with too many preconceived notions. If I become fixated on one particular theory, I'm afraid I'll develop tunnel vision and I might miss the nuances of the true murder scenario.

After Duffy snaked through downtown, the traffic thinned and he zipped through the southside—South Central to the west of the freeway and its more depressed neighbor, Watts, to the east—then past the oil refineries of Wilmington that belched clouds of acrid smoke, white against the black sky, the horizon resembling a photographic negative.

I leaned back on the seat, closed my eyes, and recalled that afternoon when my paratroop unit was searching a terrorist's house in the West Bank. While I waited in the living room, I leafed through a Koran with Arabic on one side of the page and English on the other. I still remembered one of the passages, although it hadn't meant much to me at the time: *Does there not pass over every man a space of time when his life is blank?* That's how the past eleven months had been, I thought. An utter blank. Serving subpoenas, tracking down witnesses, and shepherding people to depositions for my brother's law firm was a bore. I occasionally studied the LSAT prep book, but with little enthusiasm. I felt lost, drifting in a miasma of self-flagellation and anger. I was angry at Duffy. Angry at the department. Angry at myself.

Now I realized how much I had missed this part of the job: riding to the crime scene, adrenaline pumping, not knowing what I would find when I arrived, what clues would be apparent, what evidence would be discernible, what traces the killer left behind. I missed the unpredictability of the call-outs, how they came at any time, any day, any hour, and how they would immediately send me hurtling into the unknown. I missed encountering the parts of the crime-scene puzzle; they were always different and I never put them together the same way.

Most of all, I missed the life, the life of a homicide detective in which the stakes of a case are always high and everything else seems unimportant by comparison. This all-consuming nature of the job had always been a balm for the bullshit in my life; the challenge of the chase demanded so much from me, I simply did not have the luxury of dwelling on anything else.

Duffy pulled off the freeway in San Pedro and parked behind the Harbor Division station. We nodded to a group of cops smoking in the parking lot and traversed a long, scuffed linoleum hallway that smelled of vomit and urine and unwashed bodies, past detention benches with burglars, rapists, wife beaters, gangbangers, psychos, crackheads, and muggers cuffed to the metal rings; past drunks blowing into breathalyzer machines; past vice officers wearing jeans and Hawaiian shirts pushing screaming hookers into interview rooms. We entered the watch commander's office and greeted the p.m. shift lieutenant, who sifted through his desk drawer and handed Duffy an envelope with the key to Relovich's house. We left the station, drove toward the water, and then climbed a steep hill.

Relovich lived near the end of a cul-de-sac, in a ramshackle pale blue clapboard bungalow with peeling paint and a sagging roof. When I was a kid, this had been a working-class neighborhood, populated mostly by Croatian fishermen. But now, homes with a view of the water were at a premium in Los Angeles and property values had soared. Most of the fisherman had sold to investors, who viewed the modest homes as teardowns, replacing them with mammoth two- and three-story monstrosities, spanning lot line to lot line. Relovich's house, which was encircled by yellow crime-scene tape, was flanked by two gray and white clapboard Cape Cod-style McMansions that could sell for more than a million dollars.

I pulled out a pair of latex gloves, a few small Baggies, and a flash-light from a wooden box in Duffy's trunk, stuffed them in my pocket, and walked to Relovich's front porch, which faced the harbor. Linger-ing for a moment, I looked out at the inky black water laced with streaks of silver from the three-quarter moon. Lights atop the graceful span of the Vincent Thomas Bridge, which connected San Pedro to Terminal Island, twinkled in the distance. An offshore wind, brisker here than in the central city, blew off the water, carrying the smell of seaweed, brine, and a hint of diesel fuel.

Duffy opened the front door and flipped on the lights. I followed him inside. The house had an air of dereliction. In the living room, newspapers, unopened mail, fast-food wrappers, and empty Dr. Pepper cans were strewn on the nicked hardwood floor. Fingerprint powder streaked the wooden arms of the sofa, the chipped coffee table in front, two chairs beside a picture window, and every other smooth surface. I took a deep breath and nodded. After a year of disorientation, I finally felt at home again. Yes, this is what I've missed. Homicide.

I left Duffy in the living room and walked through an archway to the kitchen, where dishes were piled up in the sink. More fingerprint dust stippled the white cabinets and Formica counter. The faint smell of cooked meat and stale cigarette smoke lingered in the house. I walked down a narrow hallway from the kitchen to Relovich's bedroom. The double bed was unmade, the sheets a dingy white. An old gray blanket covered the window.

Walking across the hallway to the other bedroom, I was surprised because it was neat and the narrow bed—covered with a *Little Mermaid* bedspread—was made. Taped to the wall above the bed, was a child's finger painting of a rainbow. A small bookcase on the opposite wall was lined with children's books, and the bottom shelf was stacked with kids' videos. I figured he was divorced and had weekend custody of his daughter.

I walked over to a wooden desk next to the bookcase. The top drawer was lined with coloring books and a Crayon box. The bottom drawer was stuffed with cancelled checks, phone bills for the past month, a calculator, and a roll of stamps. I grabbed the envelopes containing the cancelled checks and phone bills and returned to the living room. I found Duffy staring out the window at the harbor lights. He turned around when he heard me and said, "Our killer entered from the—"

I cut him off with a karate chop in the air.

"Okay, okay," Duffy said. "I'll leave you alone."

A few brick-colored smudges glimmering on the hardwood floor in front of the sofa caught my eye. I crouched and studied them. Even now, after so many murders, I am still surprised at the color of dried blood. I still expect it to be bright red; maybe it was all those detective shows I had watched as a kid. As it dries, blood loses much of its vividness and looks more brown than crimson, but it keeps its arresting sheen. Looking at this patch from different angles, I watched it flicker in the dim light.

I flipped on my Maglite and, rising, slowly turned, illuminating the walls. Behind the sofa, about waist high, was what looked like a miniature pointillist portrait: blood spatter.

I walked over to a chair a few feet from the sofa. Sitting down on the ripped upholstery, I extended my arm toward the sofa, lifted my right hand—thumb up, index finger extended—and said softly, "Bang."

"This was no B and E, no junkie hot prowl," I said to Duffy. "Relovich knew his killer."

Duffy raised an eyebrow. "The Harbor Division detectives say otherwise."

"Look at the blood splatter pattern," I said impatiently. "Look at the directional tail. Look at the trajectory. It was a straight shot to the sofa. Asshole is sitting on a chair, across from Relovich, who's lounging on the sofa. So they're obviously comfortable with each other. They're probably chatting. And then, before Relovich can move, asshole pulls out his piece and drills him in the melon."

I stood up and paced beside the sofa. "A street-wise cop like Relovich would have been on his feet, making for a door if this was some junkie ripping him off. And no junkie would be sitting on a chair chatting. He'd be jumpy, too nervous to sit."

"Those Harbor detectives had their heads up their asses," Duffy said.

"No. They've just been working the same kinds of murders too long. Too many drive-bys. Too many street corner drug shootings. Some of 'em have never worked an indoor crime scene."

"Any neighbors hear the shot?" I asked.

"No."

"Did they do a good canvas?"

"The lieutenant said they talked to everybody on both sides of the street."

I sat on my heels a few feet in front of the sofa and studied a few tiny ovals of dried blood.

"Did the lieutenant say Relovich was found on the sofa or the floor?"

"Floor," Duffy said.

"But that's not where he died." I stood and turned toward Duffy. "Relovich is on the couch," I said pointing. "The force of the slug propels him backward. So how does he end up on the floor? It's contrary to the laws of physics."

"Somebody moved him."

"Right," I said. "But why?"

"I don't know," Duffy said.

"Neither do I," I said. "Let's ninhydrin the wall behind the sofa. Asshole might have touched the wall for balance before he moved the body."

I spent another hour in the living room, carefully examining the floor, the walls, and each piece of furniture. In the kitchen, I studied the contents of the refrigerator, which contained only a brown banana, a loaf of bread, a jar of mustard, a half gallon of milk, and a bottle of steak sauce. Typical bachelor cop who eats most of his meals out. Like me, I thought.

I checked the drains in the kitchen sink, the bathroom, and the shower for blood. I dumped out the bathroom wastebasket, sifting through an empty soapbox, rusted razor blade, a balled up Kleenex, two cigarette butts, a few wads of toilet paper, and a section of dental floss. I dropped them into different Baggies and zipped them shut.

"Let's test it all for DNA and fingerprints," I said. "Remember that case in Venice where I emptied the trash in that enormous garbage can, bagged it up, and sent it all off to the lab?"

"Yeah," Duffy said. "There was so much crap to test, they had a fit."

"The prints on an aspirin bottle led me to a hooker."

"As I recall, she didn't kill the john."

"That's right. Her pimp did." I handed the Baggies to Duffy and said, "Why don't you send these out for testing on Monday morning. Lean on someone to expedite it."

After I scoured the house but didn't find an answering machine, I tossed Relovich's bedroom, examining every piece of clothing in the drawers, peering beneath the bed, running my hand under the mattress, sifting through the closet. Then I walked outside, and while Duffy followed, circled the back of the house and the yard, a ragged square of grass bordered by a six-foot pine fence. I edged my way through a thick hedge and studied the back window, which had a jagged hole punched in the center.

I returned to the front porch and pointed to the scarred wooden railings and said, "I'm going to call SID and have them come back tomorrow and dust the railings. This should have been done."

I pulled out my cell phone. "I'm going to get a bloodhound out here."

Duffy fixed me with a skeptical look. "We're in the twenty-first century, Ash."

I had always been frustrated by the LAPD's inflexibility and suspicion of unorthodox methods. The canine unit always gave me a hard time when I wanted to use one of their dogs for tracking an urban homicide suspect, but I knew a dog handler who volunteered his services for a few Southern California police departments. He was more cooperative. Fortunately, I still had his number programmed in my phone. I called his cell, chatted with him for a few minutes, and said to Duffy, "He's out on another scene tonight. He's meeting me here tomorrow at eight."

"Won't the scent be cold by then?"

"Those dogs can pick up a scent weeks, even months, later. I want to get an early start tomorrow. Can you have the local detectives who caught this case meet me tomorrow morning at nine at the Harbor Division station? I want them to brief me, and I want to get the murder book from them."

"They won't be happy coming in on Saturday morning. But I'll talk to their lieutenant and make sure he drags their asses in there."

"When's the autopsy?" I asked.

"Sunday at ten. You want anyone with you for a second set of eyes?"

"Not necessary."

"Listen, Grazzo brought you back on temporary, but there's some administrative crap you've got to take care of on Monday so you're full-time again. You've got to take a physical from the city doctor, meet briefly with a background investigator, and write a letter to the chief about why you're coming back. Typical bullshit. Then you got to see a department shrink next week. I'll make you an appointment."

"Christ," I mumbled.

"You know the department. Gotta jump through the hoops if you want to come back."

We walked back to Duffy's car and he drove down a narrow, winding street to the bottom of the hill. He was about to pull onto a shabby thoroughfare that led toward the freeway, but before he could turn left I said, "Cut the engine and lights."

I scanned the pawnshop, grimy taco stand, shuttered liquor store, and then pointed at a Hispanic teenager on the corner, across the street, wearing a black raincoat, standing under a streetlight, his head swiveling from side to side. Grabbing a pair of binoculars from the glove compartment, I focused on the corner and noticed the kid had a crude spider-web tattoo on his neck.

"Jailhouse tattoo," I told Duffy. "Probably one of the gangbangers from the projects."

A few minutes later, a black man driving a dusty Honda pulled over at the corner. The gangbanger reached in the window, nonchalantly grabbed a few bills, and dropped a Baggie onto the passenger seat. After the driver sped off, a Hispanic couple who looked like street people walked up; the man slipped the seller a bill, and stuffed the Baggie down the front of his pants.

"Probably slanging tar heroin," I said. "Probably selling rock, too. A full-service operation."

Across the street, a few blocks away, I spotted another sidewalk entrepreneur pacing on a corner. I handed Duffy the binoculars.

"I didn't see these clowns when we drove up the hill," Duffy said.

"Probably came out here a while after we arrived," I said.

"Around the time Relovich was killed," Duffy said.

"Right. His street's a dead end. There's only one way down the hill and out of the neighborhood." I rapped my knuckles on the dashboard. "And that's through here."

"These characters might have seen the knucklehead," Duffy said.

"Can you get somebody from Harbor vice down at the station tomorrow morning? Maybe the sergeant of the buy team?"

Duffy nodded.

"I'll meet with him after I talk to the homicide dicks. I'll make sure he floods this street during the next few days and busts sellers *and* buyers. These guys are good repeat customers. You never know who saw what. When they're looking at some time in the joint, they might suddenly become talkative. And let's see if we can get the City Council to pony up a reward."

"I'll talk to Grazzo. He can get it done."

Duffy circled around to the freeway and then sped north at well over ninety miles an hour—a perquisite of the badge—and reached downtown in less than fifteen minutes. He exited at 4th Street and drove east, then south, through a derelict neighborhood at the outer edge of a district known as the Historic Core. Commercial buildings in various states of disrepair, most constructed in the early twentieth century, flanked the street. Some were shuttered, their ground-floor windows boarded up with plywood.

I rolled down my window and watched a few seedy hotel lobbies roll by, the faint smell of Lysol wafting out the doors. Crackheads and elderly pensioners shuffled about barefoot or in house slippers. The streetlamps cast a sickly yellow light on the sad landscape of check cashing offices, passport photo shops, and small markets that sold single cigarettes and short dogs to the rummies who jammed the corners.

Los Angeles was decades behind most major cities in attracting residents to live downtown. There had been efforts in the past, with scattered buildings that featured lofts, but they generally failed. Most people in L.A. assiduously avoided the area, which they regarded as a forbidding wasteland, a repository for the detritus of the city. During the past decade, however, numerous stately old commercial buildings had been renovated and converted into lofts, drawing renters and buyers. Still, those who chose to live downtown were viewed skeptically by many in Southern California, where a manicured front lawn and a backyard with a barbecue are considered a birthright.

Duffy screeched to a stop in front of one of the old bank buildings, an imposing Beaux Arts structure. Four massive, pale green marble columns border the filigreed brass door. The building was constructed of cream-colored stone and at the top is an ornate, swirling cornice shading a dozen stone griffins, eyes bulging, surveying the skyline.

"I like the building, but your neighborhood's a shithole. You can't find an LAPD cop who lives in the city, yet you move downtown," Duffy said, snorting.

"After Robin left me, this is where I wanted to be," I said.

"I been divorced three times," Duffy said. "This your first, right?"

I nodded. "But the divorce hasn't gone through yet; we're still separated. I'm waiting for her to file the judgment forms and all the final documents with the court."

"Is it really over?"

"Yeah. It's really over."

"You'll need this," he said, handing me the keys to an unmarked LAPD detective car. "You can pick it up tomorrow."

I flipped the door handle, but before I could climb out, Duffy grabbed my arm.

"I've got something for you, Asher," he said, opening his briefcase. In the center, gleaming from a fresh polishing, was the stainless-steel-and-copper badge that I had turned in eleven months before. "I made sure your number wasn't reassigned."

I took the badge from Duffy and nodded. I felt my throat catch. Getting the detective badge had been one of the greatest moments of my life. Handing it in had been one of the worst. Now, feeling the heft of it in my palm and running my fingers along the outline of City Hall, my resentment toward Duffy began to dissipate a bit.

Duffy extended his hand.

I shook it and said softly, "Thanks LT."

At the front door, I punched my code into the keypad, slipped inside, and took the elevator to the top floor. I unlocked my door and set the badge on a small wooden table. My loft, a spare, cavernous expanse, has exposed brick walls, polished concrete floors, and two gold-trimmed skylights streaked with dust. Suspended from metal hooks near my bed are a mountain bike and a surfboard. One large window faces west, the lights atop the skyscrapers on Bunker Hill twinkling in the distance; a smaller window on the other side of the loft faces east, offering a view of the rooflines of hundred-year-old brick and stone buildings.

I grabbed a beer from the refrigerator, flipped on my CD player, and eased into my leather chair. Studying the lights of the skyscrapers, I listened to the Miles Davis cut "So What." For the past eleven months this had been my melancholic anthem. Night after night, month after month, I sat here, unable to sleep, watching ESPN with the sound off, listening to "So What," while I stared dully at the obscure sporting events the network showed from midnight until dawn. I was lost; I just didn't care anymore. As we used to say in the IDF, I was *zayin nishbar—* my dick was broken. I winced, thinking about one tortured night, about a week after Latisha Patton was killed, when I was on suspension. I was so enraged at the asshole who had shot her, so infuriated that I had been prevented from tracking him down, so incensed at my own impotency, that I vowed I would never feel that kind of agony again. I pulled out my Beretta, slipped the barrel into my mouth and listened to the bittersweet, silky-smooth horns of Miles, Cannonball, and Coltrane, the plaintive piano of Bill Evans, thinking that if I was to pick the last thing I would ever hear on this earth, it might as well be the opening bars to "So What." I'd first heard "So What" when I was discharged from the Israeli army and had descended into a similar funk. Disillusioned, angry, and confused, I had found that the cut was the only thing that gave me any comfort.

When I was nineteen, I decided to move to Israel and volunteer for the army. I always thought of my relatives who were murdered in the Holocaust—and even my father, who had survived a concentration camp as a boy and had a string of pale blue numbers tattooed on his forearm—as victims. I wanted a different kind of Jewish identity for myself.

For so long, the Holocaust had been the focus of my Jewish identity, the focus of my *entire* identity. Growing up, my house was a place populated by ghosts and demons. Ghosts—the dozens of murdered relatives. Demons—the Nazis who murdered them. Sometimes, lying in bed, right before falling asleep, when the duplex creaked in a Santa Ana, I could hear the screams and gasps of my relatives; sometimes, when the refrigerator slammed shut, I could hear the clanging door of a gas chamber. Sometimes, walking home from school, I would see a guy wearing a dark coat looking at me and I would panic, convinced he was a Nazi who was going to capture and torture me, and I would run home, out of breath, jump into bed, and cover my head with pillows.

My house was a place of long, brooding silences and sudden angry eruptions. The sadness was something so palpable that I felt that I could actually touch it, like a patch of fabric. As a child, letting myself experience any emotion, was simply too painful, so I chose not to feel anything. And I didn't. But then, some little thing would set me off in school, and I would rage in the classroom, screaming at the teacher or pummeling a student who had irritated me, or throwing pencils against the blackboard. My mother would have to come to school and pick me up at the principal's office. When my mother later told my father what had happened, he would snort contemptuously and say, "What have you got to be upset about? When I was your age I saw my father shot in a ditch."

Since visions of murdered relatives had tormented my childhood, I figured that in order to purify myself as an adult, I would do some killing of my own. I flew to Tel Aviv and, naïve and idealistic, enlisted in the Israeli Defense Forces. After two months of intensive Hebrew instruction and four and a half months of *Tironut*—basic training—I was selected for an elite *Tzanhanim*— paratrooper—unit. More than four hundred soldiers in my group started the brutal training. Only forty-three earned their red berets and wings, which we were awarded after a fifty-six-mile forced march, carrying full packs, from Tel Aviv to Jerusalem.

I then spent eleven months with a paratrooper recon unit patrolling the border in South Lebanon, ambushing Hezbollah guerrillas trying to slip into northern Israel. One frozen dawn, my ambush was ambushed. Blood streaming down my back from a shrapnel wound, I believed I was dying. But as my blood pressure dropped precipitously, I felt a light-headed, eerie calm. If I was going to die, this was the way I wanted to go—trying to protect the lives of Jews.

When I was released from the hospital, my unit was sent to the West Bank to deal with the first Intifada. My perception of the Israeli army—and of my own role as a soldier—was turned upside down. I spent my days chasing teenagers with rocks through the streets of *their* towns, not terrorists with AK-47s crossing into Israel; I was viewed by the Palestinians as a sadist, not a savior. I felt I was no longer protecting people, but repressing them. Still, whenever I hear about a suicide bombing on a Jerusalem bus, or a Palestinian walking into a restaurant, maneuvering through a maze of strollers, and blowing up babies, young couples out for the evening, and pregnant women, I feel the urge to rejoin my old unit and mow down terrorists. Now, sipping my beer, listening to the music, I tried to expunge the images of severed limbs and shredded flesh.

"Damn," I grumbled. Duffy should have contacted me earlier. I was irritated that I had caught the case twenty-four hours after the murder, that the Harbor Division detectives had first crack at the fresh blood crime scene and the neighbors. I hoped Relovich's relatives would provide me with some leads.

If I could bag and tag this one quickly, maybe I would have time to work on the Patton homicide before I caught my next case. Fuck Duffy and his warnings. I would do it on the down low. During the past eleven months, I spent countless hours at home pouring over a Xerox copy of the murder book on my lap, searching for some trace, some hint of a lead that would spark a revelation. One afternoon, I decided to hit the streets and see what I could unearth. I started with Patton's daughter. But before I could ask a question, she'd screamed at me, blamed me for getting her mother killed, and threw me out of the house.

Apparently, she'd reported me to Internal Affairs, because the next day an I.A. lieutenant called me at home and warned me to stay away from the Patton case. I told him that because I was no longer a cop, I could look into any case I wanted—as a private citizen.

"If I get another call about you nosing around, I'll write a search warrant for your place," he told me. "And if I find you've stashed any pages from the murder book—or anything else connected to the investigation—I'll write you up myself for theft of city property."

That shut me up and kept me away from the investigation for a while. But the past few weeks, I had been thinking about ways to interview people connected to the case without I.A. finding out. Now that I was back on the job, I wouldn't have to worry about that any more. I had the entrée I had been searching for.

I downed the rest of the beer in a swallow, crossed the room to the sofa, and pressed replay. I stretched out and listened to the dazzling opening bars of "So What." Closing my eyes, I thought about the blood splatter pattern, the broken window in the back of the house, the dried blood on the floor, the dealer on the street corner. And I thought about Relovich. He was not some anonymous, faceless victim, one of several dozen killed every month in the city. He had been a cop, a brave cop from what I had heard. I felt a kinship with him, a responsibility to a fellow officer.

And I felt a kinship with his daughter. I knew what was ahead of her, the emotional scars she would bear, the pain she would endure. I knew that her father's murder would be the defining element of her life. Just like the murder of my grandparents, my dozens of aunts and uncles and cousins had been the defining element in mine.

I had investigated enough homicides to know that solving Relovich's murder would bring no closure to his young daughter. Every homicide detective soon learns that closure is a myth, a sound-bite word people use to try to describe the ineffable. Still, I believed that solving the case would bring some solace to her. If I caught her father's killer, it would provide her with a sense that there was some justice and order and meaning in the world—something I never had as a child—that terrible acts did not occur in a vacuum; that people who committed them were caught and punished. I wanted her to know that the killer who had created such sorrow in her life would suffer, too; that at least one man cared enough about her father to avenge his murder.

CHAPTER 3

I woke up, heart hammering in my chest, sweat streaming down my back. I quickly closed my eyes, but could not erase the image of Latisha Patton, her eyes as lifeless as a puppet's, the side of her head blown off, her right arm extended, and her fingers splayed, rigor keeping them stiff until I arrived at the scene. As if she was reaching out to me, imploring me to help her.

I glanced at my alarm clock: 3:15. I popped two Ambien, thrashed on the bed for about twenty minutes, until I finally dropped off.

I awoke a few hours later, feeling feverish and exhausted. I lay on my back, head on my pillow, arms clasped behind my neck. When I began to see that corner of 54th and Figueroa again, I blinked hard. I mumbled to myself, "Enough!" If I was to keep my sanity, I had to get it out of my head. If I was going to make any headway with the Relovich homicide, I had to focus. I couldn't afford to be crippled by the Patton case. I forced myself to exchange the images of one homicide scene for another, to contemplate the smudges of blood on Relovich's floor, the blood splatter pattern on the wall, the broken window in back. A few minutes later, my alarm began to beep. I jumped out of bed, showered and shaved, and gulped down three Tylenol. When I finished dressing, I opened the door of a wooden cabinet, reached into the back, pulled out my .45-caliber Beretta Cougar, which was encased in a leather shoulder holster, and slipped it on.

When I worked patrol I always carried a backup gun: a hammerless .38-caliber two-incher Smith & Wesson Airweight, which I kept in an ankle holster. But when I made detective, I stashed the gun in a drawer. I didn't want to be sitting across from a timid witness, cross my legs, and have the pistol peeking out from underneath my pant legs. Most cops, when they left the street and made detective, abandoned their backup guns. Some became so blasé that they even left their service

weapons in their desk drawers when they left the building for interviews. I was always the more paranoid type. When I started working as
a detective trainee and exchanged my uniform for a suit, I purchased a
little two-shot .22 caliber derringer that I kept in my pocket as a backup.
I reached into the cabinet, pulled out the derringer from a dusty corner,
balanced it on my palm for a moment, then jammed it into my right
front pocket.

By seven, I was walking toward Little Tokyo. It was sunny and clear and
the sky, not yet veiled with the inevitable sand-colored scrim of smog,
was a radiant blue. The office workers were at home, and the streets
were deserted. There was an anomalous sense of calm, a welcomed
respite from the usual downtown frenzy. I could even hear the occasional chirping of a bird. It felt good to start out a day with the distrac-
tion of something important to do.

　　I knew that people who passed me on the street wouldn't have
guessed that I was a cop. I wore a muted green Zegna suit, pale blue
Egyptian cotton shirt, and Armani silk tie. Few detectives who worked
downtown paid full price for their clothing; most, like me, shopped at
the handful of fashion district wholesale outlets that sold LAPD officers
suits at a discount. I bought my suits at Glickman's Menswear, a small
shop on Santee Street. The owner, Murray Glickman, a stooped over
man in his eighties, was so surprised and pleased that a homicide detective was a member of the tribe that he provided me with designer
clothing that he normally wouldn't sell for the cop discount.

　　During an argument, Robin once had claimed that I dressed so well
to overcompensate for the fact that I had disappointed my parents and
became a cop, to prove to the world that although I was not a professional, I could afford to dress like one. I disagreed. My father was in the
schmata business—a pattern maker for a dress company downtown—
and always made comments when we were out on the street about the
lines, the cut, the bias, the drape of dresses and sport coats that passersby
wore. Now, I simply could not wear a cheap suit. If I cared so much
about appearances, I asked Robin, why was I still driving a ten-year-old
Saturn station wagon in the most car-conscious city in the world?

　　On First Street in Little Tokyo I stopped for a few minutes and
watched through a shop window as an elderly man made tofu, then

passed a bonsai nursery, inhaling the resinous scent of the tiny pine trees. As I walked I felt my Beretta jangle against my ribs. It had been almost a year since I had worn the gun and it felt odd, like when I first slipped on my wedding ring at the temple and fiddled with it all evening.

At a small corner Japanese restaurant I sat at the counter and ordered breakfast—rice, miso soup, nori—dried seaweed—broiled mackerel, and green tea. I dipped a few strips of nori in soy sauce, rolled them up with dollops of rice, and munched on them while I read the *Times* and waited for my fish. After breakfast, I walked over to the LAPD parking structure on Main Street, checked the license plate number on the key ring, found the green Chevy Impala with 163,000 miles on the odometer, and headed back down to San Pedro.

When I arrived at Relovich's house, I walked up to the porch and looked out at the harbor. Fog shrouded the horizon and a brisk breeze rippled the water. The mournful bellow of a tanker steaming out of a berth toward the open sea echoed in the distance. I leaned against a wooden railing, heard a bark, and spotted Ray Persky's van pull up at the curb and his bloodhound, Ruby, licking the back window. I shook hands with Persky on Relovich's porch.

"Thought you'd quit," Persky said.

"I did. But I came back yesterday."

Persky fixed me with a sympathetic look. "I really felt bad when the papers blasted you after that girl got killed." He put a hand on my shoulder. "I know you. I know how careful you are. It couldn't have been your fault."

I felt my temples throb. The first person I encountered on the job mentioned the murder, and I got a splitting headache. I knew the Patton case was going to keep coming up. I knew I was going to be stressed. And I knew I had to confront the reminders with some equanimity. I spit in the gutter.

"Thanks for the support, Ray." Eager to change the subject, I led him inside the house and briefed him.

"Anything you're sure the killer touched?"

I pointed to a chair a few feet from the sofa. "I think he sat here for a bit."

"That'll work," Persky said.

He pulled a small, plastic vacuum cleaner out of his duffel bag, flicked on the power, and slowly ran it over the sofa for several minutes. Then he removed a gauze pad from the vacuum cleaner, thrust it beneath Ruby's nose, and slipped it into a plastic Baggie. He patted Ruby on the ribs and murmured, "Do your thing, old girl." The dog jumped up, sniffed the carpet, scampered out the front door, around to the back of the house, sniffing the ground by the broken window, and then to the front porch and onto the sidewalk, as Persky and I followed. The dog barked, nose down, and ambled off, straining against the long leather leash.

"Shit," I shouted as Ruby urinated on my left shoe.

"You *have* been away a while," Persky said. "Don't you remember? She pisses when she picks up a trail."

We followed Ruby down to the bottom of the hill. She paused and then veered left, speckling the sidewalk with urine. This spot was across the street and down the block from where the gangbanger with the spiderweb tattoo was selling drugs.

She ambled down the sidewalk, swung left, began to climb a hill and suddenly stopped, sniffed the sidewalk and the curb for a few minutes, occasionally lifting her head and yelping.

"Why's she stopping here?" I asked.

"This is where the scent ends," Persky said. "This indicates that, more than likely, your suspect got in a car and drove off. Does that fit with your suspect's MO?"

"I wasn't thinking that last night, but now it makes sense. That's kind of a narrow street by Relovich's house. Neighbors would have noticed the shooter's car. He probably figured it would be safer to park here, walk over to Relovich's street, climb the hill, take care of business, and then slip back to his car."

I patted the dog, then clapped Persky on the shoulder and said, "I appreciate it, Ray."

As we slowly traipsed back up the hill, the sun began to bleed through the fog and golden shafts of light slanted through the mist. While Ruby stopped to sniff a tree, I admired the view up the hill. May was my favorite time of year in Southern California—after the winter rains, before the June gloom, when shades of purple graced every neighborhood. A lush canopy of jacaranda trees led up to Relovich's house, the lavender blossoms in full bloom. Pendulous clusters of lilac wisteria

cascaded over eaves and violet stalks of Mexican sage sprouted from gardens. As I climbed the hill, the sidewalks stained from the jacaranda
blossoms, I felt as if I were floating on a purple cloud.

When I reached the top, I scanned the harbor, which looked entirely different in the light of day than it had the previous night. Unlike
much of the Southern California coastline, San Pedro has a working
waterfront, an industrial jungle dotted with two hundred-foot-high
cranes used to transport goods to and from the ships. Metal cargo con-
tainers as big as railroad cars were lined up on the docks and fishing
boats traversed the channels.

I returned to Relovich's house and slowly strolled through the
rooms, not knowing exactly what I was looking for, just hoping something would catch my eye. I realized, again, how every room was a mess,
except for the daughter's. Walking out of the house toward my car, I was
left with the impression that Relovich didn't care much about his own
life, but he loved his little girl and probably found her visits the only
meaningful part of his week.

I cruised down to the Harbor Division station, a bland, blocky, orange
brick structure hard by the freeway, facing the railroad tracks, where a
freight train rumbled by. I walked through the station to the scuffed
prefab trailer in the parking lot that housed the homicide unit: a
makeshift squad room with frayed blue-gray carpeting. Eight battered
metal desks were bordered by metal filing cabinets topped with brown
cardboard boxes overflowing with case files. Fluorescent lights cast a
pale green tint over Detectives Hank Savich and Victor Montez, who
were waiting for me at their desks. Neither stood up when I introduced
myself; neither extended a hand.

I sat down on the edge of a desk and said, "I really appreciate you
coming in on Saturday morning to help—"

"First of all, I don't like getting bigfooted," said Savich, who had a
pale, narrow face pockmarked with acne scars. "I don't like outsiders taking my cases."

I was well aware that divisional detectives often resented it
when Felony Special—or one of the other specialized units from the
Robbery-Homicide Division—took over an investigation. Some were
able to put their resentment aside, act professionally, and provide the

downtown detectives with a proper briefing. Others, like Savich and Montez, apparently could not overcome their wounded pride. I understood how they felt. Still, I wasn't in the mood to take any shit from them.

"I didn't *take* this case. It was assigned to me by my lieutenant."

"I thought you'd quit, Detective Le-*veen*," Savich said, intentionally mispronouncing my name.

"It's Le-*vine*."

"Whatever," Savich said.

"I did quit. But now I'm back."

Montez, pear-shaped and cocky, stood up beside his desk and looked down at me. "Witnesses like Latisha Patton might not get protected at Felony Special, but here in the Harbor, we make sure *our* wits don't get capped." He smiled malevolently. "So if we tell you what we've got, you've got to promise to be real careful, Detective Le-*veen*."

I clenched my teeth, trying to control my anger. But almost against my will, I found myself jumping to my feet and, with a quick backhand, I swept everything off Montez's desk, a half-filled coffee cup and pens, pencils, and paper clips scattering on the floor, the cup shattering on a desk leg and the coffee pooling on the carpeting. I kicked a coffee cup shard across the squad room and shouted, "I came here to be briefed! Not to listen to your sarcastic fucking comments!"

I took a few steps until I was just inches from Montez, forcing him to take a step back. "Hand over the murder book, and I'm outta here."

Montez glanced nervously at me and whispered to Savich, "He's a fucking psycho."

I knew they couldn't afford to let me grab the murder book and walk. If they refused to help me—a Felony Special detective on a case that the chief was personally interested in—they might be consigned next week to the purse snatching detail.

Savich flashed a forced smile at me. "We're just messin' with you. No offense meant. Let me tell you what I know."

Feeling drained, I eased into a chair next to Savich's desk. *I've got to get a grip*, I thought. I can't be going off on people like that.

Savich opened a desk drawer and pulled out the murder book—a royal blue, plastic, three-ring binder—briefly leafed through it, and set it on the corner of his desk. He then updated me, describing the crime scene, how the body was found, and what trace evidence technicians from the department's Scientific Investigation Division had gleaned from the house.

"Get anything from the canvas?" I asked.

"Nobody saw anything," Savich said. "Nobody heard anything."

"Any ideas why no one heard the shot?"

"Lots of ways to minimize the sound of a gunshot," Savich said. "Not many of these clowns on the street can get ahold of a silencer. But you can make one out of a plastic soda bottle. Course, you know all that."

He reached across his desk and handed me the murder book. I opened it and studied the photographs of Relovich's body, the Preliminary Investigation Report, the crime scene diagram, the property report, statements from neighbors and patrol officers, and the chronology of the investigation, which ended at: "0900: Meeting with Felony Special Detective Ash Levine, who assumed responsibility for the case."

"Talked to any family members?" I asked.

"The ex-wife," Savich said. "But she didn't give us much."

"Anyone he was close to?"

"We heard the uncle. He's a fisherman. He was out for halibut when we called. His phone number's in the murder book."

"Any thoughts on why Relovich pulled the pin after thirteen?"

Montez motioned as if he were tipping a bottle toward his mouth.

"That why he was living like a rookie cop?"

Montez nodded.

"What do you guys think happened up there?"

"Junkie hot prowl," Savich said. "A shot, a grab, and a run for it."

"I agree," Montez said. "I used to work CRASH down here and I used to follow the homies from the projects up to the houses on the hills where they'd fill their trunks with big screens, iPods, and laptops."

"How about you?" Savich asked solicitously. "What's your take?"

"I don't have a handle on it yet." I picked up the murder book and walked off, calling out over my shoulder a halfhearted, "Thanks." I crossed the room to the vice section, which was empty, with all the desks vacant. Glowing under a flood of florescent light, it had the forlorn air of a windswept football stadium an hour after the game ended. The room would not begin filling up, I knew, until dark.

I was reaching for a phone, when Randy Walker, a rangy sergeant with a crew cut and jug ears, who headed the division's buy team, hustled toward me. "Accident on the freeway. I was stuck in traffic. Hope you haven't been waiting long."

"I just got here."

"Good. What've you got for me?"

I told him that I believed the killer had parked on the flats, climbed the hill, shot Relovich, returned to his car, and sped off. Fortunately, Walker was friendlier than Savich and Montez and too polite to bring up the Patton case.

"We spotted some brisk business on two street corners," I said.

"That's becoming a hot spot for the Rancho Thirteen Boyz—the gang from the projects that controls the tar trade," Walker said. "We don't have enough people to shut these mutts down. You know how it is. It's like pushing down on a balloon. We stop 'em in one area and they just pop up in another."

"How about blitzing the area during the next few nights," I said. "Can you get your undercover buy team to haul in sellers and buyers?"

Walker grinned. "I was informed the chief is personally interested in this case. So you name it, you got it."

"What I want to do is shake the tree and see if any fruit falls to the ground. So I'd appreciate it if you'd ask every collar if they've heard anything about the murder up on the hill Friday night. Or if they saw anything unusual on the street late Friday night. Let 'em know that for the right information we might be ready to deal. If you get any interesting responses, call me. Anytime. Day or night."

I pulled out a clump of cards that had been stuck in the back of my wallet for the past year, handed Walker the frayed one on top, and asked if I could use a desk for a few minutes.

"Take your pick," Walker said, pointing to the empty unit.

I called Relovich's ex-wife and set up an appointment for the late afternoon. Fortunately, I also caught the uncle at home. He said he would be heading down to Berth 73 in an hour to work on his boat. I knew the spot was near Canetti's Seafood Grotto, a small restaurant on the docks. I could eat a quick lunch and walk over to Relovich's boat.

When I was a rookie patrol officer, my first training officer gave me some valuable advice, which I always tried to follow: "When you're on the job, never get wet and never go hungry."

·   ·   ·

I drove from the station to the waterfront and pulled up in front of Canetti's, a low-slung building that looked like a warehouse, and sat by the window next to a table of fishermen grumbling about the week's catch. I deboned the grilled rex sole and ate my fish and fried potatoes while I watched the bulky refrigerated trucks rumble to the loading docks at the wholesale seafood market. Brazen seagulls circled overhead, swooping for scraps.

After lunch, I walked down the cracked asphalt dock speckled with bird droppings, past the long-liners that hauled in the big swordfish and the smaller purse seiners and draggers. The breeze carried the ripe smell of gutted fish. I stopped in front of the *Anna Marie*, a rusty, fifty-foot gill-netter with peeling white paint and chipped blue trim. A huge pile of nets and orange buoys was piled up on the dock, covered by a green tarpaulin.

"In those nice, shiny shoes, you gotta watch the bird shit," Goran Relovich shouted, motioning for me to come aboard. He grabbed two deck chairs, unfolded them, and as he climbed down to the galley, said in a gravelly voice, "I'll get us some coffee."

I lugged my briefcase aboard, sat down, and looked off into the distance. Tugs and Coast Guard skiffs chugged past, leaving frothy wakes in the gray water. Across the channel, I could see the sprawl of shipyards on Terminal Island, ringed by tatters of fog.

Relovich emerged from the galley carrying two steaming metal mugs of coffee. He was a tall, wiry man in his seventies with a bristly shock of salt-and-pepper hair and a face as leathery and lined as an old wallet.

He pulled a pint of plum brandy out of his pocket and, hand trembling, poured a dollop into his coffee. "I don't suppose you want an eye-opener."

"Some other time."

I took a sip of the coffee, which smelled as strong as diesel fuel, and said, "I want to extend my sympathies to you. Pete was a good cop."

Relovich stared out at sea. We sat in silence until I asked, "After Pete left the force, what'd he do?"

"Went out with me on the boat sometimes. Helped around the dock."

"Why'd he leave the LAPD?"

Relovich set his coffee cup on the desk. "I don't really know."

"Why couldn't he just take some time off? Why couldn't he hang on seven more years and get his pension?"

"Since his mom and dad died, we became close. But he never told me why."

"What's your guess?"

"Maybe he left to get sober. His drinking was getting worse and worse. It broke up his marriage. He had custody of his little girl every other weekend, but it got so bad she didn't even want to see him. Maybe he figured if he was ever going to beat the bottle, he had to quit the LAPD."

"So after his wife left him—"

"Who said *she* left *him*?"

I took a sip of coffee waiting for him to explain.

"Pete's the one who took a hike. As bad as the drinking was, she didn't want him to leave. Even after they got divorced, I think she was still pissed, still jealous as hell. She'd drive down here all the time and bang on his door at all hours of the night, trying to see if she could catch him in bed with some other broad."

"Jealous enough to kill him?"

He stared out to sea, watching the wind from the west whip the whitecaps, the foam floating in the air like snowflakes. "Who knows."

"She ever threaten him?"

"Don't know." He pulled a dirty handkerchief out of his back pocket and blew his nose with such force it sounded like the blast of a foghorn. "Pete was a sharp kid. Could have gone as far as he wanted in the police department. But somewhere along the line, he lost his way. Why? I have no damn idea."

He poured another splash of brandy into his coffee and said, "Pete's father—my brother—was the smart one. He knew this"—Relovich pointed to the line-up of fishing boats—"was a dying business. He got himself a good job at the LAPD with a pension. All I got was arthritis in my hands from all those cold mornings at sea." He held up his gnarled fingers, the nails of the thumbs cracked like broken windshields. "Too many damn catch laws. Too many damn government regulations. Too many damn fishing season restrictions. And they've overfished the hell out of these waters. Christ, I can remember when the sea here was thick with sardines. Now you couldn't find a single one if your life depended on it."

He downed most of his coffee and tossed the dregs overboard with a flick of his wrist. "If I'd followed my brother in the police department I could be back on the Dalmatian coast right now, snoozing in the sun, collecting my monthly pension check, instead of busting my hump every day for a haul that doesn't even pay for my fuel."

I tried to steer him back to the murder. "Was Pete security conscious?"

"He was still a cop at heart. Suspicious as hell. He never opened the door without peeking through the front window to see who was there."

"Even when he was drinking?"

Relovich cracked a gnarled forefinger. "He hadn't touched a drop in three months."

"Any enemies from his days as a cop? Anyone he was concerned about? Any cases that were real problems for him?"

"Don't think so."

"Any idea who could have killed him?"

Relovich coughed and spit into the water. "Probably some wetback from the projects."

After the interview, I headed to my late afternoon meeting with Relovich's ex-wife, Sandy, in the high desert. Lancaster, the northern tip of the county was more than a hundred miles from San Pedro, the southern tip. Fortunately, because it was a weekend, traffic was light. I sped through downtown, cut over a few freeways, and began to traverse the San Gabriel Mountains. I rolled down a window and inhaled the rich acorny scent of the chaparral. But after I reached the summit and started to slalom down the mountain, I was hit with a blast of desert heat and quickly rolled my window back up and flipped on the air conditioner. San Pedro had been cool and misty, in the low sixties; now it was at least thirty degrees hotter. Southern California, I thought, must have more microclimates than a Brazilian rain forest.

At a roadside lookout bordered by spiky Joshua trees, I stopped and stretched my legs. Everything seemed outsized here: the vast dun-colored expanse; the big sky, scorched white at the horizon and electric blue overhead; the limitless vistas. I looked back at the San Gabriels, the escarpment veined with snow that sparkled in the brilliant light.

I hopped back in the car and continued my descent. When I reached Lancaster, I exited the freeway and swung down a road rippling with heat waves, past lizards darting across the asphalt, past a few isolated ranches studded with metal grain silos. I had never visited this edge of the county and was amazed at the beauty of the high desert in spring-time. Entire hillsides were thick with orange poppies, ablaze in the late afternoon light. When I spotted a rural mailbox flanked by bales of hay, I juddered down a pitted dirt road and stopped in front of a weathered white clapboard farmhouse with a broad wooden porch. I climbed out of the car and stretched. The air was still; then a hot puff of wind from the Mojave riffled the leaves of the cottonwoods that shaded the house.

"Quiet out here, isn't it?"

Startled, I whirled around and saw Relovich's ex-wife, Sandy, walking around the side of the house, clutching a can of Bud. She was a big woman, not fat, but definitely packing too many pounds to be wearing tight jeans and a sleeveless blouse. From a distance, she looked like she was in her twenties, but when she approached me, I saw the fine lines around her eyes and mouth and the crinkling at her neck from too much desert sun and realized she was about forty.

"Come on," she said. I followed her to a wooden deck behind the house. I set my briefcase down and we sat side by side on canvas lawn chairs, looking out onto a vast furrowed field. She finished her beer in a swallow, flipped open an ice chest, grabbed two more, and handed one to me. I shook my head.

"Smart cop," she said. "When we were still together, Pete got caught drinking on the job one afternoon and got suspended."

"Today they're so hard-assed they'd probably fire him," I said.

She popped open her beer, twisted off the tab, and tossed it into the dirt. "I'm not really a drinker, despite this," she said, raising the can. "At least not a drinker like Pete. It's just—the past few days. Well, you know."

She slurred her words and her eyes were glassy and bright. I figured she was mixing antidepressants with her beer. There was something brittle about her manner, and I sensed that if I started peppering her with questions she might shatter.

"What do you grow here?" I asked, motioning toward the fields.

"Onions."

"Doesn't smell like onions."

"We just planted last month. Don't start harvesting until late summer. When I married Pete and I moved to Pedro, there were still some tuna canneries out on Terminal Island. I'd smell that tuna and think of the onion fields back home."

"You grew up here?"

She lit a Winston and waved away the smoke. "Yeah. This is my folks' place. After I left Pete, I moved back home with our daughter."

"You really came from different worlds."

She took a few nervous drags and said, "I was going to college in the Valley. Pete was working patrol. He came to my apartment building to break up a party. We started dating. I moved down to Pedro with him." She stubbed out the half-smoked cigarette. "I hated the place. Too foggy down there, too cold. I'm a desert girl. I missed the sun."

She told me what a happy marriage they had, what a good father Pete had been, until his drinking worsened. "Things got so bad I had to leave him."

"So *you* left *him*."

"That's right. I didn't want my little girl growing up like that."

Recalling what the uncle had told me, I knew either she or Relovich's uncle was a liar. My guess it was her. But I wanted to keep her talking, so I didn't press her.

When I asked her about Relovich's days on the force, the cases he handled, and collars who might have wanted revenge, she stared at me, eyes unfocused, and launched into a disjointed monologue, jumping from subject to unrelated subject. Finally, after finishing her beer she said, "I'm sorry Detective Levine. I'm having a hard time concentrating." Her lips trembled and she said softly, "This has been very, very hard for me. I'm going through a lot right now."

She dropped her head and began crying, the tears falling onto the ground, stirring up tiny puffs of dust.

Watching her cry, I thought of Bud Carducci, the salty old cop who taught me the rudiments of homicide investigation when I was a young detective trainee. Bud used to always say, "Before searching for the outlaws, take a good look at the in-laws."

I leaned back in my chair, crossed my arms, and studied Sandy, trying to discern if her emotion was real or feigned. Was she crying because she was truly disconsolate about Pete's death, or because she was frightened and concerned she'd reveal something to me that would spark my suspicion?

She lifted her head, coughed a few times, and dried her eyes with her palms. "Our daughter's freaked out. I'm just trying to keep it all together."

"How old is your girl?"

"Ten."

"Is she at home?"

"She's in her room. But please don't interview her. She's not ready for that."

"It's really important, at this point, to talk to everyone. It would be very helpful for me to talk to your daughter."

"I'm sorry. I can't allow that."

"Okay," I said, already planning to return for a follow-up interview. I was determined to talk to the daughter. I wanted to know if she recalled her mother being home on Thursday night—about the time Relovich was killed.

"Do you have any idea why Pete retired after thirteen years?" I asked.

"Not really."

"Did he have any enemies? Anybody you can think of who might have had a reason to kill him?"

She shook her head.

"Any old cases he was worried about?"

"He never really talked to me about his work." She dug a balled up Kleenex out of her pocket and blew her nose. "I still miss Pete. I miss him so much." She began sniffling and crying again.

I knew I wasn't going to get much more out of her today. "Before I go, I'd like to know if you have any family pictures that were taken at Pete's house?"

She lit another cigarette, inhaled deeply, and stood up. "About eight months ago, Pete gave our daughter, Lindsay, one of those disposable cameras for her birthday. She spent the weekend with him and took a lot of pictures at his house. I'll get those for you," she said over her shoulder as she walked toward the house.

A few minutes later a screen door screeched open, slapped shut, and she returned, carefully making her way down the back steps, gripping a banister for balance. I rose and she handed me an envelope stuffed with photos. "Why'd you want these?"

"I can study the pictures and compare them to what I see now in the house. Sometimes I can spot things that are missing, things that were stolen. I've had a few cases where I've done pawnshop runs and tracked down the people I was looking for."

I slipped her my card and said, "If you think of something that might be helpful, please give me a call."

She studied the card and said, "Your name sounds familiar."

My stomach clenched.

"Didn't you catch some serial killer?"

I nodded, relieved.

"I think I read about you in the paper." She glanced at the card again. "Levine," she muttered to herself. "That ends in a vowel. You I-talian?"

I shook my head.

She turned her head and studied me out of one eye. "You look I-talian."

"When I was a young patrolman, Italian suspects would call me *paisano*. Once I was investigating a Greek loan shark, who dropped some of his mother's baklava off at the station for me. He thought I was a landsman, so I'd cut him some slack."

"Yeah, you could get lost anywhere in that part of the world." She took a deep drag off her cigarette, exhaled, and fanned away the smoke. "Pete looked a little like you—when he was younger and thinner." She dropped her cigarette, ground it into the dirt with her big heel and stared off at the onion fields, tears sluicing down her face. When I put my hand on her back, she began to sob, her chest heaving. She looked up at me and said, "Pete was a good guy. He just had his problems, like everyone else." She kicked at the dirt with the toe of her boot. "Shit. I want you to find that son of a bitch."

I nodded and said, "I will."

I drove back to the freeway at dusk as the sun curled over the Tehachapis, the ridges lit a burnished gold in the dying light. The last light lingered on the western horizon, streaking the sky charcoal and crimson. Overhead, the first stars glinted and the moon shone like a chunk of ice in the crystalline desert sky.

Speeding back down the San Gabriels, I pulled a small, digital, voice-activated recorder out of my briefcase, which was rigged with a microphone in the corner. All the way home I listened to the interviews of Relovich's ex-wife and uncle.

CHAPTER 4

I drove through the desolate downtown streets early the next morning, past crackheads dozing under bus benches and winos sleeping in cardboard boxes, and parked in Chinatown, which was bustling with families arriving for dim sum breakfasts. After picking up a cup of jasmine tea and a bag of *bao*—fluffy steamed buns brushed with syrup and stuffed with mushrooms and ginger—from a Chinese bakery, I headed back to César Chávez Avenue and crossed the bridge over the Los Angeles River, a thin stream of brackish water purling down the graffiti-scarred cement banks. I headed to the coroner's office, a bland, two-story tan building off a dreary East Los Angeles street lined with fast-foot restaurants.

I parked and munched on the *bao* and sipped the tea. When I finished, I cut through the back entrance, pulled powder blue scrubs over my clothes and booties over my shoes, and then slipped on my breathing-filter mask. I walked down a hallway, which was the same color as the scrubs, past the fluorescent lights that zapped the insects drawn to the corpses, and entered the autopsy room. I grimaced as I was assaulted by the distinctive amalgam of formaldehyde, decaying flesh, and disinfectant. A dozen bodies were lined up on shiny steel gurneys, and pathologists and technicians were bent over the corpses, probing, peering, cutting, snipping, dissecting, and slicing. Metal troughs and chrome counters gleamed under the bright overhead lights. The brown tile floor was stained with blood and stippled with tissue.

"Busy weekend?" I asked Dr. Ramesh Gupta, who was examining Pete Relovich's waxy, gray body.

"Quite hectic, Ash," Gupta said, in a lilting, melodious East Indian accent. "Eleven homicides last night, plus three suicides. One was a jumper." He frowned and shook his head. "From a freeway overpass. At rush hour. Very messy. Anyway, glad you're back. God knows, the LAPD can't afford to lose a man as perceptive as you."

"Thanks Doc. I'm glad you're on this one."

Relovich was a big, beefy guy with broad shoulders and a thick neck. But on the metal gurney, naked, streaked with blood, he looked victimized and vulnerable. Relovich's brown eyes glittered under the fluorescent lights, as lifeless as imbedded marbles.

The countless corpses I had seen rarely had looks of terror or horror on their faces, which had surprised me when I finished basic training and saw my first dead bodies. Often, they looked simply confused or disoriented. But Relovich had a curious expression: his mouth was open and his eyes were slightly narrowed as if he was about to raise an index finger and say, "I disagree."

I bent over the body and spotted a thick scar on the side of his nose. That must have been where the bullet fragment entered his nasal cavity before landing in his mouth. I don't think I would've had the balls to spit it out, carry my partner to safety, and then return fire.

When I pick up a case late—like this one—the victim is an abstraction for the first day or two. It is not until the autopsy, until I see the victim splayed on the gurney, cold and gray, the dangling toe tag, that the murder becomes palpable to me.

Now, looking down at Relovich's corpse, I felt a great responsibility. To him. To securing justice. And I felt a great burden. I knew that if I didn't solve this case, it would never be solved. It's all on me. I looked around at the other bodies on the gurneys and thought of my murdered relatives. They never had a proper burial. Nobody investigated their deaths. Their killers were never brought to justice. Not one of them even has a tombstone.

Gupta snapped his fingers and said, "Wake up, Ash." He pointed to the neat, round hole below Relovich's lower lip. "A clean entry wound." He then lifted Relovich up, and I spotted at the base of his head the jagged, star-shaped exit wound.

"I've got a complicated diagnosis for you," Gupta said gravely. "Cause of death, mode of death, and manner of death can be summed up like this: B.B.T.S."

"I don't know that one," I said, perplexed. "You better explain."

"Brains blown to shit," Gupta said with a high-pitched giggle. Still smiling, he grabbed a scalpel off the counter and made a large Y-shaped incision from Relovich's shoulders to his navel. An autopsy technician, wielding a huge pair of clippers, crunched through Relovich's ribs and removed the sternum.

"No matter how many times I hear it, I hate that sound," I said.

Gupta lifted the rib cage and peered inside, like a mechanic searching for a missing spark plug. Pointing to an expanse of brown, pitted tissue he said, "Very dirty lungs."

"Well, he *did* work in Los Angeles."

"No. He was a smoker."

After deftly trimming out Relovich's heart and other internal organs, weighing them, and logging the information on a clipboard, Gupta grabbed a metal ladle, dipped it into the open chest cavity, and poured a small quantity of blood into a glass vial. "See how easy that blood pours? Your victim expired quickly. No thickening or clotting at all."

"Coroner investigator estimates time of death at about twenty-three hundred," I said. "But I don't trust their estimates. What's your take?"

Gupta jabbed at the stomach contents with the scalpel. "I'd say the investigator was pretty close." He pointed to a checkerboard of partially digested brown meat fibers and what appeared to be white potato chunks. "He probably ate dinner a few hours before he was killed. That food had just started working through his digestive system."

Gupta dissected Relovich's neck, snipped out the larynx, and then with a few deft slashes just above the throat, removed the U-shaped hyoid bone, which was encased in pink tissue. He pointed to a jagged edge of bone and said, "The hyoid's cracked. Your guy was probably strangled."

I pointed to Relovich's hands. "No defensive wounds at all. An ex-cop like him would have been fighting to his last breath. Doesn't make sense."

"I agree."

"So what's the cause of death. Gunshot or strangulation?"

With tweezers, Gupta lifted Relovich's lips and studied the gums. He then examined the tissue inside the eyelids, bent over, and peered into his eyes. "No sign of petechiae at all. Which is also very curious. If someone's been strangled, you'll see those distinctive red specks inside the mouth or eyes."

"What do you think?" I asked.

"You, Ash Levine, are the homicide detective, not me."

"Hard to figure," I said, adjusting my mask. "Maybe our killer fires the shot, ransacks the house, and right before he's about to split—even though Relovich was dead—our shooter wants to make sure, to give him a coup de grace. But he doesn't want to risk another shot and tip off the neighbors. So he strangles him."

"You should have been a doctor."

I laughed. "You sound like my mother."

Gupta dropped his scalpel on the counter. "Indian mothers are the same as your Jewish mothers. My mother was so proud when I became a doctor. But when I chose to become a pathologist, she wanted to cry. She wants me to have a nice office in Artesia, so all her friends can make appointments with me and see how important I am. Now she's embarrassed to tell them where I work. She thinks I'm crazy."

"Tell me about it," I said.

"Any other ideas why your perpetrator wished to strangle this gentleman after he was already dead?"

I shrugged. "I'm still trying to figure that out."

I changed my clothes at home, hopped into my Saturn, drove across town, and pulled up in front of my mother's duplex. Before I could ring the bell, my nephew, Ariel, a skinny, wide-eyed seven-year-old wearing a *Sponge Bob* T-shirt, opened the door and jumped into my arms.

"Where we going today, Uncle Ash?"

"It's a surprise. Get your jacket and we're off."

As Ariel ran back into the duplex, my mom emerged from the kitchen. "Had breakfast?" she asked.

I nodded.

"You want an early lunch?"

"Not hungry. Just came from an autopsy."

"That's disgusting."

"It's part of the job."

"Don't get me started on that. Anyway, Ariel hasn't eaten anything all morning. He was too excited about seeing you."

She shook her head, looking somber. "He can't go the entire day without food."

I rolled my eyes. "You don't think I'll be able to find a restaurant in the entire city of Los Angeles that's open on Sunday?"

She limply held out her palms. "I just don't want him—or you— eating *chozzerai* all day."

"Don't worry about it, Mom." I then whispered, "When's Marty getting out of rehab?"

"A few more weeks."

"Any chance that marriage can be saved?"

She shook her head glumly. "I hope so. It's been very hard for Ariel. So these Sundays with you are very important to him." She handed me a booster seat and patted his cheek. "You're a good boy."

Ariel slammed the front door of the duplex and ran down the pathway to the car. I opened the back door, dropped the booster seat inside, and strapped him in.

"Aren't you forgetting something?" my mother said, leaning through the back window.

He kissed her.

"Okay, *einekl*," she said. "Don't give your Uncle Asher any trouble."

As I drove down the Harbor Freeway, Ariel said. "*Now* can you tell me where we're going?"

"San Pedro. We're taking a boat ride in the harbor. I've just been down there for work and thought about you. Thought you'd like seeing all those big ships."

"Grandma told me you're a policeman again."

"That's right."

"Why are you a policeman?"

"Because I want to help people."

"Mama said it's because you didn't try in school, and that's what happens to boys who don't try in school, because they can't get a good job, and that's why I should try in school, or I'll end up like you, but I told her I want to end up like you, and I want to be a policeman when I grow up, just like you, so I can carry a gun and shoot bad people, and she got mad, and she told me I should be a lawyer like my father or a psychologist like her, and I told her I wanted to be a policeman, and she told me to be quiet and go watch *Rugrats*."

"You should listen to your mother."

"Why's my father in the hospital?"

"Well, um," I sputtered. "I know he's sick, but I don't know much about it. You better ask your mother to explain."

When I pulled off the freeway I headed away from the harbor, up a steep hill, and stopped in front of Relovich's house. I climbed out of the car and unbuckled the booster seat.

"Hey, I thought we were going for a boat ride," Ariel said.

"In a few minutes. I wanted to check on something."

"Why does that house have yellow tape around it?" Ariel asked. "It looks like the ribbon around a present."

I put an index finger to my lips and whispered, "Shh. Follow me and be real quiet." We walked around to the back of the house and waded through a hedge to a window that had a jagged hole in the center.

"Who broke the window?"

"A man lived here and he forgot his key so he had to smash the window to get into his house. But I've been thinking about this window the past two days and something bothers me."

Ariel nodded, wide-eyed and serious, flattered that I was talking to him like a grown-up.

I pointed to the shards on the sill and then the tiny specks of glass that speckled the dirt at the base of the hedge.

"You know that book I bought for you, where you look at a drawing and there are ten things wrong with the picture and you have to pick all of them out?"

Ariel nodded.

"Well there's something wrong with this picture." I pointed to the window. "Say the man smashed the glass, opened the window, and then crawled inside. Where would all the glass be?"

Ariel squinted, concentrating hard, and said, "Inside the house."

"Right." I crouched and pointed to the dirt. "If he crawled inside the house right after he smashed the window, why are there tiny pieces of glass here and not any inside the house?"

Ariel tugged on my pants. "I'm bored. Can we go now and see the ships."

Ariel hugged the railing during the harbor cruise and marveled at the big fishing vessels at dock, their spotting towers silhouetted against a

scoured blue sky; the huge white cruise ships pulling into port for the afternoon; the cargo vessels lined up under the soaring cranes that cast
enormous shadows on the splintery docks. The boat steamed around
Terminal Island, through oil slicks, reflecting rainbow prisms in the sunshine, past the federal prison encircled with double chain-link fences
and topped with razor wire. A few of the prisoners, lined up for yard
time, waved at the boat passengers.

"Did you arrest any of them?" Ariel asked, excited about seeing his
first criminals.

"Naw," I said. "This is a federal prison. I only send people to state
prisons."

"What's the difference?"

Ignoring him, I pulled a sweatshirt over his head as the wind picked
up. Watching him grip the railing, smiling, enjoying the boat ride, I felt
a sudden, piercing tenderness toward him. I picked Ariel up and hugged
him.

I thought of my father, living with his parents and younger
brother—who was about Ariel's age—in a small German town on the
North Sea. In 1941 they were sent by cattle car to the ghetto in Lodz,
Poland, then on to Treblinka. They waited patiently at the station, under
the impression that they had arrived at a labor camp. The Nazis sent
most of the Jews—including the children and the elderly—to one line.
A few dozen of the young men, who looked like they'd be good workers, waited in the other line. My father was sent with the young men. He
watched his father, mother, and brother marched to a corner of the
camp. His father panicked at leaving his oldest son and ran toward him.
He was shot in the back. My father never saw his mother and brother
again.

I leaned over, kissed Ariel's cheek, and thought of my father's little
brother. Asher. My namesake.

"Why aren't you married anymore?" Ariel said.

"That's a long story."

"You miss Aunt Robin?"

"I guess so."

"I miss my dad."

"He'll be home soon."

"Maybe Aunt Robin will too?"

"I don't think so."

After Robin left me, investigating murders became a much more dismal, onerous task. The interviews with grieving relatives, the autopsies, the crime scenes with walls splashed with blood and imbedded with bone and tissue, all weighed more heavily on me. Whenever I picked up a new case, I could feel a tightness in the pit of my stomach, as if the spirit of the newly departed had remained to pressure me, to insure I did not forget my duty. Robin had always been a countervailing force; spending time with her had helped alleviate the strain of the job, ease that pressure in my gut.

After the cruise, Ariel was hungry so we ate fish 'n' chips at the harbor, and then bought ice cream cones and walked along the docks. I helped Ariel with his spelling by having him read the names on the fishing boats—many of them the first daughters of the skippers. At dusk, as Ariel snoozed in the backseat, I drove back to the city, thinking about Relovich's broken hyoid bone and the smashed bedroom window.

When I returned home, I removed from my briefcase the envelopes containing Relovich's cancelled checks and phone records, and spread them out on my dining room table. Most of the cancelled checks covered routine expenses and none of them piqued my interest. I examined his phone bills from the last few months. His cell bills didn't list any numbers called, just the amount owed; but his home phone bills recorded all the toll calls, which I highlighted with a yellow marker. Relovich had not made many repeat toll calls, but one phone number with a 213 area code stood out because during the past two months he'd called the number more than a dozen times.

After clicking on my computer, accessing an LAPD site, and checking a reverse directory for the address, I discovered that it was a business listing a few miles west of downtown: L.A. Elegant Escorts. A woman by the name of Ann Licata was registered as the owner. I decided to see what she had to say.

CHAPTER 5

I cruised down a side street a few blocks north of Olympic lined with small, shabby apartment buildings. The night was damp and columns of mist glowed a sickly yellow under the streetlights. When I double-checked the address, I realized that the establishment with the genteel name of L.A. Elegant Escorts was located in a rundown dingbat—Los Angeles's grim contribution to urban blight. I was particularly incensed about dingbats because the street where I grew up was once composed of gracious Spanish-style duplexes. But when I was in grammar school, developers began tearing them down—the story of L.A.—and throwing up hastily constructed dingbats: stripped down two-story stucco boxes with rows of parking spaces in front, the exteriors adorned with flimsy metal lamps and cheesy decorative starbursts. Dingbats are the residential analogues of strip malls.

I walked along the side of the dingbat, up a dank staircase, the steps dotted with specks of stucco that had fallen from the walls, and stood on a landing flanked by two front doors. I rang the bell of apartment number four. I waited about thirty seconds and rang the bell again. I heard rattling in the back of the apartment and then a sleepy voice call out, "Who is it?"

"LAPD. Open up."

"Do you have a search warrant?"

"I'm not interested in searching your place. I just want to talk to you. I'm investigating a murder."

An obese woman with stringy hair, wearing a ratty yellow bathrobe, opened the door a few inches. "ID," she barked.

I showed her my badge. "You Ann Licata?"

"Yeah. But I want you to understand something right off the bat. First of all, any money that changes hands between my girls and the gentlemen who contract for their services is simply for companionship," she said, as if she was delivering a memorized speech. "Anything that might occur during their time together is a matter of personal choice between two consenting adults over the age of eighteen. There is never, at any time, any written or verbal guarantee involving the exchange of sex for money. Is that clear, officer?"

"I don't care if you're a hooker booker. That's not why I'm here. I'm investigating a homicide. I don't plan to inform vice of our conversation. If you're honest with me now and help me with my case, I promise you I'll leave you alone to run your business."

"All right then," she said, turning around, taking a few steps, and flopping on a threadbare sofa. I followed her into the small living room and sat across from her. Her robe inched up, revealing two enormous blotchy thighs that enveloped an entire sofa cushion.

"Do you know Pete Relovich?"

"Never heard of him."

"Again, let me give you the ground rules. Be honest with me, and I'll walk out the door and let you run your business. Bullshit me, and I'll call vice right now, and they'll shut down your operation and haul you out of here in handcuffs. What'll it be?"

She squirmed on the sofa for a moment. "Yeah, yeah," she said wearily. "I knew Pete. He was a driver for one my girls. What's going on with him?"

"He was killed."

She pulled her robe tight and muttered, "Jesus."

"Which girl did he drive for?"

"Her name's Brittany."

"What's her real name?"

"Jane."

"Last name?"

"Granger."

"Address?"

She reached into an end table, riffled through a spiral notebook, scrawled down the address on a page, ripped it out, and handed it to me.

"What's a driver?"

"He takes the escort to her appointment, checks out the place to see if it seems safe, waits in the car for her to finish her date, and then either drives her home or to her next date."

"How long's he been doing that?"

"About a year."

"How did he end up working for you?"

"You'll have to ask Jane. She brought him in."

"Is it possible he made some enemies? Maybe crossed the wrong customer?"

"We call them clients."

"Crossed the wrong client?"

"Again, you'll have to ask Jane. But I really doubt it. We run a very professional operation."

"I looked around the dingy apartment, strewn with empty Coke cans, greasy McDonald's wrappers, and *National Enquirers*, and said, "I can see that." I pulled a card out of my wallet and handed it to her. "If you hear anything that you think I might find useful, give me a call."

I walked to the door as Licata struggled to her feet. "A deal's a deal," she said. "You're not calling vice on me, right?"

"As long as you continue to cooperate with me—no."

On Monday morning, I called Pete's uncle and he agreed to meet me at his boat. I wanted to do a little research on Pete's driving job before I door-knocked Jane Granger.

When Goran Relovich saw me walking down the dock, he climbed down below and emerged carrying two cups of coffee. We eased into our deck chairs and I said, "Did you know Pete was driving girls for an escort service?"

Relovich blew on his coffee. "Yeah, I knew."

"Why didn't you tell me?"

"'Cause it's none of your damn business."

"Everything Pete was involved in is my business. How the hell can I find who killed him if the people close to him aren't honest with me?"

He set his coffee cup on the deck. "I'm sorry. It's just that I don't want the newspapers to get ahold of it. I don't want that to be the last thing written about my nephew. He wasn't proud of it."

"How did an ex-cop get involved in a sleazy deal like that?"

"Ever since he left the force he's been hurting for money. He had a few security jobs early on, but he was drinking so much back then he ended up getting bounced. I put him to work when I could, but most of my favorite spots are fished out, and I'm getting too old to make a lot of long runs. The last year or two, Pete was having trouble making his child support payments. When he missed two months in a row, it hurt him real bad. He vowed it wouldn't happen again. He loved his little girl, loved her more than anything in the world, knew he hadn't been a good father. Figured the least he could do was send that check and provide for her."

He stared morosely out at sea, rubbing the gray stubble on his chin.

"So how did Pete get involved with that escort outfit?"

"He met one of these gals. I don't know where he met her, or if he was putting the wood to her, or how she got him to drive for her."

"You sure there isn't anything else you haven't told me, anything else about Pete that might be embarrassing?"

"That's it. But you don't have to spread it around the station house, do you? I'd hate to have everyone at the LAPD know about this."

I opened my briefcase and tapped the murder book. "It stays inside here."

"You think driving those gals around could have got Pete killed?" he asked.

"At this point, Mr. Relovich, I have no idea."

Walking down the dock toward my car, I checked my watch: it was a few minutes after eleven. If I stopped for lunch, by the time I was through I could head up to the desert. School would be out by then, and I might have a chance to interview Relovich's daughter. Sandy had refused to let me talk to the girl the last time I was there. But maybe if I ambushed Sandy, I might catch her in a vulnerable moment and persuade her to change her mind. I still hadn't ruled her out as a suspect; the daughter might know something that could prove useful.

The first time I interviewed Relovich's uncle, he had told me Sandy was extremely jealous—it almost sounded like she'd been stalking him— and Pete had walked out on her. But when I interviewed her, she told me she had left him. Lies always merit a follow-up.

I walked down the dock to Canetti's, ate lunch, and flipped through the paper, but there was nothing on the Relovich murder. Then I sped off to Lancaster.

When I descended into the desert, a harsh wind blew in from the west, kicking up clouds of topsoil, sandblasting my windshield, and bending the cottonwoods that fringed Sandy Relovich's house. I rang the doorbell and watched the cottonwood bloom swirl down the furrows of the onion fields while I waited on the porch. Finally, Sandy came to the door and I followed her into the kitchen. She grabbed a can of Bud from the refrigerator and a pitcher of iced tea. Her eyes were glazed and her hands trembled—sloshing the iced tea in the pitcher—so I figured this wasn't her first beer of the day. She opened the can, took a swig, and set the pitcher on the table. She filled a glass and handed it to me.

My mouth felt dry and gritty from the dust, and I took a few long swigs. "Sorry to barge in on you like this," I said, pulling up a chair at the kitchen table, "but I need to talk to you about a few more things."

"Okay," she said warily.

"Did Pete have any problem making his child support payments?"

She nodded. "A few times he was short, but he made it up within a few weeks. Two or three times, he missed payments altogether and couldn't get the checks to me for months. That really hurt him. He felt like he was letting his daughter down. Once, about a year and a half ago, he drove out here to tell me he couldn't come up with the cash. Second time I ever saw him cry. First time was when he told me he was leaving the LAPD."

"Why'd he say he was leaving."

"Said I wouldn't understand. We were separated by then, so I couldn't get much out of him about anything. Anyway, after he missed that payment, he vowed he'd never be late with child support again. And he wasn't."

"Did he have a new source of income?"

"Don't know. All I know is that he was working on his uncle's boat."

"You ever hear of him driving for an escort service."

"I don't know where you heard that, but it's bullshit," she said angrily. "Pete was a straight arrow. He wouldn't sink that low."

She finished her beer in a long swallow and, reaching under the sink, stuffed the can in a paper bag.

"Anything else you can think of that might be helpful?"

"If I do, I have your card and I'll let you know."

"You know, I'm talking to everyone connected to Pete. I really think it would be helpful if I talked to your daughter, too."

"I told you last time you were here: *no*," she snapped.

"I wouldn't press you if I didn't think it was important," I said softly. "But you're a cop's wife. You know it's important that I speak to all the family members. When Pete was on the job, he had to interview the children of crime victims. He probably didn't like doing it, probably thought of his own daughter. But he knew it was important, so he did it. And he did it because he was a good cop and that was part of his job. Well, I'm trying to be a good cop, too. And I'm just trying to do *my* job."

"I don't know," she said uncertainly. "You have kids?"

"No," I said, embarrassed. There aren't many bachelor cops my age at the LAPD, and when anyone asks me about kids, I always feel uncomfortable, as if I'm still a boy, unwilling to take on an adult's responsibility.

"I have a nephew I'm very close to. I promise, I'll be as careful with your daughter as I would be with my nephew."

"It always really got to Pete."

I nodded, encouraging her to continue.

"When a parent was murdered. When he was on the job and we were still together, he'd come home at night and talk to me about it how bad he felt for the kids. Said that was the saddest thing in the world. Now it's happened to our daughter."

Her eyes welled up and she began sniffling. She grabbed a Kleenex off the kitchen counter, blew her nose, and threw open the back door.

"Lindsey," she shouted. "Come on in."

I looked out the kitchen window and saw a girl sitting on a swing hung from the branch of a sycamore. Slowly shambling to the door, she plopped into a chair and stared at her shoes. She was a skinny girl with freckles on her nose and a long blonde braid that reached the middle of her back.

"This man wants to ask you a few questions about Daddy. You up for that?"

"I guess so."

"Hello Lindsey," I said. "My name is Ash. I'm a policeman, just like your father was."

She continued to stare at her shoes.

"Did you ever see your father's badge?"

"I can't remember."

"Do you want to see mine?"

She looked up for the first time. "I guess so."

I unclipped my badge from my belt and held it out. I pointed to the top and said, "Can you read this word?"

Moving her lips she said, "Detective."

"Do you know what this tall building is in the center of the badge?"

She ran her fingers along the outline. "It's Los Angeles City Hall."

"That's pretty good. How'd you know that?"

"My school went there on a field trip."

"Lindsey, I'm going to ask you a few questions."

"Okay."

"Did your dad call you at night sometimes."

"Yeah."

"How often?"

"Pretty often."

I turned to Sandy.

"A couple times a week," Sandy said. "Every other night. Something like that."

"Lindsey, do you remember the last time your father called you?"

"On Thursday night."

That was the night, I knew, he was killed.

"How do you remember that it was Thursday night?"

"Because I had a science test on Friday and he promised to call on Thursday night and explain some things to me."

"What time did he call?"

"Right after dinner."

"What time was that?"

"About seven."

I didn't want to ask Sandy where she was Thursday night. She might realize she was under some suspicion, throw me out, and deny me access to her daughter. So I thought I'd do an end run around her and hope she was too drunk to figure out what I was searching for.

"Do you remember what you did the rest of the night?"

"I finished my homework."

"Did anyone help you?"

"My mom."

"What time did you go to bed?"

She smiled. "About ten thirty."

"Did your mom put you to bed?"

"Yes."

"Why so late?"

"My mom and I stayed up and watched *Desperate Housewives*. She TiVoed it on Sunday night. She said if I studied hard all week, we could watch it on Thursday night."

Looking embarrassed, Sandy said, "She'll be eleven pretty soon. I think she's old enough. Don't you?"

"I'm sure you know what's best for your daughter," I said, feeling a twinge of disappointment. The coroner estimated that Pete was killed on Thursday night. It was a long drive from Lancaster to San Pedro. This ruled out Sandy as a suspect.

"Did you spend a lot of time at your father's house in San Pedro?"

"Every other weekend."

"Was that fun?"

"I liked going there."

"What did you do?"

"Sometimes we'd go out on my great-uncle's boat. Sometimes we'd go to the aquarium in Long Beach or fish off the jetty. In the summer, we'd go to the beach."

"Did you ever meet any of the people your father knew?"

Biting her lower lip, she looked up at her mother. Sandy nodded.

"One friend."

"Was this a man or woman?"

"Woman."

"Was this his girlfriend?"

"I guess so."

"What was her name?"

"Jane Granger." She said it quickly, without a pause, as if it was a single name.

"Was she nice?"

"Sort of."

"Did you meet any other people your father knew?"

She reached behind her, twirled her braid for about thirty seconds, and asked, "Is this an important question?"

"It might be, why?"

"I don't want to answer it."

Sandy reached over and took her daughter's hand and patted it. "Why not, honey?"

"Daddy made me promise not to tell anyone."

"Why didn't he want you to tell anyone?" Sandy asked, looking perplexed.

"He said that if you found out, you wouldn't let me visit him anymore."

"It's okay now," Sandy said. "You can tell us about it."

Lindsey clasped her hands tightly, stared at them and, racing to get out the words, said, "On Saturday night and Jane and Daddy were making dinner in the kitchen and someone rang the doorbell. Jane opened it without asking who it was. Daddy said never to do that, and he got mad, and the man at the door yelled at Daddy and waved a gun at him. Daddy pushed him out the door and locked it, and the man went away."

Sandy stared at her daughter, stunned, mouth open.

"How long ago was this?" I asked.

"About a month or two," Lindsey said.

"Did your father or Jane ever mention the man's name?"

She shook her head.

"Did you hear what the man said?"

"No."

"What did he look like?"

"He had a bald head."

"Can you remember if he was tall or short."

She shook her head.

"Fat or thin?"

"No. I just remember the shiny bald head and the shiny gun."

"Do you remember his race?"

"Race?" she said, confused.

"White, black, Hispanic, Asian?"

"White. But his skin was sun tanned."

"Do you know the difference between a rifle and a pistol?"

"A pistol is what my dad carried when he was a policeman. A rifle is what grandpa uses when he goes hunting."

"That's right. Did this man have a rifle or a pistol."

"A pistol."

I spent the next twenty minutes talking to Lindsey and her mother, but was unable to glean anything else about the man with the gun. As I drove back toward the city, I realized that although I'd just ruled out one suspect, I'd gained another.

It was late afternoon by the time I reached Jane Granger's apartment in Redondo Beach. She had to be making good money in the escort business because she lived in a luxury complex only a block from the beach. The property was lushly landscaped with banana plants and giant birds of paradise bordering the front and magenta bougainvillea spilling over the railings.

I rang the bell, and a few seconds later someone checked me out through the peephole and said, "The sign in lobby says: *No Solicitors*."

"I held up my badge. "I'm an LAPD homicide detective."

She opened the door and said, "Is this about Pete?"

"How'd you know?"

"There was short story in the *Times*. A friend of mine saw it and called me. Ann Licata also called. Told me to cooperate with you. Come on in."

The living room was tidy and spare, with just a white canvas sofa, a gleaming glass and brass coffee table in front, and, on the opposite wall, a white brick fireplace with an empty mantel. In the corner was a sad-looking ficus tree with withered leaves. The room had the featureless, generic quality of a motel.

Granger was a tall redhead with tired eyes and too much makeup. She was dressed as if she was about to leave for a date with a client: black Spandex miniskirt, high heels, and pink Angora V-neck sweater revealing the lacy edge of a black push-up bra that showed a lot of cleavage. In her twenties she had probably been beautiful. Now in her mid-thirties, she was still shapely, but the life she'd led was starting to take its toll.

We sat on opposite ends of the sofa and I asked, "How'd you meet Pete?"

She reached into her purse, lit a cigarette, crossed her legs, and leaned back. When she caught me checking out her legs, she smiled slyly. "I don't want to say anything that might get me into trouble. You understand what I'm saying, detective?"

I gave her the same spiel I gave Licata, assuring her I was not interested in prostitution, only homicide.

"Pete was a good guy. I've been real torn up about this."

I studied her for a moment, watching her take languorous drags of her cigarette. She didn't seem particularly upset.

"So how'd you meet Pete?"

"I'm just about to make a stupid mistake," she said.

"What's that?"

"I'm going to be honest with a cop." She took another long, slow drag of her cigarette and fanned away the smoke. "My girlfriend and I were having drinks one night at a restaurant on the water in San Pedro. Pete was at the bar, drinking a beer. We talked. I found out he was really hurting for money. Said he had to come up with some cash in a few days for his child support. Pete was a big boy. Seemed street smart, like he knew how to handle himself. I told him I needed a driver because my regular driver just moved to Houston, that he could make a few hundred bucks for a couple of hours work. He agreed." She uncrossed her legs. "I didn't find out until later that he was an ex-cop."

"What, exactly, did he do?"

"He took me to the date, walked me to the door, checked out the place, made sure it seemed safe. We each had our cells. I'd text him with codes. We had a code for: the call was cancelled; I was in danger; I suspected the client was a cop; the date was over; call the office; send over another girl. All kinds of things."

"Wasn't he worried about getting busted?"

"Well, he wasn't doing anything illegal. He just dropped me off, picked me up, and drove me around. He made it a point never to handle any money or negotiate with clients."

"How long did he drive for you?"

"Started about a year ago. Stopped driving a few months ago."

"Why'd he stop?"

"He never felt right about it, him being an ex-cop and all. So when he caught up on his child support, he bailed."

"Did he drive for anyone else?"

"No. Just me and Adriana." She flashed me a coy look. "I only do doubles."

"You'll have to explain. This isn't my area of expertise."

"That's two girls and one client. We start with a show. Me and Adriana get it on. Then, when the client's ready to roll, I retreat to the bathroom and Adriana finishes him off." She pulled back her shoulders and smoothed her skirt. "I'm *not* a prostitute. I don't have sex with clients."

I decided not to engage her in a philosophical discussion on what qualified as prostitution. "Was your relationship with Pete strictly business?"

"It was at first. But we started dating just about the time he stopped driving for me."

"Can you think of anyone he might have encountered when he was driving who might have a reason to kill him?"

She shook her head. "Like I said, he had nothing at all to do with the clients."

"Did you ever see anyone threaten Pete?"

"Not that I can remember."

"Let me describe a scene to you. It's a Saturday night. You and Pete are cooking dinner at his house. Pete's daughter is there. A man comes to the door. He pulls out a gun. He threatens Pete. Does that refresh your memory?"

She stubbed out her cigarette. "Yeah."

"Then why didn't you tell me when I asked you?"

"Because this whole thing is turning out to be a big fucking mess, and I don't want to get involved in a murder investigation."

"You *are* involved."

"I can see that."

"Listen, I understand your concerns. But if you keep things from me, I'll keep digging and digging. I'll keep coming back over here. I'll end up questioning everyone you know. The easiest way for you to do this is to just tell me the truth. Because if you do, I'll be out of here, I'll move on to the next step of my investigation, and I won't come back."

She slipped an unlit cigarette in her mouth. "His name is Ray Abazeda. He owns the escort service."

"I thought Ann Licata owned the escort service. The business and the phone number are registered in her name."

"She's the front man, the straw man, whatever you call it," Granger said. "Ray's the real owner, the one who rakes in the cash. Ann's just an employee. Ray's smart. He doesn't want vice cops or the IRS on his back, so he keeps a low profile and pays other people to take the risk. Fucking camel jockey."

"Where's he from?"

"One of those places back in the Middle East. I can't remember. But he's been here for decades."

"Why'd he threaten Pete?"

She sighed theatrically. "I was Ray's girlfriend. At least one of them. But I got to know Pete pretty well when he was driving me. We started dating. He didn't want me doing the escort thing anymore. So I left the business. I left Ray. He was jealous, but that wouldn't have been enough for him to go after Pete. What really pissed him off was he thought that Pete was stealing one of his girls. He thought Pete talked me into leaving Elegant Escorts because he was trying to set up his own escort service—a competing service—and I'd be one of his girls. That really pissed Ray off. Even though I didn't make it with clients, I was one of his best earners," she said with a hint of pride. "I really put on a show. I've got a lot of repeat clients."

"Any truth in what Ray was accusing Pete of?"

"No way. But Ray's a crazy motherfucker. He wouldn't listen. He was afraid that if someone poached one of his girls and went out on his own, he'd be seen as weak. And this is a tough business. He was afraid that other competitors would start poaching his girls and stealing his clients. So he had to show that he was a hard guy. So that night he confronted Pete with the gun. Told him that if he didn't stay away from his girls and his business, he'd fucking kill him."

"What'd Pete do?"

"Pete just marched to the door, smacked the gun out of his hand, shoved him off the porch, and slapped the shit out of him. While Ray was sprawled on the lawn, Pete told him the next time he saw him at his house he'd take his gun and jam it up his ass."

"Do you think Ray killed Pete?"

"Who knows?"

"Do you know what kind of gun Ray was carrying?"

She shook her head. "I don't know anything about guns."

I pulled out my Beretta. "This is a semiautomatic. See, the back is smooth, there's no hammer to cock. A revolver has a hammer and a round cylinder where the bullets are loaded. Was Ray carrying a semi-automatic or a revolver?"

"I think it was a semiautomatic."

"Did Ray ever threaten him again?"

"No. Ray's a bully. When he saw that Pete wasn't afraid of him or his gun, he slinked off."

"After Pete stopped driving for you, did he get another job?"

"The only thing I knew he did was work on his uncle's boat."

"So Pete talked you into leaving the business."

"Yeah. I went to cosmetology school years ago. He encouraged me to take it up again. I had some money saved. So I went back to the school."

"So you're out of the escort business?"

"I was."

"Was?"

"After Pete was killed, I guess I've been really turned around. I lost some of my motivation. I'm kind of hard up for cash. So I'm back with a service."

"L.A. Elegant Escorts?"

"That dickhead Ray wouldn't take me back. He's a grudge-holding scumbag. He threatened to have me blackballed in the business, spread the word that I was a snitch, just because I'd been dating an ex-cop. I hope you throw his ass in jail, and shut down his sleazy operation. I found work with a new service." She checked her watch. "We better wrap this up pretty soon. I've got an early job today. I'm leaving in a half hour."

"You find a new driver?"

"Life goes on." She reached down, ran her fingers along the edge of her right high heel and then fiddled with a thin gold anklet. "If you ever need a little off-duty cash, I can always use a good driver."

Ignoring the offer, I said, "Where can I find Abazeda?"

She grabbed a pen off the coffee table and scrawled on the back of a matchbook. "Here's his address. But he's not in town now. He's got escort services in Phoenix and Tucson. He spends every Monday, Tuesday, and Wednesday in Arizona, taking care of business. What day is it today?"

"Monday."

"You can catch him Wednesday night. He always flies in from Arizona on Wednesday night."

I pulled a card out of my wallet, scrawled down my cell phone number, and handed it to her. "If you think of anything else, give me a call."

She dropped it on the coffee table.

"You sure Abazeda will be back on Wednesday?" I asked.

"He's a creature of habit. He'll be back."

CHAPTER 6

A cold, rosy dawn in southern Lebanon. I'm part of a three-man patrol hidden behind a boulder on a rocky promontory. Three Hezbollah guerrillas wearing flowing keffiyehs, aiming Kalachnikovs, pop up on a ridge behind us. A fourth guerrilla is about to pull the plug on a grenade. I swing around. I aim my Gallil at him, but the assault rifle jams. The two other soldiers shout to me: "Esh"! Shoot. But the gun is still jammed. "Esh! Esh! Esh!"

Ring! Ring! Ring! I jumped out of bed and reached for my phone. "Hello," I said groggily.

"Are you naked?" someone asked in a falsetto voice.

"Who is this?"

"I got a sidewalk hostess for you to meet. She's even got most of her teeth."

I recognized the voice. It was Sergeant Walker of the Harbor Division buy team.

"We just rounded up a passel of ho's, in addition to some crackheads, junkies, and street-corner dealers. A couple might have something for you."

"I'm on my way," I said.

I met Walker in the squad room and shook his hand. "Good work. I appreciate it."

"No problem. Pete was a local boy. Anything I can do to help, you just let me know."

I asked him if I could run a suspect before the interviews. He rolled a chair over to the computer, and I printed out a DMV picture of Abazeda, jotted down his address, and ran his record. He had one arrest for passing bad checks in San Diego and two others for pandering seven years ago. That must have been when he decided the smart way to go was to set up a phony front and run the operation from the shadows.

I slipped Abazeda's booking photo into a sheet, along with five other olive-complexioned suspects—a six-pack—and inserted it into my murder book. Maybe I'd get lucky; maybe someone would pick out Abazeda.

I signed off and Walker escorted me through the station, past the dim, dank holding cells to a small, windowless interview room with two padded chairs flanking a metal table. "I'll have the jailer bring out the ones who are willing to deal."

I shook his hand. "Good work. I appreciate it."

A few minutes later, the jailer returned with a skinny, black woman with blotchy skin and impossibly long red fingernails that were chipped at the edges. She wore a ragged sundress, was missing a bottom tooth, and her greasy hair, reddish at the ends, flared out at the sides like the wings on Mercury's helmet. The gold border around a front tooth winked under the harsh lights.

"Coffee?" I asked.

"Sound good to me."

I brought her a cup of coffee, a packet of creamer, and four sugar cubes—because I knew most junkies liked the sugar more than the coffee. I sat across from her and watched while she dropped all four cubes in the coffee and stirred.

"Tough night?" I asked.

"Ain't that the truth."

She sipped her coffee and then leered at me "You cute. You and me could get along just *fine*."

I laughed and said, "What do you have for me?"

"What you *want*, honey?"

"Sergeant Walker told you about a murder late Thursday night. He said you might have heard something on the street."

"Before I tell you, I want a deal to get my kids back. One of my babies tested positive for cocaine. But other than that he was healthy. He weighed almost nine pounds."

"The weight's irrelevant," I snapped.

"Anyway," she said, ignoring me, "they took my other two kids away. I want 'em back, too."

"What did you hear about the murder?"

"I heard whatever you want me to hear," she said, smiling slyly. "I saw whatever you want me to see. You get me my kids back, and I'll pick *anyone* you want out of any lineup. And I'll go to court for you, too."

"This interview is now over," I announced. I walked into the hall-way and called for a jailer, who escorted the woman out of the room and returned with an Hispanic teenager wearing a stained wife-beater, black, crepe-soled winos, and black Dickies so oversized they looked like a parachute. His forearms were scrolled with gang tattoos.

"Coffee?" I asked, standing up.

"This is bullshit! I didn't know about that rock in my pocket."

I motioned toward a chair. We both sat down.

The teenager leaned across the table and said earnestly, "My girl-friend must have been wearing my pants earlier today."

"Those pants might be a little big for your girlfriend," I said.

"That *pinche puta's* fat."

"So what do you have for me."

"What do you have for *me*, ese?"

"If you've got information that helps me solve the murder, I can talk to the DA before the sentencing. I can write a letter to the presiding judge. It all depends on your information."

"Check it out. My information's good. You can take that to the bank and cash it, 'cause it won't bounce."

"You hear about that murder on the hill Thursday night?"

"The white cop?"

"Ex-cop."

"Yeah. I got a line on who shot him. I heard it was a guy from the Wilmington Insanes. Guy named Spanky. I normally wouldn't drop a dime on a *vato*, but Spanky's a buster, a total fool." He stared at me for a moment. "Hey, you Mexican? Or half-Mexican? You look a little Mexican."

I shook my head. "Who do you claim?"

"I don't claim."

I flashed him a skeptical look and pointed to the RBZ tattooed on his forearms.

"Don't mean shit," he said without much conviction.

"But you live in the Rancho Boyz's 'hood," I said.

"Yeah."

"And they're warring with the Wilmington Insanes?"

"So?"

"So you might have a reason to want Spanky off the streets. Anyway, is Spanky usually strapped?"

"Yeah."

"What does he carry?"

"A three fifty-seven."

I knew Relovich was shot with a forty, so I hustled the kid out of the interview room. The jailer led him down the hallway and returned with a skinny, jittery, black man in his forties wearing shorts, a Clippers T-shirt, and house slippers. He collapsed into a chair.

"For the last few hours I been thinkin' on it," he said. "I need help. I'm a dope fiend. I want rehab, but every time I get picked up they give me county time. Now, I know I'm facing *hard* time in the joint. They got me red-handed."

"What were you holding."

The man extended both his arms. "I had me a motherfucking smorgasbord. I had rocks to get my head up and some tar to get *down*. Gonna make me a speedball. Even had some chronic in my back pocket. So you can see why I'm ready to deal."

"You hear about that murder Thursday night?"

"I heard about it. And I was out that night. I saw sumpin'."

"About what time?"

"Midnight."

"What you see?"

The man chewed on his thumbnail. "'Pends."

"Depends on what."

"'Pends on how you help me."

"If you've got solid information, I'll try to work it out so you can get treatment at Norco instead of doing prison time. I'll talk to the DA on your case and I'll talk to your probation officer."

"Awright, then," he said, chewing the cuticle. "I didn't think much about what I saw that night until the next day when I hear this white cop been shot up on the hill. I needed a taste that night, you feel me? I don't live but three blocks from that corner. I walk down, get me my taste, and woo, woo, woo. You know how it is. And I'm walkin' back when I see these two mens makin' for their car parked at the bottom of the hill.

But they didn't heavy through the 'hood. They kinda light-stepped it to their car, lookin' around."

"Can you tell me where their car was parked?"

He described the spot where the bloodhound's trail ended.

"What did they look like?"

"The dude walkin' toward the passenger side of the car was skinny and kinda tall. He looked Mez-can. The guy by the driver's side was shorter and stout. Couldn't get a good look at his grille, though."

"Was he Mexican, black, or white?"

"Couldn't tell. It was too dark."

"Could you ID either of them if I showed you a picture?"

"Doubt it. Got only a glancing look at the Mez-can and no look at the other guy."

Abazeda had dark enough skin to pass for Mexican. But, according to the DMV printout, he was five foot nine and weighed one hundred ninety pounds. He could hardly be considered skinny. Maybe he was the driver.

"Let's give it a try," I said, sliding the six-pack across the table.

The junkie squinted at each picture, before finally saying, "Can't pick him out. Sorry."

I pressed him, but he couldn't provide more detailed descriptions. He did, however, recall that both were wearing dark stocking caps.

"Maybe them dudes were sailors, wearing lids like that," he said.

"Were they carrying anything?"

"Mez-can guy wasn't. Driver had something under his arm, like a box or sumpin'."

"You see where they went after they got in the car?"

"Whipped around and busted a right. They gone."

"Can you describe the car?"

"Dark car. Dark night. Couldn't really tell."

"You think of anything else, call me. Here's my card. Memorize the number and rip it up. I don't think you'd be too popular in here if someone saw that in your pocket."

"That how you get yourself a righteous ass whuppin'. Or shankin'."

I walked out of the jail and through the station to Walker's desk. I told him about the two men the junkie described.

"You believe that junkie?" Walker asked.

"He may be holding something back. They usually do. But I think what he told me is on the level. Do these two guys fit the MO of any teams you know about?"

"No. But I'll ask around."

"You tired of interviewing crackhounds?"

"You got any more for me?"

"One. Young Mexican gal. Doesn't fit the mold. Works as a secretary at a Torrance engineering firm and goes to community college at night. She's not really sure she wants to deal. Kind of on the fence. I'll bring her in. You'll have to convince her to talk."

I returned to the interview room and a few seconds later the jailer brought in the woman, who was in her early twenties and looked too clean to be a crackhead. She was dressed like a preppy and wore khaki slacks with a sharp crease, suede loafers, and a pale green V-neck Polo sweater. She had large, liquid brown eyes and wore her hair in a long ponytail.

Looking frightened she said, "I've never been arrested before. I've never even been in a police station before."

"Why're you here now?"

"This guy. I only dated him twice. He sent me down to the corner to buy some rock. We were going to party tonight." She blinked hard, fighting tears. "I'm such a dang idiot."

"I might be able to help you."

She looked at me hopefully. "Any way you can keep this off my record?"

"Maybe. If you tell me something that'll help me."

"About what?"

"I'm a homicide detective. I'm investigating a murder. I want to ask you a few questions about what you saw on the streets before you bought that dope."

She looked terrified. "I don't want some drug dealer or some killer coming after me. If I tell you what I saw, can you protect me?"

As she leaned across the table, fixing me with a hopeful, trusting expression, my throat went dry.

I thought about that call last year from the 77th watch commander who told me that someone stuck a pistol in Latisha Patton's ear and blew the side of her head off. I remembered standing on the corner of

54th and Figueroa, looking down at her, her head encircled by a viscous puddle of blood, knowing that it had been my job to protect her, and that I had failed. She had provided information about a case. And it cost her her life. If I couldn't protect her, how could I protect the young woman in the interview room? Could I endure the murder of another young woman on my conscience?

I pulled a handkerchief out of my back pocket and dabbed at my brow. "I don't know if I can protect you. But I promise you that I'll try."

I saw that the woman sensed my unsteadiness. She chewed on her lower lip and nervously squeezed her thumb. "To tell you the truth, detective, I didn't see much of anything."

I left the Harbor Division at dawn, wondering how I was going to survive as a homicide detective. If I couldn't get it together and learn to lean on witnesses again, to promise them—with conviction—a measure of security and safety, I'd be no good on the street. I might as well get a job with a PI firm with a lot of other washed out ex-cops and start taking surreptitious photos of workman comp cheats.

I drove back downtown and was thinking of stopping for breakfast, but after the interview with the young woman, and the echoes of the Patton case, I didn't have much of an appetite. I parked in the LAPD structure on Main Street, and walked to the Police Administration Building, which everyone called PAB. When I spotted the gleaming, L-shaped glass and limestone structure, I felt a pang of nostalgia for Parker Center, which had been the police headquarters for most of my career, until it was considered obsolete and we moved here. Every morning, I'd walk through Parker Center's back entrance, stroll through the basement, past Dr. Dave the shoeshine man, his transistor radio blaring, past the evidence room, the air thick with the pungent smell of marijuana, up on the rickety elevator to the third floor squad room, and make my way down the scuffed linoleum tile floor to my battered metal desk, beneath a stuffed elk head, bagged by one of the hunters in the unit. The new headquarters is modern, spacious, energy-efficient, and bland. I still missed Parker Center.

I took the elevator up to the fifth floor and entered the Robbery-Homicide Division squad room, a massive expanse of cubicles and carpeting, fluorescent lights glaring overhead. The room had all the personality of a credit union. Felony Special is one of a number of specialized RHD units with citywide jurisdiction that handles difficult or high-profile cases, including Rape Special, Robbery Special, and Homicide Special. Felony Special investigates all the cases that are a priority of the police chief and half of the murders deemed too complex for the divisions. The other half are investigated by Homicide Special, which is on call alternate weeks with Felony Special.

The dozen Felony Special detectives were assigned to cubicles on the south end of the fifth floor. After being away for a year, I felt jittery as I made my way to my old desk that was, surprisingly, empty. My coffee cup was still on a shelf. I sat down, opened my briefcase and pulled a small picture of Latisha Patton out of a folder and slipped it under the clear plastic sheeting on my blotter. I quickly covered it with a steno pad, so Duffy wouldn't see it when he passed by. Hearing a loud, gravelly voice, I turned around and spotted Mike Graupmann. I groaned. Graupmann and a few other new detectives had been brought in since I left. When I was a young slick-sleeved cop in the 77th Division, a boot fresh out of the academy, I had clashed with him a number of times. Graupmann rode me constantly when he discovered I was Jewish.

"Hey, if it isn't the Semitic Sherlock, the Hebrew Holmes," Graupmann called out in a Texas twang, his eyes gleaming with malice when he saw me walk through the door. He stood up and crossed the squad room.

Graupmann was about the same height as me, but much broader, with a thick weightlifter's neck that tapered to a narrow head. His eyes were slits, and a web of broken blood vessels streaked his nose. He looked like a mean drunk.

"Aren't you happy to see me?"

I ignored him.

"I'm as happy as a fag in a submarine to see you."

"I see that it's not just the cream that rises to the top, but the scum too," I said.

"Isn't it sweet," Graupmann said. "Once again, we're working in the same unit."

"Fortunately that's the only thing we have in common."

"Other than my grandparents throwing your grandparents into

cattle cars," said Graupmann, whose father, I recalled, married a German woman when he was a GI stationed in Frankfurt. He was about to slap me on the back with phony bonhomie.

"You put a hand on me and I'll knock you on your ass," I said.

"I thought Jews only knew that one kind of self-defense—I-Su-U," he said in a mock Asian accent.

I saw Duffy storm out of his office. "Okay, guys, break it up. I see you two know each other."

Graupmann smiled broadly. "Oh yeah. We're old friends from the Seventy-seventh."

"I remember," Duffy said dourly, grabbing my elbow and leading me into his office.

I sat down and said, "How the hell did a moron like Graupmann get to Felony Special?"

Duffy leaned back in his chair and pointed to the ceiling, toward the tenth floor—the offices of the LAPD brass. "He's got a buddy up there. Wasn't my decision. He was foisted on me."

I shook my head with disgust. "Any luck with the reward?"

"We're going to the City Council today and see what we can get." Duffy crossed his legs. "What do you got?"

After I told him about the trail the bloodhound followed and the broken glass leading to the backyard, I described my interviews with Relovich's daughter, Ann Licata, Jane Granger, and briefed him on Abazeda.

"When's he get back into town?" Duffy asked.

"Tomorrow night."

"You think it's worth chasing him down in Arizona today?"

I shook my head. "I don't want to get in his face right away. I'd rather low-key him."

"Fine. Sounds like you've made some real progress," Duffy said, looking pleased. "That's why I brought you back. But is Graupmann going to be a major problem for you?"

"Naw. I can handle it."

"Don't forget to take care of that administrative crap today. I made you a ten o'clock appointment tomorrow morning with a shrink—one of your landsmen, Dr. Blau." Duffy slipped off his glasses and set them on his desk. "This homicide of yours is going to be a pain in the ass. In addition to the chief, Commander Wegland's interested in the case. He wants to be kept up to date."

"Isn't Wegland in charge of Missing Persons and some of those other sixth floor units?"

Duffy nodded.

"He's got nothing to do with Felony Special. Why does he need to know about this investigation?"

"He was a buddy of Relovich's old man. It's just a courtesy. Tell him what you've got and update him every so often. It's good politics. Felony Special may need his support on something down the line. Paganos told me to give Wegland what he wants."

Captain Paganos headed RHD. I wondered why he wasn't nosing around this case. "Where's Paganos?"

"He's in Greece scoping out some island where he wants to retire. He checked in this morning and I filled him in."

"If I was in Greece, I'd have better things to do."

"You know Wegland?" Duffy asked.

"Yeah. When I worked patrol at Pacific, he was a detective. Kind of a plodder. Everything by the book."

Duffy motioned toward me with his glasses and said, "After he okayed you, Grazzo, apparently, had some second thoughts. But Wegland had your back. He told Grazzo you were the right detective for the case. That's another reason to play the game and be nice to him."

"I see my desk is empty," I said.

Duffy grinned. "I was always lookin' for an angle to bring you back."

I walked back to my desk. Some of the detectives shook my hand and clapped me on the back. But a few did not leave their desks. I could tell by the way they wouldn't look at me that they were uncertain about why I had returned and not all that happy about it. Everyone knew that Duffy had been my mentor, had recruited me to South Bureau Homicide and then to Felony Special, had often cut me more slack than the others. I knew that kind of favored-son status engendered resentment.

At crime scenes—sharing insights, tracking trace evidence, plotting strategy—I felt a bond with the other detectives. But I had been unable to overcome the ill will and jealousy in the squad room because I did not have much in common with the detectives, other than the job. Most were married with kids; I lived alone. Most lived far from Los Angeles, in suburbs at the edges of the county, or in distant counties; I lived downtown. Most were Catholics or WASPS; I was a Jew. Most were hunters or fishermen; I surfed. Most rode Harley-Davidsons on weekends; I drove a Saturn. Most ate lunch together and socialized after work and on weekends; I had only one friend—Oscar Ortiz.

And then there were the dinosaurs like Graupmann. For too long, guys like him survived and thrived in the LAPD, which was one reason the department had been reviled in black and Latino neighborhoods. During the last decade, the LAPD changed dramatically, with an increasing number of women and minorities, but Felony Special was still a holdout, primarily a redoubt for middle-aged white guys, and Graupmann fit right in. An ex-Marine who had been stationed at Pendleton, he was raised in Texas. It was widely known in the 77th that Graupmann was a racist and had been written up a few times for slapping around black and Hispanic suspects and calling them niggers or spics. It was aggravating to see that a cop like Graupmann, whose package was filled with personnel complaints, had been promoted to an elite unit like Felony Special.

For the rest of the morning, I hunched over my desk, arranging my murder book, summarizing the interview tapes on LAPD statement forms, and putting together my own case chronology. I was interrupted by Detective Robert "Bible Bob" Grigsby, who stopped by my desk and asked if I wanted to grab a cup of coffee. Grigsby was a fundamentalist Christian, a deacon at his church, and a tireless proselytizer. He'd approached me in the past.

I was wary about joining Grigsby for coffee, but on my first day back I did not want to alienate another detective. I followed him to the break room, he poured us two cups of coffee, and we rode down the elevator in silence. We walked outside and stood at the edge of a patch of grass, across from City Hall.

Grigsby placed a hand on my shoulder, stared intently at me and asked somberly, "How are you doing, Ash?"

"Okay."

"Not here," Grigsby said, tapping his head. "But *here*," he said, placing his hand over his heart.

"Okay," I said warily.

"I know those difficulties you endured last year were trying. And I know you tried to handle it alone. But there *is* another way. And if you embrace His way, you'll never be alone again."

Grigsby's eyes had a feverish sheen. I took a step back and gulped my coffee, hoping to quickly finish the cup and get back to the fifth floor.

"Have you ever considered accepting Jesus as your personal lord and savior?"

"Not really."

Grigsby jabbed at me with his Styrofoam cup, spilling coffee on his shoes. "Consider it!"

"Look. I'm a Jew. I'm happy being a Jew. I have no intention of changing religions."

Grigsby raised a forefinger and said, "Christ is the *only* path to salvation. God Almighty does *not* hear the prayers of the chosen people."

"Who says?"

"The leader of our Southern Baptist Convention told the faithful that some years ago. He was criticized mightily for that heartfelt statement, but I, frankly, agree with him. I stand by his statement."

I tossed my coffee cup in the trash and said, "Thanks for the sermon, Ron, but I'll stick with the religion Jesus was born with."

"Jesus loves me and he loves—"

"*Jesus* might love you," I said. "But everyone else thinks you're an asshole."

When I returned to my desk, Oscar Ortiz strolled through the door, spotted me, stopped theatrically, threw out his hands, and called out, "Ash Levine, my hero. Took the longest vacation in the history of the LAPD—eleven months."

He pulled up a chair beside my desk and said softly, "Glad you're back, homeboy. How's it going?"

"It's going."

During the past year, Ortiz was the only detective I'd stayed in touch with. He'd call me occasionally to see how I was doing, and ask me to meet him for a beer. I always found some excuse not to go. Quitting was painful enough; I didn't want any reminders of what I'd lost.

I noticed that Ortiz, an aggressively bad dresser who refused to purchase suits at the fashion district wholesalers, had not shopped for clothes during the past year. He wore a short-sleeved plaid shirt, brown corduroy sports coat, and a Yosemite Sam tie. Short and stocky, with a Zapata mustache that was so luxuriant it violated several department guidelines, Ortiz bore such a striking resemblance to the cartoon figure that the other detectives in the unit called him Sam.

"I just got back from coffee with Grigsby," I said. "He tried to convert me again."

Ortiz laughed. "Bible Bob's gone after me a few times, too. I think he gets bonus points for converting a Mexican Catholic to a born-again Christian. But you're the big prize. He gets a double bonus for bagging a Jew. Now if we had a Muslim detective, Grigsby would drop you in a hot minute. That would be his ultimate prize."

Ortiz hung up his suit coat and dropped his briefcase at his desk. "So Duffy talked you into coming back."

"Something like that."

"He's one persuasive motherfucker. He could have been a hell of a detective. But as long as I've known him, he's been a lieutenant. Didn't you work with him when he was still a detective?"

"Yeah. At Pacific. I was a uniform at the time, but I'd help out on some of his cases. He was devious as hell, just like now."

"I know he wasn't a detective long."

"Only a few years. He knew that wasn't his future. He was sharp, but he was drinking too much, staying out late, chasing women, dragging into the squad room every morning with the Irish flu. So he got sloppy."

"If you're sloppy as a lieutenant, you misfile a report," Ortiz said. "If you're sloppy on the streets, you can get someone killed."

When Ortiz saw me tense, he gripped my forearm. "I'm not talking about your situation. You know that."

I nodded.

"I think that's why Duffy never made captain," Ortiz said.

"I agree."

"But he's more capable than most of those pencil pushers with stars on their collars."

"He's damn smart, but when he goes on one of his binges—stand by," I said. "Don't think the brass hasn't noticed that. But they know he delivers. And as long as his detectives are clearing cases, they're not going to move him out."

"Hey, for your first day back, let me take you to lunch."

"Don't have time. Since I came back in a rush, I've got to take care of all the LAPD bureaucratic bullshit. Let's do it another day this week."

"All right, brother. I heard you're flying solo on this case. If you need some backup, I'm there."

For the next hour, I worked on the murder book and dashed off the required letter to the chief, listing a few cursory reasons why I had decided to return. I visited the city doctor for a quick physical, and in the mid-afternoon I met with a dour LAPD background investigator from personnel division who asked me a number of bizarre questions, including: "During your eleven months away from the LAPD, did you ever have sex with animals?"

"Only when I was drunk," I said, staring at him poker-faced.

The man looked through me, checked the "No" box and asked, "During your eleven months away from the LAPD, did you ever have sex in public?" I shook my head, but recalling that barren stretch of self-imposed exile since Robin left, I wanted to say that I wished that I had the opportunity.

Shortly before four, I returned to PAB to meet with Commander Wally Wegland. In the anteroom adjacent to his office, Wegland's adjutant, Conrad Patowski, extended both his hands, wrapped them around my right hand and shook it. "It's been too long, Ash," he said. "*Too* long."

We were classmates at the academy and had crossed paths over the years, although I usually tried to avoid him. I didn't like adjutants. Most were sycophantic strivers, desperate to ride in the slipstreams of their powerful bosses. In the army we called them jobniks. And I found Patowski particularly smarmy. Although he was my age, his face was pale and unlined and there was a boyish, unformed quality to him, as if he had managed, somehow, to avoid life experience. His shoes were buffed to a gleam, his shirt was heavily starched, and his pants had razor-sharp creases. His outfit looked more like a military uniform than a business suit.

"We only work a few floors from each other," Patowski said. "Let's get lunch one of these days."

"Sure, Conrad," I said without enthusiasm.

"I meant to call you, during this past year, Ash," Patowski said in a hushed tone, rubbing his palms together. "So glad you managed to work it all out and come back. I've always admired you, and the remarkable way you clear your cases. We can't afford to lose good people like you. And I want you to know that my heart really went out to you. I know it was a difficult time."

Patowski nodded sympathetically and then picked up the phone and whispered into the receiver. Opening the office door he said, "Okay, Ash, the commander will see you now."

Wegland came around his desk, tightening his tie. He was an unlikely looking cop, I thought. Skinny and sallow, with an aquiline nose, and nervous, twitchy gestures, there was something birdlike about him. Even his bad comb-over, which swirled atop his balding pate, looked like a nest.

"Thank you for stopping by, Ash," he said, extending a hand.

I shook his hand while surveying the office. On one wall were two shadow boxes filled with patches from police departments from throughout the country. On another wall, a dozen midnight blue LAPD coffee mugs stamped with various unit insignias were lined up on a shelf. After Wegland pulled a chair from the corner of the room for me, he walked back around his desk, sat down, and placed his hands primly on his lap.

At Pacific, I had been struck by how Wegland, grim-faced and humorless, always went about his job with a robotic efficiency. Later, Wegland began quickly climbing the LAPD ladder. He was one of those LAPD officials who rose through the ranks, not because he was a good patrol officer or skilled investigator, but because he studied like a fiend, tested well, and never took any chances on the street that could precipitate a complaint.

Wegland cleared his throat, poured himself a half glass of water from the pitcher on his desk, and took a few gulps. "I wanted you on this case because I know your track record. I know you can do the job."

"I appreciate that."

"But I have a question for you. Because of the, the—" he paused, searching for the right word, "calamity you were involved in last year, well, I wondered. Do you think because of the questions you might be asked by other detectives and maybe even witnesses, because of the questions you might even be asking yourself, and because of the fact that your judgment might be challenged, well, will all that hinder your investigation? In other words, do you think you can become a highly effective detective again?"

"I think I'm a highly effective detective right now," I said sharply.

"I think so, too," Wegland said, lifting his hands from his lap and clasping them on his desk. "So that's settled." Wegland turned and studied a shadow box for a moment. "I knew Relovich's father. When he retired he asked me to keep an eye out for his son. I don't take a request like that lightly. So I just want to stay in touch with you, make sure you've got everything you need, insure that Felony Special is doing right by old man Relovich's son. That's the least I can do for my late friend. So you'll keep me apprised of the investigation, I'd appreciate it."

I stood up and said, "I'll keep you posted."

I returned to the squad room and began plotting my next moves. I was frustrated that I couldn't question Abazeda right now. I had stumbled on a good lead and I wanted to run it down.

I had to be patient, but tomorrow night I planned to find out if Abazeda had dropped by Relovich's house, pulled out a .40-caliber semi-automatic, and shot him in the face.

CHAPTER 7

Early the next morning, I arrived at the squad room before most of the detectives had started work. Oscar Ortiz rushed up to me and said, "Let's get a cup of coffee."

"What's that shit on my desk?"

Ortiz stood in front of me to block my view. "I just called maintenance. They're on their way to clean it up."

I craned my neck for a better look. "What is it?"

Ortiz grabbed my arm and tried to lead me out the door. "You don't want to see it."

I pushed past Ortiz, and when I reached my desk I dropped the murder book on the floor, the photographs scattering on the linoleum. Someone had crudely slashed red paint in the shape of a swastika. Next to it, taped to the desk, were a picture of Hitler and a magazine photograph of the liberated survivors of Buchenwald, walking skeletons streaming through the barbwire fences.

I felt as if I'd been slugged in the gut. Just then Graupmann ambled by, glanced at the desk and asked, "Fan mail?"

Swinging from the heels. I landed a right cross flush on Graupmann's jaw, hitting the sweet spot like a batter pounding a fastball on the meat of the bat. Graupmann wobbled to his knees.

"You crazy motherfucker," Graupmann shouted. He grabbed the side of a desk and was pulling himself to his feet when he dove for me. I sidestepped him, but Graupmann reached out, clutched a pant leg and tugged. I lost my balance and tumbled to the ground. Graupmann, straddling me, tried to punch me in the face, but I jerked my head to the side and he only grazed my cheek. I reached around and, in a windmill motion, slammed him flush on the ear with the heel of my hand. I heard him yelp with pain.

I pushed myself up with one hand and with the other punched him in the Adam's apple. With a strangled cry, he fell on top of me.

Duffy, who was just coming into work and still clutching his briefcase, separated us with a couple of swift kicks, as if he were breaking up a dogfight in an alley. He grabbed my shirt with a meaty hand, jerked me to my feet with ease, and dragged me into his office, slamming the door shut.

"Are you out of your fucking mind?" Duffy shouted, stabbing a finger in my face.

"Did you see my desk?" I rasped, trying to catch my breath.

"I caught a quick look at it. But how do you know Graupmann did it?"

"Who else? I worked in this unit six years and never had a problem. All of a sudden he's here and my desk looks like a Nuremberg war crimes museum."

"Got any proof it was him?"

I flashed him a you've-got-to-be-kidding look.

"What's the proof?"

"It's circumstantial."

"Then let it go," Duffy said.

After I stomped out of his office, I spotted a janitor scrubbing my desk with paint remover. I knew I was too pissed off to get any work done, so I snatched the murder book from under my desk and took off.

Ortiz stopped me at the elevator, patted me on the shoulder and said, "Ride it out, Ash. Just chill for the next few months. Then, when you're back in the groove here and they can't fuck with you, take care of your business with Graupmann."

I was still so enraged I was unable to speak. I just nodded and slammed my palm on the elevator's down button.

I had an appointment with a department psychologist this morning, and I had about ninety minutes to kill. So I drove aimlessly around downtown, swearing to myself, envisioning a number of scenarios where I could drive my fist into Graupmann's smirking face.

At nine forty-five, I parked in front of the Far East National Bank building on north Broadway in Chinatown and spent a few minutes calming myself down. Then I walked up to the third floor, where the LAPD's Behavioral Science Services Section is based. A few cops, who looked distinctly ill at ease, fidgeted in the waiting room. I checked in with a receptionist who was protected by bulletproof glass.

While I waited, I remembered the photographs that Sandy Relovich had given me. Lindsey had taken them on her birthday at her father's house. As I began flipping through the pictures, the receptionist called my name. She buzzed me through the door and led me down the hallway to Dr. Nathan Blau's office.

I had first met Dr. Blau when I was a twenty-five-year-old patrolman in the Pacific Division and had just shot and killed a suspect. Shrink time is required by the LAPD after all officer-involved shootings. My partner and I had pulled over a Monte Carlo speeding down Washington Boulevard. I had my hand on the butt of my Beretta when I bent down to ask the driver, a man in his early twenties with stringy blond hair, for his license. When the passenger reached for his waistband, I already had the Beretta out. When I saw the flash of chrome, I blasted the man in the chest. I had no remorse about the killing, probably because after two years in the IDF, I had been blooded; I had already worked through the roiling emotions after taking a life.

Blau had asked me why I was so wary about the occupants that I had my hand on my gun before I even exchanged words with them.

I explained that I had heard the dispatcher announce a bank robbery earlier that afternoon, although no descriptions of the suspects were available. I knew that experienced bank robbers often carried buckets of water in their cars because tellers slip die packs in with the stolen money; sensors by the front door activate the packs within thirty seconds. But robbers dunk the money in the water before the die packs explode. As I approached the car, I had seen a large circle on the carpeting by the back seat, which looked like it could have been the impression of a bucket. My hunch saved my life. I later learned that during a previous heist the man I'd killed had gunned down a guard.

After we talked about the shooting during that first session, Blau had asked me if anything else was troubling me.

"I only have two problems," I deadpanned. "My mother and the Holocaust."

Blau snorted with amusement.

Later, when Robin left me, I made an appointment with Blau, who looked more like a truck driver than a psychologist, which seemed to reassure cops who were spooked about seeing a shrink. He had a thick chest and arms corded with muscle from regular weight-lifting sessions at the academy gym, close-cropped black hair, and a broad, sunburnt, impassive face. Although he was Jewish, he could have passed for Navajo.

Blau sat on a sofa in his sparsely decorated office, sipping coffee. I slumped onto an overstuffed chair across from him, next to a metal end table with a small fountain on top, a trickle of water splashing over polished rocks.

"We haven't seen each other for a while, Ash," Blau said. "How are you doing?"

"Not so well this morning." I told him about how my desk had been defaced.

"Is that going to make your return problematic?"

"Naw. When I first left the academy I got used to dealing with a lot of anti-Semitic shit. You know, LAPD dinosaurs. But a lot of these guys have retired. Things have changed. I remember my first training officer at Pacific. He made some crack about Jews. I got in his face and asked, "What do you have against us?" He looked me up and down and said, "What I've got against you is that you people are never happy, no matter what. Hell, Jesus Christ wasn't even good enough for you."

Blau and I chuckled.

I described how Duffy stopped by my mother's house on Friday night and asked me to return to Felony Special and take over the Relovich case. For the next twenty minutes Blau asked me a series of pro forma questions about my drinking habits, appetite, work, financial situation, state of mind, and relationship with family members.

"Been dating?"

"Not much. Still a little gun-shy since I've been separated."

"How are you feeling?"

"Pretty good. Except for one thing. During the past year I've been getting a lot of headaches. They're pretty intense sometimes."

"I'd recommend you see a neurologist. If the doctor says there's nothing medical or neurological going on, then you and I can deal with it."

"I know what's going on. They're caused by stress."

"Where'd you go to medical school?" he asked, raising his eyebrows.

"Okay. I'll go when I have time."

"How are you sleeping?" he asked.

"Sometimes fine. Other times not so well. Lately, I don't know why, I've been dreaming about the old days in the army, about being on patrol."

"The VA has an excellent sleep disorder clinic," Blau said.

"I'm a veteran," I said. "But wrong army."

"Right. I remember." He ran his palm over his bristly hair and said, "Let's talk about why you left the department last year."

"Just didn't want to deal with all the crap," I said.

"Can you tell me a little about the precipitating incident."

I listened to the burble of the fountain for a moment. "Korean guy named Bae Soo Sung operated a small market in South Central. He worked sixteen hours a day, three hundred sixty-five days a year. Unlike some of the market owners in the 'hood, everyone liked this guy. He gave people credit; he was friendly; he smiled at the customers; he gave money to the local Boy's Club. One afternoon, a guy wearing a Shrek mask charges through the door waving a pistol. Sung steps away from the counter. He keeps his hands up. He follows instructions. He dumps the cash from the register into a paper sack. Asshole grabs the sack and starts to walk out. But he pauses at the doorway, whirls around, and for no fucking reason at all, plugs Sung in the chest."

I recalled the flickering black-and-white images on the store video, the look of terror and surprise on Sung's face as he crumpled to the ground. "Sung did everything right. He cooperated completely. He couldn't even identify the shooter because he was wearing a mask. Shooting him made no sense. Asshole was just having some fun, some target practice. So now Sung's wife's a widow and his three young children have no father."

"That's a terrible thing," Blau said. "But why were you investigating the case? I didn't think Felony Special handled South Central market shootings."

"We don't. But the case went unsolved, the detectives moved onto other homicides and wouldn't even return Sung's wife's calls. So she started pestering that new Korean city councilman. He either felt sorry for her or decided that this was a good political issue to run with and get some ink. So he held a press conference and contended that the LAPD doesn't care about Korean victims. He called the chief and complained about the investigation's lack of progress. The chief had the murder book sent from South Bureau Homicide over to us. I ended up with the case."

My head ached sharply and I asked Blau for a glass of water. I drained it in two gulps.

"I read about the death of the witness in the paper."

"I'm sure you did."

"Did they ever find out who killed her or who killed Sung?"

"Both unsolved."

"Does Felony Special have any leads?"

"We're not handling either case anymore. Because of my suspension and all the bad pub Felony Special got after the hit on the witness, the case got sent back to South Bureau."

"You have any ideas?"

"The only thing I know is *why* my wit was killed. Because of me, because of my actions, she got taken out."

Blau frowned and shook his head. "A lot of witnesses get killed in gang areas. It's not always the detective's fault."

"It was mine."

"Can you honestly say that it was one hundred percent your fault? That no other factors were involved?"

After a moment I said, "There were other factors involved."

"Can you tell me about those factors?"

I sighed wearily. "I'd just like to get back to work and forget about it."

"But you haven't been able to forget about it."

I shook my head.

"Then it'll probably help to talk about it."

"Maybe some other time. But for now let me ask you something. Let's say I've got to deal with another witness. What if I keep thinking of what happened to my last wit? What if I melt down and start to lose it?"

"Take a break. Go the bathroom. Breathe deeply. Remind yourself that it wasn't your fault, that you did all you could, despite the way you're beating yourself up over it."

"I'll give it a try," I said without much conviction.

"So after you got suspended, you quit."

"The next week."

"It seems that quitting was a pretty dramatic response."

"I didn't get into this business to kill people."

Blau looked at me for a moment. "I think you know that you didn't kill anybody."

"Well, she ended up dead."

"That's a very different thing."

I could feel my head pound. When had I taken my last Tylenol?

"You felt the suspension was unfair?" Blau asked.

I massaged my temples. "I needed the support of Duffy, my lieutenant. I was going through a lot of shit. But instead of him backing me up, he told me to take a hike for a few weeks. Then he slipped a letter of reprimand into my file."

"As I recall, he was your mentor."

"*Was.* I felt betrayed. I was getting hammered in the papers. I just didn't want to deal with it anymore. I knew her family was filing a civil suit against the department. I was dreading the hostile depositions and the media circus trial. Fortunately, I was spared that when the family settled with the city out of court, after I'd left the department. But at the time, I thought it would be easier away from the job."

"Was it?"

I chewed on my thumbnail. "Probably not."

"How did your family handle this?"

"Well, my marriage was circling the drain. But you know all about that. We talked about it last year. This finished it off. And you know about my brother Marty. He was too fucking wasted to care. For my mother, it was just confirmation that I shouldn't have become a cop in the first place."

"How did that case finish off your marriage?"

"It's complicated."

"Take all the time you need."

"Fact is, it's over. I don't want to talk about it. I just want to move on."

Blau studied me for a moment and said, "How does your mother feel about you returning to the LAPD?"

"Not happy. And I know it sounds sick, but I was glad my dad wasn't alive to see all those bullshit articles about me."

"Isn't he a survivor?"

"Yeah. He died a few years ago."

"You seem too young to be the child of a survivor."

"He was only fourteen when he was sent to Treblinka. And he was in his forties when I was born."

"I have a lot of admiration for people like him."

"So do I," I said. "It's a miracle he survived. It's a miracle I'm here." I rocked for a moment, lost in thought. "He was big for his age, strong and athletic. The Nazis figured they could make use of him and some of the other young men and work them to death, instead of just murdering them right off. They were spared the showers, but not many of them survived. My dad was starved, beaten, God knows what else. I think he was eighty-five pounds when the camp was liberated. He rarely talked about it, so I don't really know everything he went through."

"Is your mom a survivor, too?" Blau asked.

"Her parents were refugees. From Lithuania. They got out, but her grandparents and a lot of other relatives were murdered." I reached inside my suit coat, tapped my Beretta, and said, "I've shot a Glock and I like it better than what I'm carrying. Smoother trigger-pull. Action is a little quicker. Lighter. No exposed hammer. Overall, a better made weapon. But I won't pack a Glock because it's Austrian. And I won't pack the Heckler & Koch because it's German. That's crazy, I know. After all these years."

"Israel does a lot of business with Germany today. And you know the Beretta is Italian. And they were aligned with Germany."

"I'm not making a political statement. I just can't carry a German gun."

"Or an Austrian gun?" Blau asked.

"My dad always told me that since the war, Austria's been trying to convince the world that Beethoven was Austrian and Hitler was German. He thought the Austrians were almost as bad as the Germans. He told me that half of all the concentration camp guards were from Austria. I guess I got that mentality from him. But that might be the only thing I got from him. He was kind of a remote guy. Always working overtime. Always tired and grumpy. He spent all day in a hot downtown dress factory, cutting patterns. My mom told me after he died that when he was a kid he dreamed of going to art school. He wanted to be a commercial artist. But when he arrived in the U.S., he didn't speak English and he needed work. His uncle got him a job in the *shmatte* business and he never left. He wanted a better life for me. He was angry when I dropped out of college, even more incensed when I joined the army. But when I became a cop, he *really* got pissed. He wouldn't even come to my academy graduation. When he first saw me in my uniform, he looked me up and down, and walked out of the room."

I reached inside my suit coat and adjusted my leather shoulder holster strap. "But I'm not here to talk about my father."

"You can, if you you'd like."

"Some other time."

"That's fine," Blau said. "I want to get back to something, Ash. Are you angry with the LAPD?"

"Sometimes. But I'm most angry at myself. Because my actions led to her death."

"How, exactly, did your actions lead to her death?"

I stared into my empty water cup.

After a minute of silence, he said, "It might be helpful to tell me about it."

"Might be. But right now I just want to get your seal of approval so I can return to work and get back to the Relovich murder."

"I don't want to push you, but I really think we should talk some more about this."

"I'm not ready for that."

"When things settle down for you, make sure to give me a call. I'll be glad to see you any time."

"I appreciate that."

"You told me that Duffy asked you to come back," he said. "Why did you?"

I stared out the window and watched the light glisten on a varnished palm frond. "The only thing I know anything about is killing—how to do it; how to investigate it." I smoothed the end of my tie. "And I feel it's important. The most important thing I can do. The investigating part."

"That year away from the LAPD must have been hard for you."

"It was."

Blau, his face a blank mask, sat there, without moving, lithic. He had an uncanny ability to intuit when I wanted to say more, to just wait silently for me to continue.

"These last few months, a lot of stuff has been bothering me, stuff that I've managed to put out of my mind for a long, long time. For decades."

"For example?"

"When I was a kid, I was haunted by all these terrible images. I'd think about the horrible things my father endured. I'd think about how hopeless and helpless his father felt, marched with his family to the cattle cars. I'd think about how my grandmother and her children were murdered, naked, coughing, and gasping for breath in the gas chambers. I'd think about the Nazis, pulling the teeth from their corpses for the gold." I rubbed the bridge of my nose. "Then when I was about ten or eleven, I managed to bury all these thoughts and emotions. And I buried them for decades. But I guess you could say that there was some collateral damage—because I buried *all* my emotions. I wanted to feel nothing because feeling anything was too fucking painful. And that seemed to serve me pretty well as a soldier and as a cop. But during the past few months, it's been hard for me to stay on an even keel. For the first time in decades I've been thinking a lot about all that Holocaust shit again. Just like when I was a kid. And I've been losing my temper a lot lately. On Saturday, a detective made some cracks about the Patton case and I went off on him, knocking stuff off his desk and screaming at him. Then this morning I decked Graupmann."

"I think the murder of your witness really seared you to the core. You felt helpless, terrified, confused, angry. Yes?"

"Something like that."

"I imagine that's how you felt as a child when you were dealing with what happened to your father and his family. So since you're having some of the same emotions now that you had as a child you're, again, starting to focus on some of those same issues that troubled you as a child. Those kinds of things stay with you forever. They have a way of hiding in a little corner of your mind and emerging when you least expect it."

"I wish they'd stay in that little corner of my mind."

"This may sound trite to you, Ash, but this is a great opportunity."

"Opportunity for what? Admittance to a mental institution?"

Blau smiled. "An opportunity to be a more open person."

"I think it's easier to do my job when I'm a closed person."

"Maybe easier for your job, but not for your life."

"That's what Robin used to tell me."

Blau stood up, stretched, and said, "I can understand that. But you know, I disagree with you on something. The best detectives I've talked to—and I count you among them—aren't always so closed off when they do their job. It's those strong feelings, that vulnerability that comes from caring so much about a case, that makes them so good at what they do. Yes, sometimes you have to turn it off. But it's that willingness to lay it all on the line—emotionally, viscerally—that makes you what you are. Witnesses can sense that. That's why they trust detectives like you. Because you care so much when something happens to them."

Blau sat down and tugged at his pants, which were bunching up at the thighs. "Ash, I'm going to recommend that the department accept you back. But, like I said, I really think we should talk some more about the death of this witness. Also, I'd like you to keep an eye on your temper. That could be a problem in your profession. And don't let your work take over every aspect of your life. You have to learn when to let go and leave the job behind. Find something you like to do outside the job. Something you really enjoy. Something that helps you relax. Do it occasionally and enjoy yourself."

I lifted my sleeve and checked my watch.

"We've got a few minutes left on the meter," Blau said. "Anything you want to talk about?"

I shook my head.

"I read an article recently by an English professor," Blau said, "and he had an interesting insight. The professor contended that novelists just write the same book over and over, even though they seem, on the surface, to be different. That makes me think of you."

"Me?" I said, surprised.

"Your cases are all different," Blau said, uncrossing his legs and inching forward on his chair. "But I think you're really investigating, over and over, the same crime."

CHAPTER 8

When I returned to the squad room, Graupmann was gone. A few detectives offered words of support; others ignored me. When Ortiz finished a phone call, he walked over, sat on the edge of my desk, and said softly, "How you doing?"

"I just got back from the bank." Because the shrinks were based in the Chinatown bank building we all referred to it as "the bank."

Ortiz rapped on my head with his knuckles. "Did the good doctor find any sign of intelligent life in there?"

Duffy shouted from his office, "Ortiz, quit bullshitting and sit your ass down at a computer. Your sixty-dayer is three weeks overdue. And Ash, the City Council approved a twenty-five thousand dollar reward because Relovich was an ex-cop."

When Ortiz walked off, Duffy sauntered over and rapped his knuckles on my desk. "Grazzo's adjutant just called me. The squint says Grazzo wants to see you ASAP."

"About what."

"He's pissed about something, but I don't know what it is. Just be careful in there."

Before I could even enter his office, Assistant Chief Grazzo pointed a pencil at a chair across from his desk and shouted, "Sit!" as if he was training a poodle.

Just to be contrary, I leaned against the door jamb, crossed my arms, and said, "How can I help you?"

"You're pulling the same old shit that resulted in your departure a year ago."

"What are you talking about?"

"You're back a few days and you act like a whack job, throwing down on Graupmann and scrapping on the squad room floor."

"How does that compare with what happened last year?"

"In both incidents you comported yourself unprofessionally, displayed unbalanced behavior, and violated LAPD guidelines. Launching an unprovoked attack on a fellow officer is grounds for—"

"The *provocation* was what he spread all over my desk."

"You have no proof it was Graupmann. I expect LAPD detectives, especially the best and the brightest from Felony Special, to have the discipline to withstand a little provocation. If you can't deal with the heat in the squad room, how can I trust you to conduct yourself professionally on the street?"

"You're *not* going to suspend me and yank me off this case. And I'll tell you why. Because if you do, I'll file an official complaint against *you* for neglect of duty."

"You're out of your mind," Grazzo said, his face flushing with anger.

"I don't think so. You know LAPD regulations. If a supervisor hears about any racist or sexist acts in a squad room, he is supposed to conduct a preliminary investigation, interview the victim and witnesses, complete a complaint form, send it up the chain of command and over to Internal Affairs, and get a form number. You knew all about all that shit on my desk. Yet you didn't conduct an investigation. You didn't complete a complaint form. You didn't do *anything*. So I'm well within my rights to file a complaint against *you* for neglect of duty. At the very least, you'd be suspended for that."

Grazzo tugged on the collar of his uniform, which looked as if it was strangling him. "That was Duffy's responsibility."

"You're the senior officer."

"I will not sit here and listen to a detective threaten me." Grazzo was so angry he sprayed spittle across his desk, and the corners of his mouth were flecked with foam.

I sat down and crossed my arms. "If you interfere with my investigation, this is what I'm going to do. After I file the complaint against you, I'm going to the *L.A. Times*. Then I'm going to talk to one influential member of the Police Commission, and I think you know who I'm referring to—Rabbi David Cohen. You can guess who he'll side with."

I walked to the door and said, "If I file that complaint, then there's no way you can suspend me and pull me off the case."

"That's bullshit," Grazzo barked.

I pulled out of my back pocket a folded up sheet of paper. "I brought this with me in case I needed it. I'm sure you're familiar with Special Order Number Eight." I smoothed out the paper on the door and read the first sentence: "Every employee of the Los Angeles Police Department has the right to work in a professional atmosphere and without fear of retaliation that may result from bringing a formal or informal complaint alleging any type of misconduct."

I folded the paper back up and stuffed it into my pocket and said, "I think pulling me off my case and suspending me could be construed as retaliation for the informal complaint I just filed with you. So let me work my investigation without interference and I'll forget we ever had this conversation. But if you don't, I'll go after you for both neglect of duty and violation of Special Order Number Eight."

I slammed the door, jogged down the stairwell, and paced on the grass outside PAB, muttering to myself and cursing under my breath. When I calmed down, I returned to the squad room.

Duffy intercepted me. "You must have been pretty persuasive in there."

"What do you mean?"

"I just got off the phone with Grazzo. He wants you to know that after considering all the variables of the situation, and taking into account the stress you were under after being exposed to that little Teutonic display, he decided that you can carry on. No suspension will be forthcoming." Duffy grinned. "You must have pictures of Grazzo screwing farm animals."

When I returned to my desk, I spotted my red message light blinking. It was Relovich's ex-wife.

"You find out who threatened Pete with the gun?" she asked.

"I've got a lead I'm tracking down."

"Will you let me know when you put the SOB away?"

"Sure." I heard what sounded like her opening the pop-top of a beer. "How you holding up?"

"Since Pete's death I've been so wasted every day, I haven't been able to string together two coherent thoughts. I guess I haven't wanted to. But I've got to be there for Lindsey."

She paused for several seconds. I waited for her to continue.

"Remember you told me if I thought of something to call you? When you asked me that, I was in kind of a fog. But after Lindsey told you about the guy who came to Pete's door with a gun and threatened him, well that gave me a jolt. I'd never heard that before. To think that Lindsey was there when that happened—that scares the hell out of me. Anyway, this morning I remembered something. It might be something you can use. It might not. But I thought I'd pass it along anyway. A few weeks ago, I was talking on the phone with Pete. We were making weekend plans for the upcoming month about how our daughter would get from Lancaster to Pete's place in Pedro. He mentioned in a kind of casual way that he wouldn't be able to pick her up on one of those Fridays because he'd made an appointment with Internal Affairs. Said he couldn't come and get her until Saturday. I don't know if it means anything, but I thought I'd tell you."

"Which Friday was it that he had the appointment?" I asked.

"Can't remember. I should have written it down. But it was within a few weeks of the call."

I thanked her and hung up. I was reluctant to stop by Internal Affairs because of my brush with the investigators after the Latisha Patton murder. Still, I knew I had to suck it up and check out Relovich's appointment.

Because Parker Center was such an outdated, overcrowded structure, a number of LAPD units were scattered in office buildings throughout downtown L.A. After PAB opened, a few of them remained in their buildings, including Internal Affairs.

The unit is now officially known as The Professional Standards Bureau, but most cops still call it by the old name. When I first got my shield, Internal Affairs moved to the Bradbury Building—a landmark structure built in the 1890s—an anomalous place for an LAPD squad room.

I walked down Broadway, spotted the unremarkable, boxy, brown brick building in the distance, and entered through the archway squeezed between a Subway shop and a telephone company. But once inside I was dazzled, as I am every time I linger in the elegant interior courtyard, a breathtaking five-story vault of open space flooded with sunlight from the massive glass roof. I admired the glazed brick walls, the marble stairs, the filigreed wrought-iron railings that look like hanging vines, the ornate birdcage elevators. I'd seen a magazine article recently and learned that a young draftsman had designed the building after he read a science fiction story describing the typical office building in a city of the future as a "vast hall of light received not alone by the windows, but from a dome overhead." A perfect building for this city of dreams, I thought, a city in the thrall of the movie business, where fantasy often dictates reality.

After wandering around the courtyard for a few minutes, I walked up to the third floor and, trying to appear casual and unconcerned, walked through the Internal Affairs squad room. It seemed like all the investigators in the room froze and cast suspicious looks my way; it was probably my imagination, but I definitely felt a hostile vibe. Maybe they heard about my return to Major Crimes and weren't happy about it. I recognized several detectives who had questioned me about the Patton case. I avoided them and approached a young Asian detective who had probably been hired by I.A. after I'd quit. When I asked him if he knew anything about Relovich's appointment, he jerked his thumb toward a desk in the corner and said, "Saucedo took the guy's call."

I stopped by Detective Virginia Saucedo's desk, and she stood up and shook my hand. I had met her years ago on a case when she was working the robbery table at Hollywood Division. Saucedo was slender with a long, graceful neck and shimmering black hair that she wore in a French braid pinned under the nape of her neck. Her top was cut a little lower than LAPD regulations allowed. Drawing attention to the cleavage was a moonstone cross on a silver chain. She rolled a chair over for me from another desk. Unlike the others in the office, Saucedo was amiable and cooperative.

I sat down, briefly told her about the case, and asked about Relovich's appointment.

"Not much to tell, really," she said. "He just called, wanted to set up an appointment, and they put me on the phone."

"Did he say what it was about?"

She shook her head. "I asked him, but he said he'd prefer to talk about it in person."

"Did he sound upset? Stressed? Depressed?"

"Couldn't really tell. We just had a very brief conversation."

"When was his appointment?"

She sifted through her desk calendar and pointed to the entry: *Det.*

Pete Relovich. Retired. Wants to talk. About—??? The date was for this
Friday—a week after his death.

"You think there's any connection between the appointment and
what happened to him?"

"Not sure," I said.

Staring at the calendar, she said softly, "I hope I'm not out of line,
but I want to tell you that I really felt bad for you last year. I know that
was a very painful thing to go through."

I nodded, feeling uncomfortable, unsure of what to say.

She gazed into my eyes for a moment with a look of pity and concern, an almost maternal expression. "Coming back, I know, can't be
easy. If you ever want someone to talk to, call me." She scrawled her
home number on the back of her business card and deftly slipped it to
me, so the other detectives wouldn't see.

She was a pretty girl, with lustrous black eyes and a nice body. I took
the card and slipped it into my pocket. But when I thought about the
way she had looked at me, I didn't know whether I would call her.

I walked back to PAB, climbed into my car, drove down to San Pedro,
and parked in front of Relovich's house. I lingered on the sidewalk for a
moment, enjoying the sunshine and looking out at the sea, the whitecaps iridescent in the bright light. For the next few hours I walked up
and down the street interviewing neighbors, but it was a fruitless afternoon. No one had heard anything; no one had seen anything; no one
provided any useful information about Relovich.

When I returned to the house, I noticed that the living room walls
were streaked purple—the color of the jacaranda blossoms that I could
see outside the front window. The fingerprint technicians had dabbed
the walls with ninhydrin, which reacts to the amino acids in the fingers'
sweat patterns, leaving a purple residue.

Sitting in my car outside Relovich's house, staring at the sea, I
reached for my cell. I called a clerk at the Harbor Division jail and discovered that Theresa Martinez, the young Hispanic woman who dressed
like a preppy, had made bail a few hours after she'd been busted and I
had questioned her. The clerk gave me her address and I drove down the
hill to where she lived, a generic 1960s-style, two-story complex with
the small apartments encircling a kidney-shaped pool.

I walked up the stairs to her apartment and rang the bell. She looked through the keyhole and opened the door a few inches.

"Yes," she said suspiciously.

"I'm detective—"

"I remember you."

"Can I come in?"

"No."

"When we last talked, I thought you might have seen something that night that might help me."

"I didn't."

"Look, I'm a homicide detective. I'm investigating the murder of a retired cop. I'm hoping you might be able to tell me something that could help my investigation, something that—"

"Well, I can't," she said, slamming the door.

"If you do think of something, call me."

I pulled a card out of my wallet and slid it under the door.

I had a few hours to kill until I figured Abazeda would be home. So rather than risk the freeway during the crush of the evening commute, I stopped by Ante's, a landmark Croatian restaurant two blocks from the harbor. A few years ago I had investigated the murder of a harbor commissioner who was carjacked and shot a block away. It took me six days to clear the case, and I had lunched at Ante's each day.

"Welcome back, Detective Levine," the hostess said when she saw me. "I've got a nice quiet booth in the corner for you."

The dining room was homey, with high-backed red leather booths, a wood beam ceiling, Croatian handicrafts on one wall, and a colorful mural of the Adriatic coastline on another. I hadn't eaten since breakfast and I was ravenous. I started with a salad of iceberg lettuce, cabbage, cucumber, and octopus and a side dish of fried smelt, and then polished off a plate of *Sarma*—seasoned meat and rice rolled in cabbage leaves—served with mostaccioli.

I was about to ask for the check, when the hostess, carrying a tray, stopped by and said, "A little something for you—on the house." She brought me a piece of sweet, flaky strudel and a glass of Croatian plum brandy, the same kind of brandy, I realized, Goran Relovich had been drinking on his fishing boat.

After I finished the strudel, I sipped the brandy and I recalled the photographs that Lindsey Relovich had taken during her birthday at her father's house.

From a flap in the back of the murder book, I removed the photographs. I sifted through the packet, spread the pictures out on the table, and divided them into piles—each pile representing a different room of the house. Apparently, Lindsey had followed her father through the house that day and snapped pictures while he mugged for the camera. There were a few pictures of Relovich posing behind his daughter, towering over her. I knew Relovich's life during the past few years had been troubled, but he looked truly happy in the pictures with his daughter.

After studying the photographs, I finished the brandy in a swallow. Then I tried to recall how each room looked when Duffy and I had inspected the house. I would visit the place again for a more thorough inspection, but I wanted to see if any of the photographs provided me with some insight.

One did.

The little girl had photographed her father in the spare bedroom, pulling her birthday present out of a closet. I remembered the desk and figured that Relovich used the room as an office. In the photo, a laptop computer sat on a corner of the desk.

I closed my eyes and recalled the desk with the coffee cup filled with pens and pencils. Riffling through the murder book, I located the property report compiled by the Harbor Division detectives. Now I was certain. Whoever killed Relovich had pinched his laptop. Because when I had searched the house, it wasn't there.

If Abazeda had killed Relovich, that would make sense. He was worried that Relovich was stealing his girls and his clients. The laptop might contain that information.

CHAPTER 9

Abazeda lived in West L.A., a few blocks south of Pico and west of Robertson. While many houses on the street were classic one-story Spanish-style cottages, Abazeda's place was a monstrosity, a three-story stucco palace with a flat roof, three balconies festooned with gold iron-work, and four giant concrete columns flanking the front door. The lot was modest-sized, but the house was so enormous there was no room for landscaping. Instead of a front lawn, there was just a cement parking slab. There were no cars in front, and the house was dark. I parked across the street and decided to wait.

It was a warm evening, and as I rolled down my window, the breeze kicked up dust along the gutter. The gritty smell of the dust cut with the faint scent of orange blossoms suggested something that I couldn't quite recall, an event hovering at the fringe of my memory. I closed my eyes for a moment.

Summer. A West Bank checkpoint at the edge of an orange grove. I was about to relieve a young South African immigrant named Danny, when I saw a Palestinian teenager approach the checkpoint. He walked robotically, stopped, and looked through Danny and the other soldiers. The Palestinian was curly haired, his skin was dark—the color of mahogany—but his eyes were an arresting pale green. Crusader eyes, the Palestinians called them. There was something about those sea green eyes that alarmed me: a curious unfocused lifeless look.

"Jible hawiye," Danny ordered—the two Arabic words every Israeli soldier learns: Give me your identity card.

The Palestinian stepped forward, reached into his back pocket—a movement so casual he might have been reaching for a handkerchief—and removed a shiny aluminum RGN Russian hand grenade. He pulled the pin, blowing

himself up, along with Danny, blasting the branches of the olive tree high be-
hind them with bloody strips of clothing that flapped in the breeze like flags.

As I instinctively flexed my calf, where slivers of shrapnel were still em-
bedded, I saw a man park a Lexus SUV in front of the house. I flipped
open my murder book and checked Abazeda's DMV picture. It was him.

I walked over and said, "Mr. Abazeda, I'm an LAPD homicide detective. I'd like to ask you a few questions."

"It's nice to finally meet you, Detective Levine. Ann Licata told me
that she has spoken with you."

Abazeda was a solidly built man with sharp features. Bald, with just
a horseshoe-shaped fringe of black hair, he stared at me with a slightly
popeyed expression. I couldn't tell if he was nervous or he had some kind
of optical condition. He wore a pale blue silk shirt, black linen slacks,
and tan loafers with no socks.

"Why don't we go inside," I said. "It'll be easier to talk."

"No problem," he said, opening the door with a key and punching
a code into the alarm panel.

I followed him into an entryway with pale blue marble floors and a
massive skylight veined with gold. He opened the door to an office off
the entryway with white shag carpeting and a desk that was half the size
of the room. Four video screens in the corner of the office offered exterior views of the house from rotating surveillance cameras. Abazeda sat
in an overstuffed leather chair behind the desk. I pulled up a chair opposite him.

"Ann Licata told me you and she have an arrangement," he said in
a slight accent that sounded vaguely Middle Eastern.

"Where are you from, originally?" I asked.

"Is that really important?"

"Not really."

"As I was saying, Ann told me that she cooperated with you and you
agreed to leave her business alone."

"From what I understand, it's *your* business."

"Your understanding is incorrect. She's inexperienced in the ways of
finance. I'm an advisor. That's all."

"At this point, as I told Ms. Licata, I'm not interested in the business—whoever owns it. I'm only interested in the murder of Pete Relovich."

"I extend my condolences. I understand he was a former member of the LAPD—one of your brothers in arms."

"You ever meet him?"

"I can't say as I've ever had the pleasure."

"Did you know he was working for your business, or should I say, the business that you're an advisor for?"

"I didn't know that until Ann told me when I talked to her yesterday."

"You sure you never met Pete Relovich."

"I'm sure."

"That's not what I've heard."

"You probably heard something from Jane Granger. Am I right?"

I stared at him without acknowledging his question.

"We used to go out, but when I ended the relationship she became very angry, very vindictive. I heard she started to date Mr. Relovich. It would be just like her to try to claim I was a jealous ex-suitor."

"Do you own a gun?"

He smiled. "Of course not. Why would I need a gun?"

I stared at him thinking that this interview was a complete waste of time. Everything he'd said after "hello" was a lie, and if someone could lie saying "hello," it would be him.

"Can you recall what you were doing on Thursday night?" I asked.

"I can. I was playing poker at the Kismet Casino in the city of Commerce."

"How many hours did you play?"

"I got there about eight and played until well after midnight."

"What game?"

"I used to play a lot of stud and draw. But I've recently become intrigued by the game of Texas Hold'em."

"Do you remember what table?"

"The high-limit table."

"What are the stakes?"

"One hundred-two hundred. Four bet cap."

If he lied about what he was doing on Thursday night when Relovich was killed, I might have enough to arrest him, or at the very least, to get a warrant to search his house and look for the murder weapon.

I stood up and said, "I'm sure we'll talk again."

He smiled broadly. "I hope not."

I navigated several freeways until I hit the 710 South, exited in Commerce, and parked in front of the Kismet Casino. I showed the doorman my badge and asked him to take me to the head of security. We walked through the club, a cavernous vault of stale air dotted with dozens of round tables. The only sounds were the click of chips and the raises and calls of tired men with poker pallors who murmured over their cards.

The doorman led me to a large room in the back of the club filled with video screens tracking the action at every table. He knocked and a wiry man in his fifties with a military-style buzz cut shook my hand and said, "Dickie Jenkins, head of security. Retired Torrance P.D."

He led me into the room and we chatted for a few minutes about the cops he knew at the LAPD and a few Torrance homicide detectives I worked with on a case years ago.

When I told him I was investigating the murder of an ex-cop, he narrowed his eyes and said, "Whatever you need, you'll get from me."

I handed him the DMV photo of Abazeda. I told him that Abazeda claimed that on Thursday night he was playing at the high-limit Texas Hold'em table. "Can you roll back the video and see if you can spot him there between seven and closing?"

"Sure I can. We've got a camera trained on that table all night." He pointed to one of the video screens, and I could see a half dozen men crowded around a table gripping their cards. "But that's a lot of hours of tape, and I've got to examine it frame by frame. Might take me a while."

"How long?"

"Since this is a homicide case, I'll hunker down and get it done as fast as I can. But it still might take me a few days to go through it all."

"Any chance I can get the tape and go through it myself?"

"I wish I could. But the club won't release it. That's *their* policy, not mine. I could lose my job if I give it up to you. You'll either have to get a warrant or wait for me. I'm truly sorry."

"Then I'll wait."

"And I'll get it done as soon as I can."

.   .   .

I heard the ringing phone as I unlocked the door to my loft and picked it up on the fifth ring.

"Hey, brah. Meet me tomorrow morning at Point Dume."

It was Razor Reed.

I was a young patrolman answering hotshot calls on the Pacific Division p.m. shift when I met Razor. On a warm summer night he had just left a Venice restaurant when two Sho'line Crips jumped out of the shadows and pistol-whipped him after he refused to turn over his watch. My partner and I just happened to be driving by the restaurant. I jumped out of the car, drew down on the Crips, hooked them up, and called an ambulance.

I stopped off at the hospital that night and questioned Razor, who had suffered a concussion and a fractured jaw. When I asked why he had refused to give up the watch, Razor lifted it off the end table and showed me the engraved back: FIRST PLACE HUNTINGTON BEACH OPEN.

"My first win in a surf contest," Razor had told me. "Got the watch and fifteen thousand dollars. Sentimental value, brah."

Razor had been a professional surfer, and when he retired from the circuit more than a decade ago, he had opened a surf shop in Santa Monica. A few weeks after the beating, he stopped by the station with a gift: a custom surfboard he had shaped for me. "You're wound pretty tight," Razor had told me. "This'll mellow you out."

The board was beautiful: a sleek expanse of foam and fiberglass with a Canadian poplar stringer flanked by two swirling turquoise panels. In the center, Razor had played off my first name and airbrushed a custom insignia: a fiery wave raining smoldering ashes on the pale green water.

Razor had designed a hybrid for me, a board that was long enough, wide enough, and stable enough so a beginner could easily paddle, catch waves, and build up some speed, but streamlined enough so he would be able to maneuver a bit once he knew what he was doing. The tri-fin was eight-feet long with a full nose for flotation, slightly kicked up for steep drops, a rounded pintail, hard rails at the bottom, and softer edges in the middle.

At the time, I was in my mid-twenties, living in a one-room studio a few blocks from Venice Beach. I was still reeling from my army service, still confused and aimless, still unsure I wanted to be a cop, still struggling to occupy my days until it was time to start my four o'clock shift. I figured I might as well try surfing; I had nothing better to do.

I started out in the early mornings near the Venice breakwater riding the bumpy white water straight into shore. The other surfers razzed me, shouting, "Straight off, Adolph." But I always had pretty good balance, and I soon felt comfortable on the board. I started to paddle farther out and give real waves a try, but for a week I continually misjudged the breaks and pearled, catching the nose of the board during my descent and tumbling into the water. To avoid the other surfers, who cut me off and cursed at me, called me a kook and a barney, I surfed at dawn, beating the crowds. Occasionally, I would judge it just right, catch the wave as it was breaking and angle across the face. The exhilaration was exquisite.

I soon found that surfing in the early morning was the perfect antidote to the insanity at night. I spent my shift lurching from crisis to crisis, breaking up fights between coked-out men and doleful women with Southern Comfort on their breath, jamming street corner junkies, cuffing fractious drunks, speeding to drive-bys, barroom shootings, alley stabbings. Waking at dawn, driving up the coast, slipping on my wet suit, and paddling out into the glassy surf, helped me unwind, washed away the tension of the previous night. Since I returned from Israel, I had trouble sleeping and often awoke during nightmares, sweating and shouting. Knowing I would be surfing the next morning calmed me, helped me fall back asleep as I envisioned gentle swells peeling off a point.

A few months after Razor had dropped the board by the station, I called him at the shop, told him I had been using the board every day, and thanked him. Razor said there was a nice northwest swell and asked me if I wanted to go surfing. The next morning, Razor picked me up and drove up the coast to Silverstrand beach in Oxnard. I had trouble with the hard-breaking waves, which were overhead with paper-thin walls; I continually tumbled off the board and ended up in the surf with my leash tangled around my legs. Razor showed me how I was taking off a fraction too late. "Commit yourself fully to the wave," Razor had said. "If you hesitate, you're lost." I knew he was right. During my next few rides, for the first time that day, I stayed with the waves all the way and finished off with flourishing kick outs. Since then, we surfed together a few times a year. I still had the board with the fiery wave in the center.

During the past year, Razor had called a number of times, but I always put him off. I wasn't interested in surfing or seeing anyone connected to my days as a cop.

Now, Razor was trying to lure me out again. "A south swell just rolled in. The outer reef by Little Dume is cranking."

I had surfed the outer reef with Razor in the past. But only in the summer and fall. South swells in the spring were rare. A hurricane from Baja must be blowing up the coast, I figured.

"I got a case, Razor. I don't think I can break away."

"Dude, I've been worried about you. You've got to get out of your own head."

I thought about what Dr. Blau had said: *You have to learn when to let go and leave the job behind—*"

"Okay, Razor, you've worn me down. What time tomorrow morning?"

"Six. And get your stoke on."

CHAPTER 10

My alarm woke me at four fifteen. I grabbed my wet suit and board and tossed them into the back of my station wagon, which I had bought when I started surfing. Now I was glad I hadn't sold the Saturn.

By four thirty, I was on the freeway, speeding by the first morning commuters.

When I emerged onto the Pacific Coast Highway from the Santa Monica tunnel it was still dark, but I could see the iridescent spray of the white water crashing against the shore. The moon was full, casting milky shards of light farther out at sea.

I cruised up the serpentine highway, hard by the rocky cliffs, past Sunset, Topanga, and a few other surf spots that caught the swell and were jacking good-sized waves near the shore. After I passed Malibu and Paradise Cove, I dropped down the hill to Zuma, pulled into the lot, drove down a frontage road, and parked next to Razor's van. I could hear the waves of the Zuma shore break before I saw them: a thunderous roar that pounded the sand.

I banged on the window of the van and Razor emerged, naked, wearing only sheepskin-lined Ugg boots, rubbing sleep from his eyes. From the neck down, Razor looked like a teenager: he had a washboard stomach, wide shoulders, arms and chest corded with muscle from a lifetime of paddling. But his shoulder-length hair was as silver as a chrome pistol, and his bushy mustache and soul chip beneath his lower lip were bleached white from the sun.

"Surf naked, brah," Razor said.

"I don't think so," I said, pulling my wet suit out of my trunk.

"Just kidding. Some of these waves are double overhead. Good way to lose your crank in the drink."

After we slipped on our wet suits and grabbed our boards, we climbed the steep bluff that separated Point Dume from Zuma. The morning dew raised the pungent smell of sage and sumac. Flowering white yucca as tall as a surfboard—called Our Lord's Candle—bordered the path. At the top of the bluff, we stopped for a moment. In the smoky early morning light, I could see the entire sweep of the Santa Monica Bay, from Point Dume below me, to the tip of the Palos Verdes Peninsula in the distance.

Little Dume, a short, rocky point, was a half mile down the coast. About six hundred feet from shore, just beyond a kelp bed, I could see the waves breaking off the outer reef. The faces were huge, slowly rising from the deep water, pausing for a moment as they caught the reef, frozen in time, glassy and deep green in the faint light, before crashing and crumbling into a mountain of white water.

We climbed down the bluff and set our boards on the wet sand. Razor lovingly ran his hands along the rail of my board and said, "That's one sweet stick."

We dropped to our knees and began waxing our boards, the bubble gum smell filling the air. The presurfing ritual—climb into the wet suit; check out the surf, tide, and wind; wax the board; pick the right spot to paddle out—reminded me of my old prepatrol routine. Clean the Galil. Slip on the flak jacket and helmet. Fill the canteen. Hook on the grenades. Then get going and look for moving shadows.

"Wake up, Ash," Razor said. "It's thumping out there."

I waded out to my waist, board under my arm, the cold water chilling me as it seeped into my wet suit. Then Razor and I hopped on our boards and began paddling out at an angle to avoid the turbulent water. We circled around the outer reef and pulled up just beyond the break. Pale bands of orange and pink streaked the eastern horizon; the sky overhead was neon blue. There was not even a hint of mist or wind, and first wave of the set that rose from the reef was a velvety wall of water. Razor took off and I saw him disappear down the huge face, spotted the top of his head a few seconds later, and then lost him again as he ripped up and down the wave, the lip feathering, catching rainbows of light.

I paddled for the last wave of the set, looked down, and felt as if I was standing atop a skyscraper staring at the street below. I quickly pulled out and swiveled around. When Razor paddled back he said, "Don't be such a puss."

"It's been a while since I've been out," I said sheepishly.

When the next set broke, bigger than the last, Razor pointed at me. I paddled for the first wave. When I saw the steep drop, I felt like pulling out again, but I muttered, "Fuck it" to myself and soared down the face as I climbed to my feet, carved a clean turn, and jetted through the silky face, just ahead of the roaring white water. I could see the wave beginning to close out, so I crouched slightly, grabbed the outside rail for balance and powered through the tube; for a moment I was completely engulfed in water, locked in, unable to see anything but a flash of green and a cloud of foam, the hiss of the surf in my ears, then I rocketed out of the wave into the sunlight, and just as the breaker began to peter out, I caught another good-sized wave, skimming along the shallow water until I ended up near the shore and caught my fin on a rock. I couldn't help grinning as I paddled back out.

As the sky lightened, other surfers joined us, but because the south swell was a surprise in the spring, the outer reef was not as crowded as the usual Southern California surf spot. After another fast rumbling ride, I paddled back out, feeling a world away from the L.A. sprawl. Steep rocky cliffs, studded with thick stands of eucalyptus, banked the shore. Looming in the distance were the Santa Monica Mountains, the escarpment purple in the morning light. A sea lion barked in the distance.

I straddled my board and stared at the sharp horizon line, the water cobalt, the sky the palest blue, with just the single brushstroke of a ragged cloud. A faint wind began to blow in from the west, rocking the red bell buoy off Zuma, the clanging echoing out at sea. The water was so clear I could see the underwater kelp beds and tiny schools of fish swim past my toes.

The sun was rising over the mountains and beams of light dappled the water, still roiling and flecked with foam after the last set. I studied a patch of water for a moment, transfixed: a clean square of foam outside a smooth square of water. The water like the Mexican tiles on Relovich's kitchen floor. The foam like the grouting.

I whipped around and furiously padded toward shore.

"Too early to book," Razor called out.

"Just thought of something. Got to go."

*　　*　　*

I snaked back down the Pacific Coast Highway, crossed town on the Santa Monica Freeway in rush hour traffic, showered at home, changed, and headed south on the Harbor Freeway. I went straight to Relovich's kitchen and studied the grouting around a corner tile.

Relovich's daughter had taken a picture of her father picking up a piece of French toast that he had dropped on the floor by the corner tile. Initially, I had not noticed the tile, but as I sat on my board, studying the play of light on the ocean and the foam, I recalled the photograph and realized in a flash of insight that the floor looked different. The grouting around one of the tiles appeared new in the photograph, whiter than the grouting around the other tiles. Now it was the same beige color as the rest of the grouting. I figured that at the time the picture was taken, Relovich must have just installed a new tile.

Crouching on my hands and knees, I rapped on several tiles with my knuckles. A dull thud. Then I rapped on the new tile. It echoed like a ripe watermelon. I removed a screwdriver and a small hammer from the trunk of my car and carefully chiseled out the grouting until I popped out the tile.

In the hollowed-out space beneath the tile, I pulled out a ragged green towel, wrapped around a metal box. Inside was a wad of dusty cash—$4,800 in hundreds—a .38-caliber snub-nosed revolver, and a small felt jewelry bag secured with a drawstring. There were two small objects inside the jewelry bag. I emptied them onto my palm. The larger one—about the size of my badge—was an intricately carved ivory figure of a fierce-looking man with a flowing beard, dressed in a billowing robe, clutching a sword. The smaller one—about the size of my thumbnail—was also a carved ivory figure and had horns, yellow fangs, and bulging red eyes. Muscular, clad only in a loincloth, with pointed ears and long claws, it looked like a demon or a monster.

I had no idea what the objects represented. But because they were so beautifully carved and seemed to represent mythological figures of some sort, I figured they were old, from some country in Asia, and valuable.

CHAPTER 11

Driving back to PAB, I considered who might know something about the ivory figures and immediately thought of Dave Papazian, who had been the art cop for the past nine years. He had the reputation of being knowledgeable and having good contacts in the art world. Papazian worked in Commercial Crimes, which was on the same floor as Felony Special. I had chatted with Papazian a few times in the hallway and at retirement parties at the academy, but never talked with him about a case.

I double-parked near the back entrance, took the elevator to the fifth floor, walked over to the west wing of the building, and past the Cold Case Unit. I was relieved to see Papazian at his desk. He was a man in his forties who had a narrow face composed of mismatched angles—sharp cheekbones, high forehead, long, spindly nose, razor lips, jutting jaw. I always thought he looked like one of those angular, abstract Picasso portraits—all slashes and sharp corners. A perfect look for an art cop.

Papazian was talking on the phone, but when he spotted me lingering in the doorway, he covered the receiver and whispered, "I'll be off in a minute."

I remained standing and surveyed the office. One wall was lined with posters from recent shows at Los Angeles's Museum of Contemporary Art. Another featured an abstract painting by Laddie Dill—a series of intersecting trapezoids—and one by Ed Moses, which resembled a Navajo weaving.

When Papazian hung up the phone, he said, "What do you think?"

"Contemporary art doesn't really appeal to me. I heard it once described as imagination without skill. But I got to like Dill, Moses, and a bunch of other Venice artists. I used to check out the galleries there on slow afternoons when I worked Pacific Division."

"I was fortunate enough to begin collecting their works while they were still affordable." Papazian smiled and nodded. "It's nice to talk to that rare cop who knows the L.A. art scene."

"A lot of artists live in my building."

"Don't you live downtown?" Papazian asked.

"Yeah. I can walk to MOCA and the Geffen."

"My wife's a patron at both museums."

Years ago I had heard that she was a high-powered real estate agent and had made such a killing selling high-end properties on the westside that Papazian could afford to start his own collection.

In a department where many cops' passions were limited to their motorcycles, their NRA memberships, and their hunting trips, it was not easy to be different. Papazian was an aesthete, passionate about art and California cabernets, which he collected and stored in a temperature-controlled storage unit. He never tried to fit in. I respected that.

Papazian waved me to a chair next to his desk. "So what's up? You probably didn't come here to talk about art."

I sat down and said, "Actually I did." I briefly told him about the murder, and explained how I found the objects underneath a tile at Relovich's. "I thought maybe you could help me out and tell me what they are."

I emptied the jewelry bag into my palm and placed the figures on the desk. Papazian picked them up and studied them. He tapped the larger figure and said, "This is a *netsuke*. Japanese. It's a decorative piece used to attach a pouch to the sash of the kimono. It's very collectible." He rolled the smaller object between his thumb and forefinger. "This little one I've never seen before. I can't tell you what it is."

"How old is the *netsuke*?"

"Could be a few hundred years. I learned about them a few years ago when a collector who lived up on Laurel Canyon had a bunch of them stolen. I arrested his gardener when he tried to pawn them."

"I don't even know if these figures mean anything," I said. "They might have no connection whatsoever to Relovich's murder. But the way they were hidden interests me. And I don't have a hell of a lot at this stage of the investigation. So I might as well track them. Any way to find out where they came from? Any way to see if they were stolen?"

Papazian swiveled around, hunched over his computer for a few minutes—typing with two fingers—printed out a half dozen pages and handed them to me. "I've listed a few databases for stolen art and some *netsuke* associations I worked with on my case. You can search their Web sites and see if there's any record of them."

"Thanks for the help," I said. "I appreciate it."

"Before you go, let me mention something to you. Since you live around a lot of painters, let me know if you come across any promising ones who're still flying under the radar. I'm always looking to pick up pieces by artists before they're discovered by those westside collectors who drive the prices out of sight."

"Will do. And thanks again."

I cut through the squad room to Felony Special. There was a note on my desk from Duffy: "Wegland called. He wants you to stop by his office."

I took the elevator to the sixth floor and stood in the doorway of the anteroom adjacent to Wegland's office. The commander's adjutant, Conrad Patowski, was staring at his computer screen.

I knocked on the open door. Patowski jerked around, surprised, and looked up at me.

"Yes, Ash," he said, sounding irritated.

"Is Wegland free?"

Patowski frowned as he perused a daybook.

"You really should call ahead for an appointment," Patowski said, frowning.

"Wegland wants to see me."

Patowski rubbed his palms together. "That's different."

He slipped into Wegland's office, returned a minute later, and intoned somberly, "The commander will see you now."

Wegland must have had a busy morning because his comb-over, usually carefully sprayed into place, was disheveled and peaked at the top of his head like the wick on a candle. "So how's the investigation coming?"

I explained how I found the Japanese figures underneath the tile at Relovich's. "I just talked to Papazian. I'm trying to figure out where they came from. If they were stolen, that might be a lead."

"Pete Relovich was no thief," Wegland said indignantly.

"I'm not saying he was. Maybe someone else hid them. Maybe Pete didn't know they were there."

"Fair enough."

"Before you go, I want to talk to you about something. I'm not your commanding officer and you're not working for me, so I can't tell you how to conduct this investigation. But I know from a friend of mine at Internal Affairs that they're not happy about you nosing around there."

"I'm not nosing around," I said, irritated. "I'm conducting a murder investigation."

"Well, the Internal Affairs people think you're pursuing this angle because you're pissed that they nailed you with that suspension Duffy recommended. They think you're following this lead so you can dig up something on *them*. Some sort of vendetta."

"That's bullshit and you know it!" I snapped.

"You do what you have to do. I'm just giving you a heads-up." He lightly touched his hair with his palms. "Something else I wanted to mention. I heard about what happened the other morning with Graupmann. You can scrap on the squad room floor with anyone you want. I don't really care. But that kind of thing's going to hurt your credibility. It'll hurt this investigation. And that's something I *do* care about. So let me give you some free advice—"

"Save it," I said as I walked to the door. "You heard about my desk?"

"I did. But how do you know it was Graupmann?"

"It's pretty damn obvious."

Wegland walked over and slapped me on the shoulder. "Good work finding that stuff beneath the tiles. Bottom line is we're both on the same side; we both want the same thing. I care about this investigation—just as much as you—and I just don't want anything hindering it."

When I returned to the squad room, I flipped on the computer. As I searched art theft and *netsuke* sites, I heard Graupmann tell his partner how much he missed the LAPD's good old days. "We used to be a *real* police department. Now we're just a division of the fucking ACLU. The guys on the street are castrated. They pull over some asshole and say, 'Excuse me sir, would you please put your hands behind your back.' If the guy doesn't comply, they don't know what to do. They call their sergeant, their lieutenant, their captain, like they're running to their mommy for help.

"When I came up we *asked* them to put their hands behind their backs. If they didn't, we *told* them. Then we *showed* them. Then we *beat* them. Then we *choke*d them. And if they still hadn't complied, we *shot* them."

A few detectives chuckled. But I had spent so much time around badge-heavy cops that I was bored by the macho rap.

Graupmann then launched into a disquisition on his number one travel rule when he visited other cities to search for a fleeing suspect. "I immediately check out the maps and find out where Martin Luther King Street is. Every city has one. Then I make a point to avoid it. Because there's one thing I know—that it'll be one of the most high-crime streets in the city, where people are peddling drugs on every other corner, where the odds are you'll be carjacked, ripped off, robbed, or beaten, before you go a dozen blocks."

While I was trying to tune out Graupmann, Papazian stopped by my desk. "I thought of something else that might help you." He handed me a piece of paper with some names and phone numbers scrawled at the top. "Here are two gallery dealers. They're both knowledgeable about Asian art. They'll be able to help you out with those objects you found. I gave them both a heads-up that you might be calling. One of 'em is an old fag who's got a gallery in Westwood. The other one's a babe who's got one in Venice. Either one should be able to fill you in. If you need anything else, I'll be glad to do what I can."

I thanked him, and returned to my computer. I finished searching the Web sites, but could not trace the *netsuke*. After studying the names on the piece of paper Papazian had given me, I called the woman in Venice and set up an appointment with her in the late afternoon. Then I called the old guy, but a woman at the gallery who answered the phone told me he was out of the country until the end of the month. I asked if there was anyone else at the gallery who was knowledgeable about Japanese art.

"There is not," she said curtly, and hung up.

As I walked out the door, Duffy waved me into his office. "I hear you had a cordial visit with Commander Wegland."

"I couldn't believe it. He was giving me a hard time about visiting

Internal Affairs and about my fight with Graupmann. He's got his head up his ass."

"It's good to keep him on our side."

"Doesn't seem like he is."

"Oh, he is. Let me tell you something." He tapped his temple with a forefinger. "Deputy Chief Grazzo thinks you're fucking unbalanced. Quitting the department in a snit, along with your other crazy habits. But on my recommendation, he goes out on a limb and brings you back. Then he hears about you going fist city with Graupmann. He wanted to bounce you off the case. But Wegland stepped up big time and persuaded Grazzo to stay the course with you. Wegland might be a pencil-neck geek, but he's very well connected in this department. He's got a lot of clout. And he's with us—with you—on this one. He's convinced—in fact he told me this—that the best way to clear this case is to turn you loose on it."

Duffy clasped his hands and said, "He's not the most personable guy in the world. But I think he laid that shit on you about Graupmann and Internal Affairs because he was trying to let you know that you don't have much of a margin for error anymore. I also think he was trying to warn you and, when you get right down to it, I think he was trying to protect you."

I started to walk out, but lingered in the doorway for a moment and then turned around. Duffy was leafing through a sixty-dayer. "You mentioned that South Bureau Homicide was handling the Patton case," I said. "How about the Bae Soo Sung homicide?"

"I had to ship both of 'em back to South Bureau," Duffy said, without looking up.

"When we picked up the Sung case, they hadn't done shit," I said.

"Well, we didn't do so well on it either, did we?" Duffy said, finally pushing the sixty-dayer aside and looking up at me.

"It's important to me that—"

Duffy slammed his palm on his desk. "Leave it alone, Ash. That case got you suspended, sunk your marriage, and almost ruined your fucking life. Now you're back with a clean slate. Be smart. You don't want any part of it. I wish they'd never sent it over to us in the first place. As far as I'm concerned, those South Central homicide dicks can have both cases."

• • •

I drove to Venice to see Nicole Haddad, the gallery owner referred to me by Papazian. The gallery was flanked by an antique store and a herbal medicine/massage clinic. I opened the door, a single shimmering sheet of stainless steel, and walked inside. The long, narrow gallery was a sleek, spare space with blonde hardwood floors, and brightly illuminated by overhead track lighting. It housed an eclectic array of artwork, ranging from jagged cement sculptures to huge canvases displaying Rorschach test pen-and-ink swirls.

"Can I interest you in anything?" a woman asked.

Startled, I swiveled around. She was almost six feet tall, about the same size as me, with an olive complexion and startling eyes that I initially thought were brown, but then flickered with specks of green when she turned her head, catching the gallery's overhead lights. Her hair was cut in a bob with the sides sharply sheared just below her ears, two parallel black slashes. She wore black pants, a black silk jacket with a Chinese collar, and a pale green blouse that matched her carved jade earrings.

"I'm looking for Nicole Haddad."

"Oh," she said, looking surprised. "You must be Detective Levine. I didn't think you were a—"

"A cop?" I interrupted.

"Yes," she said flatly.

"So what do I look like?" I asked, smiling.

"You look like the kind of guy who might buy some art."

I handed her my card, and she studied it for a moment, nodding with recognition. "I know who you are. I just Googled you." For a moment, she stared at me so brazenly that I felt a bit exposed. She lightly touched my chest with the tip of a long red fingernail and said, "You've been in some trouble."

Unlike Virginia Saucedo, the Internal Affairs detective who slipped me her card, Haddad did not gaze at me with that maternal expression of concern. She seemed to find something alluring about my brush with notoriety.

"But I know you're not here to talk about that," Haddad said, grabbing my arm and leading me back to her office.

She sat behind a small, antique desk, inlaid with arabesques of mother of pearl, and said, "Detective Papazian said you might be calling. He said you've got some interesting things to show me."

"Do you know much about Japanese art?"

She extended her hand toward the gallery and said, "The westside buyers only want contemporary art. But my knowledge is a little broader. I have a master's in art history from UCLA. I was in the Ph.D. program, but dropped out. Japanese antiquities are one of my passions." She dropped her chin and gazed up at me. "Do my qualifications meet with your approval?"

I pulled the jewelry bag out of my pocket, and emptied it on her blotter. She studied the objects through a jeweler's loupe. Then she picked up the *netsuke*, flicked on a small flashlight, and examined it and the smaller object. As I leaned over, watching her work, I caught the herbal scent of her hair.

"I don't want to bore you, Detective Levine, with too much background, so tell me how much you want to know."

"Take it from the top."

She carefully set the object at the corner of her desk blotter. "Okay. During the Edo and Meiji periods in Japan everyone wore kimonos."

"What time period are we talking about?"

"Roughly, from about sixteen hundred to just after nineteen hundred. Kimonos were wonderful. They were exquisite creations, functional works of art. They were only missing one important thing: pockets. Women usually tucked their personal items into their sashes or in their sleeves. Men created their own pockets. They had cases for things like pipes and tobacco, sake, and knives, and hung them from their kimono sashes with a cord. The cord was secured to the sash by a kind of toggle—the *netsuke*. A bead was used to slip down the cord and secure the pouches." She picked up the smaller object found at Relovich's house. "This is that slip-bead. It's called an *ojime*."

"They're both beautifully made," I said.

"The Japanese have a very interesting attitude toward beauty, form, and function. They believe the practical should be aesthetic and the aesthetic should be practical."

"What can you tell me about these particular pieces."

She picked up the *ojime*. "See the horns, the fangs, the terrible scowl, the menacing red eyes, the hands with three fingers, the feet with three toes. This is what the Japanese called an *Oni*. He represents bad luck and sickness and evil. He's a devil."

She set the *netsuke* next to it. "Now look at this stout fellow with his long robe and his sword and his purposeful expression. He's a demon queller. The Japanese called him *Shoki*."

"Were *Oni* and *Shoki* always together on the kimono?"

"No. But sometimes they are. These two pieces are probably a set."

"Are these pieces worth much?"

She held the *netsuke* and then the *ojime* to the light. "The most valuable ones can sell for more than thirty thousand dollars. But most of the good ones I've seen run between five and ten thousand. These are probably in that range."

"I checked some computer sites Dave Papazian told me about. But I couldn't track them."

"Let me give it a try." She held up my card and then flicked it down on her desk like a blackjack dealer hitting a player. "If I come up with anything, I'll call you."

"I'd appreciate it."

A bloodcurdling scream suddenly echoed from next door. Then another scream, even louder. And another.

I instinctively tapped the side of my suit coat, over my Beretta.

Haddad reached over and rapped on the wall with her knuckles. "This isn't another murder case for you. Just primal scream therapy. A hundred bucks an hour. Welcome to Venice, Detective Levine. When I get home, I scream every night for free."

I placed my hands on my thighs, about to stand up, when I paused and said, "Haddad. A Lebanese name."

"Very good. How'd you know?"

"I spent a little time in that part of the word."

She turned her head, studied me with one eye. "Levine. A Jewish name."

"That's an easy one."

"I'm glad to help you with this case so I can do my part for Arab-Jewish relations," she said, flashing me an arch look.

There was something about her that reminded me of those beautiful Israeli women who had intrigued me, with their black hair, green or deep blue almond eyes, and dusky, flawless, makeup-free complexions.

She also had the bold, confrontational demeanor of so many Sabra women I'd met.

"You Muslim or Christian?" I asked.

She patted her hair and gave me a coquettish look. "Do I look like the type who'd ever wear an chador? Lebanese Christian, of course. But now, the way people in this country view the Arab world, I'm reluctant to even tell people I'm Lebanese. I think I should call myself," she said with an amused expression, "a Phoenician-American."

I decided to change the subject. The less we discussed Arab or Jewish issues—in light of Israel's recent history in Lebanon—the better off I would be with her. "Any suggestions on where I can go from here to get a line on that *ojime* and *netsuke*?"

"Let me do my own search first."

"If you come up with anything," I said, standing up, "let me know."

I drove home through rush hour traffic and walked up to the roof of my building. The pollution and lights of downtown usually obscured the night skies, but it was unusually clear tonight with a dusting of stars overhead. To the east, I could see the back of the old soot-stained Rosslyn Hotel, its enormous neon sign buzzing and snapping. A police helicopter zipped by—the *whap-whap-whap* reminding me of nighttime assaults on Hezbollah garrisons—its spotlight scanning the streets for a dirtbag they probably would never find. When it passed, I could hear the contrapuntal blare of sirens, car horns, and rap and cumbia from the passing cars. Below me, two crackheads argued over a cardboard box, a room for one.

Staring up at the stars, I thought about the Shoki and the Oni. A demon and a demon queller. Isn't a detective's job, at its core, to quell demons, or at least chase them? Isn't it curious that those two objects were found in the house of a retired cop? A retired cop who was killed.

When I was a detective trainee, Bud Carducci, the salty old cop who taught me the rudiments of homicide investigation, once told me: "Rule one of the homicide dick: there are no coincidences. Rule two: there are no rules." I interpreted that to mean that coincidences are highly unlikely, but not impossible. Was it a coincidence that Relovich, an ex-cop, had a demon and a demon queller in his house? Did these objects have any connection—even tangentially—to his murder?

I then thought about the way Nicole Haddad had tapped me on the chest with her fingernail and that jolt I had felt. But I had always made it a point not to date women I met during the course of an investigation. At least until the investigation was finished. Maybe after this case was cleared I'd give her a call. But I knew I probably wouldn't. The Jewish-Arab thing might be too much to overcome.

CHAPTER 12

The next morning, I decided I wanted to contact Theresa Martinez, the young Hispanic woman who'd been busted in San Pedro. I had two witnesses. And one was a crackhead. I had to find a way to persuade her to talk.

When I saw her last, I had been reluctant to lean on her. I had leaned on Latisha Patton, and that had got her killed. I didn't want to pressure another young woman to talk. But I realized that I had to either push every witness to the limit, or give the murder book to a detective more ruthless than me, a detective who was willing to do whatever it took to clear the case.

I remembered that Martinez worked as a secretary for a large engineering firm in Torrance. I figured that she hadn't told her employers about her arrest and her involvement as a witness in a homicide investigation. In the past, I'd persuaded a few witnesses to talk to me simply by showing up at their jobs. They'd agreed to cooperate just to get rid of me before their employers discovered who I was. I thought this might work with Martinez.

I drove down to Torrance, parked in a lot a few blocks from the 405 Freeway, and waited for the receptionist to finish a call. When she hung up the phone, I asked for Theresa Martinez.

"And who should I say is here to see her?"

I made it a point not to identify myself as a detective. I would hold that out as a threat if she wouldn't agree to talk. "Just tell her it's Ash Levine."

The receptionist punched a few numbers on the switchboard, muttered into the phone, paused, and said, "Ms. Martinez says she doesn't know any Ash Levine."

"Tell her I want to talk to her briefly about a purchase she made in San Pedro last week."

The receptionist repeated the message, looked up at me and said, "She'll be right down."

About twenty seconds later, Martinez entered the lobby, cast a nervous glance at me, and motioned to follow her out the front door into the parking lot.

"That's not right to bust in on me at my job like this," she said. She was still dressed like a preppy, wearing khakis and a pale blue short-sleeved Polo shirt. She looked very young and very nervous and very vulnerable. Just like Latisha had looked when I interviewed her the first time. I could feel my heart pounding in my chest.

I leaned against a car in the parking lot and took a deep breath. "If you cooperate, agree to meet me at the station, and tell me everything you saw that night, I'll walk straight through the parking lot to my car, and I won't bother you at work again."

"And if I don't?"

"I don't think you want your boss to know why I'm here."

"*Christ.*"

"So you'll cooperate?"

"I got no choice."

"What time you get off?" I asked.

"I'm working part-time. I'm off at one."

I remembered she attended community college. "You have class this afternoon?"

"No. Tonight."

I told her to stop by PAB after work. I gave her directions and I walked across the lot to my car.

At two, Martinez arrived, and I ushered her into an interview room. "You want coffee or a soda?"

She shook her head. "Look, I've still got that drug case pending. If I can help your case, can you help mine?"

"If you give me information that leads to an arrest, I'll talk to the DA before your sentencing. I'll also write a letter to the presiding judge. I'll push hard for leniency. I'll go to the wall for you."

"Promise?" she asked in a quavering voice.

"I promise to do what I can for you."

"Okay. I think I might of seen something that could help you."

"What?"

"I saw two guys on the street."

"When?"

"A Thursday night. A few days before I was arrested."

"Why do you think that could help me?"

"Because the next day I read in the San Pedro paper where that ex-cop was killed. I remembered seeing these two guys that night right down the hill from where he lived."

"Why'd you think they might be involved?"

"Something about the way they were moving. They weren't exactly running, but they were really hustling down that hill. And they were checking out their surroundings, suspicious like."

"What time was this?"

"Almost midnight."

The coroner estimated the time of death at approximately eleven p.m. So these two fit the profile. "Can you tell me exactly where you spotted them?"

"Across the street from where the guy was selling drugs. They were getting into a parked car."

I pulled a yellow legal pad out of my briefcase and drew a diagram of the streets where Relovich lived, winding down to the bottom of the hill, and the corners where I had watched the dealers. "Show me where the car was parked?"

She tapped a fingernail on the spot where the trail had ended for the bloodhound.

"What happened next?"

She gripped her right index figure and nervously tugged at it. "I brought this up last time. The first time I was ever in a police station was the night you saw me. I've never been a witness before. I'm very scared of these kinds of people. Will they come after me if I help you?"

For a moment I just stared at her, stunned. I didn't know if I could protect her. And I couldn't lie to her. I tightly clasped my hands on my lap. I thought of what Blau had told me to do if I started to lose it with a witness. *Take a break. Go to the bathroom. Breathe deeply—*

"That's something I can definitely address." I tapped my cell phone and said, "But let me make a call first. It's kind of an emergency. I'll be back in a minute."

I hustled through the squad room, into the bathroom, and clutched a sink for support. To do this job, I've got to be able to handle witnesses. Without losing it. I took ten slow, deep breaths. Then I turned on the faucet, leaned over the sink, and splashed water on my face for about thirty seconds.

When I returned to the interview room, I eased into a chair and said slowly, trying to sound reassuring, "I'm a very experienced detective. I've been at this a long time. I've dealt with hundreds of witnesses, witnesses who've been in very dangerous situations, situations much more dangerous than yours. I promise you, I'll do everything in my power to keep you safe."

I pulled a card out of my wallet and scribbled a number across the top. "My work phone number is on this card. I just wrote down my cell number. If you ever feel in danger, call me. I promise I'll get back to you immediately. I'll send a unit over or come by myself to take care of you."

She bit her lower lip and stared at me across the metal table, eyes wide. "I'm scared."

"A good man has been killed. He was a retired police officer. He's got a little girl. She's crying herself to sleep every night. She's scared, just like you. And she'll never feel safe until I catch the man who killed her father."

She took a deep breath and exhaled, making a whistling sound. "Okay. It was real dark that night. I was on the street, kind of hesitating about approaching the dealer selling at the corner. That's when I saw these two guys coming down the hill. I couldn't really see the guy who crawled into the driver's side of the car. But I got a better look at the other one. I saw him climb into the car."

"What was he wearing?"

"Jeans and a stocking cap. A dark one."

"What was his nationality?"

"I think he was Mexican."

"Could you ID him if you saw him again?"

"Maybe."

I opened my briefcase, pulled out the six-pack with Abazeda's photo in the bottom right hand corner, and handed it to her. She studied each photo.

"Sorry," she said, shaking her head, "I don't recognize anybody."

I leaned across the table and said softly, "There's something you can do that's important and might help me solve this case. I'd like you to work with an LAPD sketch artist and try to put together a portrait of this guy. Can you do that for me?"

She nodded.

"How about in a few minutes, when we're done talking?"

"I guess so," she said in a weak, little girl voice.

"That could really be a help. Now can you tell me how tall this guy was?"

"I couldn't tell. But he was taller than the driver. And thinner. He was slender."

"Tattoos?"

"I don't remember any."

"Can you describe the car?"

"Not really."

She was cooperating with me. She was answering my questions. Still, I had the feeling that she was holding back on me. But I didn't want to polygraph her and alienate her further.

"What did you see after they got into the car?"

She looked embarrassed. "Nothing. I turned my attention to my... my," she said, struggling for the right word, "my business transaction with the guy on the corner."

"What happened after you bought the drugs?"

"I never bought that night. I got spooked and split. This guy I was with, he kind of persuaded me to go back again on Sunday night. That's when my problems started."

Everything she said was consistent with what the black junkie had told me. I was more determined than ever now to find the Mexican partner.

I drove her to the Piper Technical Center—where the department's Scientific Investigation Division is based—and introduced her to Vicky Ochoa, a civilian sketch artist the department contracts on individual cases. She uses a computer program to help witnesses construct the features that match the suspect's. I told them I would be back later in the morning to pick up a copy of the sketch.

I headed to the Nickel Diner on South Main for a late breakfast, but I had no appetite and just took a few bites of my eggs. I thought of

Martinez, sitting across from Ochoa, working on the sketch. She was probably safe now, but what if I arrested a suspect? I would have to convince Martinez to testify in court. Then she certainly could be at risk. I would relocate her. I would try to protect her. But could I really protect her?

You work homicide because you want to get killers off the street, because you want to protect people. But to do the job right, sometimes you have to gamble with people's lives to save other lives. And when you lose, you have to live with it. For the rest of your life. That's as real as it gets. You have to have the stomach for that kind of brutal calculus. I thought I did. Until Latisha Patton. No wonder so many cops at the divisions transferred out of homicide after a few years.

Pushing my plate away, I shook out three Tylenol and downed them with a swig of coffee. I returned to Piper Tech and thanked Martinez for cooperating and reminded her that she could call me if she was worried about anything. She nodded, lips tightly pursed. After I climbed inside my car, I studied the sketch. It wasn't much to go on, just a drawing of a Mexican in his twenties with a broad forehead and narrow eyes, wearing a dark watch cap.

I sped down to the Harbor Division, gave the sketch to the captain and asked if he could run off a few hundred copies and pass them out to patrol cops and detectives. If the officers could show them to snitches, street sources, hookers, drug dealers, and the inmates in the division's jail, maybe someone could ID the suspect for me.

When I finished, I sped back up to Lancaster, hitting almost a hundred on Interstate 5. When Sandy came to the door, I was surprised that she was carrying a cup of coffee; this was the first time I had seen her without a beer in her hand. I followed her into the breakfast room and sat down. After she poured me a cup of coffee, I pulled a pouch from a flap in my murder book, opened it, and rolled the *netsuke* and *ojime* onto the kitchen table. "Ever seen these before?"

She shook her head. "What are they?"

I explained where I found them and what they represented.

"The only art Pete was familiar with was that picture of the mountains on the side of a Coor's can," she said. "I have no idea what he was doing with those things."

I then told her about the gun I found. "Was it a throw down?"

"Might have been," she said. "But he wasn't involved in any questionable shootings, any cases where there was any doubt that the guy was armed. So I doubt he used it."

"I also found under those tiles about five thousand in cash. Any idea why he had that?"

"No."

There was something about her response that troubled me. Maybe she answered too quickly. Maybe I was just looking for something that wasn't there.

"It just doesn't make sense," I said. "He was so hard up for cash, he couldn't make his child support payments. Why didn't he just grab some of that money? Or why didn't he just sell those Japanese figures? The two of them are probably worth more than ten thousand bucks."

"Maybe he just recently got the cash and those little thingamajigs."

"Think about it for a moment," I said. "You sure you don't have any idea where he might have got all that cash and why he stashed it under a tile?"

"It could have had something to do with the divorce," she said, twirling a cameo ring. "He might not have wanted me to know about it." She sniffled, coughed, and blew her nose. "This has been very hard for me. First I find out some maniac with a gun threatened Pete while my little girl was there. She could have been killed for God's sake. And then you tell me about the little Jap figures, the gun, the money. It's all so crazy. I don't know what to think anymore."

Her eyes welled with tears and she dabbed at them with a Kleenex.

I realized I wasn't going to get much more out of her. I still wanted to have another go at her and press her about the cash. Maybe in a few days. When she stopped wiping her eyes, I apologized for intruding on her, and she walked me to the door.

I drove back downtown and returned to the squad room. After searching art-theft Web sites, I called a few *netsuke* collectors, but I still couldn't trace the provenance of the *netsuke* and *ojime*.

For the next few hours I slogged through the tedious process of examining San Pedro hot prowl reports and pressing the crime lab, unsuccessfully, for fiber and DNA results. I then received the disappointing news on the fingerprints lifted at the scene—negative. No matches.

In the late afternoon, Nicole Haddad called me. My mood was immediately buoyed.

"I need some good news," I said.

"I wish I had some for you," she said. "I checked all the sites, talked to several collectors, and even called the Art Loss Register's New York office. They've got one of the biggest databases of stolen art in the world. Nothing. That *netsuke* and *ojime* might have been smuggled out of Japan. I can't think of any other explanation."

"Well, thanks for trying. I really appreciate you taking the time to help me out on this."

After I hung up, I caught Ortiz's eye and called down, "Let's go downstairs."

I poured two coffees in the break room, and we took the elevator down to the ground floor. As we stood in front of PAB, blowing on our burnt coffee, I told him about the *netsuke*s and *ojimes* and my meeting with Haddad.

"I've never gone out with any woman I've met on an investigation—until the investigation was over. But I'm kind of wavering now."

Ortiz wagged a forefinger at me. "That kind of wavering is gonna get I.A. on your ass. You're not supposed to date someone connected to a case. You know that."

I stared into my coffee. "Yeah, but I'm in bad shape. I'm in such bad shape I was even thinking of hitting on Relovich's ex-wife when I was out there." I extended my arms. "And she's pretty damn hefty."

"You're a pathetic motherfucker. You're single; you're straight; you got a good job; you live in L.A." Ortiz slapped me on the chest. "You're meat on the hoof, prime-grade USDA beef. There're millions of available women out there. Yet you're gonna hit on the one girl who can get you tagged by I.A. Why you have to chase this one? Does she have a gold-plated pussy?"

I thought about her brown eyes with the glittering flecks of green, the jab of her finger on my chest. "I don't know. I just kind of felt a jolt when I was with her."

"That's 'cause you've been holed up in that cave of yours the past year. You'd wanna jump *any* halfway decent-looking woman."

"Maybe."

"My advice is to find someone else. You can't afford another beef with I.A. Wait until the case is cleared before you call her."

When I returned to my desk and spotted Ortiz grabbing his murder book and heading out of the squad room, I reached for the phone and called Nicole. Fuck I.A. and its petty rules and vindictive investigations.

"I appreciate you helping me out on the case," I said.

"You mentioned that."

"I'd like to show my appreciation."

"Yeah?" she said, sounding skeptical.

"You free for dinner tonight?"

"No," she said flatly.

"How about tomorrow?"

"No."

"Sunday?"

"Can't do it."

What a mistake, I thought. A detective hitting on and then badgering a source. If Grazzo heard about this, he'd yank me off the case. Now, I knew, was the time to back off, deftly extricate myself from the situation, and not talk to her again until the case was cleared.

"How about Monday night?" I asked.

"Sorry."

"How about New Year's Eve? That's seven months from now."

She didn't answer. What the fuck is wrong with me? I wondered. I need to inject some discipline back into my life. Before I get fired.

"Wednesday," she said softly.

"What?"

"Why don't we have dinner Wednesday night."

"What time?"

"Seven."

After she gave me directions, I hung up. A few minutes later Dickie Jenkins, the head of security at the Kismet Casino, called. He'd viewed the tape of the high-limit table on the night Pete Relovich was killed. And he never caught a glimpse of Ray Abazeda.

I was on a roll.

CHAPTER 13

As I headed west on the Santa Monica Freeway, I tried to figure out how—or if—Abazeda was connected to the cash and the Japanese figurines stashed under the tiles in Relovich's kitchen. Did they have anything to do with the homicide? Was Relovich dirty when he was a cop, or did he get hold of the cash and the figurines when he began driving for Jane Granger?

I parked in front of Abazeda's house, but his Lexus SUV wasn't in front and no one answered when I rang the bell. I planned to cruise by again in a few hours.

I returned to my car and when I saw the streetlights flick on, I realized it was almost sundown. I was late for Shabbat dinner. I snaked in and out of lanes on Olympic, hung a left on Fairfax, and headed north. The Hollywood Hills were just a faint silhouette, a charcoal sketch in the dying light. I found a parking space around the corner from my mother's duplex and jogged down the street. When she answered the door, she scowled at me.

"Mr. Big Shot Police Detective is so important now he can't even make it to Shabes dinner on time. I invited Uncle Benny and Ariel and they're both very disappointed in you." She muttered a hmpph, spun around, and I followed her to the dining room.

"Good Shabes," said my great uncle Benny, extending a hand. "It's been too long." He fingered the collar of my suit. "Lookin' good, boychik."

"Shabat shalom, Uncle Ash," Ariel said, hugging me.

When I sat down I was relieved to see they had not yet finished dinner.

My father's cousin Mort, Benny, and I were considered the family misfits. Me because I'm a cop. Mort because he was a Republican. Benny because he'd been arrested a few times for bookmaking decades ago and served a month in county jail. Benny eventually joined my father in the *shmatte* business, working as a showroom rep in a ladies' sportswear mart downtown—while occasionally handling football and horse racing bets from the workers in the nearby clothing factories. Benny was eighty-four now, bald, wizened, and bent over like a question mark, but he was still sharp and enjoyed needling me.

"When you going to stop being a schmuck and get a *real* job?" Benny asked.

"When are you going to get a presidential pardon and clear your gambling conviction?"

Benny wagged his fork at me. "Those gonifs in vice—half of 'em are on the take—should be looking for real criminals, instead of wasting their time on people who are just giving the public what it wants." He pointed the fork at Ariel and asked, "You know what the sport of kings is?"

"Basketball?"

"No. Horse racing. I used to make a good business on the ponies," he said wistfully.

My mother, who looked horrified, whispered, "He doesn't need to know about all this."

"About all *what?*" Ariel cried.

"This doesn't concern you," she snapped. She rushed off to the kitchen and returned with half of a baked chicken, a mountain of kugel, and a bowl overflowing with green beans. I cut a piece of challah and salted my plate. I dipped the challah three times in the salt, quickly whispered a prayer over the bread, and took a bite.

"Why such measly portions," I said to my mother with mock outrage. "I'm hungry!"

"You want more, I'll get you more," she said, rising from the table.

"Sit," I said. "I was just kidding."

After dinner, I helped Ariel clear the dishes. My mother brought out coffee and then staggered back, balancing an immense honey cake on a glass platter.

When we finished dessert, I said the prayer before the *Mayim Acha-ronim*—the washing of the fingertips. Washing off any dirt you pick up while eating the meal is a way to show respect for the blessing. After pouring some water into a cup, I dribbled over the *laver*—a ceramic basin—a few drops on the fingertips of both hands. Uncle Benny then said the *Bir Mat Hamazon*—grace after the meal. When Benny finished, he shuffled to the living room, fell onto the sofa, and loosened his belt. "Wonderful meal, as usual, Estelle. Thanks for the invite."

I went to the kitchen, rinsed the dishes, and deposited them in the dishwasher. When I had finished the last one, my mother barged into the kitchen, pulled a plate out of the dishwater and held it up to the light, pointing to a few flecks of gravy around the edges.

"Mom, you're supposed to be relaxing in the living room."

"How can I relax when I see you put a plate like *that* in the dishwasher."

"What's wrong with it."

"It's *dirty*."

"Of course it's dirty. That's why it's in the dishwasher."

"That's how you get bugs," she said, pushing me out of the way.

She flipped on the hot water and began vigorously scrubbing the dish with a sponge. "I'm going to have to redo all of these dishes," she said, dismissing me with a flick of the sponge, a few beads of water hitting me on the chin.

When I returned to the living room, Benny said, "I got three tickets to the Dodger game on Wednesday night. Dugout seats. From one of my old *customers*," he said, winking at me. "Down payment on a long overdue debt. You want to join Ariel and me?"

"Can't make it."

"Why not?"

"Got a date," I said.

"With who?" my mother called out from the kitchen, over the din of the running water and the clatter of dishes.

She marched into the living room, drying her hands on her apron. "What's her name?"

"Nicole."

"Last name?" she asked, narrowing her eyes suspiciously.

"Haddad."

With one hand, she gripped her neck, stricken; with the other, she grabbed a lamp for support. *"Haddad!* Is she an *Arab?"* she asked accusingly.

"Lebanese," I said.

She raised an index finger and said, "Hear that sound? It's your grandparents rolling over in their graves."

"I married a Jewish woman," I said. "That, obviously, didn't work out too well."

"But an *Arab*?" she said, cradling her head in her hands. "Why don't you just take your gun out of your holster and shoot me right now? Because that's what you're doing to me. You're *killing* me."

Ariel jumped out of his chair and stood in front of her, arms extended. He burst into tears. He shouted, sobbing, "Don't shoot Nana!"

I lifted Ariel onto my lap and tousled his hair. "Your grandmother's just playing."

"See what I have to put up with," she said to Benny. "You don't know the half of it."

She turned to me and asked, "Have you lost your marbles?"

"It's just a date."

"You taking her to happy hour at the local mosque?" Benny asked.

"She's not a Muslim. She's Lebanese Christian."

"But she's still an Arab, you schmendrik!" She snorted with disgust. "For God's sake, you're still married."

"Not really."

She crossed her arms and barked, "Are you divorced?"

"Technically, no."

"Then you're still married. Robin's a nice girl from a nice family. Why can't you two work it out?"

"Look," I said impatiently, "the separation wasn't my idea. She's the one who filed for divorce, not me."

"So you're separated. Big deal. That doesn't mean the marriage is over. My friend Dottie Feldman's son was separated for almost two years, but he just got back together with his—"

"It's over!" I shouted.

"Don't you raise your voice to me," she said, turning on her heels and storming back into the kitchen.

"My nephew dating an Arab," Benny muttered. "That's the worst news I've had since off-track betting put me out of business."

Typical night at the Levine house, I thought. Every discussion ends in hysteria. Eager to flee, I walked into the kitchen to say goodbye to my mother.

She flipped off the water, turned toward me, and said, "The only reason I'm so upset about all this is because I want you to be happy. I'm only thinking of you."

"You're only thinking of *yourself*," I snapped.

She angrily slammed the dishwasher shut. "That's entirely untrue."

"You want me to get back with Robin so you can have more grand-children. Having only one puts you low woman on the totem pole at your Hadassah chapter."

"How could you say such a thing," she said, looking hurt. She lightly touched my forearm and said, "Your father, as you know, had a very hard life. But you know what made him happy?"

I shrugged.

"You and Marty made him happy. You two were his whole life. He felt that raising you two boys made everything he went through worth-while."

"He said that?" I asked, my voice catching.

"Yes he did."

"I felt like I was a disappointment to him."

"How?"

"When I enlisted in the army. When I joined the LAPD. He was so angry."

"Yes, he was angry. That's because he was worried about you. Yes, he envisioned something else for you. But he never stopped being proud of you."

"I never got that sense."

"Well, he *was* proud of you. He didn't agree with some of your choices, but he respected you."

I felt myself getting choked up. Grabbing a sponge from the drain, I dabbed at the edge of the sink. "He said that?"

"Yes, he did. He respected your dedication to what you believed in. And so do I."

"I appreciate you saying that. And I appreciate your concern, Mom. But I'm old enough to make my own decisions. So please, no more advice on my personal life, okay?"

"I'll try."

I took her arm and led her toward the dining room. "Will you promise?"

"I promise I won't give you any more advice on your social life. Unless, that is, I think it's extremely important."

I laughed. "Now we're back where we started."

I shook hands with Benny and said, "Next time you get Dodger tickets, I'll join you and Ariel."

Benny gripped my bicep. "Listen to me. Don't be a schmuck. Stick with your own kind."

I tousled Ariel's hair and said, "See you Sunday?"

"Can't. Mama's taking me to a birthday party. But *next* Sunday will you teach me to surf?"

"I don't know if you're ready for surfing. But we'll do something fun at the beach."

I turned to my mother and said, "Thanks for dinner."

She walked over, stood on tiptoes, and kissed me on the cheek.

As I opened the front door, my cell phone rang.

"He came after me!" a woman shouted hysterically. "He beat me up. I had to protect myself. I think I killed him."

"Who is this?"

"Jane Granger."

"You okay?"

"I think so."

"I'll be right there."

CHAPTER 14

Reaching under my police radio, I flicked on my lights and siren and sped to Redondo Beach. I skidded to a stop in front of Granger's complex, ran up the stairs to her apartment, and banged on the door. She flung it open, and I followed her into the living room.

Abazeda was slumped on the sofa. He had a nasty purple bruise above his right eyebrow, and streaks of blood ran down the side of his face. Granger, who was holding a .32-caliber semiautomatic by her side, began to pace. "This cocksucker comes barging into my place and starts slapping me around—"

"That cunt coldcocked me with the butt of her pistol," Abazeda shouted. "I never laid a finger on her."

For the next thirty seconds, both shouted at the same time, so loudly I couldn't make out what either of them was saying.

I slammed my hand on a wall. "Shut the fuck up! Both of you!"

I pointed to a little patio with a sliding glass door across from the kitchen. "Go out there," I said to Granger, "and wait until I'm through talking to him."

"In my own apartment I'm entitled—"

"Go!"

"But—"

"Now!"

She flipped Abazeda off and trudged off to the patio.

I pulled up a chair next to him. "What're you doing here?"

He gingerly tapped his eyebrow with a pinkie. "I just came here to ask the bitch why she sent you after me."

"How do you know it was her?"

"Who else?"

"I've talked to a lot of people connected to this case."

"Why're you wasting your time talking to me when—"

"I'm asking the questions here."

"I'm not sure I want to answer them."

"You can answer them here or at the station."

He lightly touched the bruise over his eyebrow with a fingertip and grimaced. "Go ahead."

"You told me you spent last Thursday night—the night Pete Relovich was killed—playing Texas Hold'em at the Kismet Casino's high-limit table."

"That's right."

"You're a lying sack of shit. I just talked to the head of security there. He studied every player at the high-limit table, and he didn't see you."

He started at me with that disquieting popeyed expressed for a moment. Then he laughed. "You probably gave this security fellow my picture and he tried to identify me, right?"

"That's right."

"Have him try again."

"Give me a reason."

"I'm a damn good poker player. Sometimes too good. People at the L.A. card clubs are big gabbers. A few have spread the word and told some marks, 'If you see a bald guy who looks kind of like a towel head, don't play with him.' So I pull a little switch. At all the other clubs, I play like this," he said, rubbing his shiny pate. "But occasionally I play at the Kismet Casino, and when I do, I always wear a black toupee. That's why some of the insiders, the money players, call me 'Toupee Ray.' A few of the marks figure it out; but a lot don't. So tell your security guy to check the tape again and look for me—but with hair. I think he'll spot me."

I hoped he was bullshitting me, because he was the best suspect I had. "You better be right. Because if you're not, I'm coming over to your place and hooking you up."

"Am I free to leave?"

"Yeah. Get out of here. But I'm putting you on notice that there's now a record of you busting in here. If anything should happen to her, you'll be my number one suspect. So stay away from this place."

When he left, I motioned for Granger, who was staring at me through the sliding glass door, to come in. She quickly crossed the room and threw her arms around me. "Thanks for coming right over. I'm very afraid of that man."

As she ran a fingernail down my back, I felt a stir of interest. My hands lingered around her waist for a moment, then I pushed her away. *Am I out of my mind? What the fuck am I doing?*

"When you called me, you claimed he was slapping you around."

"He was."

I tapped her cheeks with my index fingers. "There's not a single mark on your face."

She gave me a half-smile. "I heal fast."

"I can see that," I said skeptically.

"Let me think of a way to thank you for coming all the way over here. While I'm thinking, how about a drink?"

I shook my head.

She took a step toward me.

Holding up my palms, I took a quick step back, hurried out the door and to my car.

When I returned to my loft, I called Dickie Jenkins at the Kismet Casino and asked him if he would view the video of the high-limit table again. But this time instead of searching for my guy with a bald head, I asked him to find the same guy—but with a hairpiece.

Jenkins didn't sound too happy about it, but he agreed to do a quick search.

An hour later he called back.

"I found this character with the beaver pelt. Actually it's a damn good piece. I never would have known it was a piece if you hadn't tipped me off. He arrived shortly before eight and I fast-forwarded and he didn't split until about two in the morning."

"I wish you'd have told me that before. Would've saved me a lot of time."

At my desk on Saturday morning, I realized that I was stumped. When I'm at a dead end, I often like to review a case away from the squad room, a conventional place that fosters conventional thinking. Sometimes I like to ponder the whys and wherefores of a homicide in a setting where I can let my mind wander.

I walked out of the PAB, down First Street and entered the Kyoto Grand Hotel, a drab white tower in the heart of Little Tokyo. Crossing the lobby filled with Japanese businessmen and tourists, I took the elevator to the third floor. Above the bustle of downtown, with Bunker Hill's skyscrapers looming in the distance, the hotel featured a traditional half-acre Japanese strolling garden. In the center was a six-foot waterfall flowing into a reflecting pool filled with darting koi, surrounded by blooming red and white azaleas, pink hydrangeas, and trellises laced with bugle vines. The hotel called the spot "the garden in the sky" and claimed it was designed to incorporate seven principals of Zen: spirituality, asymmetry, austerity, subtlety, simplicity, naturalness, and calmness. When I first began visiting the spot to get a respite from the squad room, I'd decided that the best way to solve a homicide was to clear my mind and incorporate those seven principals.

After wandering through the deserted garden for a few minutes, I grabbed a chair and set it down at the edge of the pond, beside a patch of grass that was as satiny as a putting green. Listening to the splash of the waterfall and the wind rustling the leaves of a sycamore, I felt a world away from downtown.

I spread the murder book on my lap and studied the crime scene photographs and diagram, the statements from neighbors, my autopsy notes, and the preliminary investigation report written by the Harbor Division officers. But after an hour of sifting through the murder book, I realized I was no closer to finding Pete Relovich's killer than when I had picked up the case the week before.

On Sunday, I returned to San Pedro, walked through Relovich's house again, traversed the backyard, and wandered down the hill and back up again. By Sunday night, I was afraid that I had picked up the case too late. I wished Duffy had contacted me the night of the murder, not twenty-four hours later.

When I walked to work on Monday, it was warm and clear, a late May morning with a warm breeze from the east and a hint of summer in the air. I could smell the oil stains on the street baking in the sun.

As I entered the squad room door, Ortiz, who liked to parrot the stock Hollywood detective clichés, called out, "Who's the perp? Is an arrest imminent?"

I ignored him, and as I sat down at my desk, my phone rang.

"Detective Levine, it's Walt Jenkins from SID serology."

"What do you have for me?"

"We got a hit," Jenkins said.

"Don't leave me hanging."

"The DNA results just came back. You got the hit on the Kleenex."

"From the bathroom wastebasket?"

"Yeah. The snot gave us the sample. We got a match in the database. His name is Terrell Fuqua."

CHAPTER 15

I hung up the phone, clenched my fist, and said to myself, "*Yes!*"

Duffy walked by and I called out, "We got a cold hit!"

"On Relovich?"

"Yeah."

Duffy clapped his hands once. Then he walked over to my desk and said, "You're a marvel, Ash my lad. I never had a doubt you'd put this one together. I just didn't think you'd do it so quickly." He pulled up a chair in front me. "What'd you get the hit on?"

"The Kleenex."

"Amazing."

"Not really. Next to blood, mucus has about the highest concentration of DNA."

Ortiz, who overheard the exchange, called out, "The Case of the Golden Booger."

"Who's your guy?" Duffy asked.

"Terrell Fuqua."

"Sounds like an interior decorator from West Hollywood," Ortiz said.

Duffy waved him off. "What do we know about Fuqua?"

"At this point, nothing," I said.

"Let's jack his ass up by the end of the day and we can make the five o'clock news."

"I've got to track him down first."

I slid my chair over to a computer and called up the system we called Cheers because of its acronym—CCHRS (Consolidated Criminal History Reporting System). I printed out Fuqua's rap sheet—listing all his arrests in Los Angeles County—which was an impressive nine pages. Next, I clicked onto the CII—the Criminal Index Information—which detailed Fuqua's convictions and prison sentences. Then I checked

CAL/GANG, a state-wide computerized gang file for law enforcement agencies to determine Fuqua's street name—C-Dawg—and the set he ran with—the Back Hood Bloods.

After about twenty minutes, I had compiled a fairly comprehensive criminal biography for my suspect. Terrell Fuqua was a thirty-four-year-old ex-con who was one of the founding members of his South Central gang. He had been arrested numerous times by Southeast Division cops for narcotic sales, car theft, burglary, rape, selling stolen property, but he beat most of the charges because it appeared that witnesses had been intimidated into backing down, or his gang associates were willing to take the rap for him. He had been convicted of only two felonies: once for attempted burglary and once for robbery when he stuck up a liquor store and made off with $900.

During the attempted burglary, patrol officers had caught him trying to climb inside a window after a neighbor called 911. He spent a year in county jail.

And there was no way for him to wriggle out of the robbery because a detective recovered from Fuqua's house a bottle of Tequila and a carton of cigarettes stolen from the liquor store, as well as a ski mask used during the heist. He spent five years at Folsom.

I called R & I—the Records and Identification Unit—and asked for all of Fuqua's arrest reports. After I took the elevator down to the first floor and picked up the files, I started reading the copies while walking back to the elevator, bumping into a commander, who flashed me a withering look. For the next hour I perused the files and gleaned several facts that quickened my pulse: Fuqua had once been arrested on a South Central street corner carrying a .40-caliber semiautomatic pistol—the same type of gun that killed Relovich. And Fuqua's robbery arrest five years ago was even more interesting. The liquor store was in San Pedro, which established his familiarity with Relovich's neighborhood. And the detective on the Harbor Division robbery table who put together the case against Fuqua was—Pete Relovich.

This confirmed what I had believed all along: Relovich knew his killer. Although it seemed unlikely that Relovich would let a dirtbag like Fuqua into his house, maybe there was an explanation. I just couldn't fathom what it was.

Fuqua had an obvious motive—revenge—because although he had

an extensive criminal history, Relovich had been the only detective to put together a good enough case to send him to state prison. But I knew that sometimes an obvious motive was a red herring.

I called a state parole office in Sacramento and picked up the name and phone number of Fuqua's parole officer. He provided me with his charge's South Central address. I then contacted the Southeast Division captain and arranged for two uniforms to back me up when I jammed Fuqua. I headed down the Harbor Freeway, with Duffy in the front seat and Ortiz—whose partner just left for vacation—in back. We pulled off at Florence and met the two patrol officers in the station's roll call room. I showed them a booking photo of Fuqua. Duffy worked out the logistics, telling the uniforms to storm the front door, while Ortiz and I guarded the back. Duffy said he would monitor the bust from the sidewalk.

We drove out of the station lot and parked a half block from Fuqua's house. Ortiz and I slipped on our Kevlar vests and blue LAPD windbreakers and followed the officers. The street was barren, without a single tree or bush, lined with slum apartments and ramshackle bungalows with splintered porches. Sandwiched between a front house, which was encircled by a dry patchy lawn, and an alley, Fuqua lived in small gray guest cottage with two stained mattresses stacked against the side.

While the uniformed officers pounded on the door, I kept my hand over my .45. In the distance, I could hear an out of sync rooster crowing. The officers continued to knock, but no one came to the door. I peeked in a back window. The apartment was vacant. Ortiz and I circled around to the sidewalk. I thanked the officers, who had missed lunch and were glad to leave, and motioned to Duffy. We walked to the house in front and rang the doorbell.

An elderly black man wearing faded denim overalls opened the door. He looked us up and down and glared with an expression of contempt. "Yeah?"

"We're LAPD detectives and we're looking for a former tenant of yours, Terrell Fuqua," I said.

"Do you have a warrant for *this* house?"

"No."

"Am *I* under arrest?"

I shook my head.

"Then I ain't talking to no damn detective." He slammed the door.

I rang the doorbell again.

The man angrily swung open the door. "What part of *no* don't you understand, Mr. *LAPD*," he said, spitting out the letters.

"I assume you rent that back house out," I said.

The man stared at me without expression.

"My guess is that it's not up to code. I'm sure if I notified city building and safety, an inspector could find a dozen violations and shut that rental down. It may be years before you could get a tenant in there again."

The man slumped his shoulders and wearily opened the door. While Ortiz, Duffy, and I squeezed onto a sofa, the man carried a wooden chair from the kitchen and sat down across from us. "What you want to know?"

I showed him Fuqua's booking photo. "Do you know this man?"

"Yeah. That Terrell. He lived out back."

"When did he move in?"

"When he got outta the penitentiary. 'Bout six months ago."

"Weren't you reluctant to rent to a guy who just got out of prison?" I asked.

"Naw. I tell him, 'Don't you bring that trouble around here.' He didn't. And he pay his rent on time."

"When did he move?"

"Few weeks ago. I got a new tenant moving in on Monday."

"Where'd he move to?"

"Don't know. One day he say he got a new lady, and next day he out."

"Where are they forwarding his mail?"

"He ain't never got no mail."

"Anybody around here might know where he moved?"

"He stay to himself. I don't pay no mind to where he go and with who. As long as he pay his rent on time."

I gave the man my card and asked him to call Felony Special if he heard anything about Fuqua. Driving back downtown, I told Duffy, "Interesting that he moved a month ago."

"That's right before Relovich was popped," Duffy said. "Probably figured he'd do the job and then disappear."

"Any guesses where he is?" Ortiz said.

"Fuqua," I said, swirling my index finger, "is in the wind."

I returned to R & I and picked up all of Fuqua's 510s—LAPD forms that we fill out after the arrest report, and include personal information such as the addresses and phone numbers of relatives, girlfriends, and ex-spouses, and other random data. I discovered that Fuqua's mother and four sisters lived in South Central. A brother lived in San Pedro, which would explain why Fuqua pulled the burglary there. I figured that if I door-knocked the family, they would warn Fuqua and he would be even harder to find.

Back at my desk, I called the state Department of Motor Vehicles office and asked for the date of birth for Fuqua's mother and sisters. One of Fuqua's sisters would be celebrating a birthday on Friday. Now I had the opportunity to try an approach that had worked a few times for me in the past. On Friday afternoon I would stake out the sister's house. If she had a birthday party, and if Fuqua showed up, I would be there in the shadows, waiting.

In the meantime, I had plenty of work to keep me busy. And if I was lucky, maybe I could even pick up Fuqua before Friday.

I slipped Fuqua's booking photo into a six-pack, grabbed my murder book, and drove up Interstate 5 to the Pitchess Detention Center. I decided to see if the skinny junkie who I had interviewed at the Pacific Division station after the drug sweep could identify Fuqua. The junkie had described the man climbing into passenger's side of the car at the end of the bloodhound's trail as a tall, skinny Mexican and the other as shorter and stocky. Fuqua was listed as five foot ten and two hundred twenty pounds, so he fit the description of the driver. I decided that there was no point in showing Fuqua's picture to Theresa Martinez because she said she didn't get a look at the driver.

Pitchess is a sprawling jail complex set in the parched Castaic foothills about twenty miles north of downtown. I passed through the gates, deposited my Beretta in the metal locker, and waited in an interview room. A few minutes later, deputies brought out the junkie. The last time I had talked to him, he was extremely jittery, nervously tapping his feet, and picking at his nails. Now, wearing loose fitting jail blues, he walked across the room so slowly and sat down so deliberately he looked as if he were moving underwater. After deputies uncuffed him, I slid the six-pack across the table and asked if he could pick out one of the suspects. He carefully studied each picture.

"Now if I pick out someone, will you give me a Get Out Of Jail Free Card?" he asked, smiling slyly.

"Doesn't work that way. I can talk to the DA, but I need you to be *sure*. If you can't identify anyone, don't worry about it. I won't forget you. They'll be other six-packs to check out. This isn't your last chance."

The man, again, studied each picture. He slid the six-pack back across the table. "Dang! I wish I could, but I can't. Don't know *any* of them dudes. I don't even know if the guy I saw was a brutha. It was too damn dark."

I returned to the office and spent the rest of the day studying Fuqua's file. First I tried to determine if Fuqua had ever been arrested with a Hispanic so I could show the junkie witness the suspect's picture. But I had no luck. Then I searched through the computer for all the information gleaned from field interview cards, which listed everyone at a crime scene, from witnesses to neighbors to suspects. Still no Hispanics were identified at Fuqua's arrest.

After I made fifty laser copies of Fuqua's photo, I drove over to the Southeast station and passed them out during the p.m. shift roll call. "Anybody who finds Fuqua," I announced, "gets a case of beer of their choice."

When I was done, an old-timer in the gang unit, a black sergeant named Chester Pinson, said he wanted to talk. I followed him to his desk and he pulled up a chair for me.

"I've been keeping tabs on Fuqua since he was a fourteen-year-old pooh butt. As you know, he did a nickel at Folsom a while ago. Since then, a whole new generation of gangsters have hit the streets. But I remember him pretty well when he was coming up."

"What do you remember about him?" I asked.

"He's one cold motherfucker. When C-Dawg's moving down the street, everyone takes a step back."

"What's the C for?"

"Capone. The number one gangster."

"Was he?"

"Well, he dropped eight people before he was eighteen. Who knows what the tally is now."

"Who was he killing?"

"Mostly rival gangsters."

"Ever get close to popping him for murder?"

"Naw," he said, disgusted. "Those gang-on-gang hits are tough to put together." Pinson grabbed a pencil off his desk and slapped it on his palm. "All those stupid fucking movies with the serial killers knocking off one vic after another in crazy-ass ways, taunting detectives, sending them cute little notes. You and I both know that's bullshit. You get one of them dudes every decade—maybe. Now C-Dawg is your *real-life* version of a serial killer."

"I got some information that Fuqua might have been working with a Hispanic guy. That sound right to you?"

"I don't know. He just did a stretch at Folsom. The blacks and Mexicans are at *war* there. They fucking hate each other. If I know Fuqua, he cliqued up there right away. At Folsom, if a black hangs with a Mexican, he'll get a shiv in the liver. From his own peeps. So he might be kind of hesitant, as soon as he's kicked loose, to partner up with a cholo. You might see a black and a Mexican gangbanger capering in a place like Oakwood, where everyone's on top of each other. But it's a little unusual for South Central."

"You said it's unusual. I take that to mean it's possible that Fuqua was working with a Mexican dude."

"It's possible."

"You know that Relovich was the only detective who ever put together a good enough case to send Fuqua to the joint?"

Pinson nodded.

"You think that could be enough of a motive for Fuqua to gun Pete down?"

Pinson pushed his chair away from his desk and crossed his legs. "Could be, but I wanted to tell you something else. When I heard you found Fuqua's DNA at the scene, I wanted to fill you in. Pete's ex-partner is an old-timer name of Sam Doukas. When Sam was promoted to D-III, he got transferred over here to Southeast, so him and Pete had to split up. I got to know Sam, and he talked about Pete some. And he told me a story that I wanted to pass on to you. After Pete nailed down that robbery case against Fuqua that landed him in Folsom, him and Sam went over to Fuqua's place to hook him up. Fuqua was with some of his homeboys and he was putting a good show on for them, mother-fucking Pete and Sam this way and that. He told them that if they didn't have their badges and guns, he'd kick both their asses."

Pinson chuckled. "So Pete handed his badge and gun to Sam and told him and the homeboys to wait outside. While they were outside they heard some whacks and some thwacks and some furniture breaking. Three minutes later, Pete had Fuqua—who was out cold—over his shoulder and tossed him into the backseat of the squad car. He knocked the black right outta that boy."

"That's hard-core," I said.

"Pete fought Golden Gloves when he was a kid. At the California Police Olympics, he was the light heavyweight champ."

"How come you didn't tell me about this when I picked up the case?"

Pinson held out his hands. "I've been on vacation. Just got back this morning and heard about Pete."

"I'd like to talk to Doukas."

"You can't—he died of a stroke last year. Two months after he retired."

"So what do you think?"

"Fuqua claimed that Pete cold-cocked him when he wasn't looking. But nobody believed that—not even Fuqua's homies. As you know, on the streets, rep is everything. And Fuqua's rep took a hard fall. So he lost a lot because of Pete. He lost his rep and he lost five years. Maybe during that stretch in Folsom Fuqua stewed and stewed, and decided that when he got out, he'd put getting even with Pete at the top of his to-do list."

CHAPTER 16

On Wednesday evening, I pulled off Washington Boulevard, drove through a confusing labyrinth of streets, parked, and walked to Nicole Haddad's house, which fronted one of the Venice canals. I was surprised how the area had changed.

When I was working patrol in the Pacific Division, the canals were filthy, with a sheen of scum on the surface and garbage littering the banks. Now they had been immaculately restored, and some of the small, ramshackle homes and vacant weed-choked lots had been replaced with two- and three-story villas. I had heard about the changes and now was relieved to see that they had not entirely destroyed the area's idiosyncratic charm. Invisible from the major thoroughfares and accessible to only a handful of cars because of its narrow streets, the canals remained an anomalous L.A. island, cut off from the homogenous sprawl.

Unfortunately, the Italian-style resort, built in the early 1900s on marshland, was doomed—like so many city landmarks—because of Southern California's slavish obeisance to the automobile. In the 1920s, when people began driving to the beach instead of commuting by trolley, city officials decided that Venice needed more roads and parking spaces. They ordered the inland lagoon filled in, converted it into a traffic circle, and paved over most of the canals. Soon, the remaining canals fell into disrepair. Later in the century, when land values in Venice and nearby Santa Monica skyrocketed, the scruffy neighborhood was rediscovered and gentrified.

I lingered for a moment by Nicole's front gate. She lived in one of the original homes, a white clapboard beach bungalow with faded green trim and a weathered front porch made of rough-hewn redwood. Out front was a small dock with a rowboat tied to a post. Feathery cattails banked the fence that encircled the property. The tufts of star jasmine on the patio filled the air with an intensely sweet fragrance.

When Nicole peered through the blinds and saw me on the patio, she opened the front door. I could barely see her face because the living room was so dark; only the ruby studs in her ears were clearly visible, and they flickered like flames against her olive skin.

"How about a cruise?" I asked, jerking my chin toward the boat. "When I used to patrol this area, I always wanted to ride in the canals."

"Sure," Nicole said, walking to the edge of the dock. She wore black leather pants and a red 1940s jacket, cinched at the waist, with large black buttons.

We climbed in and I rowed down a canal, under an arched Venetian-style wooden bridge. I winced slightly because my shoulders were still sore from surfing.

"Sorry I don't have a motorboat for you," she said, a mocking gleam in her eyes.

"I think I can handle it. I went surfing a few days ago. First time in a long time. I'm out of shape."

"A surfing cop?" she said. "Two diametrically opposed cultures."

I set the oars in their hooks, leaned back, and watched the boat glide under another bridge. A soft, salty breeze blew from the sea, and the only sounds I could hear were the occasional quack of a duck and the tinkle of wind chimes. The faded blue sky was soon daubed with gold and tangerine, the rippled water reflecting the sunset. I closed my eyes for a moment, feeling the tension beginning to ease a bit from my knotted up neck and shoulders.

"You know why the sunsets are so great in L.A.?" she asked.

"The smog."

"Right. It's interesting when you examine Southern California landscape paintings from seventy-five years ago and compare them to more current works. The sunsets in the older paintings were more subdued than the sunsets in the current ones. That's because as the smog worsened and the chemicals coalesced on the horizons, landscape artists began replicating those colorful, sulfuric sunsets."

"Art imitating smog?"

Nicole laughed. "Something like that."

I resumed rowing and said, "It's amazing they haven't paved this area over, like so much of L.A."

"Where do you live?"

"In a loft downtown."

"Oh, the forbidding Downtownistan. I've lived in L.A. fifteen years and I don't think I've been downtown more than a couple of times. Let's go to *your* 'hood for dinner. Give me the downtown tour. Maybe L.A. will finally make sense to me."

When I opened the Saturn's passenger door, she said, "A station wagon in a hybrid world. I haven't been in one of these since I was in the fourth grade."

I returned to the Santa Monica Freeway, drove back downtown, and parked at Union Station. We walked to Olvera Street, a faux Mexican *mercado* lined with nineteenth-century brick and adobe buildings and filled with stalls where merchants hawked sombreros, serapes, leather wallets, small guitars, and other cheesy souvenirs. She followed me to a stall filled with the statues of Aztec warriors. A few feet away, a small section of the street was laid out in a zigzag pattern of brick and stone.

I tapped my foot on the pattern and said, "This is why L.A.'s such a mess." I led her to La Golondrina, housed in a two-story brick building built in the mid-1800s, the first Mexican restaurant in L.A. We sat in a street-side patio and watched the German and Japanese tourists shuffle by. The waitress brought us the beer, corn tortillas, and nopales salad I had ordered.

I gazed intently at her, dazzled by how the flecks of green in her dark eyes glittered under the lights.

She waved both palms in front of my face and laughed. "Didn't your mother ever tell you it's not polite to stare."

"She warned me about everything else—at least fifty times. I think that was the only admonition she ever forgot."

I filled my tortilla with the nopales. When she gazed at it skeptically, I said, "Nopales is cactus. They marinate it and slice it up. It's the chopped liver of Mexico."

She laughed, covering her mouth with her napkin.

Since she said she couldn't figure out the city, I decided to give her my why-L.A.-is-so-fucked-up-rap. I told her how the zigzag pattern I just showed her is where a section of the *zanja madre*—the mother ditch—brought water to the first settlers from the L.A. River about a half mile away; and the river is why the city was established here; but the river was eventually paved over to control the flooding and now is just a cement channel with a thin trickle of water most of the year. I told her how you could have an office on the top floor of a downtown office building and not even see a patch of water no matter what direction you looked; how the architect who designed the new cathedral downtown said the grand cathedrals in Europe were all built beside rivers and the best equivalent he could come up with in L.A. was the traffic-choked 101 Freeway; how the city has no real reason for existing because downtown is landlocked, the harbor more than twenty miles to the south and the ocean fifteen miles to the west.

We finished the nopales, and as we walked back to my car, I said, "My dad worked downtown for thirty-five years. He used to take me with him sometimes in the summer and show me the different buildings. When I was a kid, I thought about being an architect."

"But you ended up as a homicide detective. Isn't that a depressing gig?"

"Whenever I get called out on a case, I think about a quote from Ecclesiastics that I still remember from Hebrew school: *It is better to go to a house of mourning than to go to a house of feasting, for death is the destiny of every man; the living should take this to heart.*"

She gave me a quizzical look.

"Everyone knows they're not guaranteed tomorrow, but we all get so wrapped up in the daily drivel it's easy to forget it," I said. "But when you see a body out on the pavement, with the blood dripping into the gutter, well, that has a way of bringing it home to you. I feel sorry for people who are so insulated from death."

"So when a body is—"

"I'd rather talk about L.A. history."

"I'd rather eat."

"What kind of food do you want?"

"Don't cops know the best spots? How about a cop place?"

"Okay. But there's no turning back."

I drove south, through a canyon of office towers, to the edge of downtown, hung a left, past a string of fashion district sweatshops and warehouses—the walls covered with savage graffiti, the tops bristling with razor wire—and stopped in front of a vacant lot overgrown with wild fennel, the breeze scented with the smell of licorice. A lunch wagon was parked across the lot, next to a liquor store, its windows opaque with soot.

"You wanted Mexican and you wanted a cop hangout," I said. "This is both. It's a roach coach, but they make the best tacos in the city."

"I've been wined and dined at the finest restaurants in Santa Monica and West Hollywood," she said, surveying the gritty landscape. "But none of them has the ambiance to compare to this place."

I bought two cans of Tecate from the liquor store, slipped them into brown paper bags, and handed her one. We walked to the lunch wagon and waited behind a dozen Hispanic people in line. Ranchera music blared from inside the lunch wagon, and the smell of sizzling beef and cilantro filled the air. I had to kick several mangy dogs that tried to sniff Nicole's pants. A woman behind the grill cranked out freshly made corn tortillas with a small hand roller.

When we reached the front of the line, I ordered, in Spanish, four tacos. I slipped in some cilantro and a few sliced radishes and sprinkled on peppery salsa thick with chopped chilies. We returned to my car and munched on the tacos, leaning against the trunk and hunched forward so the juice did not spill on our pants. We washed the tacos down with slugs of beer. I asked her if she liked the first taco I gave her. She nodded, her mouth full. I told her it was a *sesos*—cow brain—taco. She took a long, theatrical pull of her beer.

I drove over to 4th and Main and parked in a lot. We walked past a menacing-looking wino, shouting and swearing at a shopping cart, and into a restaurant located on the ground floor of a turn-of-the-century building that was once a cigar store, but had recently been renovated. We sat in the bar, ordered beers. I glanced at Nicole and watched her move her head to the sound of the jazz quartet, her eyes half-closed, her tongue peeking through her lips. I realized that tonight, for the first time in a long while, I didn't have a lingering headache, a knot in the pit of my stomach, a tightness in my chest.

She asked me about growing up in L.A., and then told me she was born and raised in Detroit, but moved to Venice to attend grad school at UCLA.

"Both parents Lebanese?" I asked.

She shook her head. "My mom's French."

"Both parents Jewish?" she asked in a challenging tone.

"Very."

"You don't seem too religious."

"I'm not. I'm Jewish culturally, I guess you'd say. The thing that ties me to Judaism, more than anything else, is the Holocaust. That, unfortunately, kind of shaped my Jewish identity. So I don't go to synagogue much and my relationship to God is pretty tenuous. The Holocaust made a lot of Jews skeptics. I figure, if there was a God, what good was He?"

"You sound like a Jewish agnostic."

"I wouldn't say that. There's some symbolism in the Kabala that suggests that God, like the Jews themselves, is in exile. That captures where I'm at. How about you?"

"A Lebanese-French atheist. You ever been to the Middle East?"

"Yeah—Israel."

"What do you think about what the Israeli army did to Lebanon in '06?"

"Let's discuss it another time. That's a topic that could ruin our evening." I decided not to tell her about my army patrols on the Lebanese border. "Any priors?"

She laughed. "One. He was another grad student. But the marriage didn't last long. You?"

"One. Five years. Then she walked. But I always thought we'd eventually get back together."

"Why'd she walk?"

"Irreconcilable differences, as they say in divorce court."

"So was there another woman who alientated your affection, as they also say in divorce court?"

"Yeah, but it's more complicated than that."

"It usually is."

"Let's blow this place. You ready to go home?"

"I'd like to see your building. Finish off the architectural tour."

I downed the rest of my beer in a few long gulps, stalling for time. I knew that, because of department regulations, I shouldn't have asked her out; when she said no, I knew I shouldn't have pressed her; and now, I knew I shouldn't take her back to my place. A date was just an LAPD rules infraction; an affair would be something more. But I had a buzz from the beer, and she was looking damn good.

I pulled out of the lot, parked behind my building, walked around to the front, and punched my code in the keypad. We walked through the lobby, with its stamped tin ceiling, and entered the elevator, paneled in burnished mahogany. We rode to the top floor in silence. When we were inside the loft, Nicole stopped, and looked around. "I like the space. But you're not much of a decorator. I'd call it Monk Modern. We need to get you some art on the walls."

I flipped on the CD player and skipped past "So What" to the second cut—the bouncy, bluesy "Freddie Freeloader." I grabbed beers from the refrigerator, and joined her on the sofa.

"The CD collection," she said. "The window to the soul. What's playing on the box? I like the sound?"

"It's a Miles Davis album. I play it over and over. Whatever mood I'm in, there's a cut on it for me."

"And what kind of mood are you in now?" she asked, sipping her beer, but keeping her eyes on me.

"I used to be in a 'So What' mood. Tonight I'm in a 'Freddie Free-loader' kind of mood."

"This a very old CD?"

"The album was recorded before we were born."

"What's the name?"

"*Kind of Blue.*"

"Good title for a cop like you."

She closed her eyes and listened to the interplay between horns, piano, and drums. She opened her eyes when she heard the next cut. "What's the name of this one?"

"Let me tell you a story about it. When I was a boot, my training officer and I were talking about music. He was an old salt who liked Tony Bennett and people like that. I figured he could relate to Miles. So I told him about this cut, "Blue in Green," and how much I liked it. He told me that's because it was the story of a young cop like me who didn't know shit, only the words were twisted around. He said they should have called it, "Green in Blue."

"So you're really into jazz."

"No. I'm really into 'Kind of Blue.' Most jazz today is too crazy for me. Space music. I like the straight-ahead sound. Not much of that around today."

She walked over to the window and pointed to the crumbling St.

Vibiana's Cathedral, the cream-colored cupola catching the moonlight. "Pretty," she said.

I walked up behind her, clasped my hands around her waist, and kissed her neck. She sighed and turned around. We kissed, standing by the window, for several minutes. She pulled away, looked into my eyes for a moment, then took my hand and led me across the room to the bed. She pulled my shirt over my head, kissing my neck, licking my nipples, running her forefinger along the jagged shrapnel wound beneath my ribs.

"I'll bet there's a story to explain the scar."

"Actually a short one. About a hundredth of a second." I lightly touched her cheek and said, "I'm not really ready for this tonight. I don't have any protection here."

She walked across the room, opened her purse, and tossed me a Trojan like she was flipping a Frisbee, the metal packet sweeping across the loft in a long, slow ellipsis. I stood there, frozen, as the Trojan seemed to hang in the air forever. Finally, I reached up and snatched it.

When she walked back to me, I began to unbutton her jacket, but she turned around and flicked off the lights. Then she kicked off her shoes, slipped off her leather pants, tossed her jacket on a chair, and unhooked and dropped her bra on the floor. It was dark, but she was back-lit by a faint nimbus of moonlight shining through the window, and I could see her silhouette: slender, high-breasted, her metal navel pierce shimmering when she turned toward me. After she slipped her arms around my back and kissed me again, I guided her down to the bed, but she resisted.

"I want you to do something for me," she whispered.

"Yeah."

"Hurt me."

I took a step back. "I'm not into that."

"No big thing."

"It is to me."

She ran her finger down my chest. "I *want* you to."

"No."

She reached back and slapped me across the face.

"What the hell is wrong with you?" I shouted.

"I told you what I want."

I shook my head.

Then she slapped me again, so hard that blood began to bead at the corner of my mouth.

My face burned. I grabbed her shoulder so hard that she fell to her knees. Her eyes were shiny with a wild look of abandon and defiance. She leaned over, licked the blood off my lips, and kissed me, probing deeply with her tongue.

I pinned her wrists to the corners and held her legs down with my knees.

"I want you to —"

"Shut the fuck up."

She wriggled her legs free and wrapped them around my waist. As she pulled me toward her, I could see the reddish outline of my palm print on her shoulder.

The bedspread and sheets were twisted on the floor. The mattress was half off the box springs. She wiped my brow with her fingertips, daubed the moisture on her lips and kissed me. "I like that voodoo that you do," she said, crawling out of bed and dressing.

"What's going on?"

"Having some work done at the gallery early tomorrow morning. Got to get back."

I wearily climbed to my feet, feeling hungover, dressed, and drove her home. She rested her head on my shoulder and dozed. At her door she kissed me and said, "I had a swell time."

"So did I. But what's up with this?" I said, swatting the air.

"You're a little numb for my taste."

"I don't know," I said.

"I do."

"If that's what you need."

She shut the door and called out as I walked to my car, "Maybe it's what *you* need."

CHAPTER 17

I drove home thinking about the night. I didn't know if it was the violence or the intensity, but Nicole had tapped into some part me that drew me to her. I didn't know why, and I wasn't sure I wanted to know. I just knew I wanted to see her again.

When I was at my desk in the squad room, I called her and left my home, work, and cell numbers on her answering machine. As I hung up, Ortiz pulled a chair over and sat down. "Let me lay out the facts as I see them." He pointed to his watch and said, "You're ninety minutes late for work. I called you three times last night, and you didn't answer your phone. And when I check out your demeanor and body language right now, I notice that you're not wound as tight as usual. Now I'm a detective. So putting all these leads together I come to one conclusion: You ignored my advice, went out with that broad last night, and nailed her. Am I right?"

"Let's go downstairs," I said.

As we stood outside PAB, sipping our coffee, Ortiz extended an arm toward me, wiggled his fingers, and said, "Give it up."

"Guilty as charged," I said.

"I hope this doesn't come back to bite you in the ass."

"Why shouldn't I go out with her? All she did was give me a little background info. She's not a witness. She's not a suspect. Big fucking deal."

"I.A. might not look at it like that. So just keep this thing on the Q.T."

"You're the only one who knows."

"Who'd you say put you on to her?"

"Papazian in art theft."

"That geek? Then she must be a real firecracker," Ortiz said sarcastically.

"You don't know the half of it."

"You're pathetic," Ortiz said. "You're so desperate, you've got Papazian pimping for you."

"She's just some art expert he met on a case. He figured she could help me."

"She helped you all right," he said, leering at me. "You know, homes, this whole deal doesn't sound like you. Pumping some broad you just met on a case."

"She's different."

"Famous last words," Ortiz said.

I tossed the rest of my coffee on the grass and walked back to the elevator.

I headed out to South Central and cruised down the street where Fuqua's sister lived, a working-class neighborhood of tidy homes and freshly cut lawns a few blocks east of Crenshaw. I hoped he'd show up for her birthday. There was an empty lot about thirty feet from the sister's house with an 18-wheeler parked in front. I parked behind the truck, which gave me a clear view of the sister's front door, but my car was obscured enough so I could take Fuqua by surprise. Setting my binoculars next to me, I rolled the window halfway down and waited.

The afternoon was warm and sunny, blue overhead, the horizons the color of burnt butter. I could see a few fleecy clouds hovering above the Hollywood Hills. I loosened my tie, pulled the six-pack out of my murder book, and fanned myself.

When my cell phone rang, I made the mistake of not checking Caller ID.

"No visits, no phone calls, no nothing," my mother said. "How am I supposed to plan for Shabes dinner?"

"Sorry, Mom. But I just located a suspect. Been very busy."

"Well?"

"Well what?"

"You coming for Shabes?"

"I'm tied up with a case."

"And you consider *that* a good excuse?" she snapped.

"Look Mom, I'm parked on a South Central side street, on a stake-out. I can't talk."

"How long have you been there? Have you eaten? Do you want me to bring you something to eat?"

"I'm trying to keep a low profile here."

"I could just drive by, slow down, and hand you a sandwich."

I massaged my temples with my thumbs. "No."

"So how was your date?" she asked coldly.

"What date?"

"The date with that Syrian person."

"Lebanese."

"Does it matter? So how was it?"

"Fine. Look, Mom—"

"I'll say it once and only once. If you're going to date a shiksa, for God's sake, make sure she's not an avowed enemy of Israel."

After hearing the phone click, I looked around. I was relieved that no neighborhood gangster was close enough to my car to hear me talking to my mother.

As I looked to the north and spotted the faint outlines of the Hollywood sign, I thought about the night with Nicole again. I wondered why she hadn't returned my call. Now it was probably too late to see her this weekend. I reached for my cell phone and checked my home answering machine. But there were no messages.

Forty-five minutes later, a Toyota pulled up in front of Fuqua's sister's house. A woman climbed out of the passenger seat carrying a bag of chips and a six-pack of beer.

When she walked inside, I reached for my cell phone again. As I was calling my answering machine, I saw a man driving a Ford Explorer park in front of the house. I studied him through my binoculars: it was Terrell Fuqua.

I didn't want to take the chance of rushing the house and losing Fuqua through a back window, so I called Duffy. "We got him. He's at his sister's house. I want some backup before I hit the door."

"I'll rustle up Ortiz and Graupmann. Both their partners are on vacation. We'll be there in a flash."

Fifteen minutes later, Duffy, Ortiz, and Mike Graupmann pulled up. I was irritated that Graupmann was part of the bust team, but it was too late to do anything about that now.

"Ash, you and I will hit the front door," Duffy said. "Oscar and Mike will deploy in back."

We slipped on our vests and windbreakers and walked to the house. I rang the doorbell. To my surprise, Fuqua answered the door. His head was shaved and his tight black T-shirt showed off his jailhouse buff. I could hear the blast of rap music from a CD player.

"Terrell, I'm Detective Ash Levine with the LAPD and this is Lieutenant Duffy. We're here to talk to you about a case."

"What case?"

"We'll explain it all back at the station."

"It's my sister's birthday. Why don't y'all come back tomorrow and we'll talk," he said, with forced bonhomie.

I feigned surprise. "Your sister's birthday? That's terrible timing. Sorry, Terrell. But we need to talk to you today."

I shouldered past Fuqua and stepped inside the living room, as Duffy followed me. Several women emerged from the kitchen and glared at us.

Fuqua waved his hands in front of his chest. "If you ain't arrestin' me, I ain't goin' no*where*, no *how*, no *way*."

"As a matter of fact, we *are* arresting you," I said.

"For what?"

"We'll tell you all about it back at the station," I said. "Now we can do this nice and easy, so you're not embarrassed in front of your family. Or we can prone you out on the living room floor and carry you out by your cuffs."

Fuqua staggered back a few steps, stunned. "What the fuck is this about?" he shouted.

"Like I said, we'll talk about it back at the station," I said.

Fuqua turned around and scanned the living room, looking for an escape route. Although he was rocked up from years of prison weightlifting, Duffy, who towered over him, spun him around as easily as if he was a mannequin. I cuffed his hands behind his back. We led him down the street while several women ran from the house and stood on the sidewalk, giving us the finger and shouting, "LAPD 'necks. Motherfucking cops. White devils."

When the detectives reached the car, Duffy said, "Oscar and I will drive back to the station. Ash, you ride with Mike."

Duffy hopped in his car before I could protest. This was probably Duffy's way, I figured, to ensure that we learned to work together: stick us in a squad car with Fuqua.

For most suspects I had arrested, climbing into the backseat of a squad car with their hands cuffed behind their backs was an awkward move. I usually had to put a palm on their shoulder and guide them. But Fuqua jerked away when I reached out for him. He had been cuffed and dropped into police cruisers so many times over the years that he knew precisely how to dip his head, turn half way, and slide into the backseat in a single fluid motion, as gracefully as an Olympic figure skater whirling through a double axel.

While I drove north on Normandie, Graupmann winked at me and turned around to face Fuqua. "You strike me as the kind of guy who likes a hairy pussy."

Fuqua ignored him, staring glumly out the window.

Graupmann winked at me, leaned over the seat, and poked Fuqua in the stomach. "Well, do you?"

"Don't know."

"Well *I* like a hairy pussy. Makes me feel like I'm in a jungle. Makes me want to *attack!*" Graupmann roared like a lion. "Hey, Terrell, let me ask you another question. "You like to *eat* pussy?" Graupmann crossed his eyes and waggled his tongue.

Fuqua stretched, wincing when the cuffs bit into his wrists. "I don't eat *nothin'*," Fuqua said, shaking his head, "that can get up and walk away."

I checked my rearview mirror. Fuqua was staring at Graupmann, eyebrow raised, with an expression that seemed to say: *top that, dickhead.*

We rode the rest of the way in silence. When we walked through the squad room, Duffy called Graupmann and me over and whispered, "Ash, you and Mike handle the interview. Mike, this is Ash's case. You're just there to help out."

Graupmann punched his open palm. "I say we knock and talk this fool."

"Just let me handle the questions," I said. "I'll let you know if I need your help."

I flipped on the video recorder and we entered the small, window-less interview room. The walls, the carpeting, and the hard plastic tables and chairs were battleship gray. Fuqua sat on one side of the table and Graupmann and I sat across from him. I walked behind Fuqua and un-cuffed him. Then I removed my card from my wallet and set it on the table. "We want to talk to you about the murder of an ex-LAPD offi-cer by the name of—"

"WHAT?" he shouted, jerking his head back.

"His name is Pete Relovich."

Fuqua's eyes were clouded with fear. "I din't kill no motherfuckin' cop."

Graupmann leaned across the table toward Fuqua, until he was just a few inches from him, and shouted, spraying spittle at his face, "You're a fucking cop killer!"

I grabbed Graupmann's arm, pulled him away from Fuqua, and slashed an index finger across my throat.

"Okay, okay," Graupmann said.

A street-wise ex-con like Fuqua was savvy enough to end the inter-view at any point and ask for an attorney; Graupmann's approach just heightened that risk. I wanted to keep Fuqua talking, and the best way to do that was to approach him in a low-key manner.

The DNA in the Kleenex was enough to convince a deputy DA to file charges. But I'd arrested enough killers who walked after trial to know that I should never stop buttressing my case.

"I think it's in your interest to talk to us, give us your side of the story," I said. "But first I've got to read you your rights. After that, if you want to talk, we'll be happy to listen."

"I can't believe this shit," Fuqua said with disgust.

"Believe it," I said. "I'm going to read you your rights now, so listen up. You have the right to remain silent. You understand that?"

Fuqua, who looked dazed, mumbled, "I'm trippin'. I can't believe y'all layin' this on me."

"Please answer the question. You have the right to remain silent. Do you understand that?"

"Yeah."

"Anything you say may be used against you in court. Do you un-derstand?"

"Yeah."

"You have the right to the presence of an attorney during any questioning. Do you understand?"

"*Before*," Fuqua said.

"What?" I asked, confused.

"You said I have the right to the presence of an attorney *during* any questioning. Should be before *and* during any questioning."

"That's one for the books," Graupmann said sarcastically. "A scumbag cop killer knows Miranda better than the great Ash Levine."

"He's probably heard it more times than me," I said. Turning to Fuqua I said, "Let's finish this. If you cannot afford an attorney, one will be appointed for you *before* and during any questioning, free of charge. You understand?"

"Yeah, I understan'."

"Okay," I said. "I just want to get your side of the story. First of all, where were you on Thursday night, three weeks ago?"

Fuqua brushed his jaw with his palm. "Probably in my house, drinkin' some eight ball, and watchin' TV."

"That was in the house you rented behind the main house, right?"

"Yeah."

"Anybody with you that night."

"Naw. My girlfriend was in Oakland visiting her sister."

"Your landlord see you that night."

"Naw. He always turn in early."

"Did you know Pete Relovich when he was working as a detective in the Harbor Division?"

"Sure I knew him," Fuqua said. "He popped me and sent me to the pen."

"Were you angry with him?"

"*Hell* yes I was angry with him. 'Cause I didn't do what he say I did."

Graupmann muttered, "Sure. Folsom's full of innocent—"

Cutting him off, I asked, "Have you ever been to Relovich's house?" This was a critical question, because if he denied it, then I knew the Kleenex would doom him in front of a jury. But if he was a step ahead of me and could come up with an innocuous explanation why he visited Relovich—but left before the time of the murder—the evidence against him might be negated.

"I never been to his house."

Relieved, I asked, "You're absolutely sure you've never been to his house?"

"Hell, no!"

"Know where he lives?"

"How would I know that?"

"Is that a no?"

"Yes."

I held up a hand. "Let me clarify. Do you know where former Detective Relovich lives?"

"No."

Now that I could use the Kleenex against him, I figured I would try for a backdoor confession. "Listen Terrell, I know you're lying. I've got evidence that puts you right at Relovich's. DNA evidence. And DNA doesn't lie. But I know that every story's got two sides. I want to hear yours. Maybe Relovich asked you to come by to provide info on an old case. When you were there, maybe he came after you. Maybe he pulled a gun. Maybe you felt your life was in danger. If it went down like that, you can claim self-defense."

"Don't play me like that."

"I'm not playing you," I said. "I'm serious as a heart attack."

Fuqua dropped his head on the table and closed his eyes.

Graupmann banged his fist on the table. "Wake up, shitbird. We're talking to you."

He opened one eye.

"Look," I said, "I know you didn't go to Relovich's alone. Maybe you had no idea what your partner was going to do. If it was your partner who shot him, save yourself and let us know."

Fuqua shook his head disconsolately.

"You got a chance right now," I said. "But when we pick up this other guy, he'll roll over like a circus dog. Then it'll be too late for you."

"You tryin' to *do* me."

"I'm not trying to do anybody." I rapped my knuckles on the table. "Terrell, this is a death penalty case. And juries don't like cop killers. Right now, you're looking at the choke chamber. Give me something. Anything. And I'll try to help you."

Fuqua glared at me, eyes as cold as bullets. "You jammin' me for a murder I didn't do. You playin' me for the fool, like you LAPD cops do."

He grabbed my card off the table, and studied it for a moment, reading with his lips. "Le-*viiine*," he said, stretching out the second syllable. He angrily threw the card on the ground. "Damn! Had a public defender once whose name was Le-*viiine*. He was a motherfuckin' Jew. I learned about Jews when I was in the joint. Became a Muslim in there. I go by Tariq Ahmed Fawaz now. My cellie give me one of our minister's writings. He called y'all bloodsuckers. He called your religion a gutter religion."

Fuqua leaned over and spit on the floor. "I learned from him how y'all controlled the slave trade back in the day, and how now ya'll now control Hollywood, trying to keep the bruthas down, making us look like clowns, makin' us look like degenerates in front of the whole world. This minister said Hitler was a great man. Maybe if Hitler finished the job, you wouldn't be here persecutin' me like this."

Graupmann laughed so hard that he choked. "This guy's the black Mel Gibson."

I jerked my thumb at the door. Graupmann followed me into the hallway.

"I can handle it on my own now," I said. As Graupmann returned to the squad room, I shut down the video so the hidden camera wouldn't record our encounter.

When I returned to the interview room, I kicked the bottom of Fuqua's chair so hard that he tumbled over. When he tried to stand up, I stepped on his wrist, increasing the pressure until he grimaced in pain.

"When I brought you in here, I treated you with respect. I expect to be treated the same way. When you say things that are disrespectful, there are consequences. Do you understand?"

Fuqua looked up at me, eyes smoldering.

I put more weight on his wrist. "Do you understand?"

"Yeah!" Fuqua yelped.

"Yes, what?" I asked.

"Yes, I understand."

I lifted my foot and Fuqua climbed to his feet, groaning and rubbing his wrist.

When he sat down, I said, "I'm glad we understand each other. But before I get back to my questions, let me explain something to you. You know who the biggest slave traders were, the people who really ran and controlled the West African slave trade? Not Jews. But Arabs. That's right. Muslims."

Fuqua shook his head. "That ain't right."

"After they convict your ass, you're going to have plenty of time to read history and find out the real story. And the real story is that Arabs operated all those African slave markets and made their money selling slaves to other merchants who shipped them to America. You changing your name to a Muslim name is like me changing my name from Asher to Adolf. Wouldn't be too bright, would it?"

"I don't know about that," Fuqua said, looking uncertain.

"Now getting back to Relovich, I'm giving you one final chance to give me your side of the story." I planned to flip the video back on if Fuqua said anything interesting.

Duffy barged into the interview room and said, "Come on out for a sec."

When I shut the door, Duffy asked, "Did he cop to it?"

"No."

"Doesn't matter. You've got DNA. This case is cleared." Duffy clapped softly. "Hell of a job."

Graupmann, staring at his desk, mumbled, "Good work."

"I just talked to the chief," Duffy said. "He and Grazzo send their congratulations. They're setting up a press conference at eight tonight in the auditorium. Before you write the arrest report, give me what you got. I'll send it right over to Press Relations. They'll write a release."

"What's the rush?"

"The DA will be sending out their own press release after they file charges. We don't want them stealing our thunder. We want to beat them to the punch."

Duffy shook my hand and walked back to his office.

When I returned to the interview room, Fuqua said, "While you gone, I been thinkin'. I remember that clown in your car say he ain't your partner. It come down to *you* be workin' this case alone. *You* the one tryin' to dog me out. So *you* my main problem."

"That's right," I said.

"When I was attendin' Folsom State *University*," he said with a grin that looked like a grimace, "I did myself a lot of readin'. Here's a quote I come across from a guy named Stallman: 'No man, no problem.'"

"It's Stalin, you moron," I said.

"That not the point."

"What *is* the point?"

"Now *you* the fucking moron."

I was so enraged I could barely speak. "So you're saying that if you can get someone to cap me, you don't have any problem?"

He shrugged.

I slowly leaned across the table and looked into Fuqua's eyes. When he began to grin again, I threw a punch and nailed him in the cheek, knocking him to the ground. For a few seconds he was on his back, woozy, staring at the ceiling. When he staggered back to his chair, I said, "Don't ever threaten me again or I'll crack your fucking head open." I stood up and said, "You might as well get used to following orders right now, you piece of shit, because you'll be following a lot of them after I send you to death row. Stand up, turn around, shut up, and face the wall."

I cuffed him, grabbed him by the wrists, and ferried him to the elevator. At the ground-floor jail, I fingerprinted Fuqua and then, feeling a flood of relief and exultation, booked him for Pete Relovich's murder.

CHAPTER 18

At midnight, after the press conference, after I finished writing the three-page arrest report and the nine-page follow-up investigation report, I called Nicole.

"Yeah," she said, sounding groggy.

"Did I wake you?"

"Yeah."

"Sorry."

"Saw you on television tonight."

"Yeah. If it bleeds it leads. Anyway, I wanted to stop by."

"Now?"

"Yes."

"It's too late. Some other time."

"How about tomorrow night?"

"This isn't a good weekend for me. I'll give you a call next week."

I decided to back off. "Sure," I said, hanging up the phone. I slipped the murder book in the bottom drawer of my desk, shut off the computer, took the elevator to the ground floor, and walked out into the night. I could smell the fog before I could see it, that distinctive brackish scent blowing in from the ocean. It was late May, but Southern California's traditional June gloom had descended on the city a few days early. The skyscrapers on Bunker Hill were barely visible, with just the tops of the buildings peeking through, their lights twinkling in the swirling mist. The fronds of the palm trees bordering PAB were beaded with water and dripped onto the sidewalk.

I was still charged up from the sudden windup of the case, too restive to return home, so I walked over to Hill Street, crossed the freeway overpass spanning the 101, the stream of headlights dimly flickering down the ribbon of wet asphalt. I entered a narrow courtyard at the fringe of Chinatown, where aqua and yellow paper lanterns glowed in the fog. A ginseng store, a dusty acupuncture office, and several small sweatshops were tucked away in the courtyard, one of which was still open. Two young Asian women, surrounded by bins of fabric and enormous spools of thread, were hunched over sewing machines, beneath the glare of florescent lights. The scene reminded me of my father. Another sweatshop; another part of downtown; another century.

At the end of the courtyard, I walked through a door beneath a red neon sign shaped like a lizard and into a small lobby with a black and red terrazzo floor. A wizened Asian man behind a desk scrutinized me for a moment. When he recognized me, he flashed a toothless smile. He stepped on a floor button and buzzed me through a door that led to a bar.

I discovered the Red Gecko a few years earlier while I was investigating the murder of a Chinatown jewelry store owner. The man regularly played high-stakes mah-jongg in the back room, and I originally thought another gambler had killed him. I later discovered that two members of a Hong Kong triad whacked him because he wouldn't pay their shakedown fee. The owner and employees of the Red Gecko were grateful that I had never notified vice detectives about the game in the back room. Since then, whenever I wanted a quiet drink, they welcomed me with beers on the house.

Sitting at a table near the back, I could hear the click of mah-jongg tiles in the adjoining room. The only other patrons in the bar were a wealthy Chinese restaurant owner, his young Vietnamese girlfriend, and two heavily made-up bargirls wearing carved jade pendants. One made her way toward me, but the bartender shouted at her in Vietnamese and she swiveled around and returned to her stool. He then walked over with a Tsing Tao beer and a glass.

"Every time, you always welcome here, Detective Ash Levine," he said in heavily accented English.

"Good to see you, Lam."

I handed him a few dollar bills. "How about some quarters."

Lam returned with the change, and I scanned the tunes on the jukebox, my favorite one downtown because the recordings were all vintage jukebox classics. I punched in a dozen of my favorites, including "Blue

Gardenia," and "Baby It's Cold Outside." After I downed two beers, I tried to pay, but Lam waved me off. So I walked back to the table and left a ten dollar tip.

In the courtyard the smells of garlic and sautéed onions hung in the air. I hadn't eaten since breakfast, and I realized that I was ravenous. I walked over to Broadway, sat at a corner table at Hop Woo, a brightly lit restaurant that stayed open late on weekends. When I finished my fried rice with duck and scallops, I walked back onto Broadway. The fog was now so thick I couldn't see across the street. My face and hair were speckled with mist. I felt disoriented as I struggled to find my way back to Hill Street, up the freeway overpass, and through downtown to my loft.

I flipped on the CD player and skipped through *Kind of Blue* to "Flamenco Sketches," a moody, plaintive cut that usually soothed me when I was too amped up to sleep. I played it over and over, closing my eyes, trying to relax, concentrating on Miles's and Coltrane's soaring sound, hoping I would be able to sleep tonight. But images of the case continued to flash in my mind's eye, like a slide show run at warp speed: the floor tile, the *netsuke*, the *ojime*, the blood splatter pattern, the Kleenex, the fractured hyoid bone, the broken glass behind Relovich's house, the uncle's fishing boat, the ex-wife's tears.

By five o'clock, I knew I wouldn't be able to sleep, so I left my loft and walked south on Los Angeles Street, past the sleeping homeless in small tents and cardboard boxes, emaciated hookers waving at passing cars, and street corner dealers selling rocks that contained more baking soda than cocaine. The fog was thick overhead, but to the east, I could see the faint signs of sunrise: pinpoints of light irradiating the sky a pale pink.

I cut over to Maple and then slipped into the Flower Mart, a vast, cavernous warehouse bustling with shippers, shoppers, distributors, merchants, bargain hunters, and floral designers. From end to end, wholesalers displayed their wares, acre upon acre jammed with flowers of every genus and hue.

I liked to stroll down the aisles after I cleared a case. The end of an investigation often left me—after the initial thrill and sense of accomplishment—drained, empty, and despondent, because I knew that in the next hour or day or week, there would be yet another murder; another grieving wife, child, or mother left behind; another killer to track. At the flower mart, the rush of sweet, heady fragrances; the luxuriant mélange of colors, textures and shapes; the earthy scent of freshly cut stalks was a palliative. I felt that it purified me, provided a brief infusion of grace and optimism that enabled me to regain my perspective, to ready myself for the next case.

After an hour of wandering about, I felt my head clear from the long night, the beers, the sustained adrenaline rush of the case, the disappointment about Nicole. I returned home, crawled into bed, and immediately fell asleep.

When I awoke, I checked my digital alarm clock: 6:12, but I had no idea if it was morning or evening. I looked outside and could see shafts of sunlight slanting through the office towers. The sun was setting. I closed my eyes and I began to think of Nicole, those glittering flecks of green in her eyes, the night we spent together, her bizarre needs and, now, her distant manner.

After I showered and dressed, I hopped in my Saturn and sped to Venice. The sky was still overcast and the arched Venetian bridges were cloaked in mist that rose from the canals. When I heard Nicole slam her screen door, I walked up the path and joined her on the porch.

"Do I have a stalking cop on my hands?" She smiled, but it did not reach her eyes.

"What's going on?"

"I had a great time the other night. But the on-again, off-again thing I've got with the ex-boyfriend is on-again."

I shrugged. "The old song."

"I guess so." She leaned over and kissed me, then lightly licked me on the neck. "I'd still like to see you sometimes. But not here. The weekends are going to be tough for me. I'll let you know when."

"That kind of deal's not going to work for me. If things change, call me," I said over my shoulder as I climbed off her porch and walked toward the canal.

When I heard her door close, I stopped and lingered in the pewter light, staring out at the water, feeling hurt and foolish. The last time I had been at her house, when the night was full of promise, the intoxicating fragrance of jasmine filled the air. Now an offshore breeze carried the stench of society garlic—wispy purple flowers that grew in a corner of her yard. The scent of a moldering affair.

CHAPTER 19

When I reached my desk Monday morning, I picked up a note from Duffy: "Hell of a job! Congrats on clearing the case. I knew I could count on you. I'm in meetings this morning. Let's talk this afternoon."

As Ortiz sauntered through the squad room door, he called out, in a mock newscaster tone, "Detective Levine, do you feel a sense of closure? Do you feel the unfortunate ghetto youth was compelled to commit murder because of his underprivileged childhood?"

He leaned over my desk, shook my hand, and said softly, "You did Pete Relovich right. He was a good cop. I'm glad you nailed that gangster. And I hope—"

Ortiz paused when he heard Graupmann's booming voice.

"I softened Fuqua up," Graupmann boasted to another detective. "I was like the guy at the bullfight who jabs at the snorting bull with one of those spears until he's covered with blood. You know that guy."

"The banderillero," Ortiz called out.

"That's it," Graupmann said. "Then when Fuqua was just about ready to give up, the Manischewitz matador stepped up and finished him off."

Ortiz chuckled and said, "Maybe you just got yourself a new partner."

"God forbid."

"I haven't eaten. Let's grab some breakfast."

"I don't think I—"

Ortiz wagged his finger at me. "You just cleared your case. Duffy's not here. Face it, you got no excuse this morning. And to celebrate, I'm buying."

"Okay, I'll take you up on your offer. A cheap bastard like you will probably never make it again."

•   •   •

Ortiz drove to his favorite restaurant, Astro's, a twenty-four-hour coffee shop a few miles north of downtown. As we sipped coffee, waiting for our omelets and toast, he said, "So how's that hottie that Papazian pimped for you?"

"She was all over me like a cheap suit. Then she dumped me."

"It's one thing if your wife walks out on you. That's normal. Happened to you—happened to half the guys in Felony Special. Christ, that's what my first and second ex-wives did." Ortiz sipped his coffee. "When I was at Hollenbeck, the crusty old D-3 who recruited me to work homicide said, 'Don't get married. Just find a woman you hate and buy her a house, a car, and give her half your pension. Because after you work homicide for a few years, she'll divorce your ass and take it all anyway.'"

The waitress brought our breakfast, and as I shook salt on my omelet, I said, "She mentioned something about an old boyfriend coming back on the scene."

"Sounds like a load of shit. Anyway, if your wife leaves you, it's nothing personal. That's the way it goes. But if some broad you nail once dumps you, now that's a *real* insult." Ortiz patted me on the shoulder. "Let me give you some advice, *mijo*. Next time you want to get your rocks off, don't go after some classy art gallery bitch. She's out of your league. You gotta know your limits. You know what they say about boxers: when they move up in weight, they can't take their punch with them. Well, you just moved up in weight, too, and you never had a chance. Come with me to an academy barbecue. I'll find you a nice cop groupie who'll rock your world and come back for seconds."

When we finished our breakfast, Ortiz said, "So, one case down. What's next?"

"It's not exactly down. I've still got some follow-up to do."

Ortiz laughed. "You say that about every case. They should put that on your tombstone."

As I walked through the squad room, Duffy craned his head out of his office and motioned for me to step inside. "Again, great work, Ash," he said, leaning back in his chair. "Just got calls from the chief, Assistant Chief Grazzo, and Commander Wegland. They loved the press conference. Great for the department. They all send their congratulations. And their thanks."

I sat down and said, "It isn't over yet."

"What do you mean?"

"According to two witnesses, Fuqua had a partner."

"Witnesses?" Duffy lowered his chin and raised an eyebrow. "More like a crackhead and a dumb-shit broad."

"I'd still like to find Fuqua's partner."

"The only way you're going to find the partner, *if* there's a partner, is after the prelim when Fuqua realizes death row's got a cell with his name on it. Then he'll give up his mother and his favorite pit bull to save his ass. His P.D. will talk to the D.A. and it'll be *let's make a deal time*. You had your chance with Fuqua and he didn't give you shit."

"I'd like a little more time on this one."

"We picked up a triple in Mar Vista a few nights ago. I want you to help the primaries."

"There's something about this case that still bothers me."

Duffy smacked his forehead and said, "Oh, no! Here we go again. Do you always have to pick, pick, pick?"

"You sound like the department shrink."

"You *need* a shrink. Can't you just be happy that you cleared the case and move on?"

"It's just that there's a few things—"

"Okay, okay," With a look of weary forbearance, Duffy asked, "What is it?"

"I'm still bothered with the setup in the living room. I can't see Relovich sitting on the sofa across from Fuqua. A veteran cop would never allow himself to be maneuvered into that kind of setup."

"If Fuqua's pointing a nine at him, he'll sit wherever the hell he's told to sit. What else?"

"A week before Relovich was killed he called Internal Affairs."

"It's not so unusual for a retired cop to call I.A."

"But he's killed before he ever gets to talk to them. I don't like the timing."

Duffy backhanded the air with a dismissive flick. "He could have been seeing I.A. about *anything*."

"Fuqua just spent a nickel in Folsom. The blacks and Mexicans are at war in there. A black wouldn't partner up with a Mexican after hitting the streets."

"But it looks like Fuqua did."

"Maybe."

What else?"

"A few other things that you'll just blow off. Why don't you cut me some slack. I think I've earned a second look at this case."

"Every time we clear a case in here, there're always a few things that don't add up. Fuqua's our guy. He had the motive. And you can't argue with DNA. All this shit you're laying on me, you knew about it from the get go, but you still chased Fuqua and jacked him up."

"When that DNA matched Fuqua, the case came together so well, I just rode the momentum. But now—"

"Now that the momentum's run out, you're suffering from the paralysis of analysis."

"I'm not saying Fuqua didn't do it. I'm just saying I want to find the partner."

"You think that pimp Abazeda who ran those escort girls was involved?"

"No. I don't think he's got the balls for it. He's just an asshole with a big mouth."

Duffy crossed and uncrossed his arms. "Damn it, you're a pain in the ass. Sometimes you're like the cow that gives the farmer a bucket of milk. Then kicks it over. Then pisses on it."

"I resent—"

"Let me lay it out for you. Pete Relovich's murder is cleared. Fuqua's in custody. Fuqua had a motive. Fuqua was tied to the crime scene. So the chief is happy. The assistant chief is happy. Commander Wegland is happy. Captain Paganos is happy. And I'm happy."

Duffy began pacing in his small office. "Remember what your old guru, Bud Carducci, used to say?" Duffy asked.

"Yeah. When you hear hoofbeats—don't think zebra."

"Well? Why ignore the obvious explanation and go looking for some far-fetched one?"

"Carducci's saying doesn't apply here."

"I think it does. You should be proud that you got that gangster off the streets. If you start all over on this one, you know what that means for me? I'll be pestered again with phone calls from the brass all fucking day. I'll be badgered by reporters, asking why this case isn't wrapped up. I'll be hassled by the other detectives who want to know why they keep getting paged at three in the morning for new cases, while I refuse to put *you* back on the on-call board."

"I think it would be worthwhile—"

Duffy held up both palms. "Ash, you know I respect your instincts. But frankly, you have a tendency to overthink a case. I think you're doing it on this one. Still, I asked you to come back and solve the homicide. And you did. So I'll give you one more week. I owe you that much."

I shook my head. "I need a month to put this case together properly."

"A week," Duffy said. "You're back on call next Monday."

"Three weeks."

"Ash, I'm not going to haggle with you. You get a week."

"I need three weeks."

Duffy narrowed his eyes. "One week. Take it or leave it."

"I'll take it."

"But after your week," Duffy said, pointing to the on-call board posted on a wall, "you're going back up there."

CHAPTER 20

The next morning, I opened up the Relovich murder book, but couldn't concentrate as I flipped through the pages. I grabbed my cup from my bottom drawer, walked across the squad room, filled it with coffee, returned to my desk, and tried again.

Finally, I snapped the murder book shut and called the LAPD's Behavior Science unit. In a hushed voice so no one in the squad room could hear me, I asked a secretary if Blau could squeeze me in today. She told me he just had a cancellation and could see me in a half hour.

I drove over to the bank building in Chinatown, sat in the waiting room for a few minutes, until the receptionist buzzed me in. I eased into a chair across from Blau.

"How are those stress headaches you were telling me about last time?"

"Better," I lied.

"You sure?"

"Yeah. I'm glad I'm back on the job," I said, trying to change the subject.

"That's good to hear."

"I probably never should have left."

"It seems you've adjusted pretty quickly to being back."

I listened to his fountain burble for a moment and then I said, "I think I have. But I'm still having a problem with something. Remember we talked about that case—the murder of Bae Soo Sung, the Korean market owner? And I mentioned that a witness to the shooting, a woman named Latisha Patton, was killed?"

Blau nodded.

"Well, I'm still having a lot of trouble dealing with it."

"Why is that?"

I thought about Latisha and felt queasy. The room began to blur. I filled my cheeks with air and slowly exhaled. "Okay. Here's the deal. Like I told you, my partner and I pick up the case from the South Bureau Homicide. A few days into it, his back goes out and he's off for two weeks. So I'm working it solo. But I don't have shit. The case looks like a dead end. There're a few wits around, but all they see is a guy in a Shrek mask run out of the store with a gun in his hand. He jumps into a car parked across the street and speeds off.

"Patrol found the car later that day, but it wasn't much help. Car was stolen and the shooter was wearing gloves, so we got no prints. After a few days, the case is really getting to me." I pounded my chest with a fist. "Every other day the wife calls me and asks in fractured English, 'You find who kill my husband?' And then she breaks down sobbing. She's a widow with three young children. She's working the store alone now, scared out of her fucking mind that the shooter will come back and finish her off. But she's got no choice. She's got no other way to support her family.

"I really feel for this lady and her kids. And I'm very, very pissed off. Sung cooperated completely. Yet asshole killed him anyway. For no reason. And destroyed four lives. I figure it's only a matter of time until he does it again and shatters another family. So I vow to myself that I'm going to nail this guy. The first week I'm working fourteen, sixteen hours a day, rousting and questioning crackheads, gangbangers, bag men, and strawberries."

"Strawberries?" Blau asked.

"A woman who exchanges sex for crack. I interview probably fifty people in the 'hood. But I'm not getting shit. Every day, I'm looking for a revelation, I retrace the shooter's steps, from the time he parked his car, walked down the street into the store, pulled out the gun, grabbed the cash, shot Sung, ran across the street, and drove off.

"The car was parked in front of a thrift shop run by a church. There was a woman who worked there by the name of Latisha Patton. When the South Bureau Homicide detectives first interviewed her, she told them she hadn't seen anything. When I interviewed her, she told me the same thing. But, running out of leads, I went back to talk to her again. I press her and, bluffing, I tell her that I know she was lying, that I know she'd heard the gunshots across the street and ran to her front window and got a good look at the shooter.

"We go back and forth, but I keep pressing and she keeps lying and denying. Finally, she admits that she saw a guy in a Shrek mask park the car and walk across the street. A few minutes later she heard a shot and saw him run back to his car and speed off. She insisted she never got a look at his face.

"But I know there's one thing wrong with her story. No armed robber would pull up to the scene wearing a mask. That would draw too much attention. He'd only slip the mask on right before the heist. She realizes that I had caught her in a lie. Finally, she admits that she did get a look at him when he first pulled up.

"But she's still too scared to cooperate with me. She's got a daughter. Doesn't want her involved in all this. Says she won't look at any pictures I want to show her. So I tell her all about Sung's kids, how they're crying for their daddy every night, how tormented his widow is. I lay it on thick. Latisha knew the family, had frequently shopped at the market, and they were always nice to her. She finally breaks down. Says she'll cooperate. She can't ID the shooter, had never seen him before, but says she can definitely pick him out if she saw him again. But she knows that in her 'hood, if word gets around that she's cooperating with a detective, it'll be a death sentence. She's scared as hell now.

"But I tell her that I'll move her and her daughter. I tell her I'll protect her, I'll keep her safe. So she agrees to look at stacks of pictures of local gangbangers and guys with armed robbery in their jacket that I want to show her."

I closed my eyes and massaged them with my palms. "Three days later, she's dead."

"Why do you think you were responsible for her murder?" Blau asked.

"I know that just cooperating with me, agreeing to look at pictures, trying to pick someone out, puts her life in danger. So I go to the DA, submit my request for witness relocation funds, and request to move her. I want her out of the 'hood. But without a positive ID on the shooter, their regulations won't let me relocate her.

"She hasn't IDed anyone yet, but I feel she's still at risk. And she's spooked, too, afraid to go home, but she doesn't have the money to pay for the move herself. I promise to keep her identity secret. I meet with her at Felony Special—downtown—not at South Bureau where someone in the neighborhood could see her. Still, I know word sometimes has a way of getting out when a witness cooperates with the police. I go to the DA's office again, really press the witness relocation coordinator, but he nixes the move. He says they can't come up with money for people who *might* be able to ID shooters, who *might* someday be threatened. And LAPD regulations won't let me relocate her without the DA paperwork.

"So I say 'fuck it,' find her an apartment in the West Valley myself. She sends her daughter to live with an aunt in Fresno. I pay first and last and security deposit out of my own pocket. I tell her to grab a few things, give the rest of her stuff to her mother, meet me out there, and not tell *anyone* where she's gone. I tell her that within a few weeks, after I had shown her the picture of every gangbanger and armed robber in her neighborhood—and some surrounding ones—I'm confident we'll have the shooter IDed. I'm sure asshole is a local boy who's been collared before. I'd track him down, lock him up, and she'd pick him out of a live lineup—to really nail the case down. Then I could go through the DA's office, get her and her daughter some funds for long-term relocation and maybe some job training. The Sung family would have justice. The wife wouldn't have to worry about the killer coming back. And Latisha and her daughter could start a new life."

I stood up and stared out the window, watching the cars stutter down Broadway. "Two weeks after I move her, someone kills her—I still don't know where or how—and then dumps her body at Fifty-fourth and Figueroa—a block from the Sung's market. Probably as a warning to anyone else who might have seen something the day he was killed."

I fell back onto my chair and tried to stretch my neck, which was so tight I could barely move it.

"Why did the department come down on you?"

"Her family sued the LAPD. Because I'd given her the money for the move and found her the apartment, the LAPD, Latisha's lawyers claimed, assumed responsibility for her safety. It was a liability issue. The city attorney settled before trial and paid Latisha's family a nice chunk of change. The department was pissed. I got investigated by I.A. and Duffy hung me out to dry. Instead of arguing to the brass that I was just trying to protect a wit, Duffy suspended me. I was on my own."

"I've heard of detectives doing things a lot worse, without being disciplined or having I.A. on their backs. All you did was come up with some money for her apartment." Blau inched forward on the sofa. "So why do you blame yourself?"

"If I'd just stuck with regulations, maybe she'd be alive today. Maybe no one would have known that she'd seen the shooter. Maybe no one would have known she was cooperating with us. Instead, the shooter, somehow, found out."

"How'd he find out?"

"Maybe he followed her when she drove out to the West Valley. Maybe someone saw us together at the apartment and word got out. Maybe when she made some calls, someone star eighty-nined her, found her phone number, and tracked her address."

"Ash, that's a lot of maybes. Too many for you to assume responsibility for her death."

"I just know that what I did blew up in my face and my wit ended up dead. If I'd done things differently, the way I was supposed to, she might be alive today."

"You're being too hard on yourself. You did your best to protect her." I shrugged.

"It sounds to me that you did all that you could. I'd suggest you make a real effort to be as rational and realistic as you can about the situation. Because right now you're over-assigning blame to yourself."

"I had to do the death notification. When I told Latisha's daughter her mother had been killed, well—" I swallowed hard and shook my head. "She blamed me. She was out of control. She screamed that I should have left her mother alone. I probably should have."

"You need to focus on the reality of the situation. The reality is, this woman didn't think she was safe where she was. Ultimately, you didn't either. So you tried to protect her. The fact that you couldn't keep her safe was not your fault. She might have been in danger no matter where she lived."

"But I put her in danger."

"You didn't put her in danger. She was in danger before she even talked to you. She was in danger the moment she saw the man in the Shrek mask get out of his car. You can't blame yourself, because when you moved her, you know what you were doing?"

"What?"

"Your job."

"You know, whenever I'm in the middle of breaking down a case, I think of two phrases that always come up in Talmudic study: *tsorikh iyyun*—needing further study and *b'makhloket*—still in controversy."

"Homicide detective as Talmudic scholar?" Blau asked, smiling wryly.

"I'm not giving myself that much credit. I'm just a cop who can't leave a case alone."

We sat in silence for a few minutes until I said the first thing that popped into my head. "Somewhere else in the Talmud it says something like, if you save a life, it's like you saved the whole world. Sometimes I feel like that with my job."

"You solve a murder, it's like you've solved all the world's murders?"

"That sounds like I've got delusions of grandeur."

"Leave the psychological diagnosis to me," Blau said, smiling. "But no one can dispute you have an important job." Blau tapped his chin with his middle finger. "I get the feeling you've got something more to say about this woman, Latisha."

I nodded.

"This is a good time to tell me about it. "

"I've got to be indirect about this."

"Why?"

"I don't want to lose my job. So let's say there's this hypothetical detective with a witness who—"

"We're not here to talk about the hypothetical. We're here to talk about you."

"What are your rules about confidentiality."

"Typically, confidentially is absolute between a psychologist and patient."

"*Typically?*" I asked.

"Well, I'm an LAPD employee, so the situation is a little more complicated because—"

I walked across the room, filled a cup with water, and downed it in a gulp.

"It just got too complicated for me, too."

I crumpled the water cup, tossed it in the trash can, and walked out the door.

.   .   .

I sat in my car, staring out the windshield, my heart pounding, my throat dry, my hands shaking so much I couldn't start the engine. I thought about that first night I moved Latisha to the apartment in the Valley. She told me she'd never felt so lonely in her life. She couldn't go to work; she couldn't see her daughter, her mother, or her friends. I went out and picked up a pizza, and we ate together on the sofa. She made me promise I'd return the next night. I picked up some pasta and a bottle of wine. She told me how grateful she was for the company. Robin and I had just separated, and I didn't feel like being alone either.

After dinner, when I was leaving, my hand on the doorknob, she started to cry. I put my arm around her shoulder, trying to comfort her. She looked up at me, her eyes misty, and at that moment I realized, for the first time, how beautiful she was. She had high, sharp cheekbones and almond, amber-colored eyes. She was only a few inches over five feet, but had the willowy body of a dancer, and every move she made was fluid and graceful. While Robin was sarcastic and cynical and could be devious like me, Latisha was sweet and direct. "You're my protector," she whispered to me, her arms around my waist. She framed my face in her hands and kissed me; she led me to the bedroom. I felt like I was in a trance and I stayed in that trance, oblivious to the consequences. And there were many. My feelings for her were intense, the emotions complicated. During those last few days I thought about asking her to move in with me after the case was resolved.

Did Latisha's involvement with me cost her life? Definitely. Did the fact that I was sleeping with her every night for weeks end up putting her at even more risk? Probably. I tried to be discreet, but who knows. Maybe someone tailed me from downtown. Maybe the killer attached a GPS to my engine block. Maybe Latisha told someone in the apartment complex about her dilemma. Maybe she slipped and talked to someone from the old neighborhood about our relationship or about where she was living. In the end it was on me. I convinced her to talk to me, to move, to testify against the killer if I ever caught him. I then decided to up the ante and make the relationship personal.

Robin was the only one who suspected what was going on. After I moved out, Robin, shaken by the finality of the move, had second thoughts about the separation. She called me at home, late at night, a number of times. I was never there. After Latisha was killed, I stopped by our old house. I didn't know exactly what I wanted from Robin; I just felt like I needed to be with her. She wouldn't let me in. She just stood on the porch, staring at me, frowning. She could see how Patton's murder had shaken me to the core.

"I know you, Ash, and this *woman*," she said with distain, "wasn't just another witness." She walked back inside, slammed the door, and that's the last time I saw her. I called Robin a few months ago, and she advised me to hire a divorce lawyer.

Telling Blau all this would be a big gamble. I couldn't even tell Ortiz. All I could do was wrap up the Relovich investigation and finagle some time so I could finally get to the real case that lured me back to the LAPD.

CHAPTER 21

I returned to the squad room, my head throbbing. I filled my coffee cup with water and downed three Tylenol. Moving my steno pad off the corner of my blotter, I stared at the picture of Latisha. When I started to choke up, I left the squad room and locked myself in a bathroom stall. Should I just dump the Relovich case now? No. I've got to do right by Pete Relovich. Latisha's homicide is a very cold case, a year old. Waiting another couple of days won't hurt. I'll finish off the Relovich case. Then I'll go after Latisha's killer.

After splashing cold water on my face, I returned to the squad room. Still feeling shaky, I opened up the Relovich murder book and drummed a forefinger on my leather shoulder holster. Where to begin? It was always easier to launch a new investigation than to revisit a cleared case. The difficulty was reviewing the material with a fresh perspective, envisioning a new path to follow that deviated from previous avenues of investigation.

Bud Carducci always told me to view the disparate elements of an investigation like the links in a chain. A smart defense attorney, Carducci explained, will always hone in on the weakest link and split it open. The jury won't care how strong the other links in the chain are. When it is time to deliberate, they'll focus on the broken one.

I decided to first focus on the interview summaries, including the ones conducted by the Harbor Division detectives. But when I finished reading them, I hadn't found an obvious weak link. The interview with Relovich's ex-wife, Sandy, however, troubled me. She insisted she had no idea that Relovich had hidden almost $5,000 under his floor tile. But I recalled that she seemed hinky when I told her about the cash. My instincts during interviews had been wrong in the past, but not often. I decided to pay her another visit.

•   •   •

I drove north out of the city on a cool, gray morning. As I climbed the San Gabriel Mountains, the fog thinned, and by the time I reached the summit at 3,300 feet, I could discern two distinct climate patterns: ash gray and overcast in the vast Los Angeles basin; turquoise skies and shimmering heat waves in the scorching Mojave Desert. In L.A., summer weather was still a month away. But here, in the high desert, the sun was unforgiving, parching the hillsides and withering the spring flowers.

When Sandy answered the door, she was holding a can of beer in one hand and a cigarette in the other. She stared at me for a moment, her eyes rheumy, her expression perplexed. When she recognized me, she set her beer on the floor and hugged me, the smoke from the cigarette swirling around and burning my eyes.

"I never got around to calling you, but I wanted to say that I'm grateful," she said. "Thank you for everything you've done."

I followed her into the kitchen, where she poured me a glass of iced tea.

"It's finally over. You finally got him," she said, grabbing another beer from the refrigerator and joining me at a round wooden table. "As you can see, I'm drinking again too early in the day. Maybe now that you've put the case to rest, I'll get it together."

I had worked with enough drunks to know Sandy was lying to herself. But I just nodded sympathetically.

"You've really helped me and my little girl, and I'm grateful to you for that," she said. "She believed that the bad man who killed her father was going to come after me and kill me, too. She's had a lot of trouble sleeping. But after you made the arrest, well, it helped a lot."

Sandy took a deep drag of her cigarette and said while exhaling, "What brings you all the way out to our shit-kicking little burg?"

"I wanted to ask you a few follow-up questions."

"Okay. Ask."

"Remember I mentioned that stash of cash that I found under a tile in Pete's kitchen?"

She angrily stubbed out her cigarette. "*Remember* I told you I didn't know anything about it?"

"Yes I do. But it's something I have to pursue."

"Why? I thought the case was solved. You already arrested that gangster who killed Pete."

"There might be more to the homicide than I originally thought."

"Detective Levine, this is the fourth time you've been out here. I'm sick of this shit."

Telling her about the questions I had about the case would be pointless. She'd probably just get angry. But if I mentioned the partner, it might provide enough of a scare so she'd open up to me. I leaned toward her and said, "I locked up one suspect, but witnesses have told me that he had a partner. I need to find that partner. That's the only way I can be sure this case is solved. And it's the only way I can be one hundred percent sure that you and your daughter are safe."

She gripped the edge of the table. "Do you think this partner could come after us?" she asked, voice quavering.

"No. But it'll be better for everyone if I find out who he is and get him into custody."

She wiped her eyes with a fist.

I fought back the impulse to speak. Sometimes silence was more effective in gleaning information than the most penetrating question.

Slowly lifting her head, she lit another cigarette, smoking half of it in silence. Finally, she said, "Maybe what I'm going to tell you will help you find out whatever you're trying to find out. Probably not. But I'd never forgive myself if I had some little piece of information that could help you find this partner and I didn't tell you." She stubbed out her cigarette and stared into the ashtray for a moment. "About eleven years ago, Pete was working patrol in Hollywood. He'd only been a cop for a few years. Something happened. I don't know exactly what. Pete never talked about his work. He didn't want to bring the streets home with him. But something big must have gone down. We weren't married yet, just living together in a small apartment in Torrance, trying to save up for a down payment so we could get our own place. Pete was just a young patrolman. So it was slow going. Then one Saturday he sits me down and tells me he's got $60,000 for a down payment. Those were the days when you could still buy a nice house in Pedro for $300,000. He made me promise not to ask him where he got the money. I agreed. So he bought the house a month or two later. We got married and moved in."

She downed her beer in two gulps and lit another cigarette.

"Where'd he get the money?"

"I didn't want to know then. I don't want to know now."

"Who was his partner at the time?"

"No idea. He had lots of partners over the years."

"Do you remember what month he bought the house?"

"February. I remember it was around Valentine's Day."

"Did you know about the cash under the tile?"

"No. He said the $60,000 was the whole jackpot. I guess he kept a little extra for himself."

"You think this is what he was going to tell Internal Affairs?"

"I sure as hell hope not. It was too late to do anything about the money. He'd spent it. He should have been smart enough to keep his mouth shut."

"Any idea what his appointment with Internal Affairs was about?"

"No idea."

"Last time I was here, I showed you those little Japanese figures. You said you didn't know anything about them. Are you sure that—"

"I still don't know anything about them."

"You said he got the cash about eleven years ago. You sure it was eleven years?"

"Yes. Because I remember it was the time of my mom's sixtieth birthday."

"Why didn't you tell me about all this before?"

She stared into the ashtray. "Two reasons. I don't want the IRS on my ass, seizing the place for Pete's back taxes. And I want Lindsay to remember her father as a good cop. If you start digging into the source of that cash, I'm afraid of what you'll come up with."

"I appreciate you leveling with me," I said. "I'll keep the IRS out of the investigation. And whatever I find out, I'll keep it as private as I can."

She sniffled and then blew her nose on a napkin. "I got a final question for you?"

"Yeah."

"What happens to the five thousand?"

"It's in evidence now. I don't think Pete left a will, so it'll probably go to your daughter."

I walked to the door. Sandy waved feebly, without standing up, then dropped her head and covered her eyes with her palms.

•   •   •

The first thing I wanted to do was determine who Relovich's partner was eleven years ago at Hollywood Division. A girlfriend or wife may not know a cop's deepest secrets, but there was a good chance his partner had some insight.

When I returned to the squad room in the afternoon, I called Records and Identification and gave the clerk Relovich's serial number, and requested all of his arrest reports from the year he bought the house and, just to be safe, the previous year as well.

"*Every* one?" the clerk asked wearily.

"Every one for those two years," I said.

She found eighty-seven reports—all chronicled on microfiche—which I spent the next few hours studying. Fortunately, it appeared that Relovich had only one partner during that time—Avery Mitchell, a patrolman about ten years older than Relovich. Scanning the pages of the LAPD's Alpha roster—the list of active duty personnel—I could not find Mitchell, so I knew he had retired.

I then called Regina Williamson, a Department of Pensions clerk who owed me a favor. "Regina, I need an address and phone number for a retired cop by the name of Avery Mitchell."

"You know, I'd do anything for you, Ash, but they're really tightening up on us here. So as much as I'd like to give you the info right now, you've got to follow LAPD regulations. The request's got to be in writing, on LAPD letterhead, and signed by your commanding officer."

"If I do that, I won't get the address for a week. I don't want to waste a week."

"But they don't want us to make any exceptions," she said in a plaintive tone.

"I did some rule bending for *you*." Her teenage son had been busted driving a stolen car, and I called the arresting officer and the deputy DA, who agreed not to push too hard on the case. The judge gave her son probation.

"I know, I know," she said. "I truly appreciate what you did. But this new regime is a bitch and they want us—"

"Regina," I interrupted, " I gotta have that information today. I wouldn't press you if it wasn't important."

After about ten seconds of silence, she whispered, "Mitchell, common spelling?"

"Yes."

"I'll get back to you."

Ten minutes later she called back with the information I needed. Avery Mitchell had retired a decade ago to a small town in Idaho. I called him immediately.

A man with a raspy voice and a cigarette cough answered.

"Avery Mitchell?" I said.

"Don't live here anymore."

"Any idea where he lives?"

"Don't live anywhere. Man's dead," he said in a monotone. "I just rent his house."

"When did he die?"

"And who're *you*?"

"Detective Ash Levine with the LAPD. I wanted to talk to him about some old cases."

"He died about two months ago."

"How?"

"Maybe heart attack. Probably had one when he found out *you* were looking for him," the man said sarcastically.

"Who do you rent the house from now?"

"Mitchell's son."

The man gave me the address where he sent the rent check.

Avery Mitchell Jr. lived in one of the last bungalow courts in Hollywood, a 1920s-style complex with a dozen small cottages encircling an oval of grass. A palm swayed in the center, the top of the trunk swathed in dead, desiccated fronds that looked like the tawny matted mane of a lion.

As I walked to the door, I felt weary and disheartened by the investigation.

I rang the bell several times and banged on the door, but Mitchell didn't answer, which accentuated my melancholy mood.

I returned early the next morning. Mitchell answered the door wearing a pair of tattered boxer shorts and wiping the sleep out of his eyes. He had a lip ring and an eyebrow was pierced with a slender silver rod. Both biceps were covered with bands of swirling tattoos.

When I identified myself and said I wanted to talk about Avery Mitchell Senior, I was surprised at the son's gracious manner. "Come on inside," he said. "I'm going to make some coffee. I'll bring you a cup."

I looked around the small living room. The overstuffed gingham sofa was flanked by bone-colored end tables with pale pink lamps atop doilies. Opposite the sofa were a crochet throw rug with a floral pattern and a powder blue leatherette easy chair. An amateurish oil painting of an ocean sunset hung on a wall. The décor, I thought, seemed more appropriate for one of my elderly aunts than a tattooed, pierced Hollywood hipster.

When Mitchell returned with two cups of coffee, he noticed me checking out the room. "I rented it furnished."

"I didn't think it was your style."

Mitchell handed me a cup and we sat on the sofa.

"Sorry for waking you," I said.

"I usually don't sleep this late. I'm a prop boy on *That Thing of Ours*. It's a new cable show. We're filming on the street at night now. Got to be back out there later this afternoon. Ever see the show?"

"I don't have much time for TV."

"It's a crime family dramedy. Kind of a cross between *The Sopranos* and *The Brady Bunch*. I got my dad to watch it once."

"What did he think of it?"

Mitchell nodded thoughtfully. "I'll quote him for you: 'Biggest pile of horseshit I've ever seen. Never in all my years on the street have I seen anything resembling the crap you're showing.' Right then I knew the show would be a monster hit."

We both laughed.

"You have a card?" Mitchell asked.

I handed the card to him and Mitchell studied it for a moment. "So why's the LAPD interested in my father? Especially the downtown boys from Felony Special. My dad left the department a long time ago."

"Just some old cases I'm checking out that your dad might have investigated."

He lightly touched his lip ring and eyebrow rod, and stuck out his tongue, revealing a silver stud. "Even though I walk the walk and look the look, I got nothing against cops. Believe it or not, I was even an Explorer Scout at the Hollywood station when I was in high school."

"You've taken a different career path."

"Yeah. My dad walked out on my mom, my sister, and me when I was in high school. Moved in with his girlfriend. So I guess I did a one-eighty on him."

"Where's your mom live?"

He sipped his coffee. "She died two years ago. Breast cancer."

"How'd your dad die?"

"Suicide."

I jerked my head back. I had been trained to stay poker faced during interviews, but I was so surprised I reacted without thinking. Embarrassed, I took a quick sip of coffee. "The guy who rents his house in Idaho said he thought it was a heart attack."

"He was probably pulling your chain. They don't like cops up there snooping around."

"How'd he do it?"

Mitchell swallowed hard. "The tried and true cop way. He ate his gun."

"Had he been depressed?"

"It was impossible to tell with him. He was always kind of sour and cynical. Typical retired cop, right?"

I shrugged. "Were you close?"

"Not really."

"How often did you talk?"

"He called me every month or so. And whenever he was forced to come down to L.A. to take care of some business, he'd take me to breakfast." He smiled sadly at the memory. "He always threatened to yank out my studs and rings with a pair of pliers."

"How often did he visit?"

"As rarely as possible—a couple times a year."

"Why'd he retire?"

"'Cause he hated L.A. He called it the cesspool of California. He loved the mountains. Fished every day."

"Any close friends or girlfriends up there?"

"Not really. That cunt he dumped my mom for eventually dumped him. Had some drinking partners at the local tavern. But I don't think they knew him too well. Nobody knew him too well."

"When he was still a cop, do you remember him, at any time, coming into a lot of money?"

Mitchell canted his head and studied me with a dubious expression. "Hey, what's this all about?"

"Your dad's gone, so you've got nothing to worry about. It's like I said: I'm tracking down some old cases and I thought you might be able to help out."

"If we'd been closer, maybe I could."

"Do you have his personal items, things from the house?"

He walked across the room and opened a closet. Inside were two fishing poles, a shotgun, a Finnish deer hunting rifle with a satin-walnut stock, and a Plexiglas shadow box with his father's first service revolver—a .38-caliber, six-shot, Smith & Wesson—his badge, and a few unit patches. "This is what I kept. My sister's got the rest."

"Your sister nearby?"

"Yeah. Mid-Wilshire."

"What does she do?"

"She teaches third grade."

At the door, we shook hands. "You can be proud of your dad; people always told me he was a good cop," I said, although I had never heard of Avery Mitchell until a few hours ago.

"Thanks for saying it, but let's get real. He wasn't a good father. He wasn't a good husband. And I doubt if he was a good cop. But I know one thing he was good at."

"What's that?"

"He was an awesome fisherman."

I returned to the squad room and immediately called the sheriff from the rural, sparsely populated county where Mitchell had lived. He agreed to fax the autopsy report.

"I'd also like to talk to the coroner," I said.

The sheriff laughed. "Don't have no coroner up here. This isn't Los Angle-ese," he said, a hint of derision in his voice.

"So who conducted the autopsy?"

"Our local surgeon. If he thinks the death is suspicious, he sends the body over to the medical center in the next county where they got a full-time pathologist."

"Did he think this was suspicious?"

"This was a straight suicide. It was as clear as day."

"When was your last murder?" I asked.

"Three years ago."

"I'd like to talk to the surgeon."

"He's on a pig hunting trip. You can catch him next week when he gets back."

"Did Mitchell leave a note?"

"No note. But the gun was right next to him."

"Did you print the gun?"

"Of course we printed the gun," the sheriff said. "We may be in the mountains, but this is the mountains of Idaho, not Afghanistan. Mitchell's prints—and no one else's—were all over the gun, you suspicious son of a gun."

"Did you test his hands for gunshot residue?"

"No need to," the sheriff said defensively. "The suicide was obvious. And just out of curiosity, why you so interested in this guy?"

"This is just a standard follow-up."

The sheriff laughed. "Serves me right for thinkin' I could get a straight answer out of one of you Los Angle-ese boys."

Five minutes later, the sheriff faxed the autopsy report to the squad room, and I spread it out on my desk.

> Cause of death: penetrating gunshot wound to medulla oblongata. Mode of death: suicide. Entry: one-eighth inch above center of uvula. Stippling and sooting to back of the larynx and tongue. Direction: front to back. Projectile: copper jacketed lead .32-caliber bullet, flattened nose. Exit: none; recovered from medulla oblongata; massive hemorrhage. Trajectory: level. Associated injury from fall after gunshot: left external ear contusion; left lateral neck ecchymosis; left parietal scalp contusion, abrasion.

I understood the surgeon's hypothesis: Mitchell committed suicide by sticking a .32-caliber pistol in his mouth and pulling the trigger. The bullet rattled around in his skull and lodged in the base of the brainstem. Mitchell fell to the ground, bruising his ear, neck, and head.

The surgeon might know more about anatomy and medicine than me, but he probably had conducted only a handful of suicide and homicide autopsies. I'd viewed hundreds and had read thousands of autopsy reports. I trusted my own conclusion, which was diametrically opposed to the doctor's.

I didn't believe Mitchell committed suicide for one elemental reason: the trajectory of the bullet was level. I lifted my thumb and dropped my extended forefinger on the bottom row of my teeth, as if I was placing a gun inside my mouth. The trajectory was upward at about a thirty-degree angle. It was highly unlikely that anyone sticking a gun in his own mouth would drop the barrel so low that it was level and he could blow off the tissue below the epiglottis. And it was highly unlikely, I believed, that the injuries to Mitchell's ear, neck, and skull resulted from a fall after the gunshot. I simply could not envision Mitchell suffering significant contusions in three different places from a bounce off the floor.

It was clear to me that Mitchell had been struck several times with a blunt object. When he was dazed or unconscious, the killer stuck the barrel in Mitchell's mouth—to simulate suicide—pulled the trigger, and then rolled the dead man's fingers on the pistol butt.

CHAPTER 22

What were the odds that Relovich and Mitchell had been killed within months of each other? I'd pursued the obvious leads, now was time to go after the longshots. I knew that whoever broke into the house and killed Relovich and stole his laptop was probably wearing latex gloves, since no prints had been found—other than Relovich's and a few police officers. It looked like a professional job.

While the chances now of successfully lifting prints were remote, I knew it was not impossible. I had known of cases in which people wore latex gloves long enough so that their hands perspired, and when they touched smooth, solid objects, their fingerprints seeped through the rubber. Technicians using traditional methods had been unable to lift the faint prints, but lab workers using a high-tech process called vacuum metal deposition had been successful.

A few weeks before I had quit, I had investigated a four-year-old murder and was dazzled by the results of the process. My partner at the time had recovered a rusty Coke can from a backyard pond. A technician using VMD applied a thin layer of gold to the surface and dropped it into a vacuum chamber. Microscopic specks of oil from the fingerprint absorbed gold fragments. The technician then spread zinc over the can. The zinc and gold evaporated into vapors when they were heated in the chamber. The zinc coated the entire can, except for a single fingerprint on the side, which became visible as a contrasting image. That did not lead to the killer, but it made an impression on me.

Maybe VMD would yield results in the Relovich murder. I still suspected the shooter had a partner. So if both of them were wearing latex gloves and were in the house long enough to chat with Relovich and then rob him, I figured their hands might have perspired. And if they had ripped off Relovich's laptop, they probably had rummaged through his desk as well, which meant that to open the drawers one of them had grasped the shiny metal handles—ideal surfaces for VMD.

As I pulled off the Harbor Freeway, I rolled down the window and enjoyed the ocean air, a bracing contrast to the fetid smog of the central city. The morning had been overcast again, but the sun had eventually burned off the fog and the sky was clear. From Relovich's front porch, I could see boats drifting by in the channel, their white sails vivid against the blue-gray sea. The faint offshore breeze ruffled the flags at the edge of the harbor.

I returned to my car and pulled a toolbox and a bag of latex gloves out of my trunk. After opening the front door, I slipped on two pairs of gloves and, using a Phillips screwdriver, removed the three metal handles from the desk drawers. I dropped them into separate Baggies.

The LAPD crime lab did not have VMD equipment, so the desk handles would have to be sent to an independent lab in Orange County. Because LAPD supervisors always are confronted with budget shortfalls they usually try to discourage detectives from using outside labs unless it is absolutely crucial. And, unfortunately, VMD is an expensive process. But because an outside lab—and not the notoriously slow LAPD facility—does the test, the turnaround time is quick.

When I returned to the squad room, I told Duffy I wanted to VMD the metal handles.

"You're a pain in the ass, you know that?" Duffy grumbled. "If I authorize it, I've got to deal with all that LAPD red tape. I've got to go to SID, convince a supervisor that we need the test, that it's worth spending the dough on. After all that, the *supervisor* has to authorize it."

Duffy glumly stared at the phone, as if he hoped it would ring so he could delay making a decision.

"VMD is amazing because—"

"I know all about vacuum metal deposition," Duffy said. "I've heard all the stories. But I've never heard of them getting prints through latex gloves."

"It's happened."

"In for a fucking dime, in for a fucking dollar," Duffy muttered. "Just to get you out of my hair, I'll authorize it."

*   *   *

I headed out to the mid-Wilshire area in the late afternoon to question Mitchell's daughter. Rather than calling first, I decided to door-knock her, just in case she was reluctant to talk. Since Laura Mitchell was an elementary school teacher, I figured she would be home by now.

I drove west on Beverly, south on Rossmore, pulled down a side street, and parked in front of Mitchell's drab, blocky apartment building. I watched the breeze rustle a lush jacaranda that shaded the house next door, the blooms drifting down from the branches like a purple snowfall. I climbed the steps to the top unit, but before I could ring the doorbell, Mitchell, who had been peering out the front window, opened the door. I introduced myself.

"My brother told me you'd be coming by," she said, eyeing me coldly.

Mitchell, who was heavy and fair, wore beige cords and a brown round-neck sweater. Her hair was cut short in a matronly style, stiff with spray.

Standing in the doorway, she asked, "How can I help you?"

"Would you mind if we talked inside?"

"Yes, I'd mind. But I know from my father that you cops can make things unpleasant for people who don't cooperate."

The sofa in the living room was a jumble of torn pantyhose, blouses, skirts, nail polish bottles, emery boards, and cotton balls. The coffee table was dusted with corn flakes; in the corner was a half-eaten bowl of cereal that I figured had been there since breakfast. The apartment smelled of cat urine. I pushed aside a pile of blouses and squeezed onto the sofa. Mitchell dragged a chair over from the dining room.

"My brother told me all about his conversation with you," she said. "I don't think I have anything else to add. But I will tell you that I didn't get along with my father, and I don't particularly like cops."

She stared sullenly at me, crossing her arms and legs. I knew I wouldn't get much out of her if I began firing questions about her father. So I decided to chat casually with her and then stun her with news she hadn't expected, like a boxer throwing a few tentative jabs and then unleashing a short left hook—the knockout punch.

"What grade do you teach?"

"Third."

I smiled. "I think that was when my parents realized, after getting my report card, that I'd never be a neurosurgeon."

Mitchell picked at a cuticle, looking bored.

"Did you visit your father much up in Idaho?"

"No. I hate Idaho."

"Guess you don't like to fish?"

"How'd you guess?"

"Doesn't sound like your brother was close with your father."

"Nobody was close with my father."

"Did you talk with him much?"

"He'd call every once in a while. He'd visit L.A. every once in a while."

I stared out the window and watched jacaranda petals scatter in the breeze. "Did you know your father was murdered?"

Mitchell looked as if she had been jolted with a cattle prod.

Now that I had her attention, I decided to wait for her to ask the questions.

"Nobody said anything about this before."

I nodded.

Mitchell slumped onto the sofa. "Why didn't anyone tell me this before?"

"Because nobody knew about this before."

She looked confused. "Who found out he was murdered?"

"Me."

"Are you sure?"

"I'm pretty sure."

"How come, months later, I'm just finding this out."

"I was recently assigned to investigate the murder of a retired police officer by the name of Pete Relovich. During the course of that investigation, I was looking into some of his former partners. Your father worked with Pete for a few years. I checked out the circumstances of his death. I came to the conclusion that it wasn't a suicide."

"What do you base that on?"

"I'd rather not get into the details now. I will tell you, though, that I'm basing my conclusion on solid information. Somewhere down the line, I'll be able to explain everything."

Mitchell went slack and began to cry softly. I grabbed a Kleenex from the box on the coffee table and handed it to her.

She dried her eyes and coughed. "When my father walked out on us, it hit me a lot harder than my brother. Maybe because he was younger, he grew up used to not having a father. I was devastated. My mom lost it. I had to head the family for a while." She dried her eyes again. "I hated my father after he left. On weekends, when he'd come by to pick up my brother and me, I'd lock myself in my room. I never wanted to see him again. Now this news of yours makes me look at things differently."

"Why?"

Sniffling, she fiddled with a strand of hair. "About a year ago, I kind of lowered my defenses. I let him back into my life a little bit. Seemed like he was trying to repair our relationship, make up for the past. Then, without a word to me, or any warning, he kills himself. I thought, 'What a jerk. Isn't that just like him. He's done it again.'" She grabbed a balled up Kleenex from her pocket and dabbed her eyes. "When I heard he shot himself, I felt like he just abandoned me all over again. If he was murdered, I might feel different. Like maybe he didn't just walk out of my life a second time."

"Had he seemed depressed shortly before his death?"

"I know my brother told you it was hard to tell. But I could tell. And he didn't seem depressed at all. He liked living up there, where he could fly fish in the summer and hunt in the fall."

"Did your father have any buddies from the LAPD who he stayed in touch with?"

"He was kind of a loner type guy."

"Any ex-partners he kept contact with?"

She tapped a finger on her knee. "I think there was one guy. Randy Fringa. Years ago, they worked together in East L.A. At Hollenbeck. Before my dad moved to Idaho, they used to take fishing trips up near Bishop."

"Fringa still with the department?"

She shook her head. "I don't have his phone number or know where he lives. But I remember my dad saying that after he retired, he got a job working security at some big mall in Glendale."

"Do you remember your father coming into a substantial amount of money when he was a cop?"

"I don't know much about his finances. I just know he made his child support payments on time."

"Your brother said you got some of his personal items from the house."

She nodded.

"Can I see them?"

She walked into the bedroom, returned with a small suitcase, and handed it to me. I set it on the coffee table. Inside were a few photographs of her father and mother, probably when they were dating; his army dog tags; mementos from his years with the LAPD, including promotion certificates, an LAPD silver eagle cap pin, and a plaque for ten years of safe driving; a few fishing and hunting licenses; and a brown leather man's jewelry box.

I opened it up. Inside, on a felt base, were his wedding ring, a silver cross on a chain, a gold Rolex watch, another less expensive watch, a gold money clip, and several tie tacks. Taking them out, I set them on the sofa beside me. I shook the box, but nothing rattled. With a sharp tug, I removed the felt base—which was a false bottom.

In a compartment below, in two corners of the box, secured with strips of tape, were a carved ivory *netsuke* and an *ojime*: a demon and a demon queller. They were similar, but not identical to the ones I had found at Relovich's house.

She looked confused. "What are they?"

"The Japanese wear them on their kimono sashes. You've never seen them?"

She frowned and shook her head. "I had no idea they were there— until now."

CHAPTER 23

I drove out to the mall in Glendale, parked in front of a department store, and found my way to the security office. I asked a young woman manning the counter if Randy Fringa was working today. She held up an index finger, mumbled into an old-fashioned two-way radio, and said, "He'll be back in five."

When Fringa arrived, he studied me with a sour expression and said, "Do I know you?" He was a skinny man with a bobbing Adam's apple, who wore a wrinkled short-sleeved white shirt and a stained red polyester tie.

I handed him my card and told him I wanted to talk about Avery Mitchell. He led me to a small, windowless office, sat behind a desk, and crossed him arms over his chest.

I opened a battered metal folding chair leaning against a wall. "So I understand you worked at Hollenbeck. My first training officer ended up as a lieutenant there. That guy was—"

"What do you want to know?"

Most retired cops miss the camaraderie of the station and enjoy swapping news and gossip. I was surprised that Fringa was so hostile.

"I'm looking into Avery Mitchell's death."

"I heard it was a suicide."

"I have reason to believe it wasn't."

He tapped my card on his desk. "To tell you the truth, I'm pretty damn pissed off at the LAPD. If I could've stayed for thirty, or at least twenty-five, I would've have had a decent pension. Something I could've lived off of. I might have joined Avery up in Idaho. and spent my days fishing, instead of humping my butt at this chickenshit job."

"What happened?"

"I took a poke at a some spic who was fat mouthing me."

"How'd they find out?"

"He was cuffed to a detention bench and this boot with a stick up his ass ratted me out. When I was coming up, boots kept their mouths shut or they wouldn't last a month in the department. It's a different fucking world today."

I nodded and tried to appear sympathetic.

"My captain cut a deal with me. Retire and he wouldn't write it up. I knew that poke, in today's LAPD where the politicians run the department, could get me fired. I had twenty years and change, so I pulled the pin."

"When did you work with Mitchell?"

He studied my card. "I still got buddies in the department. Before I say anything, I'm going to ask them about you. When I'm ready to talk, *if* I'm ready to talk, I'll give you a call."

I knew there was no point in trying to pressure a bitter ex-cop. All I could do was hope I passed muster with his buddies.

I paced on the roof of my apartment after the interview with Fringa. Red-rimmed clouds massed behind the San Gabriels, purple in the waning light. A lost seagull squawked overhead, skimming the rooftops, searching for food. Watching the first stars prick through the sky, I considered the links between Mitchell and Relovich: they were partners when Relovich hit the $60,000 jackpot; they had similar *netsukes* and *ojimes*; they had hidden the figures; they had both been murdered.

I knew that when retired or off-duty cops were killed, detectives invariably assumed the homicides were connected to their police work. Often they were wrong. As a result, the detectives frequently ignored key elements of their personal lives that could have led them to the killer. But these two homicides, I suspected, were connected to their days on the street when they were patrol partners. I just didn't know how.

I also believed that whoever killed Relovich had killed Mitchell. I could understand why Fuqua would want Relovich dead. But what was his link to Mitchell? At the time Relovich had arrested Fuqua for armed robbery, he was no longer partners with Mitchell. Relovich had been promoted and was working as a Harbor division robbery detective, while Mitchell remained a patrol officer in Hollywood. So why would Fuqua go all the way to Idaho to take out Mitchell? That made no sense to me.

When the last light drained from the sky, and the moon rose over the office towers, I walked back down to my loft. I was hungry but discovered my refrigerator was almost empty, with just a six-pack of ale, jars of pickles and mustard, and a can of peaches. I changed out of my suit into jeans, sneakers, and a T-shirt and was about to walk to dinner when I heard a knock on the door.

"Who is it?"

"I decided to make like a detective," Nicole Haddad said. "Just show up at someone's place without calling."

I opened the door. "So where's the boyfriend?"

"The on-again, off-again thing is off-again for a few days. He went out of town."

"I'm not into the off-again, on-again dynamic. Maybe you should find someone who likes getting jacked around." I crossed my arms and stared at her. Being Nicole's backdoor man did not appeal to me. But standing in the doorway, in her tight jeans and black crop top, revealing her tanned stomach and navel pierce, she looked damn good.

"You going to invite me inside or not?"

"No," I said, waiting a beat to gauge her reaction.

She looked hurt. As she turned to leave, I said, "I was just about ready to get some dinner. You like Korean barbecue?"

"Sounds good to me."

We walked down Second Street to the edge of Little Tokyo. The restaurant was wedged between a sushi bar and a Japanese candy shop. We passed through the smoky front room to a small patio in back, bracketed by huge stands of bamboo. A waiter fired up the grill, which was built into the middle of our table. Nicole frowned at the menu.

"Why don't you order for me."

A few minutes after I ordered, a waiter returned with a pot of roasted wheat tea and then tossed a half dozen thinly sliced strips of marinated beef on the grill, stopping by every few minutes to turn them over. When the beef was ready, Nicole, following my lead, wrapped a piece of meat in a lettuce leaf and dipped it in a dark sauce with her chopsticks.

"Hmm," she said, nodding appreciatively. "I can taste the soy sauce and garlic. What else?"

"Some oyster sauce, ginger, sesame oil, and a few other things."

The waiter brought a large stone bowl with rice and an assortment of seafood. He cracked an egg, which cooked as he stirred it into the rice, and served us. I ordered a bottle of Korean rice wine called *bek se ju*, which was laced with ginseng.

She took a few sips of wine and said, "I like being with you."

"Why do you like being with someone who is—" I paused, swirling the wine in my glass. "What did you call me that first night—numb?"

"On the surface, you are. But somewhere down there"—she reached across the table and jabbed at my solar plexus—"you're not." She smiled lasciviously. "You proved *that* the other night."

I filled our wineglasses.

"Maybe you come off like that," Nicole said, "because of all those bodies you've seen as a cop."

"I saw plenty of bodies *before* I became a cop."

"Where was that?"

"I was in the army. The Israeli army."

"So that's how you became familiar with Lebanon."

"That's right."

"I remember when Israel invaded Lebanon back in the eighties. I was a little girl and I remember how my father followed all the news."

"Did you know we were on the same side then?"

"Who's we?" she asked.

"The Israeli army and the Christians in Lebanon. We were allies. They provided us with a key intelligence network. The Israelis figured they'd drive the PLO out of Lebanon, install a Christian as president who would control the Muslim hordes, among a few other geopolitical goals. Turned into a fucking quagmire."

"I don't really know that much about that time. It was something my father followed. To me, it was old country stuff."

"The relationship between your people and my people—the Jews and the Lebanese Christians—go back a long time. In the thirties, when Zionists first made contact with them, they both thought they had a lot in common. They viewed themselves as enlightened islands of Western culture, surrounded by a sea of uncivilized Muslims. The relationship goes back thousands of years. I remember from my Hebrew school days that King Hiram in Lebanon sent the cedar trees down to Israel for Solomon's Temple."

"Why'd you enlist in the Israeli army?"

"I was just a kid, a naïve college student. I wanted to protect people. I didn't want to see any more Jewish victims."

"Your parents probably weren't too happy about that."

"They weren't. When I joined the LAPD I promised I'd go back at night and get the degree. I eventually did. When I was thirty, at night."

"Since you solved your case and got on TV the other night, you got your taste of glory. You must be feeling pretty good now that it's all over."

"Not really."

She looked surprised. "Why not?"

"Because it's not over."

"Why not?"

"There's more to the case," I said, dropping my credit card on the tray. "I'll tell you about it some other time."

We walked back to my building, and as we entered the loft, she lifted my leather shoulder holster with the Beretta and the handcuffs tucked in a pouch off the back of a chair. She pulled out the handcuffs, crossed the room, and lightly ran the metal edges across my wrists. "We could have a lot of fun with these."

"If you've seen some of the people I've hooked up, you'd have an entirely different image in your mind."

She slipped her arms around my waist and kissed me lightly on the lips. "By the time I'm done with you, I'll make sure you have a *new* image."

I dipped my knees slightly, grabbed her by the knees, lifted her over my shoulder, and tossed her on the bed. Sitting astride her, I said, "Since they're *my* handcuffs, I think I'm the one who'd better do the cuffing."

"I don't know if I can handle that," she said weakly, a rare moment when she seemed to briefly lose her composure.

I pulled the key out of my pocket and clicked open the handcuffs. But before I could slip them on her wrists, my cell phone rang.

"Sorry," I said, reaching for the phone.

"Can't you pretend you didn't hear it."

I watched her stretch on the bed, her top rising and revealing the edge of her lacy black bra, and seriously considered her suggestion. "Can't do it," I said, as I climbed off the bed and answered the phone.

"I asked around about you," Fringa said.

"Yeah."

"I'm willing to talk to you."

"I'll stop by the mall tomorrow."

"Make it tonight."

"Can't do it tonight."

"Then you can catch me in two weeks. I'm taking the RV up to Oregon early tomorrow morning. We can talk when I get back."

"How late you work?"

"Until midnight."

I looked down at Nicole, splayed on the bed, giving me a half smile, and felt so frustrated, I kicked a chair across the room. "Okay. I'll be there in a half hour."

As I slipped off my jeans and T-shirt, tossing them on the bed, and pulled a pair of slacks and button-down shirt out of the closet, Nicole crouched in front of me, licking my stomach. "Can I persuade you to stick around?"

"Wish I could," I said, my voice catching. "I'll give you a call when things clear up."

"The boyfriend's gone for a few days. Let's take advantage of our window of opportunity before it closes."

CHAPTER 24

When I stopped by the mall's security office, Fringa said, "Let's take a ride."

I followed him through the dim, deserted mall, through a side door and into the parking lot. He hopped in a small, electric cart and said, "I gotta take a last patrol before end of watch."

I climbed into the cart, and he began to cruise around the property. "Let me give you one piece of advice, Levine. Don't fuck up like me. Or you'll end up when you're fifty driving a fucking golf cart at midnight around a mall. Do your twenty-five or thirty and don't piss anyone off."

"I'm trying."

"Like I said, I asked around about you. I still got some friends in the department. Word on you is that you can act like a dickhead sometimes, but when it comes to doing the job, you're old school. You'll do whatever it takes to clear the case."

"I think that's a compliment," I said, smiling.

"In my book, it is. Anyway, I'm glad you're looking into Avery's death. When you stopped by this afternoon, I wanted to make sure you'd do a righteous investigation. Not some quickie in-and-out LAPD whitewash. Anyway, I never thought it was a suicide."

"Why's that?"

"Just not the type."

"When was the last time you talked to him?"

"A few months ago. Sounded like the same old Avery. We talked a couple of times a year. Whenever he had to come to L.A., we'd get dinner. I was up to Idaho a few years ago. Stayed with Avery for a week. Went fishing." He pulled the cart over, behind a department store. "Suicide? Naw. Just can't see it. After I heard the news, I called the sheriff in that one-stoplight town in Idaho. Told him I didn't think Avery was the suicide type. He said he'd look into it."

"Where did you meet Mitchell?"

"At Hollenbeck. We were working patrol. We ended up as partners for a few years. Best partner I ever had."

"Why was that?"

"He was funny as hell. Made those eight hours fly. And you could count on him. He always had your back."

"Before Mitchell died, was he worried about anything?"

"Avery was kind of a closed-mouth guy, so I don't know if he'd tell me."

"Was he concerned about anyone coming after him?"

"Avery could take care of himself."

"You have any ideas of who might have wanted to kill him?"

"No idea at all."

"You remember when he transferred to Hollywood Division?"

"He didn't transfer. He *got* transferred. Pissed off our captain for arguing with him about some stupid-ass thing. So the captain decided to give him some freeway therapy. Hollenbeck was only about twenty minutes from where Avery was living at the time with his family. Sending him to Hollywood added a lot of miles to his commute."

"When was this?"

He tapped his finger on the steering wheel. "Thirteen, fourteen years ago."

"Did you hear about Pete Relovich?"

"What about him?"

"He was killed at his house in Pedro?"

"Jesus."

"There was an article in the *Times*."

"I don't read the *Times*. They're always ripping the department. You think there's a connection?"

"Do you?"

"I know Pete and Avery were partners for a few years. I had lunch with them once when I had some business up in Hollywood." He started up the cart and began cruising the mall lot again. "Two partners getting waxed in the same year. That's too much of a coincidence for me."

"When they worked together in Hollywood, anything going on with Avery that sticks out in your mind?"

Fringa drove in silence for a minute of two. He stopped and turned toward me. "The homicide is what you're after, right? You're not interested in stirring up a lot of shit are you?"

"All I care about is who killed them. Anything else they might have been involved in doesn't interest me."

"Okay. When Avery was working Hollywood he came into some money."

"How much money?"

"I don't know. I just know that it must have been a nice piece of change. Because that was about the time he bought his place up in Idaho."

"Where'd he get the money?"

"That's the question, isn't it. I have no fucking idea. I'll tell you this, though. He didn't have any money before he hit Hollywood. He came into the money there."

"Can you give me a better idea *when* he came into the money? Maybe an exact year?"

"Can't remember exactly. Just sometime when he was working Hollywood."

We cruised around for another thirty minutes, but I wasn't able to find out much more about Mitchell. I had to listen to Fringa continue to complain about how he got royally screwed by the LAPD; how he wanted to sue the department but none of the shysters he talked to would take his case; how if he could do it all over again, he would have steered clear of the LAPD and, instead, gone into real estate, like his brother-in-law in San Diego, who's now a millionaire.

I was at my desk at five o'clock the next morning, eager to get started. I finally had a direction to follow, some leads that had coalesced. The money that dropped in Mitchell's and Relovich's laps was a good starting point.

Relovich's ex-wife told me that Pete purchased the house eleven years ago and the sale closed in February. I figured it was likely that Mitchell had scored his bundle of cash around that time. Previously, I had obtained from Records and Identification all the arrest reports from that year and the previous year as well. I began sifting through the arrest reports, starting when Relovich purchased the house and working backward. I didn't know exactly what I was looking for, but decided to search for cases in which it seemed possible for Relovich and Mitchell to recover large amounts of cash or the carved Japanese figures.

By noon, I had studied all eighty-seven arrest reports. A half dozen of them, I decided, merited a more thorough investigation. I wanted to see the entire case files, which included witness statements, interviews, crime scene diagrams, photographs, and everything else that chronicled the investigation. So after stopping at a hole-in-the-wall Mexican restaurant on Sunset for chicken mole, I drove to the city archives, just east of downtown. Parking on the roof, I walked over to the musty office, where documents from city departments were stored, including building permits, personnel records, planning documents, and LAPD case files. The long, narrow room was filled with researchers and historians hunched over wooden tables, surrounded by white boxes filled with files. On the walls were faded pictures of former city officials, maps of Los Angeles, and old neighborhood photographs.

I had jotted down the storage location numbers for the half dozen cases I wanted to study further. After handing the numbers to a clerk, I wandered over to a glass case in the corner that displayed the original yellowed map—almost 100 years old—for the "Venice of America" subdivision. I hunched over, studied the layout, and located the plot for Nicole Haddad's house.

When the clerk returned with the boxes, I lugged them to my car, returned to PAB, and quickly riffled through the files. One case immediately intrigued me. Relovich and Mitchell had responded to a 911 call from a neighbor who spotted a man climbing into the back window of a house in Hollywood, a few blocks north of Franklin Avenue. The officers responded, but just missed the burglar.

I put the case at the top of my priority list when I read the property report. An officer had written that in addition to some electronic equipment, a dozen pieces of "Oriental art" also were stolen. Those pieces might have included *netsukes* and *ojimes*, I figured. The man's name was Richard Quan, which sounded Chinese, but that did not preclude him from collecting Japanese art.

I headed out to Hollywood to interview Quan. He lived in a 1930's Spanish-style house with a red tile roof and a courtyard with a bubbling fountain shaded by bottlebrush trees, the bristly red blooms dappling the water and carpeting the lawn. Quan, fortunately, was home. He invited me inside and we sat around a dining room table. A half dozen antique ginger jars, with delicate rose patterns and gold edging, were lined atop a gleaming Chinese rosewood cabinet set against a dining room wall.

I explained that I was following up on a robbery. Quan's wife briefly interrupted us and asked if I preferred tea or coffee. I told her tea would be fine; she returned a few minutes later with a pot of oolong tea and two cups on a serving tray. She set it on the coffee table and quietly returned to the kitchen.

Quan filled the cups, handed me one, and asked, "Why are you interested in a case this old?"

"It might be connected to another case I'm tracking. I was interested in the Asian art that was stolen. Any of it Japanese?"

"No," Quan said stiffly. "You know, there *is* a difference between the many cultures in Asia."

Trying to placate Quan, I said, "The only reason I ask is because the property report was not specific. It just stated that 'Oriental art' was stolen."

"I find the term *Oriental* offensive," he said, frowning at me.

"I'm sorry to offend you, but I was just quoting the report. I would have written it up differently."

"I accept your apology."

I took a sip of tea. "I would appreciate it if you'd tell me what, specifically, was stolen?"

"Some things of little value; some of great value, including pieces that have been in my family for a long time—hanging scrolls on rice paper, woven silk tapestries, enamel incense burners, and some painted porcelain and carved jade pieces."

"Did you ever recover them?"

"Yes," he said, looking uncomfortable.

"I noticed from the arrest report that the two policemen on the scene—Officers Relovich and Mitchell—made an arrest later that week. They pulled over a bunch of kids who had some Asian art in their trunk—"

"Junk," Quan said contemptuously. "They showed me the items.

They weren't mine. It turned out these kids had broken into a Chinese restaurant and stole some decorative items that were on the shelves."

"How'd you recover your items?"

Quan pursed his lips and stared at his tea. "Can we talk confidentially?"

"Certainly. I'm only interested to see if there are any links with my *other* case. If what you tell me doesn't connect, it'll go no further than you and me."

Quan finished his tea and said, "The person who broke into my house and stole these things—it turned out I knew him."

I waited for him to continue. After a minute of silence, I asked, "Who was he?"

"He was my daughter's boyfriend at the time. A very bad boy. Associated with a Chinese gang in Monterey Park. My wife and I forbid her to see him. A friend of our daughter confided to us that this boy had sold our things. My wife and I made a deal with my daughter: If she never saw him again, we would not go to the police. She agreed. Detectives later recovered the items from a pawnshop. And that was the end of it. Until now."

I believed Quan. "Did your daughter keep her word?"

Quan beamed. He opened his wallet and showed me a picture of a young couple with a baby boy. "She married a fine young man a few years ago. This is my first grandchild."

When I returned to the squad room, I picked up the ringing phone.

"Ash Levine here."

"I read something in the *Hadassah News* that was very disturbing."

I sighed. "Hello, Mom."

"The article said that mixed marriages fail at twice the rate as the national average. Just imagine what the statistics would be if they studied Jewish-*Arab* marriages."

"Mom, I have no intention of marrying *any*one now."

"Things can change."

"Not with me."

"Are you still dating that Iraqi girl?"

"Lebanese."

"I can't keep those countries straight. Are you still dating that *Muslim?*"

"She's not a Muslim. She's Christian."

"Are you still dating her?"

"It's too complicated to explain. Let's talk another time."

"Will you be coming by for Shabes dinner on Friday night?"

"Sorry. I can't make it."

"I think you should. Uncle Benny met a nice girl in his building. Single. Very attractive. From a nice family. He wants to bring her along."

"Forget it. Tell Uncle Benny I appreciate his efforts, but to hold off."

She did not respond.

"Did you hear what I said?"

"Yes, yes," she said impatiently.

"Look. I'm just too busy this week. Please pass that along to Uncle Benny. Tell him *not* to bring the girl."

"Oh, your job is *so* important. God forbid, another *shvartzeh* gets murdered in South Central and you don't show up. That would be such a tragedy—"

"I don't work South Central anymore, Mom."

"Wherever you work, I think it's important that you have dinner with us on Friday because—"

"Got to go Mom," I interrupted.

I hung up, and returned to the files I had recovered from the archives. A homicide in the Hollywood Hills looked faintly promising. The victim was a small-time burglar named Jack Freitas who had clipped the wires to the alarm system at the home he was robbing. The owner, Lloyd Silver, was vacationing in Italy with his family when Freitas broke in. The case was a curious one because someone shot Freitas in the temple, but the killer was never caught.

Relovich and Mitchell had been on patrol in the area, heard the gunshot, and sped to the scene. They found the body and arrested a homeless man wandering down a nearby street, who, they later discovered, had no connection to the case. Homicide detectives theorized at the time, according to the files, that Freitas' partner double-crossed and killed him because he didn't want to share the loot.

What interested me was the name of the firm Silver owned—Kyoto

Import-Export. Since Kyoto was a city in Japan, it followed that Silver might have collected some *netsukes* and *ojimes*. The property report, however, did not list any stolen objects d'art. The thieves had blasted open a bedroom safe and stole Silver's wife's diamond and emerald jewelry, valued at more than $300,000.

I decided to stop by the Lloyd Silver's house in the Hollywood Hills.

CHAPTER 25

I headed west on Sunset at dusk and cut north on a canyon road, past hills cloaked in chaparral, studded with yucca and stunted fan palms. Cruising beneath a canopy of live oaks, I pulled onto a narrow, winding street, the homes bordered by oleander with pink and red blossoms, thick stands of bamboo, and cactus gardens, the prickly pears starred with pale orange blooms.

Silver's house was easy to spot, a dramatic, modern structure, all sharp angles, built of glass and steel, teetering on a hillside. After climbing fifty-one steep steps, I rang the front bell. While I waited for someone to answer, I realized how quiet it was in the hills compared to my loft. The only sounds were the breeze rattling the bamboo and the cars whirring through the canyon.

A man looked through a peephole and shouted, "Who is it?"

"Detective Ash Levine. LAPD."

"ID?"

I covered the peephole with my badge.

The door opened, revealing a short, skinny man with thinning gray hair and a little ponytail. He wore shorts, sandals, and a short-sleeved yellow silk shirt. "What's the problem, detective?"

"No real problem. Just checking out some old cases. I wanted to talk to you about that burglar who was killed at your house about ten years ago."

Silver sighed, absentmindedly fingering his ponytail.

"Can I come inside?" I asked.

"Of course."

I followed Silver into the living room, which had a sweeping view of the city, sheathed in a film of smog. The room was spare, almost monastic, with hardwood floors and a scattering of black leather and chrome furniture. The white walls were bare.

I joined Silver on the sofa and asked, "When it's clear, can you see the ocean from here?"

"A few times a year," Silver said, looking distracted. "So what's this about? Did you finally find out who killed that thief in my living room?"

"We haven't."

"Well, he was no great loss. But that means the shooter is still out there victimizing other home owners."

"With your cooperation, we might be able to get him behind bars."

"And recover my property?"

"Maybe."

"Is that what this is about?"

"Not exactly. I'm working on another homicide case and I'm trying to determine if it's related to that murder at your house."

"That was a long time ago."

"It was," I said. "But just to cover all my bases, I wanted to ask you a few questions."

"Shoot."

"I noticed from the crime report that three hundred thousand dollars worth of jewelry was stolen from your safe."

"That's right," Silver said.

"That's a lot of jewelry."

Silver flashed me a forced smile. "My wife has expensive taste."

"What kind of business are you in?"

"What does *that* have to do with anything?" he asked, sounding defensive.

"Just background."

"Okay. I'm in the import-export business."

"From what country?"

"Japan."

"What do you import?"

Silver nervously tugged on his ponytail. "Is all this necessary?"

"Got anything to hide?" I said, smiling.

"Of course not. We import Japanese electronic equipment."

"And what do you export?"

"Nothing. Why?"

"You said your business was import-export."

"It's just an expression."

I sensed Silver's growing irritation, so I shifted the interview in another direction. "Anything else stolen from your house?"

Silver lightly brushed his forefinger across his lips and said "Just the jewelry. I told the officers that at the time."

"You *sure* nothing else was stolen?" I asked.

"I'm sure."

"How about any art work or art objects?"

He shook his head.

"You sure no small Japanese figurines were stolen, or things like that?"

Silver glowered at me. "You calling me a liar, detective?"

I knew this was a critical juncture in the interview. If I was too belligerent, too combative, Silver might refuse to answer the questions and tell me to pound sand or call his attorney. I had no leverage. I would simply have to walk back down the fifty-one steps and drive off.

I didn't know if Silver was lying; I didn't know if the Freitas homicide and the jewelry heist were connected to the Relovich and Mitchell murders. Still, I was suspicious of Silver for reasons I couldn't articulate. Maybe it was because Silver's business had a Japanese connection; maybe it was because he was so testy. The murder also bothered me. Why would Freitas's partner shoot him during the heist? Why attract all that attention? Why not just wait and plug him later?

I inched closer on the sofa to Silver. "Let me break it down for you. If you don't level with me right now, I'm going to do two things. First, I'm going to obtain your insurance records and examine the jewelry purchases you made and confirm that they were truly worth three hundred thousand. If they weren't, I'm going to go after you for insurance fraud. The second thing I'm going to do is talk to the supervising detective at Hollywood Homicide and ask him to reopen the Jack Freitas murder case. If he finds you've withheld any information, I'm going to request that he prosecute you for conspiracy," I said, bluffing. "And conspiracy in a murder can get you locked up for a very long time."

I knew immediately that I had hit pay dirt. Silver blinked hard. The corners of his mouth twitched. "You've got no proof," he said weakly.

"You continue jacking me around, and I'll make sure I get the proof.

But if you level with me right now and tell me everything that happened, I'll forget about the insurance company. I'll forget about talking to Hollywood Homicide."

I checked my watch. "I'll give you one minute to decide. Then I'm leaving. By tomorrow, you won't even recognize your life anymore."

Silver gazed out at the smog, a thousand-yard stare. Dropping his chin to his chest, he said softly, "Okay."

"Okay, *what?*"

"There *were* some other things stolen." He sighed wistfully. "I had some very nice works."

"All Japanese?"

"Yes. A hanging scroll from the sixteen hundreds. An eighteenth-century two-panel screen—ink and color on silk. Some exquisite splashed ink landscapes, and a few erotic woodcut prints—all hundreds of years old."

"Any *netsukes?*"

"Yes, yes," he said, pained. "*Netsukes*, iron tea kettles, iron sword guards, *ojimes*, lacquered boxes."

"Why didn't you tell the police or the insurance company about these items? They weren't listed on the property report."

Silver reached around and tugged on his ponytail again. "You sure if I tell you the truth, you're not going to go after me for this?"

"I'm not interested in insurance fraud, art theft, or income tax evasion," I said in what I hoped was a reassuring tone. "All I care about is the murder I'm working. I just want to see if it's connected to what happened at your house."

"Okay," Silver said softly, more to himself than to me. "I couldn't talk about these items because I wasn't supposed to have them."

"Why not?"

"A few Japanese art dealers were ripped off. Some very old and very valuable items were stolen. It was too risky to fence them in Japan. So the thieves sold them to an American. The Japanese would not be too happy to see these treasures leaving their country. But if the American had an import business, he would know how to slip these items in through customs. Back in the States, he could have kept some of the items and sold some of the others."

"Just so I'm clear, this person you're talking about is you?"

"Unfortunately."

"And it was hard to launder the profits, so you kept a lot of cash in your home safe."

"How'd you find out?"

Ignoring him, I asked, "How much?"

"About two hundred thousand."

"So you inflated the amount of your wife's jewelry—which was never stolen—to, at least, cover your cash loss and some of the art. The rest, you just had to write off."

"That's pretty close to it."

"Why'd you take the chance of displaying this stuff on your walls?"

"I didn't keep them out here," he said, pointing to the living room walls. "They were in our bedroom and my home office, where guests aren't permitted." He stared out the window again. "What's the use of risking so much to secure magnificent works of art if you can't see them?"

"Any idea who ripped you off?"

"I still don't have a clue."

"Any idea why Freitas was killed?"

"Whoa," he said, waving his palms. "I had nothing to do with that. That's your area of expertise. Certainly not mine."

It was so dark when I drove back down the canyon—the moon was obscured by high clouds—that I had trouble negotiating the hairpin turns, but I relaxed when I finally hit Sunset and headed east. As I approached downtown, I decided I was too energized to go home, so I pulled into the parking garage, walked to PAB, and took the elevator to the fifth floor. I pulled the tape recorder out of my briefcase with the microphone in the corner, listened to Silver's interview again, and summarized it on a statement form for my murder book.

CHAPTER 26

Galvanized by the break in the case, I spent a restless evening at home. I tried to sleep, but kept squirming in bed, thinking about the interview with Silver. At three thirty, I finally crawled out of bed, showered, and dressed; I knew I was too charged up to get much sleep. Driving north on Broadway, I flicked on my windshield wipers. It was a typical foggy June morning, socked in from the beaches to the valleys. As I stopped at an intersection, the slick street reflecting red from the signal over-head, I decided to splurge on an expensive breakfast.

I drove a few blocks west of downtown and parked in front of the Pacific Dining Car, located on a bleak intersection, across the street from a gas station and a liquor store with a rusty metal security gate in front. I liked the restaurant even though, like so many L.A. institutions, it was more façade than reality. Built in the 1920s as a replica of a railroad din-ing car, steel wheels were bolted on and the structure was rolled to an empty lot. Still, the atmosphere was comfortable and clubby and it served some of the best—and most expensive—steaks in the city.

The twenty-four-hour restaurant, with gleaming wood paneling and polished brass lamps, was quiet and desolate. I settled in at a corner booth and ordered the breakfast filet and scrambled eggs, a short stack of blueberry pancakes, and a carafe of coffee. I ate slowly, savoring the meal. When I heard the first wave of delivery trucks grinding their gears as they rumbled down West 6th Street, I bought a paper and lingered over my coffee.

When I returned to the squad room, Duffy intercepted me. "So where are we on the case? What now?"

I decided not to brief him about my interview with Silver. I didn't want to tell him anything yet that might attract attention from the brass, who might waste my time by calling me in for meetings and updates.

"I've got a few things I'm chasing," I said.

"Well, don't do anything too crazy over the next few days, because I won't be around to run interference for you with Grazzo. We've got a department retreat for homicide supervisors this weekend in San Diego. I'm heading down this afternoon."

I left Duffy's office and Ortiz grabbed my arm and led me toward the break room. He poured us two cups of coffee and said, "Let's go outside." We took the elevator down the ground floor and sat on a stone bench in front of the building.

"So what's happening with your gallery owner?"

"She wants to see me when her boyfriend's not around."

Ortiz clapped me on the shoulder. "Don't be so gloomy. Could be the ideal relationship. You don't have to waste any time and money on going to movies, dinner, or, with this babe, boring art gallery openings. You can just nail her when her boyfriend's not around and have plenty of time left over to play golf with me."

"I don't play golf."

Ortiz swung an imaginary club. "Now's the perfect time to start."

When we returned to the squad room, I grabbed the Freitas homicide file, leafed through it, and jotted down the names of the two Hollywood Homicide detectives who investigated the murder. Relovich and Mitchell were the patrol officers who responded to the scene; I wanted to see what the investigators had to say. Searching the LAPD's Alpha roster, I discovered that one of the detectives was still with the department—he now worked as a lieutenant in Northeast. I called him and asked about the case. But he didn't remember much and he told me the case wasn't worth pursuing.

"Just one less scumbag on the street now," he said.

I asked about his former partner, and the lieutenant provided the phone number of a private investigation firm in San Jose. The former partner, however, recalled even less about the case.

I cut across the squad room to Commercial Crimes and wandered into the office of Dave Papazian, the art cop. I told Papazian about the robbery at Silver's house, his import-export business, and the man's art collection. "You ever come across this guy?" I asked.

Papazian shook his head.

"You ever hear of that heist at his house?"

"When was it?"

"About eleven years ago."

Papazian stroked his chin. "That's before my time, before I got this gig. But just to be safe, I'll check my records. If he's filed any theft reports since then, I'll let you know."

I returned to my desk, leaned back in my chair, and closed my eyes. The interview with Silver was definitely a break. The problem was I didn't know how to follow up on it, how to create a progression to the next clue, and the next, and the next. After talking to Silver, I assumed Relovich and Mitchell were dirty; I assumed they had stumbled onto the crime scene while on patrol and pocketed the cash from the safe before the homicide detectives arrived.

If Relovich and Mitchell were dirty, I didn't relish the prospect of documenting it. I knew the revelation would be devastating to their families. When Relovich's daughter was old enough to learn the truth, she'd be crushed. But the shooter, I suspected, was still out there. He'd already killed two ex-cops. He might kill another.

I thought about Terrell Fuqua, who was facing San Quentin's gas chamber. I didn't believe he killed Relovich. Even if he was a scumbag, I couldn't let him go down for a crime he didn't commit. I leaned back in my chair and closed my eyes. If Fuqua didn't kill Relovich, who would want to set him up? And why?

I decided to listen to Silver's interview again. I slipped my headphones on and pressed play. Was Silver more culpable than he acknowledged? I wondered. Was Silver telling everything he knew? Probably not. Everyone who confesses always leaves something out. I pressed the pause button. Would it be worth my while to question Silver again? What points should I follow up on? I realized that another interview with Silver was pointless. I pounded my palm on my desk in frustration.

"What the hell's wrong with you," Ortiz shouted across the squad room.

I tossed the tape recorder and headphones into my bottom drawer. "I can't think."

"Remember that psycho who was doing his Benihana routine on those downtown transients? Sliced and diced about six of them."

"The Spring Street Slasher," I said.

"Yeah, that's the one. What did you do when you hit a dead end on the case?" One day, you were sitting here agonizing just like this. Couldn't figure what he was using for a weapon. Then the next day you knew it was a . . . a . . . What the hell was it?"

"A ceramic dimpled meat slicer," I said. "Made in Germany. Went to a kitchen supply store. Looked at about a hundred knives. Saw that one. It matched the wound pattern on the body. Started interviewing chefs downtown until I found one who—"

"So how'd you get that burst of inspiration?"

"I got away from the case for an afternoon and cleared my head."

"Why don't you do that now?"

"Good idea," I said.

A cruise down to the harbor and a walk along the water might do me some good. I wanted to talk to Relovich's uncle anyway, so I called him and arranged to meet him at his boat.

The sky at the harbor was so overcast that the horizon line was obscured and the sky and ocean melded in a sweep of sidewalk gray. The oil tankers steaming north were just faint one-dimensional silhouettes drifting in and out of the fog.

I climbed aboard the *Anna Marie* and sat on a deck chair beside Relovich.

"Want some coffee?"

Before I could respond, Relovich bounded below deck and returned with two metal cups, sloshing coffee on the deck.

"Never got a chance to say thanks for doing right by Pete," Relovich said. "I read about you arresting that no good son of a bitch."

In order to avoid a complicated explanation, I said, "There might have been an accomplice. So I've still got some work to do on the case. Would you mind if I asked you a few more questions?"

Relovich shook his head.

"I want to ask you about one of Pete's ex-partners, a guy named Avery Mitchell. What do you know about him?"

"Met him once. Long time ago. Maybe more than ten years ago. They were down here one afternoon and I took 'em to lunch. I didn't care for this Mitchell character. He had this thin, greasy little mustache. I don't trust a man who can't grow a decent mustache."

"Anything else about him you remember?"

"Not really. Just that he seemed kind of shifty looking. And I don't think Pete liked him."

"Why's that?"

"Just a feeling I had when I saw the two of them together. Pete seemed to just tolerate the guy."

"Did Pete ever talk about Mitchell, ever say anything about him to you?"

He shook his head.

"Did Pete have any artwork around his house?"

Relovich looked confused. "Artwork? What do you mean?"

"You know, like paintings or pieces of carved wood or ivory. Maybe art objects. Maybe Japanese-type artwork."

"You gotta be kidding me. Pete? Not a chance. He wouldn't know Japanese artwork if he chipped a tooth on it." Relovich swatted the air. "I was talking to Pete's ex-wife the other day. She wanted me to ask you something. I've been meaning to call you. Since her daughter inherited the house, she wants to know when the LAPD will release it. She wants to rent it out."

"Why didn't she call me herself?"

"She's a touchy bitch," he said. "She's tired of you going out there and asking her questions. But I understand. You're just doing your job."

"Did Pete seem worried about anything these last few months?"

Relovich blew on his coffee a few times, before taking a sip. "One thing."

"What was that?"

"He worried that he hadn't been a good enough father to his little girl. 'Cause of his drinking. During the past few months he tried to change that. But Pete didn't talk much about it. He was a pretty closed-mouthed guy. These Americans, all they do is gab, gab, gab about their *feelings*," he said, as if he found the word distasteful. "Pete was more like his pop and me. More Old Country. Kept things to himself."

I questioned the old man for a few more minutes, but learned nothing useful. As I climbed down from the ship, Relovich called out, "Don't stop until you find that accomplice. He deserves to pay for what he did."

I returned to my car, removed the tape recorder from my briefcase, and walked down the dock alongside the channel, dodging bird droppings. When I found a bench on an isolated stretch, I plugged in my ear-phones and listened again to the interview with Silver.

As I was finishing the interview, the sun pierced a slit in the fog, streaking the shimmering water with specks of honeyed light. Looking out at sea, I felt disheartened. I had no idea how I would identify the shooter.

CHAPTER 27

I drove back downtown in a sour mood. I could feel the case stalling out, heading for unsolved purgatory. I was close to the truth, but I had no idea what to do next, how to take that final step to IDing the shooter. It was Friday evening, I was at a dead end, and I had only a few days left to work on the case. On Monday, Duffy would put me back on call, and I would soon be jammed up with another case, another cluster of characters to interview, another set of priorities and pressures, another mystery to unravel.

I pulled into the parking garage, walked to PAB, and took the elevator to the squad room. At my desk, I opened the murder book, but immediately shut it. I felt exhausted and couldn't concentrate. If I could sleep for a few hours, maybe I would have the energy to return to the squad room and have another go at the case tonight. I locked the murder book up in the bottom drawer and returned to my loft. After undressing, I crawled into bed and closed my eyes. I tried to relax, but the horns, the squealing tires, the hydraulic hiss from the buses, the music blaring from passing cars kept me awake. I grabbed a pair of earplugs from the end table and slipped them in. But disconnected images from the case continued to flash in my mind: Relovich on the autopsy table; the crime scene photos; the blood splatter pattern on the wall; the *netsukes* and *ojimes*, their eyes glowing like coals.

In an attempt to relax, I forced myself to think about surfing, and tried to recreate the magnificent ride I had the morning at Point Dume with Razor. Finally, I dozed off.

I'm on the flank of a T-formation, searching for land mines and booby traps. My sergeant is in the center. The first thing an Israeli soldier learns is to fill his canteen to the top before going on a patrol because a sloshing sound can give him away. But I forgot. And now every step I take I hear the splash of water against metal. And every step it gets louder and louder and louder,

*until it sounds like huge waves pounding the shore with a deafening roar. Fi-
nally, my sergeant holds up his right hand, silently halting the unit. He grabs
my canteen and pours out the water, steam rising from the desert sand. The
steam becomes thicker and thicker. It soon envelops the unit. I hear footsteps
in the distance, but I can't see through the thick mist. I hear shouts in Arabic.
Then the metallic click of a magazine shoved into an assault rifle. Then rapid-
fire shots. Panicked, I run, but I'm blinded by the mist.*

The ringing of my cell phone woke me. I bolted up, covered with
sweat. Grabbing the sheet, I wiped my face, brow, and the back of my
neck.

I picked up the phone. It was the vacuum metal deposition tech at
the Orange County laboratory.

"Any luck getting a print off that desk handle?" I asked.

"It ain't luck, my man," the tech said. "We raised a latent for you."

"And?" I asked.

"You don't sound too excited."

"Just a routine check. Probably a patrol officer at the scene."

"It usually is. Give me a minute. I've got to find the file. Okay. I've
got it right here."

I yawned and wiped the sleep out of my eyes.

"A cop named Velang."

"First name?"

"Sorry," the technician said. "I can't read my own writing. It's Wegland. Wally Wegland. He's a commander."

So Wegland was at the crime scene. Why didn't anybody tell me? That's
strange. But maybe it isn't. He was good friends with Relovich's father.
When the old man retired, he asked Wegland to keep an eye out for his
son. It would make sense for Wegland to head over to Relovich's as soon
as he heard about the homicide.

I remembered scanning the crime scene log, but couldn't recall seeing Wegland's name on the list. I decided to scan the names again.
Maybe I'd missed Wegland. Maybe it would be worth looking through
the log again and checking the other names on the list.

The murder book, unfortunately, was at my desk. I decided to walk
over to PAB and read the log again.

I took a quick shower, shaved and dressed, and headed out the door.

CHAPTER 28

I swung open my front door. I was about to jog down the steps.

But standing a few feet down the hall, dressed in khakis, a polo shirt, and a blue blazer, holding a Heckler & Koch .45 at his hip was Wally Wegland.

"Let's head back inside," he said. "No sudden movements."

I glanced at the stairs, calculating how quickly I could avoid the trajectory of his shot. Wegland jammed the HK in my back and said softly, "Move. Now."

I slipped my key into the lock. Wegland followed me inside and slammed the door.

As I moved toward my shoulder holster, which was slung over a chair, Wegland said, "You take one more step, and it'll be your last."

Wegland was aiming at the center of my chest in a perfect Weaver Stance: right arm partially extended, gun supported by his left hand, knees slightly flexed, left foot forward.

He motioned with the gun for me to sit on the couch. "Take it real slow."

I sat on the edge. Wegland eased into a chair across from the couch.

"So I guess you've got a contact at the VMD lab," I said.

"*Fortunately*, they caught me while I was at my desk. *Fortunately* you're only a few minutes away. *Unfortunately*, they called you first."

Wegland studied me for a moment and then shook his head sadly. "If you weren't so damn obsessive, if you could have just left well enough alone, we wouldn't be here at this painful juncture."

He jabbed the gun at me and said, "Why couldn't you let Fuqua take the fall? Why couldn't you just follow the obvious leads and let him go directly to jail?"

My mouth was dry and I swallowed hard. "Because he didn't kill Relovich."

"So what? Who cares about a predator like him?"

"So you broke into Fuqua's place in South Central, grabbed a Kleenex out of the trash, and planted it at Relovich's," I said softly, more to myself than to Wegland. "You knew he'd been charged with rape, so his DNA would be in the state DOJ database. You also knew that Relovich had arrested him and you heard about how Relovich kicked his ass. So you assumed we'd stumble on the obvious motive."

Wegland looked at me and frowned. "It all could have been so easy, but you had to make it so hard. I knew things would get dicey when that cretin Grazzo brought you back for this case."

"When he wanted to pull me off the case, why'd you persuade him to keep me on?"

"I didn't. But that's what I told Duffy. Actually, I lobbied hard to get you *off* the case. But Grazzo wouldn't budge because the chief was already on board with you. So I tried another tack. I told him all about how you went postal on Graupmann. I convinced him to suspend you. He tried, but you outfoxed him on that one."

"So it wasn't Graupmann who put all that Nazi shit on my desk. It was *you*. Trying to provoke me. Trying to get me to do something stupid, something that would get me thrown off the case."

"Almost worked," Wegland said.

I wanted to keep Wegland talking until I could figure out a way to make my move.

"Then why come after me *now*? Why not just let things play out and hope I wouldn't be able to put it all together?"

"You were getting too close to the bull's-eye."

"I knew the VMD print was from a cop. But I just assumed they were from a *patrol* officer. I didn't realize—"

Wegland waved me off. "I'll talk my way out of that one; I'll claim I left the print on a visit months ago. But I knew Duffy had freed you up for a week to take another look at the case. I knew that once that week was up you wouldn't drop it. You'd keep chewing and chewing on this case until you came up with something else. I didn't want to see what your next surprise would be."

"So Relovich and Mitchell were in cahoots with you on the heist at Silver's house," I said.

"Not initially," he said pompously.

Wegland was no different from most scumbags I had interviewed. They talked too much because they couldn't resist showing how smart they were.

"Not many people knew about Silver's collection," he said. "But when I was a robbery detective in Hollywood, I investigated a theft at his house once. I had to toss the place and itemize what he had for the insurance claim. So I knew what it was worth. I was also aware he had a safe. He told me he kept a lot of cash in there, but the thieves never got it. Of course, I made a mental note of that."

"And you," I said, "had enough on Jack Freitas to have him locked up for a long time. But he was your informant so you were able to keep him on the streets. You took advantage of his B and E expertise and had him do jobs for you, rip shit off for you, like he did at Silver's. Then things turned sour there."

"That's right. Freitas started arguing about the split, right in the middle of the job."

"So you took him out. And you figured no one would care. A crook killed by a crook."

"That's how Hollywood Homicide played it."

"So Relovich and Mitchell hear the shots and stumble on the scene," I said. "That's for real? They didn't know this was going down?"

Wegland snorted loudly. "They had no idea. They got there as I was about to slip out the back door."

"You must have done some fast talking."

"It wasn't as hard as you'd think."

"Were you really friends with Pete's old man?"

He shook his head. "I saw him a few times at the academy shooting range, but we never actually had a conversation." He fiddled absent-mindedly with a blazer button, as if lost for a moment in a memory. "Pete wasn't a problem at Silver's. He'd only been on the job a few years. Mitchell was the senior guy. I figured Pete would follow Mitchell's lead. Anyway, I knew all about Mitchell. He'd been working Hollywood for-ever, and I had worked there for a while. He was dirty. Not filthy dirty. But dirty. Some of us knew he was checking department files and sell-ing the info to PIs. So when the two of them see me, I figure I have got a chance to talk my way out of it. Of course when you've got two hun-dred thousand in cash you can be pretty persuasive."

He stared through me; his eyes looked unfocused. I wondered if he was steeling himself to pull the trigger. I was about to make a dash for the door when Wegland said, "I told them I was doing some undercover work for the art detail. Then I pointed out Freitas with the bullet hole in his temple. Mitchell had arrested him before; he knew he was scum. I told them I'd heard Freitas was going to pull this caper at Silver's, and when I'd tried to stop him he pulled a gun on me. So I had to drop him. I convinced Mitchell not to call it in. Said I was doing the undercover work without authorization. Said I'd be in a hell of a fix if I had to deal with all those interviews and shooting boards. When I pulled out the duffel bag with cash, Mitchell was persuaded. I told both of them it was drug money and if we didn't take it, it would just get turned over to the feds. Pete wasn't too happy about it, but he was surrounded by two vets, so he went along with the program. They gave me a few minutes to get down the canyon. Then they called the station—and never mentioned anything about me."

"So why'd you have to silence Pete after all these years?"

"He never got over this thing," Wegland said, dropping the barrel of the Smith for a moment. "I think that's why he bailed out of the department. Always looking over his shoulder, thinking he was going to get jammed by I.A. for taking the money and covering up what happened at Silver's."

"That why he was drinking so much?"

"Maybe. Though he eventually did dry out and get it together. But last year Hollywood Homicide got some kind of federal grant to reopen all their unsolved cases from the past fifteen years and take another look. The feds figured that with the automated fingerprint system and DNA available now, the new technology would dig up some suspects and a bunch of these old cases would get cleared. Pete and Avery Mitchell figured it was only a matter of time before they were questioned about the Freitas homicide. It was a misdemeanor murder—just a loser ex-con who nobody cared about. But it was unsolved, so it fit the bill. I heard through a source of mine that Pete talked to one of his pals who used to work I.A. He didn't tell him the particulars of the case, just presented a hypothetical situation. Talked about making a deal—asked if he could avoid prosecution if he laid out what happened. Next thing I knew, he made an appointment with an investigator."

Wegland frowned and shook his head. "That was unacceptable."

"Why was Pete so worried?"

"He figured with the new technology, maybe I'd get IDed. Then maybe if I got cornered, I'd implicate him and Mitchell. Maybe I'd even put the murder on them."

"And after you shot him, you strangled him, to make it look personal, to—"

"Mitchell had a little more savvy than Pete," Wegland said, ignoring me. "He wasn't running scared. But about six months ago he calls me out of the blue. Asks for what he called 'a loan' to expunge his memory."

"Blackmail?"

"That's how I interpreted it."

"So you gave Relovich and Mitchell the *netsukes* and *ojimes*?"

Wegland whistled softly. "You don't miss much, do you? I remember when you were a young patrolman in Pacific and I was a detective working robbery. I said to myself, That's a sharp kid. That's a kid to watch."

"Why did you give 'em to Relovich and Mitchell?"

"After I'd investigated the robbery at Silver's, he showed me his whole collection and told me all about them, the history and what they represented." He cupped a hand, as if holding the imaginary *netsukes* and *ojimes*. "I gave each of the cops a matching pair. A Shoki and an Oni. A demon and demon queller. I told them the predators out there— like Freitas—were the demons. And us cops were the demon quellers. I told them not to forget which side they were on."

"But you did."

"I did *what*?" he said impatiently.

"You forgot which side you're on."

"No I didn't. I always know what side I'm on—*my* side."

"Why were you so sure I'd—" I paused in mid-sentence when I heard a screech of brakes, the crash of a fender-bender, the shattering of glass. Wegland flinched and briefly glanced toward the window.

I jumped to my feet, hurdled over the sofa, and zigzagged to the corner of the room, as I heard the blast of the gun and a bullet zip past my ear. Snatching my surfboard off its hooks, I held it in front of me like a shield and charged Wegland, the pop-pop-pop of shots splintering the fiberglass. I smashed into him, and with all my strength shoved the surfboard and Wegland through the window, shattering the glass.

I craned my neck and watched Wegland frantically wave his arms and legs as he and the board spiraled down eleven stories, and then he exploded on the sidewalk in a red mist.

CHAPTER 29

Two Homicide Special detectives—who investigate all cases in which officers have been shot at, assaulted, threatened, or killed—were waiting in the squad room when the Central Division patrol officers dropped me off back at the station.

One of the detectives handed me a note with a phone number on it. "Lieutenant Duffy wants you to call him."

When I saw the 619 area code, I remembered he was in San Diego.

"A hell of a deal," Duffy said. "I never would have made Wegland for a killer. But the most important thing is: are you okay?"

"I'm all right."

"I've been working the phones, trying to coordinate as much as I can from down here."

"What's Press Relations put out on this thing?" I asked.

"Just the stock release. We haven't notified Wegland's next of kin yet, so we just identified the man pancaked on the sidewalk as an LAPD officer. And we didn't release how the officer fell, just that the incident is under investigation."

"My surfboard shattered when it hit the sidewalk, so I don't think anyone could identify exactly what it was," I said. "Can Press Relations hold off on releasing that tidbit?"

"It'll come out eventually," Duffy said. "Hard to keep something like that out of the news."

"That's okay. Let's just keep the details under wraps for a little while."

"Until when?" Duffy asked.

"Just hold off tonight."

"That'll work. The chief and Grazzo are holding a press conference tomorrow morning. I told Grazzo I want to drive up for it and to check on you. But I think he's afraid I'll get too much face time on camera and steal some of his glory. He told me to stay in San Diego."

"Sounds like Grazzo."

"He'll probably ID Wegland at the press conference. And once he does, there'll be a shitstorm of media interest. Who knows what'll come out. I hear the chief's really bent out of shape. He's still trying to figure out how to spin this. A cop as dirty as Wegland makes us all look bad."

I listened to Duffy's labored breathing.

"Why the need to keep this quiet tonight?"

"I just want to tie up some loose ends. Easier to do that if the news doesn't break."

"Got you."

"Who's giving Wegland's wife the death notification?" I asked.

"Grazzo. He's just about ready to drive out there. Fortunately, he had no kids."

"What's he going to tell her?"

"He'll probably give her the usual line: It was an off-duty incident; the department has no details yet; and he'll provide her with more information as the investigation continues."

Duffy cleared his throat. "Well, I guess you were right. There was a little more to this case than it initially appeared. Which reminds me, I'd better get the paperwork going so I can kick that lowlife Fuqua—as much as I hate to. If you want to say, 'I told you so,' go ahead."

"I'm too fried to say anything."

"When I heard about what happened, I was worried as hell about you," Duffy said. "I'm damn relieved you're okay. You've had enough action for one night. You should head home right now, pour yourself a stiff one, and hit the rack."

"Can't."

"Why the hell not?"

"Got to deal with those Homicide Special detectives."

I followed the two Homicide Special detectives into an interview room. One was a short, bald detective in his late forties; his partner was a tall woman with a heavily lined face and a smoker's cough.

The bald detective nodded to his partner, indicating that she should ask the questions.

"Hey, can we finish up tomorrow?" I asked. "I've got a few things to take care of."

She shook her head. "No can do. You know that."

"Let's get this out of the way."

"So," she said with a wry smile, "how does a Felony Special detective end up attacking an LAPD commander with a surfboard and shoving him out the window?"

I gave her a brief recap of the incident. As I answered her questions, I was distracted and kept thinking about the San Pedro crackhead and the young Hispanic woman who had spotted two suspects the night Relovich was murdered. I wanted to track down Wegland's partner—if he had a partner—tonight, because once his death hit the news, people would scatter like cockroaches under a klieg light.

When the detectives finished their interview, I walked over to Duffy's office, hoping he'd gone on one of his binges right before he left town and had been careless. But when I turned the knob, I discovered that, unfortunately, he'd remembered to lock his office door. I couldn't find the Guatamalan cleaning crew, so I started on the ground floor and worked my way up. After traversing the third floor, I found them in the bathroom. I asked one of them to follow me.

Outside Duffy's office, I rattled the knob and motioned with a phantom key.

"*Eso no es permitido*," he said.

I opened my wallet and handed him three twenties. He pocketed the money and let me in.

I grabbed a PAB passkey from Duffy's desk drawer, jogged up the stairs, and unlocked Wegland's office. After sifting through the crime reports on his desk, the paperwork in his drawers, the files in his tall metal cabinet, and the crumpled papers in the trash, I realized I had no idea what I was looking for. After checking under the rug, I peered inside the dozen LAPD coffee mugs stamped with various unit insignias that were lined up on a shelf. Sinking into Wegland's chair, I opened the top desk drawer and ran my hands underneath it. I did the same with the underside of the middle drawer. And then the bottom one. In the back, underneath the drawer, I felt something. I pulled the drawer out of the desk, emptied it, and flipped it upside down. Taped to the left corner, was a key with the number *52* and two faint, barely legible words imprinted along the top two lines:

POMONA
RAGE

What the hell did that mean? I examined the paperwork from Wegland's desk, trash can, and file cabinet again, but saw no reference to Pomona. I decided to drive out to Wegland's house and see if his wife was in any shape to talk. Maybe she could tell me the significance of POMONA RAGE. If not, it wasn't a wasted trip because I wanted to interview her anyway.

After calling downtown for Wegland's home address, I drove out to Monrovia, and down a street, shaded by magnolias, of mostly tidy, single-story homes with clipped front lawns and sculpted shrubbery. Wegland's was the largest on the block, a white Colonial with a pair of sturdy pillars bracing the portico, a steeply gabled roof, and windows inset with diamond panes. The house looked so absurd in Southern California; I could picture a black lawn jockey in front.

When I rang the bell, I heard the yapping of dogs in the backyard. A thin, severe-looking woman in her late forties with extremely short black hair opened the door.

"Mrs. Wegland?" I said.

"No. I'm her sister. Who are you?"

I handed her my card.

"An assistant chief was just here."

"I know. But I'm assigned to the investigation and I wanted to ask Mrs. Wegland a few questions."

"She's in no condition to talk to anyone right now."

"I promise it'll be very brief."

"Don't you people have any shame?" she said indignantly. "My brother-in-law sacrificed *everything* for his job. He gave his *life* for your department. Can't you at least have the decency to let us grieve in peace?"

She slammed the door. I lingered on the porch for a moment, wondering how the woman would react when she discovered the truth. A moment later I heard a faint voice from inside the house: "That's okay, Bonnie. I'll come downstairs and talk to him for a minute."

The sister opened the door, and I followed her into the living room. A gleaming black grand piano covered one corner of the room, wing-backed chairs flanked a marble fireplace, and hung on the opposite wall were several pictures of panting Pomeranians. No kids, but probably a backyard full of dogs.

"I'd ask you to sit, detective, but I can only manage a minute or two."

Startled, I swiveled around. Grace Wegland was a younger-looking version of her sister. Her eyes were puffy and bloodshot, and she clutched a hankie in her right hand. With her other hand, she dug a pill vial out of her pocket and shook it like a maraca. "I hope you'll excuse me," she said, swaying slightly, carefully enunciating each word. "I'm not entirely lucid right now."

"I'm very sorry to trouble you at a time like this, but I was hoping you could tell me—"

"You worked with Wally before, didn't you?"

"Yes. At Pacific. We met once."

"Could you at least give me the courtesy of telling me what's going on. Grazzo didn't tell me a damn thing. Only that Wally was killed in some off-duty incident."

"I'm sorry, Mrs. Wegland, but that's all I know." I felt sorry for the woman. But not sorry enough to tell her the truth. And knowing that I might only have the opportunity to ask her a quick question or two, I blurted out, "I'm guessing your husband had a home office. Can I quickly check it out?"

She stared at me, eyes glassy, gripping the back of the sofa for balance.

A moment later, her sister charged into the room. "Out!" she shouted at me, jerking her thumb at the door.

Ignoring her, I asked Grace, "This might be important, Mrs. Wegland: Do you know any reason why Wally would have any business in Pomona?"

She continued to gaze at me with a slack-jawed, unfocused expression.

The sister marched to the door and swung it open.

As I drifted toward the door, I asked again, "Anything about Pomona—"

"Now!" the sister shouted.

She slammed the door as soon as I stepped on the porch. A moment later, I heard Grace Wegland utter a muffled sentence. "Storage." was the only word I could make out.

Sitting in my car, I mulled over what she had said: storage. What did that have to do with Pomona or the key I discovered?

I rolled the window down. The scent of a spring evening in Los Angeles suffused the car with an intoxicating blend of mock orange and freshly cut grass.

"Of course," I muttered to myself. "Storage."

The faint writing on the key was POMONA RAGE. But now I realized that the first three letters of the second word had worn off the old brass key.

It should have read POMONA STORAGE.

CHAPTER 30

I pulled off the freeway about thirty miles east of downtown and rolled into the parking lot of Pomona Storage, one of the ubiquitous self-storage warehouses hard by the freeway that dot the Southern California landscape. I parked on the street and walked past the small office—closed for the night—and onto an asphalt lot with a dozen cinderblock warehouses. In the corner of the lot was the warehouse for spaces 1-60, but there was a security box outside the door, and I didn't have the code.

After lingering by the back fence for fifteen minutes, I was relieved to see a pick-up truck screech to a halt in front of the warehouse. An unshaven man wearing jeans and cowboy boots hopped out, punched a code in the security box, and opened the door.

When I followed him inside, the man shouted, "What the—"

But he stopped in mid-sentence when I pulled my suit coat back, revealing the badge on my belt.

As I walked down the narrow, dim corridor lit by dusty lightbulbs, I recalled when I was a young patrolman and I was dispatched to a self-storage warehouse in Mar Vista to investigate a noxious odor emanating from a unit. My partner and I discovered a bloated, dripping, decaying body in a packing crate. Later, when I had worked the robbery table, I discovered that a few of the burglars I was tracking had stashed their loot in storage units all over town.

Pomona Storage, with its cracked cement floors, ceilings covered with tattered aluminum insulation panels, and stripped-down exterior, had been shoddily built decades ago. The warehouse where Wegland rented space, however, had one concession to modernity: climate control. Cool air blew from the ceiling vents and a digital thermostat on the wall read: 66. I figured the owners installed a heating and air-conditioning unit in one of the dozen warehouses on the property and then charged the customers—who wanted to protect their belongings from mildew—double the rent.

At space 52—a few doors down from the man in the cowboy boots—I pulled out the key, opened the padlock, raised the metal roll-up door, and flipped on the light. Inside was a cubicle the size of a large office, with a cement floor and plasterboard walls lined with metal shelves. Strewn about were dozens of empty cardboard boxes, a few bare picture frames, and mounds of balled up packing paper.

Too late, I thought. *I wonder who got here first?*

When I heard a loud rattling, I whirled around and saw the metal storage door closing and caught a quick glimpse of the bottom half of a body—just jeans and sneakers—and fingers sliding the door down. Before I could move, glass shattered on the cement floor. The door rattled to the ground. I heard the metallic click of the padlock. The moment I smelled the gasoline, the packing paper ignited, shooting flames above my head, singeing the boxes on the shelves.

I darted to the door and began kicking it, but there was little give. I banged on the plasterboard walls and began shouting for help. Suffocating from the smoke and beating on my flaming pants cuffs, I ran around the room, hammering the walls, desperately searching for a soft spot, an opening.

The boxes on the shelves had ignited and were shooting flames up to the ceiling. I wrapped my suit coat around my right hand and began knocking boxes off the shelves and onto the floor. I climbed the shelves like a ladder, my head grazing the plasterboard ceiling. The smoke was now so thick I couldn't see the door. I had investigated enough arson-murders to know I had only a minute or two left until the room was sucked of oxygen.

I grabbed my gun and blasted the corner of the ceiling, emptying my magazine, the hefty 230-grain, .45-caliber hollow-points punching a fist-sized hole in the thin plasterboard. I slammed another magazine into the Beretta and, with a few more shots, widened the hole. Gripping the opening with both hands, I realized it was a false top, a shoddily constructed ceiling plopped on top of the framing. Straining, my feet wedged against the wall for leverage, I slid the ceiling over a few feet, and climbed up and onto the metal framing. I scuttled along the framing for about twenty-five yards, struggling in the darkness, coughing through the smoke, frantically searching for a wedge of light. I was trying to gauge which unit the man with the cowboy boots had opened.

Jamming both heels on the edge of one of the false ceilings, I rammed it open slightly and peered inside. I was exultant to discover the lights were on and the metal roll-up door was open; I knew I had hit the right space. When the man in the cowboy boots smelled the smoke, he must have dashed outside without closing the door.

I wriggled through the opening, landed on the cement floor, and sprinted out the door and toward the street. Blinded temporarily by a bright light, I saw the faint silhouette of a man standing beside his car, holding a flashlight above his shoulder. A moment later I saw the muzzle flash and heard the pop. I hit the ground, ripped the Beretta out of my shoulder holster and, as the shooter hopped into his Jeep Cherokee and careened down the street, squeezed the trigger and kept squeezing, the spent casings tinkling on the cement like a wind chime, until I realized my magazine was empty.

I darted out of the parking lot and into the middle of the street. Crouching, I spotted a half dozen shards of splintered glass. One of my shots had clipped a taillight.

CHAPTER 31

I sat on the curb for several minutes, hacking, spitting, and gulping air, my lungs burning, my chest aching. Easing into my car, my knees bruised and sore, my back aching, I drove a few blocks to a mini-mart, passing a convoy of fire trucks, sirens blazing.

When I paid for a bottle of water, the teenage clerk stared at me and said, "Dude, looks like you been toasted like a marshmallow."

I checked my reflection in the glass: my face was soot stained and my eyebrows were singed. I bought a package of wipes and, in the parking lot, cleaned my face and hands and then gulped down the water. For a few minutes I leaned against my car, staring into the middle distance, brushing ashes and soot off my suit.

I bought another water for the road and headed back to PAB. I had an idea of who might have gone after me, but I wanted to do a little research, including a DMV check, first. I wanted to be sure.

When I returned to the squad room, I noticed that someone had scattered the items on my desk and jimmied open the bottom drawer, busting the lock. The murder book was still there. Why would someone want to break into my desk and riffle through my murder book? I could see the picture of Latisha Patton under the plastic sheeting on my blotter,

"NO!" I shouted. I won't lose another witness. My chest was so tight it felt like my lungs were exploding. I tried to stand up, but my legs started to buckle. Gripping the edges of my desk, I pushed myself to my feet, and ran down the stairs, across the street, and into the parking lot.

I careened down the city streets, screeching around corners, until I hit the onramp for the Harbor Freeway, already doing sixty. I flicked on my dashboard light, punched my siren, and slammed down the gas pedal until I hit a hundred. I shimmied off the freeway at a San Pedro exit and slammed on my brakes in front of Theresa Martinez's apartment complex.

I sprinted past the pool and took the stairs three at a time. Sweat dribbling from my hair into my eyes, coughing and trying to catch my breath, I pounded on her door. A moment later I heard a muffled cry.

After ripping my Beretta out of my shoulder holster, I leaned back and kicked out her front window.

As I jumped inside, slicing my thigh on the jagged glass, I saw a shadow dart to my left. Gripping the Beretta with two hands, elbows flush to my sides, I swiveled around.

"Drop the gun real slow and kick it over here," said Conrad Patowski, Wegland's adjutant. He stood behind Theresa Martinez, gripping her neck, pointing his Glock at her temple.

"Drop it!" Patowski shouted. "Or I'll blow her head off."

Tears streamed down Martinez's face and her chest heaved with convulsive sobs.

I knew if I gave up the gun, she'd be dead. And so would I.

"I said drop it!" Patowski said.

I slowly lowered the gun a few inches. I could feel the blood sluicing down my thigh and soaking my sock.

"That's a good boy," Patowski said.

I won't lose another witness. I took a step forward, raised the barrel an inch, and fired.

The boom echoed in the small room.

Martinez fell to the ground with a thud.

CHAPTER 32

I was in a fog of anguish and anger.

Then I heard the scream.

Patowski fell against the door jam and slowly slid to the ground, the blood streaking the wall in a wide, wavy swath. He had dropped the gun after my shot had blasted his shoulder, just missing Martinez. She had fainted, and was now coming to. With one arm, I cradled her; with the other, I punched in the number for Communications Division.

About ten minutes later two ambulances arrived. A crew strapped Patowski, who suffered a through-and-through shot to the shoulder, on one metal gurney and me on another. We both headed for the Little Company of Mary Hospital in San Pedro.

After two detectives from the Force Investigation Division—who investigate every incident in which a cop fires his gun—questioned me, the ER doctor who'd stitched me up stopped by the examination room and handed me a prescription for Vicodin.

"A couple of inches lower, detective, and that broken glass might have severed your femoral artery," he said, as Ortiz entered the room. "That's an unpleasant way to go. Fortunately we got you here in time." He patted my thigh. "Twenty-five stitches and you're good to go."

"Shouldn't you keep him overnight, just to make sure?" Ortiz asked.

"He can go home," the doctor said. "The Vicodin will help with the pain." I lifted myself off the table.

"I feel like kicking your ass," Ortiz said.

I limped around the room, testing my leg.

"You shouldn't have gone out there without calling for backup," he said. "You're a fucking hardhead."

"I didn't have time."

Ortiz shook his head with disgust.

"Before I leave," I said, "I'd like to question Patowski."

"That ain't gonna happen. While you were going through triage, I tried to get a statement, but he dummied up. Said the only person he's talking to is his lawyer. So let me give you a ride home. Maybe I can knock some sense into you along the way."

Ortiz drove through the deserted streets and parked at a Denny's.

"I know this doesn't meet your high culinary standards," Ortiz said, scanning the menu, "but there's not much open at this hour. And you should have something in your stomach for the pain pills."

Wincing as I reached for a glass of water, I dug the Vicodin vial out of my pocket and popped one. "How'd you know I was at the hospital?"

"I'd just come from a call-out, and one of the guys at the station heard about the shooting in Pedro," Ortiz said.

I told him how Patowski had tried to barbecue me at the storage facility.

"How'd you know it was Patowski."

"When I climbed out of that bonfire and I saw asshole shine the flashlight at me, I knew he was a cop. Nobody else holds a flashlight like that." With my right hand, I gripped my fork, knuckles up, and raised it above my shoulder, forearm parallel to my ribs. I dropped the fork and said, "I suspected it was Patowski, but I didn't know for sure—until I saw his car parked down the street from Martinez's apartment. His rear right taillight was broken. I'd shot it out as he was burning rubber at Pomona Storage."

"Good shooting."

"If it was good shooting, I'd have hit *him*, not his taillight."

"So how'd you know Theresa Martinez would be in trouble?"

"I figured that whoever had peeked at my murder book was looking for wits. One of them is in jail. Since Martinez was the only other wit who really saw anything the night Relovich was killed, I figured she was the most vulnerable target."

"No surprise Patowski was dirty."

"I should have figured it out earlier," I said, picking at my scrambled eggs and hashed browns. "Adjutants are usually aware of everything their bosses are doing. What promotions they're angling for. How they fudge their expense reports. Who they're screwing. Since Wegland was dirty, I should have known that, at the very least, Patowski would be aware of it."

"He must have emptied out that warehouse," Ortiz said. "Grazzo told me a few dicks with a warrant are at Patowski's place right now, and they found antiques, jewelry, stacks of cash, paintings, and a bunch of other artistic shit in a back bedroom."

"I'm sure he was in on it up to his ass," I said.

"Why'd Wegland rent space in a dumpy storage unit?" Ortiz asked. "He must have had some valuable things in there."

"He probably had that place for years and years," I said. "Probably had stashed stuff he'd lifted over the years. That's why the writing on that key was so worn down. He was smart. It was far enough from L.A., so nobody would recognize him there. The drive was long enough so he'd be able to pick up a tail."

"That's why he kept the key in his office," Ortiz said. "He knew that Internal Affairs always tries to take a dirty cop by surprise and searches his house first." He motioned to the waitress for more coffee. "Why'd Patowski try to torch the storage unit?"

"He'd probably been going in and out of there, helping Wegland for years. He probably figured he'd left so many prints, fibers, and hairs in there, he'd never be able to clean the place up. He might have just emptied it when he saw me roll up. Or he might have even staked the place out, expecting me. Then when I showed, he put together a crude Molotov cocktail, which couldn't have taken long to make, and figured he'd eliminate two problems at once—the storage unit and me."

As I limped to the parking lot, I said, "Drop me back at Martinez's place. I want to pick up my car."

"I'll take you home. I'll have a uniform bring your car back downtown later tonight." Ortiz jiggled his keys. "Is Martinez going to be okay?"

"She's pretty spooked. She's spending a few days at her sister's place in Orange County."

Ortiz opened my car door. "I'm worried about you, brother. Everyone's trying to take a bite out of your ass. You're not going to pull any more of that Lone Ranger shit tonight?"

I shook my head.

"And if you do anything else on this case, you'll call me to back you up, right?

"Right."

"Promise?"

"Promise."

CHAPTER 33

The Vicodin knocked me out for a few hours, but early the next morning I awoke with a shout, covered in sweat. Now that I didn't have the Relovich case to distract me, I had my first nightmare about Latisha in weeks. I sat up and massaged my temples for a few minutes. Jumping out of bed, I padded to the bathroom, shook out three Tylenol, filled my palm with water, and swallowed them.

I'd wanted to get back to the investigation for almost a year. When Duffy brought me back, he'd warned me to stay away, that South Bureau Homicide was handling it, that it was no longer a Felony Special case. I figured I would settle in, clear Relovich, earn some points, and then surreptitiously reopen the murder book. Well, as an old NFL coach once said: "The future is now."

This case was personal for me, more personal than anyone at the LAPD could imagine. I had a responsibility to protect her. I failed. If Latisha's killer was never found, I knew that this would haunt me until the day I died. I would always feel that I'd failed. Failed Latisha. Failed as a detective.

I still wanted to find Relovich's partner—if he had a partner. And I was pretty sure he did. Although Conrad Patowski was dirty, I didn't think he was with Wegland on the night of the Relovich homicide. Wegland, I was certain, drove the car. Both the junkie at the Harbor Division station and Theresa Martinez had described the passenger as dark-skinned, probably Mexican. Patowski was a pasty-faced white boy.

Finding the partner could wait. By nailing Wegland, I had bought myself some time. Duffy wouldn't return from San Diego until Monday. I had the weekend to freelance—free from his scrutiny. When he returned, I would figure out a way to buy a few more days. At South Bureau, when things were hopping, all I had was a few days to work a homicide, until my next fresh blood case. So I should be able to make some progress. Now was the time to search for Latisha's killer.

I was back in the squad room at eight o'clock, searching my computer for the cell phone number of Tommy Pardo, the South Bureau detective who was the primary on the murder of Bae Soo Sung—the Korean market owner—before it was transferred to Felony Special. He was an old-timer who had spent more than twenty years as a homicide dick. When I was working South Bureau, he was at Wilshire Homicide, and I got to know him on a few cases. We were never friends, but we were friendly. I had always considered him a solid detective and a stand-up guy. A few years after I left for Felony Special, he transferred to South Bureau Homicide.

When I took over the Sung homicide, he had a very different attitude than the Pacific Division cops who gave me a hard time after they lost the Relovich case. I had apologized to Pardo for big-footing him, but he just smiled, handed me the murder book, and said, "No problem, Ash. There's enough damn murders in South Central for all of us."

After Latisha's murder and the debacle that followed, the Sung investigation had been transferred back to Pardo. He was also handling Latisha's case. Before I quit, I had briefed him and returned the murder book. I was grateful that he was so decent to me, telling me that he'd lost witnesses before, that it was an occupational hazard of South Central homicide detectives, and not to blame myself.

I punched in Pardo's number, and he answered on the first ring. I apologized for calling him on a Saturday morning.

"You're back on the job less than a month and you've already tossed a commander out the window and fired on his adjutant," he said, chuckling.

"Word travels fast."

"It's the blue grapevine, bubba."

"I was wondering if I could come by your house and talk to you about Latisha."

"I was coming into town anyway. Caught one two nights ago. The autopsy's this afternoon. Meet me at the station."

I asked if I could talk to him away from the station, because I didn't want it getting back to Duffy that I was asking about his case. He agreed to bring the murder book and meet me at "the motel."

The motel was a lot behind a boarded up market on South Hoover. We called it "the motel" when I was at the South Bureau because during a slow p.m. shift, when we needed to coop, we'd park there and grab a quick nap.

I drove behind the market and parked beside the weed-strewn lot. A few minutes later Pardo pulled up, climbed out of his unmarked Buick, carrying two Styrofoam cups of coffee. Wiry and bowlegged, he slowly made his way across the lot looking like a cowboy who'd just hopped off his horse. Handing me a cup, he gripped my shoulder and said, "Glad you're back on the job, Ash."

We leaned against my Impala, tore holes in the plastic lids and sipped the coffee, looking out at a soot-darkened landscape of rundown apartment complexes, check cashing shops, and crumbling storefront churches.

"Good work on Relovich." He flashed me a thumbs up. "I knew Pete and I knew his old man—they were both damn good cops. I'm glad they put a pro like you on the case."

"So what's up with the Patton and Sung homicides? Any progress?"

"Hey, you're the big thinking Felony Special guy," he said with a smile. "I'm just a lowly ghetto cop."

"Now that we got that out of the way, tell me what's going on."

A cockroach scuttled past us, and Pardo ground his heel on it, crunching it into the dirt. "When the two cases got kicked back to us, me and my partner didn't have much to work with. And when Latisha was dumped down here, people figured out real fast that talking to us on this case was hazardous to their health. No one would open their doors to us; people wouldn't even—"

He stopped in mid-sentence and gave me a worried look. "You know I'm not blaming you for this. There're some careless-ass detectives out there. I know you're not one of 'em. I'd work with you again. Any time. Any case."

"I appreciate that, Tommy."

"After a few weeks of the silent treatment, we picked up another homicide. Then another. Then another. Then another. You know how it is, Ash. You worked this division. More than a hundred murders a year and only four weeks. After those first few weeks, to be honest with you, we didn't have a lot of time on this case." He made a circle with his thumb and forefinger. "That's where we're at right now."

"I wished they would have kept it at Felony Special."

"Probably should have. But when Latisha's family filed that lawsuit and their shyster lawyer started blasting Felony Special on the five o'clock news, the department figured they'd better get the case out of there, ship it back down here, and bury it."

I kicked a rock and sent it flying across the lot. "That's what I was afraid of." I stared into the distance. I knew I was only a few blocks from where Latisha was dumped. I thought about her, splayed on that street corner, half her head shot off. Sweat trickled from my armpits down my side.

"Don't worry, Ash, we'll get 'em," Pardo said without much conviction. "When things slow down a little, we'll get right back on it."

I asked him if he could spare a few minutes while I looked through the murder books. He pulled them out of the trunk, set them on the backseat, and fired up a cigar. Although Pardo had warned me, as I flipped through the pages, I felt increasingly disappointed. He and his partner hadn't done much with the case. They conducted a few fruitless follow-up interviews and rustled up a handful of gangsters who didn't know much.

After about ten minutes, he knocked on the back window. "Sorry, Ash, gotta be at the coroner's in fifteen minutes."

I shut the books, feeling frustrated. What the hell did I expect? Did I really think I could flip through some pages in the backseat of a squad car and unearth the golden key that would unlock all the secrets?"

I climbed out of the car and thanked him.

"Anytime. Next time we'll grab lunch. I'll bring the books, and you can check them out a little more leisurely."

"I want to ask you for a favor, Tommy."

"Sure."

"Let's keep this talk we've had on the Q.T. You know Duffy. He doesn't like his guys poaching on other units' cases. But this is more than just a case for me. So I want to nose around a little without him finding out."

"No problem."

"I appreciate it." As I climbed back into my car, he said, "Hold up. I've got something for you." He opened his trunk and handed me a paper bag with a flat plastic case inside.

"What's this?"

"The DVD of the Sung shooting. I know you've seen it. But I thought you'd like a copy."

As Pardo drove off, I flipped through my yellow legal pad where I'd jotted down Latisha's daughter's address. She was a fourteen-year-old freshman at Crenshaw High School named Darnella Ferguson. I recalled that although she had her father's last name, she'd never met him. After her mother was killed, she moved in with the family of her best friend, a girl she called her play sister.

When I'd interviewed her a few months ago, she tossed me out of the house and called I.A. to complain. She blamed me for her mother's murder. I dreaded seeing her again, but I knew I had to start there. If she heard about me nosing around the case, she might call I.A. again. I had to appease her, convince her that if she wanted her mother's killer caught, she had to cooperate with me. And I needed her. Family members often know details about victim's lives that are invaluable; they sometimes pick up critical leads on the street.

I cruised west on Florence, hung a right on Western, and a left on a side street, through a run-down neighborhood with cracked sidewalks and potholes big enough to crack an axle. I killed the engine in front of a white stucco box that looked like an enormous sugar cube.

I rang the bell, and as I waited on the porch, I heard rap blaring from a box in the living room. The door swung open and Darnella's friend gave me a quick once-over and yelled, "Hey girl, that police is here to see you again."

Darnella pushed past her friend, stepped out onto the porch, and slammed the front door. She had her mother's high cheekbones and amber-colored eyes. She slapped a hand on her hip and said, "How many times I got to tell you, I ain't talkin' to you. You done enough already. You pesterin' and pesterin' my mamma got her killed."

I felt so nauseous, I had trouble standing. Leaning against the wall for support, I said, "Can I come inside?"

"My mama talked to you, and look where it got her." I could see a pulse beating on her forehead. "What you need to say, you say here."

"I want to find out who killed your mother."

"Some police been here a while ago. Tell me he takin' over the case and you gone. Far as I know, he didn't do shit. Now you say you takin' over the case and he gone."

"He's not gone. And I'm not taking over the case. I'm just helping out. The more detectives you have investigating a homicide, the better."

"Y'all a little late, ain't you?"

"A murder investigation is never closed."

"So what you want from me?"

"Before she was killed, did your mother ever say anything to you that you think, looking back on it, might be important?"

"Like what?"

"Did she ever see anyone following her? Did she mention any people she might have been afraid of? Did she ever get a phone call that frightened her?"

She shook her head.

"Did you ever see her talking to any officers besides me and the detectives from South Bureau Homicide?"

"No."

I asked her a few more questions, but she had little to offer.

"Please, Darnella, I need your help," I said, feeling my throat catch.

"Why you care so much?"

"This case is very important to me."

"It's very important to me, too." For the first time, her voice didn't have a tinge of hostility.

"Will you help me?"

"I'll try."

"All right. Anybody she was friends with who's particularly plugged in?"

"Plugged in?"

"Well-connected in the neighborhood. Knows a lot of people. Hears a lot of things."

"One lady I can think of. Juanita Patterson. She manages that thrift shop where my mama worked. They were friends. She know everybody in that 'hood."

"She work Saturdays?"

"Six days a week, she there."

I sped over to Figueroa and parked in front of the thrift store. I re-called interviewing Juanita right after Latisha was killed. She didn't give me anything then; I hoped I'd have better luck a year later.

The thrift shop, which was lined with racks of shirts, coats, and trousers, and large metal bins filled with socks, belts, and T-shirts, smelled of cleaning solvents and musty clothes. I waited until Juanita, a heavyset woman with a red bandanna tied over her hair, finished ring-ing up a customer. Handing her a card, I introduced myself.

"I know who you are," she said, eyeing me suspiciously. "You the cop who got Tisha shot."

I slipped my hands in my pockets and made tight fists, trying to calm myself. "I'm trying to find out who killed her, and I was wonder-ing if I could ask you a few questions."

"I not speakin' to you. Now or ever."

"I think it's important—"

"Get," she said sharply, pointing to the door.

As I left the thrift shop, I recalled that they employed parolees from halfway houses to do the sorting. Last year, I'd interviewed a few of them. They weren't much help, but I thought I'd try again. I walked be-hind the thrift shop and spotted two hard cases wearing tight T-shirts, unloading boxes of clothes from a truck. Both had the ripped chests and biceps of ex-cons who had thrown a lot of iron in the joint.

I introduced myself and asked them if they'd heard anything in the past year about Latisha Patton's murder. They said "no" simultaneously, without looking at me, and continued to unload boxes.

I walked back to the street and was about to unlock my car, when I heard a low whistle. I looked up and saw one of the ex-cons, in the shad-ows of a narrow driveway squeezed between the thrift shop and a check-cashing shop, motioning for me with his forefinger.

"It be hazardous to a brutha's health talkin' to you in broad day-light."

"I understand."

"When I was comin' up, I knew Latisha," he said. "She friends with my big sister. She passed a few years back."

He stared off into the distance. I waited for him to continue.

"I got sumpin' for you. Month or two ago, friend of mine talkin' to a neighbor of Sweet Maxine. She a nice ol' lady who always baking cookies and such for the young 'uns in the neighborhood. It turn out that Sweet Maxine heard some fool talkin' 'bout that Chinese who got capped last year."

"You mean the Korean guy who owned the grocery store at Fifty-fourth and Figueroa?"

"Yeah. That the one. I know Latisha seen something on that killin' and that why someone take care of her."

"What did Sweet Maxine hear?"

"Can't rightly say. All I know is the neighbor say Maxine heard sumpin', but she ain't talk to no police. She scared for her own self."

The man told me where Sweet Maxine lived and disappeared down the back end of the alley. I clenched my fist and pounded it into my palm.

I drove a few miles west, through a working-class neighborhood where all the lawns were freshly mowed, and parked around the corner from Maxine's house so neighbors wouldn't see a police car in front. I walked up the steps to the porch of a tidy bungalow. When I saw the row of collard greens planted along the side of the house, I knew Sweet Maxine, like so many of the older blacks in South Central, had grown up in the South. Ringing the bell, I could see an eye peering at me through the peephole. I held my badge up.

A gray-haired woman in her seventies opened the door. She wore a powder blue cotton housedress that had frayed sleeves, but looked freshly ironed, and white orthopedic shoes. "How can I help you, young man?"

I showed her my badge. "Can I come inside?"

"Yes, you can."

I followed her to the sofa and sat next to her. The tiny living room was immaculate, with plastic slipcovers on the sofa and the chairs. Grammar school and high school pictures of two girls, who I assumed were her daughters, lined a mantel over the fireplace.

"Do you have a card?" she asked.

Handing it to her, I was relieved when she studied it for a moment and dropped it on a coffee table. She didn't seem to recognize my name or my connection to the case.

"I'm investigating last year's murder of Latisha Patton."

"That was a terrible, terrible thing," the woman said, pursing her lips and shaking her head.

"I heard that you might have some information that could help me."

She clasped her hand on her lap. "I don't think so."

"I understand that you heard something about the case."

She stared at her hands. "Not really."

"How long have you lived in this house?"

"My husband and I moved out here from Louisiana in sixty-one. Bought this place in sixty-six."

"Neighborhood was a lot different then."

"Sure was. None of this gangbanging and dope selling and gunshots at all hours of the night and young girls selling their bodies for rock cocaine and no-accounts killing each other in the street like they're dogs. Back then, this street was filled with lots of nice families. Lots of nice kids."

"You looked out for each other's kids then."

"Sure did. That's the way it was back then."

"Nobody's looking out for Latisha's daughter."

"I don't follow you."

"Her mother was murdered and nobody will help the police try to find the killer."

"It's a different world today. Back then folks around here tried to help the police."

I pointed to the pictures of her daughters. "If one of those beautiful girls were murdered, wouldn't you be angry if a witness wouldn't come forward to help the police? And what if this predator then killed another young woman?"

Maxine pulled a lacy white handkerchief out of the front pocket of her dress and gripped it in her right hand.

"Can you imagine how this would prey on the conscience of the witness?"

Maxine dabbed at her eyes with the handkerchief. "I've always been cooperative with the police. My late husband used to be a neighborhood watch captain. It's just that I'm frightened. Latisha tried to be a good citizen. She tried to help. And look what it got her."

"That will not happen to you. Tell me what you know, and I'll do everything I can to keep your name out of the investigation."

She gripped both ends of the handkerchief and pulled tight. "I just heard one little thing."

"Why don't you tell me what it was?"

She stuffed the handkerchief in her pocket. "All right then. I spend a lot of time in my backyard, tending to my roses. An alley runs behind my backyard and there's an old sofa there. A low element hangs back there sometimes. Boys and girls, smoking marijuana and putting God knows what kind of poison into their bodies.

"About a month ago, I was out there in the early evening. I heard two youngsters who were out on the sofa, gabbing."

"Exactly what did they say?"

"I heard one of them say something like, 'If there'd been a reward for the Chinaman, Water Nose might have dimed off the fool.'"

"Who's Water Nose?"

"I have no idea."

"Anything else you hear?"

"Just enough to know they were talking about the man who killed that Oriental grocer last year."

"Bae Soo Sung? Who ran the store at Fifty-fourth at Figueroa?"

"Yes. That's who they were talking about."

"Do you know who those kids were?"

"No idea. I usually make it a point to go right inside when they start gathering there."

"Ever call the police on them?"

"It's safer to just go inside and close my back window. I don't want those boys doing anything to my car, my house, or to me."

"Could you tell their race by their voices?"

"African-American. Definitely not a Spanish voice."

We talked for a few more minutes, and I handed her my card. "If you think of anything else, please give me a call."

I drove back to Felony Special, pulled up a chair in front of a computer, and checked CalGangs—a statewide law enforcement gang file—but was unable to find a Water Nose. I then walked across the squad room to the gang unit and opened a green metal filing cabinet—known as the

Moniker File—which contained the names of thousands of gang members, and included their address, street names, tattoos, and gang affiliation. But, again, I couldn't find a listing for Water Nose. Finally, I called the Southeast watch commander and asked for the cell number of Chester Pinson, the gang sergeant who'd given me some background on Reginald Fuqua.

I called and told Pinson about my interview with Sweet Maxine. "You know a Water Nose? I can't find him in the system."

"I know every O.G., banger, and pooh butt in this division," Pinson said. "But I never heard of a Water Nose."

"If you haven't heard of him, maybe he doesn't exist."

"I wouldn't say that. I'll tell my guys tonight to jam some of these gangsters and see if they can ID this guy. And I'll put the word out to some of my snitches."

"If you find anything, call me. I don't care what time."

CHAPTER 34

I returned to the squad room and spent the next few hours typing up the notes I had taken from Pardo's murder book, compiling a chrono, and putting together my own murder book for part two of my investigation into Latisha's murder. At ten, I left the station, stopped for some shabu-shabu and a Sapporo in Little Tokyo, and headed home.

My ringing phone woke me the next morning.

"One of my snitches has something for you." I recognized the voice. It was Chester Pinson.

"You're working early on a weekend, Sarge."

"I need the overtime. Got two kids in high school. I'm saving for college. Anyway, I'm sure Felony Special will authorize it."

"They will, but hold off." I told him to wait until the end of the D.P.—the twenty-eight-day deployment or pay period—until he called Duffy.

"Why?"

"It's a long story. So where do you want to meet?"

"Southeast."

"I'll head right over."

"Not so fast, homeboy," Pinson said. "With my snitch, you play you pay."

"Okay," I said, laughing. "On my way in, I'll stop by the ATM."

I parked behind the bland, blocky Southeast Division station on 108th Street and crossed the squad room. Pinson and his snitch, a stocky black man in his early thirties with long, filthy dreadlocks, waited for me in a corner interview room.

"This is Vernon Tilly," Pinson said to me, nodding toward the snitch.

"Let's get right to it," I said, sitting on a metal chair across from Tilly. "Who's this Water Nose?"

Tilly grinned sheepishly—revealing a few missing lower teeth—and rubbed his thumb against his index and middle fingers. "First, I need some remumeration," he said, mispronouncing the word.

"Vernon, Vernon, Vernon," Pinson said, as if he were mildly scolding a child. "You know it don't work that way. Tell us what you know. We'll evaluate the information. Then we'll pay you what it's worth."

"It not about the coin," Tilly said, sounding indignant. "My moms need medicine for her glaucoma, and I gotta pay for it. If it weren't for that, I'd be jawin' with y'all for free. They takin' a life these days for nuttin'. I ain't wit' dat. So I just tryin' to be a good citizen. Help make my 'hood a better place."

"We're both well aware of how seriously you take your civic responsibilities," Pinson said, giving me a surreptitious wink.

Tilly tugged on a dread and said in a conspiratorial whisper, "This is on the down-low, right?"

"Always," Pinson said. "And I can vouch for Detective Levine. He won't reveal where he got the information."

"Aiight," Tilly said.

"Now be a good citizen and tell us who Water Nose is."

"They ain't no Water Nose."

"That's not what you told me on the phone," Pinson said, irritated.

"That ain't his street name," Tilly said.

"Look," Pinson said. "It *is* his street name. We know that because a confidential informant told us. We want to find out who Water Nose is. And we want to find out where he lives."

"They don't call him that."

"You're full of shit," Pinson said.

I leaned over and patted Tilly on the knee. "Vernon, take your time. We've got all morning. Tell us what you know about the guy we're calling Water Nose."

"What a nose."

"What?" I said.

"What a nose."

Pinson impatiently drummed his fingers on a thigh.

"This is beginning to sound like *Whose on First*," I said. Leaning forward, I studied Tilly for a moment. "So you're saying his name is not Water Nose."

"That what I tryin' to tell you."

"His name is What A Nose?" I asked, astonished. I had never heard a nickname like that before.

Tilly nodded excitedly and shouted, "Yes!"

"I assume he has a large nose," I said.

"He do. He got a big monsta nose. It wide. It long. It *ugly*."

"Unbelievable," Pinson said. "I never thought I'd need a white boy to translate Ebonics for me."

I turned to Pinson and whispered, "My informant thought they said Water Nose, so I didn't get a computer hit."

"Tell us a little bit about this What A Nose," Pinson said to Tilly.

"I don't mean to dog the dude out, but he a big dummy," Tilly said.

"He's slow?" I asked.

Tilly tapped his temple with a forefinger. "Not much here."

"Does he live on the southside?"

"Yeah."

"You know where?" I asked.

"Naw."

"What's his set?"

"Five Deuce Hoover."

"What's his real name?" Pinson said.

"Don't know that."

"Does he know who killed that Korean grocer last year or the woman who was a witness?"

"You tole me you just wanted me to ID What A Nose," Tilly said. "And I ID him for you. I don't know nuttin' about what he see or hear. That ain't my bidness."

When the interview was over, I handed Tilly forty dollars.

Tilly stared at the cash, frowning, and said, "Ain't you a little light?"

"What the hell," I said, peeling off another twenty.

After we escorted Tilly out the door, I said. "His good citizen line was a load of horseshit. But what about him using the money to buy medicine for his mom's glaucoma. Is that for real?"

Pinson flashed me an are-you-kidding look. "Ash, you been away from the southside too long. His mom died three years ago."

      •   •   •

"Don't even need the computer for this one," Pinson said, opening the metal drawer of the Southeast's Moniker File. Flipping through a few cards, he immediately located What A Nose. He was a twenty-four-year-old gangbanger named Earnest Dupray who had been arrested a half dozen times and served three years at Tracy for robbing a gas station with a toy gun. He had a misspelled tattoo on his throat: Fuc It, which made it easy for police to identify him after the robbery.

Dupray lived in a tumbledown South Central duplex, with the address spray painted below the front window, next to an auto repair shop on a smoggy stretch of South Broadway lined with liquor stores and laundromats. At the door, Pinson and I could hear a cartoon blaring from the television.

"That's the gangbanger acid test," I said, knocking on the door. "If a kid over the age of twelve is still watching cartoons, he's a banger."

A few seconds later, Dupray, who was wearing boxer shorts and a red FUBU sweatshirt, opened the door and stared dully at us.

I immediately understood the provenance of his street name. His nose was long, wide, and aquiline—resembling an eagle's beak more than a nose—and probably had been broken a few times because it had several switchbacks, like a mountain road. The FUC IT tattoo on the side of his neck was clearly visible in large block letters.

I flashed my badge and introduced Pinson and myself.

Dupray continued to stare into space, eyes unfocused, breathing through his mouth.

"Can we come in, Earnest?" I asked.

Dupray shrugged and we followed him into the living room, which contained a ripped vinyl chair with the upholstery spilling out, a stained throw rug over the cement slab floor, and a few plastic milk crates, which I figured were used for chairs. There were no curtains on the windows, just silver foil taped to the glass.

Dupray dropped into his chair, reached for a can of Schlitz malt liquor on the floor, took a long pull, and was immediately engrossed in a *Blue's Clues* cartoon that was blaring from the television.

Pinson and I dragged milk crates across the floor and sat across from Dupray.

"Must be an interesting episode," I said, jerking a thumb toward the television.

Dupray nodded, without taking his eyes off the screen.

I reached over and shut off the television.

"Hey," Dupray whined. "Gotta watch my 'toons."

"We're investigating a homicide, Earnest," I said. "We want to ask you a few questions."

"Ain't no thang," Dupray said. "I got nothin' to hide."

"About a year ago, a Korean man who owned a grocery store at Fifty-fourth and Figueroa was killed," I said. "We know that you were a witness."

"How you know that?" he asked, looking genuinely surprised.

"I'm a homicide detective. I know a lot of things about you. Now I want you to tell me what you saw that afternoon."

"What if I don't?"

"Then I'll have to arrest you for withholding information from a detective," I said, bluffing. "And book you into county jail, where they don't show cartoons in the cell blocks."

Dupray scratched his nose with a knuckle and swigged his Schlitz. "If I help you, will you help me?"

"How?" I said.

"I been lookin' for a job around here, but nobody want to hire me. I think they prejudice against bruthas."

"In South Central?" Pinson said, incredulous.

"Tha's right."

"Maybe it has something to do with *that*," Pinson said, pointing to the FUC IT tattoo on his neck. "You get rid of that, and we'll talk about getting you a job."

Dupray rubbed his neck and stared out the window.

"Let's get back to what we were talking about," I said. "Can you tell us about the afternoon of the shooting?"

"Do I have to?" Dupray asked, still staring at the blank television screen.

I nodded somberly. "Yes you do."

"All right then," Dupray said, mouth open, with a blank, bovine expression. "What you want, again?"

"We want to know what you saw?"

"I seen a few things."

"Can you recount your activities that afternoon?" Pinson said.

Dupray bit his lower lip, his forehead furrowed in intense concentration, and said, "Five."

"What do you mean, five?" I asked.

"You ask me to count my activities that afternoon. I watch TV. I smoke some bud. I get a burger and fries at Jack in the Box. I walk down to the thrifty store across from that market to buy myself a belt. That five things I did."

I suppressed a smile. "Actually, Earnest, that's only four things, not five. But we said to *re*count your activities, not count. That means tell us what you did that afternoon."

"I just did."

"Okay," I said. "What did you see when you got to the thrift shop?"

"I saw a guy with a cartoon mask comin' up on the chink's store. Had a rod in his hand."

I exchanged a glance with Pinson. This was consistent with what Latisha—who had seen a man in a Shrek mask—had told me.

"Automatic or revolver?"

"Automatic.

"Shiny or dull finish?"

"Shiny."

"Did you see what kind of car he'd been driving?"

"Didn't see no car."

"What did you do then?"

"I knew trouble coming down. So I beat feet."

"Can you describe the man with the gun?"

"I just did."

"Was he tall or short?"

"Can't rightly remember."

"Slender or stocky."

"Too long ago."

"What race?"

"No race. The dude was like walking."

"Was he black, white, Hispanic?"

"Seemed black to me."

"Any tattoos?"

"Homie's wearing a tight T-shirt." He tapped his fingers on his upper arm. "But I could see right under the sleeve that the dude had a big C and a big K, with the C crossed out."

Pinson and I exchanged a glance. We knew this meant the shooter was a member of a Blood set. CK is a common graffiti in Blood neighborhoods. It means Crip Killer. And the *C*s are usually crossed out with big *X*s.

"Right or left arm?" I asked.

He patted his right arm.

"Did you see anything else interesting while you were there or while you were walking back?"

"Naw. I was movin' fast. That all I know. Now can you come up with some kind of *re*-ward for me?"

"For what?"

He scratched the side of his head with a palm. "I hear about people who tell po-lice about crime activities get some *re*-ward."

"If what you tell us leads to an arrest, we might be able to come up with something for you."

We leaned against my car and Pinson said, "You think he's holding out on us?"

"I think he's too stupid to hold out on us."

"What do you make of his story?"

I stretched, my back sore from sitting on the plastic milk crate. "What he said surprised the hell out of me. That's a Crip 'hood."

"Surprised me, too. There's a dozen Crip sets crisscrossing these streets."

"That's why, when I first caught the case, I was chasing Crips."

"I would've, too."

"It's been years since I worked the South End. What Blood set would be poaching in this 'hood?"

"Let's see," Pinson said, stroking his chin. "A couple miles north are where the Back Hood Bloods hang. That would be my guess. They're the closest Blood set to this 'hood. And they've been known to put in some work around here."

"Jesus," I muttered.

"What's up?

"Fuqua was a Back Hood Blood."

"So?"

"That's pretty fucking strange."

"What's strange about it?"

"My last two cases, I been running into a lot of Back Hoods."

"That's not so strange. Every year, there're a few dozen Back Hood hits down here. So if you're catching cases, you're going to run into Back Hood suspects."

As I drove back to the Southeast station, I said, "So now that we know it was a Blood—and probably a Back Hood—any ideas who it is?"

Pinson laughed. "That's a popular fucking tat. Might take me a few days to track the clown down." He checked his watch. "Gotta be at Jordan Downs in an hour. We're working a task force at the projects. It's going to go late and into tomorrow. My weekend's shot. But I might be able to put in some time Monday or Tuesday, before my shift starts."

The case had been stalled for a year. I finally felt like I had gained some traction. I didn't want to wait.

CHAPTER 35

I grabbed a Styrofoam cup in the watch commander's office, poured a cup of coffee, and found an empty desk in the corner of the Southeast squad room. I was still stunned by the discovery that the shooter What A Nose IDed was probably in the same gang as Fuqua. But I couldn't get a handle on why that was significant. Wegland had set up Fuqua, who was a Back Hood. And Latisha had probably been killed by a Back Hood. But what did that mean? I had no idea.

I sat up and logged on to the computer. Maybe Pinson was right. If you dig into homicides with South Central connections, there's a decent chance Back Hood Bloods will be involved.

I set my cup on the desk, and signed onto Cal-Gangs. When I worked South Bureau Homicide, I discovered that the best source of information often was the members' girlfriends. Detectives had the most leverage over them because they had the most to lose—their children. So I searched for associates of the Back Hoods. I jotted down the addresses of a half dozen girlfriends—they could be ex-girlfriends by now—and pulled out of the station in the early afternoon. I headed north on Broadway, east on Slauson, hung a few quick lefts, drove down a scruffy street pocked with potholes, and pulled up in front of a dingy gray clapboard house. Iron bars covered the windows, and instead of a front lawn there was an oily patch of dirt with an old Chevy truck in the center, its front wheels missing. I walked around the property, but could see no toys, tricycles, balls, or any other evidence of children.

I returned to my car and drove east to Watts, where the streets grew narrower, the houses more decrepit, the apartments more rundown, the commercial thoroughfares more depressed. I passed a few low-slung crumbling housing projects, and cut down a bleak, barren street—without out a single lawn, tree, or bush—lined with two-story, rickety apartment buildings. I stopped in front of one with a large canvas *We Take Section*

8 banner tacked just below the buckled roof. Fortunately, the iron security doors were open, and I walked into the chipped asphalt courtyard. In front of apartment B there was a miniature rubber football and an empty Pampers box.

I pounded on the door with the heel of my hand. Pausing, I heard rustling inside. I pounded a few more times, until I heard a faint voice: "Who is it?"

"LAPD! Open up! Now!"

A chubby black woman wearing a stained Lakers T-shirt and panties slowly opened the door. Her large brass hoop earrings were turning green along the edges. I badged her and pushed my way inside. The room was spare with just a few metal folding chairs, a splintered wooden breakfast room table, and a half dozen broken toys. Dirty dishes were piled up in the sink and pizza boxes littered the counter.

She stared at me sullenly. "What you want?"

I pointed to a chair and said, "Sit down."

I looked inside the single bedroom. Two young children were sleeping on a bare mattress on the floor next to another mattress covered with a tangle of mismatched blankets. I walked around the living room, opened the drawers to a metal cabinet, and riffled through the papers and boxes. In the kitchen, I opened the refrigerator and the freezer. Beside the stove, caked with food stains, I crouched, opened a cabinet, pulled out a metal pot, and opened the top. I removed a crushed Dr. Pepper can with holes poked in the charred top that was dusted with a film of ashes.

I set the can on the kitchen counter. "This could be a real problem for you."

"That ain't mine," she said, shaking her head and waving her hand. "I never seen it before."

I raised my eyebrows.

"One of my silly ass girlfriends probably came in here while I was sleepin' and fired up."

I stared at her skeptically.

"I'm not lyin," she said, defiant now.

I dragged one of the metal chairs across the stained carpeting and sat across from the woman. I crossed my legs and jiggled my foot.

The woman sighed. "All right now. What you want?"

"I don't have time to screw around, so I'm going to get right to it." I pointed to the makeshift pipe. "If that tests positive for cocaine, you know that I can call Child Protective Services and they'll take your kids."

Her shoulders sagged and her chin dropped to her chest. "I can't believe this shit."

"Believe it."

"Why you mess wit me?"

"Because I need information."

"Why you think I got information."

"You may not have it, but you're going to get it."

"How can I get something I don't know about when—"

I raised a forefinger and the woman stopped in mid-sentence. "Listen to me. I need you to find out something for me. And I need it by tonight."

"But—"

I raised my finger again, silencing the woman. "Just listen. There's a Back Hood Blood who's got a tattoo on his right arm with a *C* and a *K* with the *C* crossed out. I need you to identify him for me."

"Might be a few with that kind of tat."

"I've got one other way for you to pick him out. He held up a Korean grocer last year and killed him."

"Hold on now." She raised her hands above her head and shook them, like she was in the grip of divine inspiration. "This getting too heavy for me."

"Smoking crack with your kids in the house is too heavy for *me*. Now this is what I want you to do. Get on the phone this afternoon, or visit some friends, or do whatever you need to do. But by seven, I'm coming back here and I expect you to have the information for me. If you do and if your information's solid, I'll give you two hundred bucks. If you don't have anything for me, or if your information doesn't pan out, or if you're bullshitting me, I'll call a social worker I know and he'll toss your kids in a county shelter."

"Why you think I know anything about those Bloods?"

"Because a Back Hood Blood by the name of Curtis Pemberton listed your address several times on his arrest reports."

"I ain't seen that fool in a year."

"I want that information." I checked my watch. "You've got plenty of time to get it. Any questions?"

"Yeah," she said. "Why only two hundred?"

"Because that's the maximum I can get from the ATM machine. Any other questions?"

She started to sniffle. Her lower lip trembled and her eyes welled up with tears. "Why you do me like this? Say you gonna take my kids. That ain't right. Why you so cold?"

I walked across the room, said, "Seven o'clock," and slammed the door.

My stomach was rumbling and I had a few hours to kill, so I blasted north on the Harbor Freeway, exited at downtown, and parked in front of a Chinese market on North Broadway. I walked up a staircase to Pho 79, my favorite Vietnamese noodle shop. The décor was modest and utilitarian—Formica tables, gray carpeting, and paper lanterns hanging from the ceiling—but the food was excellent. I squeezed through the packed restaurant and found a table in the back. I ordered a large bowl of pho—aromatic meat broth with strips of charred beef, laced with onions and thick with rice noodles—which was served with a plate piled high with bean sprouts, stalks of Vietnamese basil, and slices of hot chilies, which I dumped into the bowl. Slurping the noodles and sipping the broth, I thought about that woman from Watts, and how I'd threatened to take her children. Then I thought about Latisha, her arms around my waist, whispering, "You're my protector." Fuck that woman from Watts. If I had to jam up and threaten every female associate of the Back Hood Bloods to get what I wanted, I would.

I left the restaurant, spent a few hours back at my desk, and returned to Watts at dusk. At seven fifteen, I knocked on the woman's front door. But there was no answer. I pounded. Still, no answer. Finally, I pressed my ear against the door. Silence. I walked around the side of the apartment and squinted through the window. The woman and her kids were gone.

"Damn that bitch!" I muttered to myself.

I decided to return to the squad room, run her, and see if I could find any other addresses from her arrest reports. I walked back to my car, climbed inside, and smacked my thigh in frustration. She'll probably put the word out that I was looking for the shooter. What if the shooter is in the wind now, too? I realized that I just lost the element of surprise. What kind of leverage would I have now? How would I force any of the gangsters to talk?

My reverie of self-recrimination was interrupted by a banging on the passenger door. I saw the woman's face, pressed to the window.

Relieved, I followed her into the house. She sat in one of the metal chairs; I remained standing.

"If I give you what you want, how you gonna p'otect me?" she asked.

"I'll put the word out that I got the information from a jailhouse snitch."

She looked up at me, eyes hooded, smiling ruefully. "What's the biggest problem a black woman have?"

"I don't know," I said impatiently.

"A black *man*," she said, tapping her improbably long pink fingernails on the metal chair. "If I hadn't got wit P-Rock, I wouldn't be in this predic-o-ment. You feel me?"

"Who's P-Rock?"

"Curtis Pemberton. When I saw that he hard with them Back Hood fools, I shoulda run. Instead I got wit him. Got one of his babies too. Somehow, you know I be with him. I guess you got yo record keepin'. So you know where I stay. You come after me to get what you can get."

"Something like that," I said. "So what do you have for me?"

"Okay now. It like this. They a nigga, name of Rip. He a youngster. He been puttin' a lot of work in to get his respect. I never met the dude, but my girlfriend say he either got that tat you describin' or he know who has. He a very active Back Hood. He know both the youngsters and the O.G.s."

"I asked you to identify the guy with the tattoo. I didn't ask you to identify someone who *may* have the tattoo or may *know* the guy with the tattoo."

"You gimme short notice. That the best I got."

"What do you know about Rip?"

She pursed her lips. "My girlfriend say he a bonehead. All balls, no brains."

"What does he do?"

"My friend say he bang, sometime he slang."

"What does he sell?"

"A little rock, a little weed."

"What's Rip's real name?"

"Don' know."

"What's his address?"

"Don' know."

"What's he look like?"

"My friend say he a little dude. Kind of on the frail side."

As I walked toward the door, the woman called out. "Ain' you gonna make it right?"

"What do you mean?"

She rubbed her index and middle finger against her thumb.

"If Rip is the guy with the tat, then you'll get your money."

From my car, I called a clerk at PAB, and she traced Rip's name through Cal-Gangs: Orlando Houston, age nineteen. I called an after-hours number for state parole in Sacramento and jotted down some background on Houston and his latest address. For the past six months, since he was released from a prison near the Oregon border for assault with a deadly weapon, Orlando had stayed with his mother, who, fortunately, lived in South Central, only a few miles away. I cruised by the house, on a street of modest, but well-kept clapboard bungalows with small front lawns and wooden porches.

To avoid spooking Orlando, I parked down the street and walked up the sidewalk. When I passed a preschooler peddling a tricycle, the kid announced in a taunting, singsong voice: "Here come the *po*-lice, here come the *po*-lice."

I quickly hustled down the sidewalk and bounded up the front steps to Orlando's mother's house. Standing on the front porch, I could hear rap blaring from the radio. I rang the bell.

When the door opened, I spotted a short, skinny teenager wearing oversized jeans and a white T-shirt. When he saw me, he crossed his arms. "I got a little surprise for you—*detective*."

Damn, I thought. The woman from Watts had warned him I was coming.

As I reached for my Beretta, a stocky black kid with a wispy goatee walked through the kitchen door aiming a .357 Magnum Colt Python at my head.

CHAPTER 36

"Get your hand off your holster or I'll blow your fucking dome off," the kid with the .357 said. His pinkie and ring finger were missing from his left hand. The flesh was jagged and scarred, like the fingers had been sawed off in an industrial accident.

Slowly, I put my arms to my side

He motioned to the little guy, who I figured was Rip, and said, "Tape him."

Rip walked into the kitchen, and I could hear him opening and closing drawers.

"Where you put the tape, Li'l Eight?"

"On the kitchen table, you dumb ass."

I pointed to his left hand. "I see where you get the name."

He gave me a cold smile, revealing a top row of very white buckteeth. "You smart. But not smart enough."

Rip returned with a pair of scissors and gray duct tape.

Both were wearing oversized jeans and white T-shirts that were so baggy I couldn't check out their upper arms for the Crip Killer tattoo.

Eight pointed to Rip and said to me, "Follow him."

He led me to a musty back bedroom.

"On your knees," Eight commanded.

"So far, you guys aren't in real trouble. You tape me up and they'll nail you for kidnapping. That's a life sentence. Get smart. You should—"

"Nobody going down for kidnapping," Eight said. "'Cause ain't gonna be no witness."

Before I could respond, Rip covered my mouth with a strip of duct tape. Then he reached inside my coat and grabbed the Beretta from my holster. "Always wanted a piece like this," he said, jamming the gun into his waistband.

He tightly taped my ankles and knees together, jammed my hands in front of me, and taped the wrists together. Eight walked over, examined the taping job, and pushed me to the ground. They walked off to the living room, laughing.

Lying on my side on the threadbare carpet, which smelled of dog piss and mold, I frantically tried to free my hands. But Rip had wrapped my wrists several times, and there wasn't any give. After several minutes trying to kick the tape loose, I couldn't free my legs either. Sweat streaming down my face, my wrists rubbed raw and ankles stinging, I looked around the room, searching for a sharp object to cut the tape. But the room was spare, with just a mattress on the floor, a floor lamp in the corner, and a large CD player on a small wooden table.

As I strained to hear what they were doing in the living room, I flashed back to the afternoon Ariel had asked me to speak to his second grade class. It was career week, and the fathers of the students gave brief presentations. Most were doctors and lawyers and accountants and businessmen. Marty was out of town on business and Ariel had asked me to speak to the class, insisting I wear my full uniform, with the Sam Browne belt and holster, ammunition pouch, baton, handcuffs, and the service stripes on my sleeves. Most of the kids asked the typical questions: Why did you want to become a policeman? How many bad guys have you arrested? Have you ever shot anyone? One little curly headed boy—who the teacher later explained was autistic—asked me a question that took me aback because I thought it was so perceptive. Arms crossed, eyes closed, rocking back and forth, the boy asked, "What are you most afraid of?" I tossed off a facile answer for the class, but as I was driving back to PAB that afternoon I contemplated the question.

And now I realized I knew the answer. *This* is what I was most afraid of. Tied up, helpless, facing the prospect of being killed without having the chance to fight back. This must have been what it had felt like for my father, his brother, his parents—and all my other relatives—packed into cattle cars, rolling along to their death, defenseless. With a groan, I tried to free my hands again. Rolling over on my back, I took a few deep breaths, exhaling slowly. Now is not the time to panic, I told myself. Conserve your energy. Wait for an opening. Then exploit it.

I heard the door open, looked up, and saw Eight and Rip standing over me.

"We been talking 'bout what to do wit' you," Eight said.

Rip smiled, his eyes glittering with malice. "What to do wit' you—
before we cap yo' ass."

"We ol' partners from the joint—Tehachapi State Prison," Eight
said. "That where we get a taste of getting a little mud for the duck."

Rip punched his palm. "You know, a keester stab."

"The ol' butt fuck," Eight said. "We gonna turn you into a punk.
Just like we do inside." He aimed the Colt at me. "Before you get a taste
of this."

They left the room, and a moment later I thought I heard Eight
talking on the telephone. Tasting blood in my mouth, I realized I had
bitten the inside of my cheek.

I had never had to use the little two-shot derringer I kept in my
right front pocket as a backup; I had never even shot it. But if I could
just loosen my wrists an inch or so, I might have a chance. My only
chance. I rolled over onto my side and tried to reach into my front
pocket. I strained, my shoulder muscles quivering, but my wrists were
tied too tightly.

Again, I tried to stuff my hands into my right front pocket, but I
could only get my pinkie inside. And I was a good three inches from
the derringer. I did a half sit-up, stomach muscles straining, reached for
my pocket, and fell over with a thud.

Eight rushed into the room, jammed the barrel of the Python between my eyes, the steel feeling cold as ice on my skin, and looked
through me with dead eyes. "Make any more noise and I'll plug you
right now."

When he left, the image of those dead eyes stayed with me. Again,
I tried to reach into my front pocket, but my wrists were simply taped
together too tightly. I was never going to get the gun that way, I realized.
I took a deep breath, slowly exhaled, and began rolling across the carpet, trying not to make any noise. I could feel the derringer, through
my pocket, clank against the ground. I continued rolling and every rev-
olution I began jerking my hips, hoping to work the derringer out of
my pocket and onto the floor.

Freezing, I heard footsteps outside the door. I thought I heard Eight
talking on the telephone again. I waited a minute, then began rolling
again, thrusting out my pelvis, as I tried to jostle the derringer out of my

pocket. A dozen more times I rolled across the floor, twisting my hips, until I was so dizzy I began to retch. But I didn't stop. Until I heard a sound so sweet it brought tears to my eyes: a solid thud. The sound of metal hitting carpet. The gleaming derringer was only a foot away. I inched over, grabbed the gun, and quickly clasped my hands together, hiding it.

I curled up on my side, breathing heavily, wheezing with exertion, my shirt soaked with sweat. I closed my eyes and tried to catch my breath. When Eight and Rip returned, I knew I couldn't afford a mistake. There were only two bullets in the barrel and they were .22-caliber. Not much stopping power. I had to make them both count.

About ten minutes later, they returned. Eight softly ran his hand along my haunches, making my skin crawl. My teeth ached from clenching them. "He gonna do you. I gonna do you. Then when I done, I gonna take care of you with this," he said, jabbing me in the ribs with the Python. "How you like that?"

"Cut his ankles and knees loose," he called out.

Rip returned from the kitchen with a butcher knife, crouched beside me, and poked me in my butt with the tip. I cried out in pain.

"That right," he said. "You gonna be yelping plenty while we grind you."

He cut the tape with the knife and rolled me onto my knees. My hands were sweating so heavily, I was afraid the derringer would slip out and onto the floor. He unbuttoned his Levis, dropping his pants to his ankles, and set my Beretta on the carpet beside him. When he crouched behind me, I looked over my shoulder and saw Eight behind him, grinning madly, laying his Python beside the mattress.

"Rip the warm up act. I gonna finish you off, punk."

As Rip reached around my waist, trying to unbuckle my belt, I whirled around, on my knees, jammed the derringer toward his face and fired.

His right eyeball exploded, spraying my face with a viscous blast of blood and tissue and bone fragments. I rolled to my side, grabbed the Beretta, and fired at Eight, missing him but splintering the door.

As I climbed to my feet, firing, he ran out. But the shots were wild because my hands were still taped together. I saw the door slam and, through the window, spotted him jumping into his car. By the time I had the Beretta aimed at him, he was careening down the street. Then he was gone.

I walked back to the bedroom and lifted the sleeves on Rip's baggy white T-shirt. I examined both arms, but all I saw was an expanse of smooth brown skin, without a single tattoo.

CHAPTER 37

I finally finished briefing Daryl Sippleman—the captain from the 77th assigned to coordinate the search for Li'l Eight—Duffy, and the two detectives from the Force Investigation Division, who asked me a series of softball questions. I had shot and killed Rip and shot at and missed Li'l Eight, who was still on the loose. I told Sippleman how the woman from Watts had set me up, how Rip and Li'l Eight were waiting for me. He said his detectives would hook her up for conspiracy to kill a police officer and try to put together a case against her.

I was too ashamed to admit to them what Rip and Li'l Eight had planned to do to me. I just told the detectives they taped me up and were going to execute me. Because the shooting was clearly a case of self-defense, I was not put on administrative leave.

When Duffy and I finally left the house, he followed me to my car and slammed his fist into an open palm. "I told you to stay away from that Patton case. I *ordered* you to stay away. Didn't I?"

I shrugged.

"You didn't listen and you almost got yourself killed."

I rubbed my wrists, which were still sore.

"You going to finally listen to me? You going to back off this case now?"

"Yeah."

"This isn't our case anymore. South Bureau Homicide's got it. You fuck with me on this again, Ash, and you're going to regret it. I'll call I.A. myself and report you for violating department policy. You can't poach on another division's case just 'cause you've got a beef to settle. You understand me?"

I nodded.

"When you got the lead, you should've let the department investigate it. No more flying solo. Understood?"

"Understood."

"I cut my San Diego trip short. All night I was calling you. Now I see why you didn't get back to me. I'm putting you back on call tomorrow night. You got too much fucking time on your hands."

"You promised me I couldn't go back on call until Monday. I've still got a lot of paperwork to finish up."

Duffy shook his head. "I changed my mind. Tomorrow night. End of discussion. So how're you feeling?"

"I may be out a Zegna suit. I think that duct tape ruined my pants."

"Listen, Ash, you got to be careful. That one gangster got away. You want a unit outside your building?"

"I can't live like that. Anyway, I'm sure this guy's laying low."

"So you think Li'l Eight's your guy?"

"At least I know Rip isn't."

"You don't know for sure that Li'l Eight was involved. Right?"

"Not for sure."

"He may have just wanted to put the hurt to a cop. And it sounds like that gal you jammed who put you on to Rip and Li'l Eight may've been blowing smoke up your ass—just to get you off her back."

"Maybe."

"Well, it doesn't matter now. Because all you can do is wait for Captain Sippleman to find Li'l Eight. Let him do his job."

I drove back downtown and returned to my loft. Grabbing a bottle of ale out of the refrigerator, I took a few long pulls and walked to a back window. I could see in the distance a patch of the Los Angeles River, encased in high cement banks, the shallow water slick and black, glimmering under a full moon, trickling to the sea. Pushing myself away from the window, I downed the rest of the ale, hoping it would calm my nerves. It had been a long time since I had felt like this: heart pounding, pulse racing, a quicksilver mood shifting from sudden exultation to anger. Exultation because I had escaped death and was alive. Anger because someone just tried to kill me. This was how I felt when I was a soldier, after a firefight, returning from a night patrol.

I had been shot at numerous times then, and when I was a young patrolman I had a few close calls. But I felt much more rattled now. Maybe it was the humiliation; maybe I'm just getting too old for this shit. After downing my ale, I was still anxious and jittery. I knew another ale would just give me a headache. One of my patrol partners at Pacific called me "The Two Brew Hebrew" because I rarely ordered a third when we went drinking after our shift. Occasionally I did, but I paid for it the next morning. I told him that the stereotype about Jews being unable to tolerate much alcohol was true. My Uncle Benny once quipped that Jews don't drink because it interferes with their suffering. But I read a more scientific explanation somewhere that Jews have a genetic mutation that increases the levels of a toxic chemical when they drink, which brings on headaches and nausea.

I jogged down the steps, climbed into my car, pulled onto the freeway, and headed toward the ocean. Fifteen minutes later I was crouching beside a window, in a stand of oleander, that offered me a clear view of Nicole reading on her living room sofa. I surveyed the room, decorated in an expensive, eclectic style, with gleaming hardwood floors, an intricately woven Persian rug, hammered-copper wall sconces and Art Nouveau floor lamps flanking the sofa. I circled the house, and when I was sure her boyfriend was not lurking about, I rang the bell.

"Who is it?" she called out.

"I'm collecting money for the Chabad Chanukah fund."

When she opened the door, she scowled at me, her face set in an expression of tight, pinched disapproval. "I thought I already told you not to come by here, that *I'll* contact *you* when I want to see you."

She tried to slam the door, but I pushed it open, and edged her out of the way with my shoulder. "I decided I don't like that plan."

"I've got a boyfriend, remember? So that's the way it's got to be." She leaned toward me and sniffed. "You're drunk."

"Not really."

She pointed to the door. "Get out."

I gripped her by the shoulders and kissed her hard.

She wriggled free and stepped back. "What's *with* you tonight?"

"Two guys just tried to kill me."

She slumped onto the sofa, looking stunned.

"Well I'm one for two. One down. One to go."

"What happened?"

Ignoring her question, I fell onto the sofa, kissing her, working my way down her neck to the base of her throat.

She looked up at me, eyes half closed. "I can see I'm not going to have to whup you upside the head *tonight*."

"Somebody," I said, "already did that for you."

A gust of wind rustling the oleander woke me. I reached for the Beretta. Gripping the gun, I realized where I was. Nicole was asleep, her hair splayed on the pillow as if she was floating underwater. I checked the digital clock on the end table: 7:05.

I dressed quietly and left without waking her.

When I entered the squad room, a half dozen detectives immediately surrounded me and volunteered to search for Li'l Eight. They may not have liked me, but if someone tries to kill a cop, everyone closes ranks.

"I appreciate the offer," I said, "but the Seventy-seventh is all over it. They're hunting this guy down. But I'll let you know if I need you."

When I returned with a cup of coffee, Ortiz strolled over. "You need some backup, homes. Let me ride with you. At least until my partner gets back from vacation."

"I appreciate the offer," I said. "I'll let you know if I need you."

Ortiz stood up and straightened his pants. "Let me pass along some advice my grandfather used to give me. It's an old Mexican saying: All your friends are false; all your enemies are real."

I fingered Ortiz's frayed, antiquated corduroy sports coat and said, "Let me pass along some advice *my* grandfather used to give me: Dress British, think Yiddish."

When Ortiz walked off, chuckling, I called Captain Sippleman. "Any luck in tracking down Li'l Eight?"

"Jesus, Ash, it's been less than twenty-four hours. Give us a chance."

"When you get him into custody, I'd appreciate it if you'd let me know as soon as possible."

"Will do. And don't worry. We'll get him. I sent out a state-wide BOLO. And every watch commander on every shift in every division in the city knows we're looking for this clown. As you know, a lot of these gangsters are too stupid to leave the 'hood. So I also gave an extra heads up to all our South Central patrol captains and Sheriff's department stations on the southside. They know this guy's a number one priority target."

I wanted to track down Li'l Eight myself, stick the barrel of my gun in his face, and pull the fucking trigger. But after my last attempt at going solo and almost getting killed, I decided that the 77th had a better chance of finding him and taking him into custody, than I did. They had the patrol officers scouring South Central, the gang officers with snitches, the vice cops making arrests and picking up scuttlebutt on the street.

Duffy wandered by and sat on the edge of my desk. "Have you seen the paper this morning?"

I shook my head.

"The *Times* has got a big spread on the Wegland dirty cop story. TV and radio is chasing. I've been sending calls all morning to Press Relations."

"They get any of it right?"

"About half right. Not much more you can do. Let Captain Sippleman do his thing. Fortunately, you're back on call tonight, so the problem of you fucking around with the Patton case has been solved."

"How about a few more days? There're some things I need to do on Relovich because—"

"I already told you this is nonnegotiable," Duffy said, walking off.

I closed my eyes and slumped at my desk, unable to concentrate, unable to keep my thoughts from drifting back to yesterday, when I was taped up, helpless, frightened. I blinked hard a few times. My head began to pound. I shook out three Tylenol and swallowed them with the dregs of my coffee.

A secretary from the captain's office called out across the room, "Ash, a cop from Metro is on the line. I'm transferring him to you."

I could feel my pulse quicken. Metro is the department's elite patrol unit. Maybe one of the Metro guys scooped up Li'l Eight. I grabbed the phone.

"Detective Levine, this is Dan Freed from the *Times*. I'm doing a follow-up on the Relovich murder. I'm trying to get some background on Wegland and Patowski and put together—"

"What kind of shit are you trying to pull? You identified yourself as a Metro cop."

"I never said I was a cop. I just said I was from Metro. I'm on the *L.A. Times* Metro staff."

"Don't play dumb. That's a bullshit con job and you know it. Call Press Relations," I said, slamming down the phone.

When I returned to my loft that evening, I was in a nasty mood. I popped open a beer and collapsed on the overstuffed chair by the window. The sun was red and low on the horizon, seeping through the venetian blinds and casting stripes on the polished concrete floor. I drank another beer, stared into space, and angrily thought about how Rip and Li'l Eight had humiliated me.

I fell asleep in the chair, and when I awoke, I checked my digital alarm clock: 6:10. Sitting up, I grabbed my remote control, flipped on ESPN, and distractedly watched a darts tournament, feeling dazed and half-asleep. After staring at the screen for about fifteen minutes, I spotted on top of the television the DVD of the Bae Soo Sung robbery-murder that Tommy Pardo had given me. I had seen it before, but the last time was almost a year ago, so I decided to watch it again.

I slipped the disk into the DVD player and studied the soundless black-and-white security video of a stocky guy in a baggy T-shirt wearing a Shrek mask and black gloves who burst through the front door waving a pistol. Sung raised his hands above his head and stepped away from the counter. Shrek yelled something to Sung. Sung nodded and waved his palms, as if to placate Shrek. He stuffed the bills from the register into a paper bag. Shrek grabbed the bag and headed for the door. But instead of walking out, he spun around, extended the barrel toward Sung. That terrified expression in Sung's eyes had haunted me since I had first seen it: in an instant he knew he had only a few seconds left to live; he knew he'd never see his wife and children again. Shrek pulled the trigger. A dark rosette burst from Sung's chest, and he fell to the ground.

For the next twenty minutes, I rewound and played the tape several times, but I didn't see anything that I hadn't spotted before. I padded off to the kitchen, made myself a cup of coffee, and brought it back to my bed. Sipping the coffee, sitting on the edge of the bed, I played the tape again. When Shrek grabbed the bag of cash with his left hand, I dropped my cup, spilling the coffee on my bed.

Staring at the screen, I was unable to move. I could hear a loud rushing noise, like the roar of the surf. I felt disoriented, like I was underwater, unsure of where the surface was, not knowing whether to swim up or down.

I jumped to my feet and shouted, "Damn! That's it!"

Quickly rewinding the tape, I froze the image of Shrek grabbing the bag. I crouched a few inches from the television and studied the screen.

When Shrek had entered the store, his left hand was in his pocket. He only removed it to grab the cash bag. In that split second when he pulled his hand out of the pocket and gripped the cash bag I saw something that stunned me.

Two fingers of the left glove flapped a bit, as if there was nothing inside.

The shooter was missing two fingers—his ring finger and the pinkie.

I knew someone missing two fingers. He'd planned to rape me and kill me.

Lil' Eight.

CHAPTER 38

I waited until eight and called Captain Daryl Sippleman, who was co-ordinating the search for Li'l Eight. I didn't want to tip him off about my discovery; I just wanted to know if he was close to arresting Li'l Eight.

"Sorry, Ash, no luck yet," he said. "But I did bust that woman who set you up."

"Where they holding her?"

"She's at the jail over at Seventy-seventh. And don't worry about Li'l Eight. It's supposed to heat up over the next few days. The natives will be restless, and they'll all be out on the streets. We'll get him."

"I don't like the idea of this guy still roaming around."

"Neither do I," Sippleman said. "We'll scoop up his ass. Don't worry."

But I was worried. And I wasn't going to wait around to see when—or if—Sippleman would finally find Li'l Eight. Sippleman had his chance. Now I was going to track him down using my own methods.

I showered, dressed, and headed down to the 77th Division. After parking in back, I hustled over to where they kept the female prisoners. I told the jailer to bring out the woman who'd set me up.

A few minutes later, she shuffled into the interview room, wearing a frayed yellow housedress. When she saw me she shouted, "All because of you that I'm here."

"No. It's all because of you. Remember when you told me where I could find Rip? Well, when I got there he tried to kill me. And he was almost able to do it because he knew I was coming. And he knew I was coming because you warned him. That's why you were arrested for con-spiracy to commit murder. That's why you won't see the sun shine for the next twenty years."

She buried her face in her palms. After I let her cry for a few minutes, I said, "There might be a way for me to help you."

She lifted her head and looked up at me, eyes red and tear-stained. "How?"

"I've got to find Li'l Eight. You let me know where I can find him, and I'll talk to the DA for you. He might cut your sentence."

"How can I find him from the jailhouse?"

"Follow me."

I led her down a narrow hallway that smelled of disinfectant to the small windowless sergeant's office, which was empty. "Sit," I ordered, pointing to the chair behind the desk.

I handed her a pen and pad, pointed to the phone, and said, "Get me an address."

During the next fifteen minutes she made a series of calls, the phone jammed between her ear and the crook of her neck, her voice muffled. After slamming the receiver down on the hook, she glared at me and jabbed her finger on a number she'd scrawled on the paper.

"There's the address right there. You put it out that I tell you where he stayin', I dead. You understand?"

I grabbed the piece of paper and said, "If he knows I'm coming, you'll never get out of here. You'll never see your kids again. *You* understand?"

After leading her back to the interview room, I left for a moment to tell the jailer not to let the woman make any phone calls for the next twenty-four hours. When I returned, I said, "I want to ask you something else before I leave. You know Li'l Eight?"

"I seen him around a few time."

"You know anything about a market shooting he was involved in?"

"Don't know nothin' 'bout that."

"You sure?"

"Sure I'm sure."

"You ever hear of a woman named Latisha Patton?"

She crossed her legs. "I heard of her."

"What did you hear?"

"I heard she a snitch."

My mouth went dry. "Who'd you hear that from?"

"It was out on the street."

"How'd it get out on the street?"

She jiggled a foot and said, "Will it help my case if I tell you?"

I slammed my fist on the metal table. "Where'd that information come from?" I shouted.

She glanced at me with distaste, pursing her lips as if she had just sucked a lemon. "A girl from 'round here, named Rhonda Davis, her sister work at your po-lice headquarters downtown. She a secretary. She work with all the kiddie cops."

"Juvenile?"

"Yeah. That's it. Well, she gettin' down with one of your big shot cops there. A guy she call the Big Leprechaun. Rhonda's sister hear it from him."

As I walked back to my car, I was so stunned I had trouble walking. I tried to sort out what I had just heard, but I still couldn't believe it. I took a few deep breaths, slowly exhaling.

I called Ortiz at the station. I tried to speak, but my mouth was too dry. Finally, I managed to croak, "Meet me on Second Street behind PAB."

I pulled up at the curb and motioned for Ortiz to get in the car. I filled him in on what the woman told me.

"You sure she was talking about Duffy?" Ortiz said.

"I'm sure. That's what the gangsters used to call him when he worked South Bureau Homicide."

"What the fuck was he thinking?" Ortiz said.

"I heard Duffy was banging some twenty-two-year-old black secretary who works in juvenile, but I didn't think he'd be dumb enough to actually talk to her about a case. He must have been on one of his fucking benders."

"When he's on one of those, he gets all drunked up and runs his mouth. What a stupid motherfucker. This is your case, Ash. It's your call. What're you going to do?"

"I'm going to drive out to this address," I said, waving the piece of paper the woman gave me. "I'm going to bust Li'l Eight. Then I'm going to front Duffy."

I shook out three Tylenol, swallowed them with a swig of warm water from a bottle in the backseat, and stared through the windshield, my head swirling with thoughts of Latisha, how I had convinced her to talk to me; how I had tried to protect her; how we'd awake in the morning, her head on my chest, our legs entwined; how I had found her sprawled out on a street corner, half her head blown off. I thought about the hellish past year. I had been so consumed with anguish, so tormented; I had blamed myself for her death and I had suffered grievously. Every single day. And then this. The anger would come later, I knew. Now, I was in a daze.

"You want me to drive?" Ortiz asked.

I slipped the key into the ignition and started the car.

"You okay?"

I gripped the wheel tightly, drove off, and didn't answer.

"For what it's worth, that bitch in juvenile got canned a few months ago. She got caught snooping into some department databases."

Pulling off Crenshaw, I headed up to The Jungle, a run-down South L.A. neighborhood crammed with seedy two-unit apartment buildings. Residents originally gave the neighborhood its nickname because of the lush tropical landscaping—fan palms, banana plants, begonias, enormous birds of paradise—that surrounded the buildings. But soon the name took on a more menacing meaning when the neighborhood began to deteriorate. Rival gangs shot it out on the streets, dealers peddled crack in the alleys, and the shoddily built apartments fell into disrepair.

I pulled up in front of the apartment where Li'l Eight was staying, we climbed the steps to the second floor, and rang the bell. When no one answered, Ortiz and I peered into a few side windows and determined nobody was home.

I returned to my car, and parked down the street, far enough away so Li'l Eight couldn't spot us, but close enough so I could keep an eye on the front door. After two hours of silence, Ortiz said, "You're great fucking company."

"Sorry. This Duffy thing's got me turned around."

"Why don't we call in this address to SIS and let them sit on the apartment. They can bring Li'l Eight in for us."

"I don't want to interview Li'l Eight at the station. I want to talk to him right here. I've got a creative interviewing approach in mind for him."

"Just don't be so creative that they fire your ass."

I turned toward Ortiz. "This was never just a homicide investigation. The stakes were always high for me. Now they're higher. I've got to take care of it in my own way."

Ortiz nodded. "I understand."

After two more hours of waiting, I said, "Let's meet downtown tomorrow morning at five and then hit him up. We should catch him in bed then."

"You got it."

I drove back to PAB, and we headed up to the squad room. Now was the time to confront Duffy.

CHAPTER 39

Duffy was in his office, hunched over a computer, typing furiously. I entered without knocking and sat down.

He pushed away from his desk, twirled his chair toward me and, with a theatrical motion, checked his watch. "It's almost two. Where the hell you been?"

"I just figured out something."

"What's that."

"That you suspended me last year because you were trying to get me to quit."

"I don't know what you're talking about."

"I think you do. You didn't contact me this past year because you didn't *want* me to come back."

"Ash," he said, his voice softening, "when you were just a kid on patrol, I pulled you off the street and brought you into homicide as a trainee. I shepherded you through and made sure you made detective. I was there when you got your shield. I brought you to Felony Special. We go too far back for you to come up with some crazy-ass conspiracy theory about me."

Thinking back to all those years with Duffy, how I had trusted him, looked up to him, worked so hard for him to curry his approval, I felt betrayed and began to choke up. I couldn't get any words out, so I just swallowed hard and shook my head.

"You're paranoid," he said.

I leaned forward and studied his face. "I know you were banging that secretary in juvenile. I know you told her that Latisha Patton was cooperating with me. I know she put the word out on the street that Latisha was a snitch. And I know, now, that's why Latisha was shot."

Duffy gripped his desk, kneading the edges. "That cunt's a liar."

"I didn't hear it from her. I did my own investigation."

Duffy's hands fell limply to his sides.

"After I was suspended last year, you didn't want me to come back because you were afraid I might stumble onto the truth. You figured you were home free when I quit. Then you heard that I started nosing around the case, that Latisha's daughter complained, that the I.A. lieutenant warned me off. You thought I'd keep picking at the case. So you decided the best way to derail me was to hire me back on the job, where you could keep an eye on me and load me up with cases so I'd be too busy to chase the Patton case. You were trying to figure out how to get me back when the Relovich homicide landed on your desk. You used the case to manipulate Grazzo into asking for me, making him think it was his idea."

He stared straight ahead, frozen, not even blinking

"Don't bother trying to weasel out of all this. I know it's true. You know it's true."

He leaned over and closed the blinds in his office. Raising both palms he said, "This is the God's honest—" He stopped in mid-sentence and abruptly dropped his palms to his lap.

"Let's stop shoveling the shit," I said.

His face was contorted, as if he was struggling with an emotion that was somewhere between anger and anguish.

"God, I'm a stupid motherfucker. Worst mistake of my life. Damn, Ash. You know how often I wished I'd never got involved with that whore? Every fucking day for the past year."

"You don't know what I've gone through," I said softly.

Duffy bowed his head. "That's what's made it so hard," he said, his voice cracking.

"You can fuck anyone you want. But why did you have to tell her about Latisha? I just don't understand that."

He wiped his eyes with his sleeve and emitted a phlegmy cough. "We were out drinking one night. Christ, I'd downed so many I can't even remember where we were or when. I don't even remember talking to her about the case. It was a total fucking blackout."

"You're pathetic."

"That's not an excuse, I know. But that's the truth. The next morning she brought up Patton's name. I realized then that I'd totally fucking blown it. I tried to piss backward. But it was too late."

"But why?"

He shook his head, frowning. "I guess I was telling her about some of the cases we were working, trying to impress her, an old man with a hard on for a young babe. She hung on my every word, and I kept gabbing." He slammed a palm on the blotter, the tears spraying the edges of the desk. "Stupid! Stupid! Stupid!"

Watching Duffy sputter out an explanation, I felt an intense hatred for him. I wanted to grab him by the throat and smash that self-pitying look off his face. "What a prick you are. You just let me take the fucking fall. You took the easy way out. And, to be perfectly safe, you sent the case back down to South Bureau. You figured those guys are so overwhelmed, so overworked, they'd never have time to get to the truth. Then you wouldn't have to deal with me or the case. You were just praying I'd never put it all together."

Duffy unclipped his badge from his belt and dropped it on his desk. "You want my badge, Ash, you can have it. I mean it. You can tell Grazzo right now about all this. I won't dispute it. I got twenty-three years in. I don't deserve a twenty-fourth."

Reaching over, I picked up the badge and walked to the door. I knew Duffy. He always liked to make the grand gesture. At the time he made a dramatic pronouncement, he usually believed it. Later, however, he invariably recanted.

I tossed the badge on the floor and walked out of the squad room.

CHAPTER 40

As I walked through the dim parking lot, I could feel my anger settling and mutating into a profound sadness. I didn't have the luxury to wallow in how Duffy fucked me over, however, because I had to focus on Li'l Eight. I didn't want to wait until tomorrow morning to sit on his apartment. And I decided that I wasn't going to call Ortiz. I didn't know exactly what I was going to do when I confronted Li'l Eight, but I knew I wasn't going to adhere to LAPD interrogation regulations. This case was personal for me, but it wasn't personal for Ortiz. I was willing to get fired over how I sweated Li'l Eight; I wasn't willing to risk Ortiz's job.

I drove out to The Jungle, parked down the street, and opened my trunk. From a metal toolbox, I removed a small silencer that I had confiscated from a Belizian cocaine dealer and slipped it into my coat pocket. Light-stepping it to the building, I climbed up the stairs to Li'l Eight's apartment on the second floor, looked in the windows, and determined no one was home. So I returned to my car, kept my eye on the front door, and waited.

I was jittery, nervously tapping my fingernails on the dash, but the longer I waited, the more I thought about Li'l Eight, the angrier I became. When I had first joined the LAPD, there seemed to be a code that criminals followed. If you held up a market and the clerk gave you the cash—you didn't shoot him simply as an afterthought. If you knew a witness was going to cooperate with detectives, you threatened him first and persuaded him not to cooperate—you didn't just blast him. If a detective came to arrest you, you'd probably run and maybe even shoot it out—you'd never tie him up and debase and assassinate him. I may not have liked some of the old-time crooks I had arrested as a young patrolman, but I realized now that many of them at least pulled their heists with a degree of professionalism, getting in and out of jobs quickly, with no violence. Li'l Eight symbolized to me the new breed of criminal. Since he'd decided to violate the code of street poker, I decided I wouldn't simply call him. I would raise the stakes.

At dusk, I drove off to a gas station to take a piss. When I returned, the fog had rolled in, so there wasn't much of a sunset, just a gradual darkening as light seeped from the veil of gray on the western horizon. At eight, I thought I saw someone enter the apartment. I climbed out of my car, but slowly crawled back in when I realized it was the apartment next door. A half hour later, I almost dozed off, so I opened all the windows and took a few deep breaths. The fog had misted up my windshield, limiting my visibility, so I kept my windshield wipers running.

Shortly after nine, I spotted a stocky black kid with a goatee, who was wearing a baggy, white T-shirt, approach the apartment. Jumping out of the car, I hustled down the sidewalk for a better look. It was Li'l Eight. As he began to climb the steps, clutching a key ring in his right hand, I slipped up behind him, stuck the Beretta in his back and said, "Put the key in the lock nice and easy."

When he reached into his coat pocket, I jammed the gun in his back and said, "Hands out where I can see them."

He opened the front door and I followed him inside.

"Surprised to see me?"

He gave me a contemptuous look.

"Sit down."

He held his wrists out toward me. "You might as well cuff me right now and take me downtown. 'Cause I ain't sayin' shit till I see my lawyer."

I took a step forward and lifted up the right sleeve of his T-shirt. And there it was on his upper arm: The big CK tattoo with the C crossed out.

I was so enraged, Li'l Eight faded into an amorphous blur. I wanted to jam the Beretta into his mouth and blow the back of his head off.

He stood up, looked at me with a half smile, and muttered so softly I could barely hear, "Shoulda finished you off when I had the chance, punk-ass bitch."

I slammed him on the side of his head with the barrel of my gun. He fell to his knees, wiped the blood off, and looked up at me with a smirk

of superiority. "No beat down gonna make me change my mind. Nothin'
you can do to make me talk."

I gripped my gun tightly and said, "You're going to tell me all about
how you killed that Korean liquor store owner and you're going to tell
me all about Latisha Patton."

I thought of my old guru, Bud Carducci, and how he used to persuade recalcitrant suspects to talk. He'd figure out what they were most
afraid of, then exploit that fear.

"Start talking—Li'l Seven."

He shook his head. "That ain't my name."

"I screwed the silencer onto the Beretta's barrel, reached over and
grabbed Li'l Eight's right wrist. I jammed the muzzle on the tip of his
pinkie fingernail and pulled the trigger, spraying tissue and nail fragments over the front of his shirt.

He let out a strangled scream and flopped on the carpet like a
landed fish, jerking his hand spasmodically.

"It will be if I have to pull the trigger again."

"Mother*fucker*!" he howled.

I grabbed a towel from the kitchen and tossed it to him.

He wrapped his finger and fell onto the chair, writhing and yelping.

"You going to tell me?" I asked.

He looked up at me—blinking hard, lips quivering—and said,
"Don't know about no Korean and no lady named Tisha."

"I just took the tip off. But next time, I'll blow the whole pinkie off.
Then I'm going for the ring finger and the index finger and the thumb.
So you either tell me what I want to know, or I'll keep blasting."

He shook his head.

I wrestled his right hand out of the towel, stuck the muzzle just
below his pinkie, and said, "You want to be known as Li'l Seven?"

"No!" he screamed. Reaching for the towel, he wrapped his right
hand. "You crazy!"

"That's right," I said. "So you better start talking."

"Just keep that piece away from my hand," he shouted.

I pointed to the chair. "Get off the floor and sit down."

He crawled to his feet and teetered onto the chair, his chest heaving with staccato coughs.

"You robbed that Korean market on south Figueroa, right?"

He nodded.

"Yes or no?"

"Yeah, I robbed it."

"Why'd you shoot the Korean guy behind the counter?"

He looked down at the towel, now soaked in blood, and shook his head.

I jabbed my gun toward the towel.

"I don't like slopes."

"That's it? That's why you shot him?"

"Didn't want to leave no wits."

"But you were wearing a mask. He couldn't identify you."

He mumbled a reply, but I couldn't understand what he was saying.

"What was that?" I shouted.

"I'd been in there before, buying shit and casing the place," he said through gritted teeth. "Maybe he could've recognized my voice or IDed me later on. I didn't want to take no chance."

"Why'd you pick that place? It's a ways from your 'hood."

"When I was in the joint, met a homeboy from that 'hood. Said the slope kept a lot of cash in his register. I remembered that. When I got out, I went after it."

"You killed Latisha Patton, didn't you?"

He gripped the towel and shook his head.

I reached over, yanked off the bloody towel, tossed it on the floor, and stuck the barrel in the middle of his palm. "Tell me the fucking truth, or I'll blow the whole hand off."

He stared at the bloody towel, turned his head, and spit on the floor. "I had to cap that bitch. She talkin' to the police. What I suppose to do?"

"Tell me where you found her?"

"I found out where she lived."

"How?"

"Through the ghetto grapevine. She tole some friend in the 'hood, who tole someone, who tole someone. So I go out to her place in the Valley."

"You shoot her there?"

"Lemme think." Crouching slightly, he balled up the towel and threw it at my face. He ran into the kitchen.

I chased after him, and cracked him on the head with the Beretta. He dropped to the floor, twitching and rubbing the back of his head.

"I'm sick of fucking around with you." I tapped the barrel of the gun on the knuckles of his right hand. "Did you shoot her there?"

"Tied her up there," he whispered. "Shot her at Fifty-fourth and Fig, cut her loose, and dumped her."

CHAPTER 41

The doctor at the Twin Towers jail downtown was able to quickly patch up Li'l Eight's pinkie, and I was able to book him there. I was relieved that I didn't have to check him into the jail ward on the thirteenth floor of County General Hospital and contend with the questions and the paperwork associated with an injured suspect in my custody.

I didn't think the methods I had used for extracting the confession would hold up in court, so I busted him for attempted murder of a police officer. Since this was his third strike, he'd get twenty-five to life—and would probably never get out. Still, I planned to pass on Li'l Eight's confession to Pardo over at South Bureau. Maybe we could work the case together when things calmed down, nail Li'l Eight for the double murder, and send him to death row.

At dawn, two tired and bored detectives from the Force Investigation Division interviewed me briefly. I told them that Li'l Eight had tried to grab my gun and I fired, which zipped off the top of his pinky. I wasn't sure they believed me, but they didn't seem too interested in trying to disprove my story.

Shuffling through the squad room, I poured a cup of coffee, returned to my desk, and fell into my chair. I closed my eyes, but jerked them open when I heard Duffy sit on the edge of my desk. He looked like he hadn't slept in days. His eyes were so bloodshot I could only see a few streaks of white in a sea of red. I smelled alcohol and Tic Tacs on his breath. His tie was askew and his hair was uncombed.

"I'd like to have a minute with you," he said.

I followed him into his office.

"I'm grateful to you—more than you can ever know—for getting some justice for Latisha Patton," he said softly, staring down at his desk. "That case was so damn important—for the department, for this unit, and for me, especially because of the way I . . . how I . . . how because of me everything turned to shit," he sputtered, still looking away from me.

I remained silent.

"I don't know how many people know of my culpability," he said, licking his lips.

Duffy was fishing. He wanted to know if I was going to file a complaint or inform the brass about his role in the Patton debacle.

"I'm not going to take you down."

"Ash, I can't tell you how much I appreciate—"

"Save it."

"So where do you want to go from here," Duffy said. "You just cleared two big cases. You're in a position to call your own shots."

I still wanted to track down Wegland's partner. I just didn't want to discuss my plans with Duffy. The power equation with him had shifted, and I knew I could use it to my advantage. That was one reason I didn't rat him out. If the chief brought in a new lieutenant, I might not be able to finish off the investigation the way I wanted. But as long as Duffy remained in charge, I had all the leverage and I could do whatever I wanted.

"I need some time to finish things off."

"No problem. I'll keep you clear of new cases for as long as I can. I owe you big-time and I can promise you that—"

I stood up, walked across the office, and slammed the door while Duffy was in mid-sentence.

By the time I finally returned to my loft, I'd been up almost thirty hours straight. I crawled into bed and slept deeply. It had been a long time since I had slept without waking up in a cold sweat, without a nightmare, without tossing and turning, without having to pop three Tylenol in the morning for a stress headache.

The next morning, lying in bed, I decided to work from home. Normally, Duffy would squawk about me being away from the squad room. But there wasn't much he could say now. And I just couldn't deal with him today. If Duffy would've simply leveled with me last year, owned up to what he'd done, instead of letting me take the fall, everything I had gone through the past year would have been—

"Damn," I shouted, jumping out of bed. If I continue to go down that road, I'll be too pissed off to get any work done today. And I might be too pissed off to return to Felony Special and work for Duffy. I didn't want to leave the unit. This was the best job in the department. If I wanted to stay at Felony Special, I had better learn to let it go; I had better learn to live with it and tolerate Duffy. Could I? If I continued to use my leverage against him to get what I wanted, maybe I could.

I showered, dressed, ate a bowl of cereal, and made a cup of coffee. Sipping my coffee, I read my synopses from the interviews with Theresa Martinez and the San Pedro crackhead. Since they were my only eye wits of Wegland's ghost partner, I decided to interview them again.

I walked to PAB, picked up my car from the lot, drove up Interstate 5 and arrived at the Pitchess Detention Center in the early afternoon. After dropping my Beretta in the metal locker, I waited in the interview room for a few minutes. When the deputies brought the junkie out, he wearily walked across the room, hunched over, hands slightly in front of him, like he was an old man pushing a walker.

He plopped down on a chair with a grunt. "I'm tired, youngblood. Too tired to do long time."

"Then you better give up the pipe."

"Soon as I get out, I gonna clean up my own self."

"Look, I appreciate you talking to me, helping me out with this case."

"Ain't no thang."

"I just have a few more questions."

He nodded.

"When I talked to you in the Harbor Division jail, right after you got popped, you told me you spotted two guys at the bottom of the hill, walking toward their car, looking around."

"Aiight. I remember that."

"Can you describe the guy who got into the passenger side?"

"Looked kinda Mez-can. Skinny and taller than the other dude. I tol' you that already."

"I know that. Anything else you remember?"

"I just seen that Mez-can for a second before I was on my way."

"I'm trying to get a little better description."

"Gonna be tough. That junk ride I was on that night done wrecked my memory. And both fools wearing those lids that sailors wear. Made it hard to see their faces."

"Watch caps?"

"Thas right."

"Anything else you remember about this Mexican guy? Think about it. Take your time."

He rubbed his palms together. A few seconds later he said, "Dang. Just can't think of nothin' else. Wish I could help you. And help myself. I'm sorry 'bout that."

"So am I."

When I returned to my car, I opened my briefcase and searched for the address of Theresa Martinez's sister. Martinez was spooked after the shooting and decided to stay with her sister down in Santa Ana. I had a drive ahead of me, but fortunately the traffic was light. I hit ninety on the 5 all the way down to Santa Ana. I parked on a cul-de-sac lined with modest ranch-style homes, many with RVs and boats in the driveway, that all looked alike. After ringing the doorbell, I could see Martinez peeking through the front window blinds. She opened the door and let me in.

She grabbed the remote and flipped off the television, which was playing a soap opera.

"Can I get you anything to drink. Coffee or soda?"

Still standing in the foyer, I shook my head.

She motioned toward the sofa. "Please come in." I sat at one end and she sat on the other.

"I been watching a lot of trash TV lately," she said, looking embarrassed. "Can't really concentrate."

"You've got to give yourself some time. You went through a traumatic experience."

I pulled a card out of my wallet, jotted a number on the other side, and handed it to her. "This is the phone number for one of the city's victim's assistance coordinators. Tell her I told you to call. She'll set you up with some counseling. It won't cost you anything."

"I appreciate it. I keep thinking of that man holding the gun to my head." She hugged herself and said, "I *should* talk to somebody."

"I promise you, it'll help."

"I never got a chance to thank you. If you hadn't shown up at my apartment, I hate to think—"

"I'm just glad I made it there in time."

She reached up, wrapped a tendril of hair around an index finger and stared at the wall.

"I wanted to talk to you about something."

She continued staring blankly at the wall.

"Remember when you told me that you saw two people coming down the street that night you were arrested."

She nodded, still avoiding my eyes.

"You said you couldn't see the driver, but you got a better look at the other guy. You said you thought he was Mexican."

"That's what I saw," she said in a soft monotone.

"I just want to make sure you're not holding out on me. Because I got the sense that maybe you saw something else, something you haven't told me. And it's very important that you tell me *everything*."

"Why's it important?" she asked, finally turning toward me. "You already arrested the guy who killed the cop. Why do you need to keep talking to me?"

"The killer, I believe, was the driver of the car you spotted. I'm still looking for his partner. The passenger. The Mexican."

She looked up at me, eyes wide, and said, panic in her voice, "You still think I'm in danger?"

"Yes," I said, unsure if I believed it. But if I had to put the fear of God into her, so be it. "The only way I can get you out of danger is to find this guy and lock him up. So if there's something you know that might help me find him, please tell me now."

She dropped her chin to her chest and cried softly, wiping away the tears with her thumbs. I grabbed a Kleenex off an end table and handed it to her.

"I was able to save you at your apartment in San Pedro. If it happens again, I may not be able to get there in time."

Crying and sniffling, she leaned across the sofa and said, "The night I was busted, I knew some pipehead was talking to you. There was some chatter around the jail that night about it. I knew he'd seen two guys with watch caps by the car at the bottom of the hill near where I was busted. I knew the guy in the driver's side was a Mexican."

"So you just parroted what he said."

"I added a little of what I'd seen that night. But it was basically a variation of what he told me."

"I'm sorry," she said, dabbing at her eyes with a Kleenex. "I was hoping you'd help me out when my case came to court. Then you pressured me at work. I didn't want to lose my job. And I figured if I told you the same story as the pipehead, I'd be safe."

"Safe how?"

She balled up the Kleenex and gripped it tightly. "If someone had to testify, I wanted it to be him. Since we told you the same story, I hoped he'd be the one to tell it in court. I didn't want to be a target. I didn't want these people coming after me." She shook her head. "But they came after me anyway."

"And the composite you worked on with the police artist?"

"Bogus," she said softly.

"But you did see something. Right?"

She grabbed another Kleenex and spread it out on her lap.

I was angry now. "*Right?*" I shouted.

She nodded. "I did see a lot of the same stuff the pipehead saw."

I gave her a skeptical look.

"For real. But I saw something else, too.

"Let's hear it."

"A lot of what I told you at the station last week was true. I was standing around, about to walk over to the dealer selling on the corner when I saw those two people coming down the hill. I didn't get a decent look at the guy who got into the driver's side of the car, but I did see the other one walk around the car and open the door. A street lamp was only a few feet away. I saw the passenger pull a gun out of a pocket, stuff it under the car seat, and then climb in."

"What was he wearing?"

"Jeans and a stocking cap. A dark one."

"What was his nationality?"

"What I said before was true—Mexican."

"Besides the gun, you still haven't told me anything I didn't already know."

"I know. There's something else I didn't tell you. Something kind of weird."

"What is it?"

"Like I said, the passenger wore a stocking cap real low, just above the eyes, so at first I wasn't sure. I just thought it was a guy with kind of delicate features. But after the passenger got into the car and whipped off the stocking cap, I saw the hair come tumbling out. I realized that the passenger was a woman."

"You sure?"

"Pretty sure. I know I should have told you all this before. But I was afraid. I was just trying to protect myself. But like you said, they might keep coming after me until you catch them. So now I'm trying to help you."

"Could you ID her if you saw her again?"

"I doubt it. "

"You bullshitting me again?"

"No."

"Anything else you remember about her?"

"Yeah. After she took off her jacket, I could see she was wearing something around her neck. It stood out because it was white. It was a good sized crucifix."

"Moonstone?"

"Could be."

She leaned across the sofa, grabbed my hand, and squeezed it. "Do you know who this woman is?"

"I think I do."

I asked her a few more quick questions and then jogged toward my car and sped to the freeway.

CHAPTER 42

As I was heading north on the 5, I called downtown for an address. I checked my GPS and made my way to the Santa Monica Freeway. Cutting north on the Hollywood Freeway, I exited near Griffith Park and drove up a winding foothill road in Los Feliz. I parked on a quiet side street, walked about fifty yards, and stopped in front of a redwood bungalow carved onto a hillside.

I could use some backup, but, at this point, I didn't trust anyone in the LAPD. Wegland and Patowski were dirty. Duffy was a liar. I had no idea who else in the department was compromised. I felt safest handling this alone.

I flicked on my Maglite, edged my way down the driveway, circled the house, and stopped at the back door. Pulling a set of lock picks out of my back pocket, I inserted the tension wrench into the keyhole and turned it slightly. As I continued to apply pressure with the tension wrench, I slipped the pick into the keyhole. I lifted the pins, one by one, unit I heard a *click*—the upper pin falling into place. Rotating the plug and opening the door, I slipped through the darkened house. Every few steps I stopped and listened. All I could hear was the ticking of a clock and the humming of the refrigerator. When I reached a large bedroom, I peered inside. There she was, curled up on her side, one arm clutching a pillow. I needed a confession. If I didn't get one, I would have to haul her back to the station. And I knew she'd keep her mouth shut until her lawyer arrived. But if I took her by surprise, knocked her off her mooring, I just might be able to extract something useful from her.

When I stopped by Internal Affairs a few weeks ago, all those old-timers were flashing me hostile looks. Virginia Saucedo seemed like the only supportive detective in the room. She was a damn good actress.

Reaching for the Beretta, I slowly removed it from my holster, the leather creaking. I walked across the room and stood over the bed. "Detective Saucedo. You're under arrest."

She twitched, opened her eyes, and reached for the drawer in her end table, where I assumed she kept a pistol. I grabbed her wrist and said, "Let's go."

She was wearing a sheer blue V-necked nightgown, and the moonstone cross around her neck glowed in the faint light. She looked younger than the last time I had seen her. Shivering on the edge of the bed, blinking hard, hugging herself, she looked like a scared little girl.

"Where we going?"

"To the living room."

Grabbing a robe from the foot of the bed, she slipped it on, and as she stood up I noticed she was almost my height. She stumbled off to the living room as I followed her. I motioned toward the couch with the barrel of the Beretta. She sat down, and I pulled a chair across from her.

I glanced around the room. This house was beautiful, too nice for a single cop on a detective's salary. An enormous hand-carved chest in front of the sofa served as a coffee table, Mexican folk art lined the walls, and a large picture window revealed a spectacular view of the city, a carpet of lights from downtown to the ocean.

I figured the best way to go would be to bluff her.

"Conrad Patowski layed you out."

She glared at me.

"Patowski is singing to save his ass. He's angling for a deal. He served you up on a silver platter."

"I don't know what you're talking about."

"Conrad tried to get the best deal for himself. So he started talking. Said you went along with Wally to Relovich's. You know the felony murder rule. You're going down."

She clasped her hands on her lap. "That's all bullshit."

"Tell me what happened. I'll go to the DA with your statement and see if he can give you a break. Since Patowski's talking, you better not bullshit me. I'll compare statements and see who's lying."

"I think *you're* lying."

I leaned forward and said softly, "Save yourself."

"Save myself from *what*?"

"You know they execute women in California."

"If you want to arrest me, arrest me."

Ignoring her, I pulled a digital voice recorder from my vest pocket, set it on the wooden chest, flicked it on, and read Saucedo her rights. "How'd it begin with Wegland?"

She fixed me with a cold stare and said, "Go fuck yourself."

Before I could react, I was staring into the long blue steel barrel of a .38 revolver that a slender, jittery Hispanic man with a thin mustache was waving at me. "Set it down on the floor," he said in a quavering voice.

I dropped the gun.

"Am I glad to see *you*, baby," Saucedo said. "Even if you are late."

"I saw through the window this *pendejo* pointing a piece at you, so I snuck in the back door. Who the hell is he?"

She leaned over and shut off the tape recorder. "Just a stupid fucking cop who doesn't know when to back away from a cleared case."

When I reached toward my pocket, she shouted, "Hands to your side!"

The guy gripping the .38 looked like he was nervous enough to pull the trigger. But I hoped he might be reluctant to shoot me if I was talking to Saucedo. "I've figured out a few things about you and Wally," I said. "Before he made commander, he was a captain in Hollywood. You were working patrol there. He probably looked out for you. Helped you make detective. Got you on with I.A. And all this time the two of you were running your games and raking in the cash. Conrad was staying behind as the errand boy while Wally and you were out there ripping off houses. And all this led to the hit on Relovich." I glanced at the guy with the gun and back at Saucedo. "What the hell happened to you?"

"How do you think I could afford this house?" she said, an angry, defiant expression clouding her features. "Around here, just the lots are selling for a million."

"I think a jury would call it justifiable homicide because the L.A. real estate market made you do it. But why did Wally do it?"

The man with the .38 called out, "Because he was pussy whipped." He pointed the pistol at me and said, "This fucking guy's a tongue jockey. He'll talk all night if we let him. Let me shut this fool up."

Crossing the room and opening a closet door, she removed a sweat-shirt and a gun from a holster hanging on a hook. She wrapped the sweatshirt around the barrel of the gun, walked over, and knelt beside me. Then she whirled around and shot the man in the chest, the gunshot muffled by the sweatshirt.

He crumpled to the ground, his mouth open, his eyes bulging with astonishment, as the .38 clattered on the hardwood floor.

She walked over to the man and kicked the pistol to the side of the room.

I knew Saucedo was going to shoot me with his gun, making sure to leave no prints. Then she was going to put her gun, which was probably a throw-down, in my hands.

"Why'd you go after Relovich?" I asked.

"You're the Felony Special hotshot. You figure it out."

I knew she let me talk because she was pumping me for information. She wanted to figure out how to play it with the LAPD after she disposed of me.

"When Relovich called I.A. a few weeks ago, you managed to take his call," I said. "That call made you paranoid. You were afraid Relovich would rat you out because you were in on Wally's scams from the get go. You went with him and his snitch Freitas to rip off Silver. And when Freitas started arguing about the split in the middle of the job, *you* blasted him."

"If you know so much, why didn't you come after me sooner?"

"I was still putting my case together. It was apparent early on that Wally took care of Avery Mitchell in Idaho, because he was afraid he'd talk. You might have done it yourself, but you'd be a bit conspicuous out there. Wally was just another middle-aged white guy in Idaho. After that, when he went after me, he had a little experience."

"Obviously, he didn't have enough," she said with contempt. "He couldn't even do that right."

"It's pretty clear that *you* killed Relovich, not Wegland."

"I see Wally was pretty fucking talkative before he took that swan dive. That was Wally. All he wanted to do was talk, talk, talk. He thought he could persuade Relovich to keep his mouth shut about the shooting at Silver's and the payoff."

"But you knew there was only one way to make sure that—"

"No more stupid fucking questions." She jabbed the gun at me and said, "On your stomach. *Now!*"

I dropped to my knees.

"*Stomach*, I said! Wally should have cancelled you out when he had the chance."

We both froze when we heard a metallic *click-clack* sound. I turned around and saw the silhouette of a man in the dim kitchen racking a Remington 870 police-issue 12-gauge shotgun.

"Drop the gun, Saucedo!" the man shouted.

Saucedo took a step toward me and raised her pistol.

I heard a deafening blast and saw Saucedo fly across the room, bounce off a wall, and topple to the floor.

CHAPTER 43

Shuffling through the squad room, I poured a cup of coffee, returned to my desk, and fell into my chair. I spotted my phone light blinking. Nicole had left a short message: "Call me." I was so exhausted I closed my eyes, but jerked them open when Duffy sat on the edge of my desk.

"You saved my ass," I said.

"Least I could do."

"So how'd you figure out where I was?"

"After all the shit that's gone down, I've been worried as hell about you working alone. Didn't want a dead detective on my watch. I wanted to talk to you, tell you that I was willing to free up Ortiz for the next few months so you could partner up with him. Anyway, a captain I know, a buddy of mine, left a message for me on my cell. Told me he heard you'd been snooping around for the home address of a cop. He knew you'd been involved in a lot of shit lately with dirty cops. So he gave me the name and address of the cop. Thought I should know.

"When I finally got the message, I rushed right over to Saucedo's house. I got there and saw your car parked down the street. I grabbed the shotgun—just in case— and saw her pointing a gun in your face."

"Who was that clown at her place?"

"Just some part-time squeeze who keeps a .38 in his trunk."

"I thought she was Wegland's girlfriend."

Duffy grinned. "I guess poor old Wally was getting two-timed."

"Well, I'm glad you put it together and showed up when you did."

Duffy reached over and slipped an arm around my shoulders. "Ash, for the past year I've been really torn up about everything. I'm still torn up about it—about the way you found out, about what you had to go through, and what I did. I'm a weak bastard—"

"Well," I said, pausing, not knowing what to say.

"Did I at least partially redeem myself last night?"

"Considering what would have happened if you hadn't showed up—yes. *Partially*."

Duffy squeezed my arm and smiled. "Patowski flipped. He didn't lawyer up, after all. He's spilling it right now. He thinks we've got Saucedo in another interview room and she's laying it all on him."

"Maybe Conrad explained something I'm still struggling with," I said. "Li'l Eight's a Back Hood Blood. He killed my witness. Flash forward a year. Wegland framed Fuqua for the Relovich hit. Fuqua just happens to be a Back Hood Blood, too. What's the deal?"

"I picked up some of what Patowski's been telling the DA," Duffy said. "When Wegland found out from Grazzo that the department was bringing you back to investigate Relovich, he calls Saucedo. They both panic. They thought the overloaded Harbor Division dicks were going to handle the investigation—and get nowhere with it. If it was an active cop, Felony Special would take over the case, but we don't handle hits on retired cops. Usually it's just some domestic beef. Or in the case of Relovich, it appeared to be a low-rent B and E. Yeah, when he was a rookie, he saved his partner's life. But there's thousands of brave, retired cops out there, sitting on their asses, hitting the bottle. And Pete was just another one of them. What Wegland and Saucedo didn't count on was the chief's friendship with Relovich's old man a thousand years ago. They didn't count on him getting involved and sending the case to us. They knew we had the resources to push it hard, and I think they got spooked when they heard you were taking over the investigation."

Duffy loosened his tie. "Your reputation, my boy, apparently still counts for something. Anyway, Wegland knew about Relovich's history with Fuqua, how he'd kicked his ass, how he'd sent him to Folsom. And Saucedo had contacts at South Bureau Homicide and knew about the Patton investigation. She heard that a Back Hood had killed Patton. So Saucedo comes up with the idea to frame Fuqua. They worked fast. Saucedo sends Wegland down to break into Fuqua's place and get something to plant. He gets lucky. Fuqua's not home, so he bags up a tissue, hits Relovich's place, and plants it. He's a commander, and commanders can go wherever they want. They always have a righteous excuse to be at a crime scene."

"They really pushed that Back Hood angle."

"Saucedo guessed that when you came back you'd figure out—

sooner rather than later—that a Back Hood Blood killed Latisha Patton. She wanted you to believe that a Back Hood also killed Relovich. By connecting the two murders, Saucedo figured you'd be so turned around chasing Back Hood Blood leads, so enraged when you got a sniff of those guys, and so damn eager to bust Fuqua, that you'd never pick up *her* trail."

"It took me a while."

"I guess she overestimated your ability as a detective." Duffy chuckled. "She thought you'd find out sooner. Saucedo knew the hit on your wit was the best way to yank your chain. So she intertwined the two cases."

"Looks like Saucedo was calling the shots," I said.

"Patowski said that she had Wegland by the balls. From the get-go. When he told her about that collection of Japanese art and cash at Silver's house, she was only a detective trainee. But she convinced him to rip off the place. It's not like Wegland was squeaky clean before he met her. Patowski told I.A. that before Hollywood, when Wegland worked narcotics on the eastside, he was skimming cash from the dealers he busted. But before he met Saucedo, he'd only rip off the bad guys. After he met her, anyone was fair game."

Duffy stood up and stretched the tail of his shirt as he attempted to tuck it in over his gut. "How'd you know she shot Relovich?"

"I didn't. I figured it was Wegland. But the more she talked, the better feel I got for her and for the crime scene dynamic with Wegland. I just guessed that she chilled Freitas. When it turned out I was right, I made her for the Relovich homicide. It fit the pattern. That bitch was devious as hell."

Duffy smiled. "But not as devious as you."

He stood up and pointed at the ceiling. "Grazzo called a little while ago. He wants to see you."

I took the elevator to the tenth floor, walked down the deserted hallway, and entered Grazzo's office.

"Have a seat," Grazzo said, with a forced grin. "After the night you've had, you deserve a little rest."

He was dressed in his dark blue uniform, his three collar stars glittering under the fluorescent lights. "You've done this department and this city a great service, Detective Levine. I hate to think how much more damage Wegland, Patowski, and Saucedo could have caused the LAPD, how many more lives would've been lost, if you hadn't risked your own life to stop them."

I was so exhausted and drained I just stared into space.

"We can't have gangsters going out and murdering a small-business owner in cold blood and then killing the witness. That tears at the fabric of a law-abiding society. More kudos for putting together that case, too."

I stood up to leave.

Grazzo held up a hand. "One more thing I wanted to mention. I know you've had a very rough week. But I just wanted to talk to you briefly. There will be a lot of attention, a lot of publicity, a lot of scrutiny after this Wegland-Patowski-Saucedo scandal. I might have to put together an extensive in-house inquiry. And I just wanted to make sure we're on the same page."

"Same page on what?"

"Remember when you were in here last? I said some rather intemperate things. Things that I now regret."

"You mean when you tried to suspend me?"

Grazzo cleared his throat and grimaced. "I was under a lot of pressure then. Lot of stress. Assistant chief is a job I wouldn't wish on my worst enemy. I think the pressure got to me. I kind of buckled under."

I stood up. "Don't worry about it. I just want to do my job. Investigate murders without any interference. You promise you'll let me do that, and I'll forget we ever had that meeting."

Grazzo leapt to his feet, looking relieved. He pumped my hand. "You got it, detective. From now on, in this department you've got a rabbi." He shook his head, looking chagrined, and said, "Pardon the expression."

When I returned to the squad room, Duffy said, "You've had quite a night. Can I take you out to breakfast at the Pacific Dining Car for a Stoli Bloody Mary and steak and eggs."

I shook my head.

Everyone looked up when they spotted Grazzo waddling through the squad room. "I forgot to tell you, Detective Levine. We're having a noon press conference in front of PAB. Lots of media interest. I mean *lots* of media interest. I need you there."

"Give me a second." I reached for the phone and punched in Nicole's number. Hanging up before she could answer, I decided to call another number.

"Yeah," Razor Reed answered.

"It's Ash. How's it breaking?"

"A pretty tasty south swell's rolling in. I'm going to cruise down to Trestles tomorrow morning."

"Can I join you?"

"Sure. Come on by. Four thirty a.m."

"I'll be there. But I got to ask you a favor. Can I borrow a board?"

"Sure. But what happened to that sweet stick I made for you?"

"It's gone. But it saved my life. I'll tell you all about it while we're heading down the coast."

I hung up. "Can't make the press conference," I told Grazzo.

Panic in his voice, Grazzo said, "What'll I tell the chief?"

I looked up at him and smiled. "Tell him I'm going surfing."

ACKNOWLEDGMENTS

I would like to thank a number of people who helped during the research of this book: Bernard Bauer and Tom Olson; LAPD Detectives John Garcia, Rick Jackson, Chuck Knolls, Marcella Winn; and retired Detectives Dave Lambkin and Pete Razanskas.

Patricia Gussin and the crew at Oceanview Publishing were terrific.

I owe a great debt of gratitude to my agent, Philip Spitzer, for his unwavering support. Lukas Ortiz was a tremendous help.

Michael Connelly is the ultimate mensch.

A special thanks to Diane and Marius.